NITS

A NOVEL

By Michele Harris

This is a work of fiction. Names, characters, businesses, places, events and incidents are either the products of the author's imagination or used in a fictitious manner. Any resemblance to actual persons, living or dead, or actual events is purely coincidental.

ISBN: 0615925863
ISBN-13: 978-0615925868 (Cinimod Press)

To my family—
Dominic, Nicholas,
Caroline and Caitlin.

PROLOGUE

January 2014

Buzzing like the woods in the middle of a cicada summer, the Lansing municipal auditorium was packed with a thousand chirpy variations of the exact same thing. There were a thousand varieties of white athletic shoes. A thousand varieties of sensible jeans bearing labels from Costco and Target and a thousand varieties of multi-colored sweaters, most older than the age of the wearer's youngest child. As the lights dimmed, a deep announcer's voice boomed over the speakers, "Good afternoon and welcome. Please silence your cell phones and refrain from any flash photography or recording of any kind. Ladies and gentlemen … Pups MacArthur!"

An attractive woman in her early 40's and dressed just slightly better than the ladies in the audience, stepped boldly onto the stage. Beaming her well-rehearsed, Middle American smile and waving with the fervor of a cult leader, her very presence sent a charge through the crowd. They stood, they applauded and they cheered so long and with such unwavering enthusiasm, she finally had to step up to the microphone to settle them down. "Thank you, Michigan! What a great state! Is it cold enough for you?" The crowd laughed like she had just told the world's funniest joke. They loved her. "You know as I've been touring this wonderful country in what we're calling the 'Who Did it and Ran Tour ... '"

The crowd erupted in a spontaneous, "Whooo hoooo" as some waved hardback copies of her book, *Who Did it and Ran?* over their heads. "I've talked to many fine citizens like yourselves. It's no secret that America's got lots of problems and I've got lots of ideas which I'll share with you today. But before I get into all of that, as you know, I'm a mom ... "

Another exuberant cheer from the audience. "And like most moms I tell some pretty good stories. I'd like to share this one with you, if I may. During World War II, there was a place called Auschwitz. It was the most notoriously brutal of the all the Nazi concentration camps. People in the camp lived under the most heinous conditions: abused by their captors, stricken with disease, malnourished, and of course, something a lot of us moms know a thing or two about ... they were horribly infested with lice."

As the audience erupted in its biggest cheer of the day, Pups waved, winked and waited patiently until they settled themselves. "Now, in one of the barracks of Jewish prisoners at Auschwitz, the people became horribly infested with lice—far worse than any other barrack in the camp. The inmates, who were already suffering at the hands of the Nazi's, suffered even more. And I don't have to tell all you moms out there how wretched that must have been."

Following her every word like she was Moses, the audience emitted a collective, "Uh huh!"

"They scratched so much their skin bled. Soon,

they had painful, festering scabs covering their bodies. They pleaded to God for mercy. Among this group of prisoners was a wise old rabbi who did his best to console them. The prisoners believed the rabbi's prayers would get God's attention, so they begged him to ask God for help. Of course, the rabbi prayed but the lice infestation only grew worse.

"Meanwhile, prisoners continued to be harassed and beaten by ruthless guards. The uncertainty of who would be the next ones dragged off to their death was constantly on these poor peoples' minds. Horrible as all that physical brutality was, the most horrifying part of living in that camp were the never-ending screams and cries coming from other parts of the camp.

"One bit of solace the prisoners in this particular barracks had was their evening prayers, led by the rabbi. One night, he surprised them by saying, 'Tonight we say a prayer of thanks ... for the lice.' The prisoners were confused. They wondered if the rabbi had gone crazy. Thank God for more suffering? Thank him for never ending itchiness and pain? However, they trusted their rabbi so they followed his wishes and thanked God for giving them lice.

"In the weeks that followed, the lice continued to plague them, but they noticed that the guards' visits became less frequent and soon they stopped altogether. Completely ... stopped. It puzzled them because awful shrieks still rose from the other barracks in the camp. They continued to pray and the lice continued to torment them until finally, the joyous day when the allies arrived to liberate the camp.

"Those prisoners never forgot what they endured and in time, they came to realize that God had been listening to them all along. He had allowed the lice to become so bad that the guards refused to step foot into their barracks for fear of becoming contaminated themselves. The very curse which had plagued the prisoners was in the end, a true blessing ... "

The auditorium erupted in thunderous applause. She had them exactly where she wanted the ... eating out of the palm of her hand.

one

NYMPHS

August 2012

On the count of three, a swarm of phosphorescent green orbs took flight, as pixies in white pleated skirts and red hair bows skipped around the courts waving miniature rackets like fairies waving magic wands. There were ten of them—each cuter than the next. Mostly blondes with a few brunettes and one red-head, the delightful little pixies (also known as stage one nymphs) all carried the same highly coveted and fiercely protected genetic code within every cell of their highly toned seven-year-old bodies. The code that ensured each of them a life full of bests: the best schools, the best neighborhoods, the best opportunities. They will have the best friends, like the ones skipping around the tennis court with them at that very moment. By the time they reach stage two, characterized by lavish sweet sixteen parties, the nymphs will know all the other bests that life has to offer: the best fashions, the best cars, and the best boyfriends.

As they mature, they will be honored for their brains, their athletic ability, and their service towards those less fortunate. They will move effortlessly from their high-ranking private school to an equally high-ranking university, signaling the third and final nymphet stage. They will spend four busy years at an institution of higher learning (preferably an Ivy), then take a year off to teach the poor in Calcutta or deliver meals to AIDS patients in the inner city. The year of service typically triggers a period of self-discovery—namely, that they really don't like serving the sick or the poor—leading latent nymphs to enter law school or a top-notch MBA program.

A few more years of study will produce impressive parchment degrees to laminate and hang on the paneled walls of upper level Washington, D.C. law firms or government relation's agencies. Soon after setting themselves up behind Ethan Allen colonial desks, the pixies (now fully formed adults) become "pickies" as they move into the imago stage of the life cycle and begin to choose their mates—limiting their selection to males carrying equally fabulous DNA. (A stellar group of such males could be found at that very moment over on the putting green chipping golf balls.)

As those masculine little three-holers grow into brawny eighteen-holers, they will lead similarly blessed lives. They will attend (but not always graduate from) good schools; the kind of schools where equal value is placed on academics, athletics and character and where godlike status is given only to the most deserving—the lacrosse players. Naturally, all of them will play lacrosse and in doing so, they will forge lifelong friendships with like-minded men on verdant practice fields. The bond between these young men will be virtually unbreakable. As girlfriends, wives and mistresses come and go, these fellows will be there to bail out, prop up and otherwise delude each other through a lifetime of errors, missteps and personality malfunctions.

Like their female counterparts, accolades will be heaped upon them. They too will move on to esteemed universities like Georgetown, UVA, UNC and other schools where lacrosse players are deified. (Ever since the Ivy League embraced diversity over legacy and true achievement over DNA potential, top-flight colleges just weren't as much fun for these fellows.) They will join the best fraternities where they will be schooled in the delicate nuances of Special K, Roofies and EZ Lay. Their year off will not be a service mission. Third nymphet stage for the males or "bros" as they are now called, will entail traveling the world with the simple yet challenging goal of sampling beer from every active commercial brewery on the planet.

After a year of international hangovers, they return to Georgetown or Chapel Hill to study business or law—as much to understand how they can get themselves out of the messes they will someday find themselves in as to make a living. When milking the system is no longer possible, the lacrosse playing, not-quite-ivy males settle themselves behind mahogany junior executive desks on K Street and spend virtually every waking moment trying to persuade their firm's metro-riding administrative assistants to settle beneath those desks—for the good of the firm. Unlike their female counterparts, latent stage three males do not move fluidly into the adult or imago stage. Rather, they hang on to their nymphood for as long as is humanly possible.

While it is abundantly clear to females of the species that twenty years from now, the tiny Junior Leaguers flitting about the tennis court will fall in love with the diminutive junior partners on the putting green, males of the species are completely unaware of their fate. Once chosen by a female, males endure a long and seemingly endless mindfuck leading them to the very precipice of sanity. In this state of dementia, the whipped young men will do anything to end their misery, triggering their reluctant move into the imago stage. Evidence of this milestone is the spectacular four-story diamond engagement ring they proffer to lure their desired mates/tormenters to join them in perpetuating the circle of preppy life.

* * * * *

Stubbie Hill understood destiny. As much as he resented the predetermined fate of his young charges, he was happy their parents were rich enough and stupid enough to shell out hundreds of dollars so he could teach their pixies how to serve and how to lob. Tennis was Stubbie Hill's life. A national champ in high school he competed with the best of them at Ohio State—not an Ivy but a really good school for tennis. He earned a degree in business administration, but Stubbie cared for nothing but the tennis court. He landed a job as a pro at a middling club in Columbus right out of college, moving up to a better, more prestigious club every other summer or so before reaching the top of the heap, Presidential Country Club. That was eight years ago. Since then, Stubbie met his wife, Courtney and fathered three children— two with Courtney and one with Bridget, his best player ever. Stubbie wasn't much of a father and he wasn't much of a husband—or a boyfriend for that matter—but he could transform an uncoordinated five-year-old into a contender for the Junior Nationals in as little as three summers, and he could woo the tennis panties off of any woman with an interest in perfecting her backhand. On a perch high above Presidential's Har-tru courts, Stubbie ordered the pixies to parade around the court while bouncing green balls off their racquets. Just a few days into summer tennis camp, the girls were still eager to please so they followed his every command. At least, most of them did.

He watched Ayn Nuttin help herself to her fifth cup of water. "Ayn, get over here," he called. She took a gulp from the cone-shaped cup, tossed it into the trash and ran to catch up with the others. Before she was halfway across the court, the clouds converged directly overhead, emitting a rumble of thunder. Throughout Chevy Chase and into Potomac, nine bottle blonds dashed to their European SUV's. Once the sound of thunder was heard, tennis camp at Presidential Country Club was over.

When the thunder rumbled, the tenth bottle blonde, Suzanne Nuttin, was paddling down the middle of the Potomac River. Even if she could get to her SUV—which she couldn't—she was not the kind of mother to pamper her only daughter. A latecomer to the mommy game, Suzanne didn't marry until she was in her late thirties. Her husband was a crafty old maverick named Corn (short for Cornelius) Nuttin— forty years her senior with grown children who were older than Suzanne. Seventy-eight-year-old Corn Nuttin was a semi-retired old school lobbyist, the kind who wined, dined and comped his way to favorable votes unlike today's candy-ass manipulators hogtied by regulations and words like "transparency" and "disclosure." Soon after marrying Suzanne, the woman whom he referred to as the "love of his retirement," Corn insisted on giving her a child; someone to keep her company when he was gone. When it didn't occur naturally, they hired a surrogate and paid her handsomely to carry his seed. They hoped for one child, were told that twins were highly likely and were pleasantly surprised when the doctor told them their surrogate was carrying triplets. Early sonograms indicated three boys, which pleased Corn and especially pleased Suzanne who feared having to teach a girl, things she knew nothing about. On the day of the birth, Corn was overjoyed when baby A turned out to be a girl. Suzanne was terrified.

Ayn had no illusions that her mother Suzanne would be picking her up anytime soon. She was used to being the last one claimed, but it seemed to bother the other girls' mothers because they were constantly shoving their cell phones at her to call Suzanne. They didn't realize that even if her mother answered her phone, she wouldn't get there any earlier because she was probably hanging off of a rock wall or inside some smelly cave or paddling some stupid kayak down the river. Her brothers thought their mom was the coolest person on the planet, but Ayn wanted the kind of mom who likes taking her daughter shopping or to get mother/daughter mani-pedi's. The kind of mom Suzanne was not.

One by one, the gas-guzzlers pulled up to the edge of the court. Magically, the silver, white or black

SUV rear doors rose up, the pixies heaved their racquets and gym bags into the vehicles and just as magically, the doors closed. As expected, there was no Mercedes G Wagon—the only SUV Ayn had ever been in that didn't have an automatic back door. Her brothers adored that G Wagon, but Ayn longed for something beautiful with shiny wood trim and soft leather seats. She packed her gear into the pink monogrammed gym bag her Aunt Mel gave her and trotted over to Mr. Stubbie.

"I think my dad is having lunch in The Grillroom," she lied.

"Go ahead," he answered, fully aware that Ayn's father was not on the grounds. He rarely ventured out to Presidential anymore, and certainly not on a scorching hot day like today. Ayn smiled sweetly to Mr. Stubbie then turned and ran at top speed towards the clubhouse. Even if Mr. Stubbie knew she was lying, he'd never run after her. He couldn't leave the two remaining pixies unattended. Their mothers would complain. She entered the building through the side door, the one without a doorman or valets. The one that leads to the casual dining room where unsupervised children were permitted. It was Tuesday so the place was empty. Her friend Mr. Winge was at the maître d' stand and her other friend, Mr. Nick, was behind the bar. A bunch of old ladies were having coffee at one of the tables by the window. Ayn dipped her hand into the large bowl of mints resting on a table by the entrance and stuffed a handful into the pocket of her tennis skirt.

"You are very hungry girl today?" asked Mr. Winge as he hung up the phone.

"These are good," said Ayn.

"Come, have a sandwich," said Mr. Winge, extending his small freckled hand towards her.

"Sandwich? Ugh. I hate sandwiches," said Ayn.

"What you like? Hot dog? Chicken nuggets?"

"Ugh! Even worse," said Ayn.

"I see. I see," said Mr. Winge as if he was trying to solve a complex mystery. "So what you like to eat, Miss Nuttin?"

"Lobster."

"Lobster bisque very, very good here," said Mr. Winge.

"Lobster bisque is disgusting. I like real lobster. With butter on the side."

"Ah, yes. Real lobster," said Mr. Winge.

"With butter on the side," she added.

"All out of butter-on-the-side-lobster today. How 'bout chicken nuggets?"

Ayn smiled sweetly at Mr. Winge like she was actually considering his offer. "Ummmm," she said, grabbing another massive handful of mints, "Poor people eat chicken nuggets," she said. "And that's why they're so fat. Chicken nuggets make you fat."

"Fat?" said Mr. Winge as he watched Ayn disappear around the corner. "Butter on the side make you fat. Chicken nuggets not make you fat," he said.

Ayn headed to the bar where Mr. Nick was busy

arranging his tray of edible drink decorations. Maraschino cherries on tiny plastic swords. Orange slices cut just right. Wooden skewers stacked with olives and pickled onions. Ayn reached for a pineapple chunk soaked in cherry juice just long enough to make it look like a fruity sunset. "Hey there kiddo. Big storm coming," said Mr. Nick. "Slow day ahead so help yourself, Darlin'. Nobody's drinkin' tequila sunrises in the middle of a stormy Tuesday."

From experience, Ayn knew that too much pineapple would make her tongue tingle so she sampled a few orange slices, two swords full of cherries and hopping down from the bar stool, she grabbed one of the olive/onion sticks for the road.

"Come back and visit later. Happy hour buffet starts at 4:00," said Mr. Nick.

"Okay," she said. She hoped her mother would be here before 4:00 when The Grillroom put out the complimentary chicken wings and mozzarella sticks for happy hour, but if not, she'd be back.

Ayn knew the floor plan of the Presidential Club intimately. The janitor's supply room that smelled like the sour towels at Aunt Priscilla's beach house, the small upstairs kitchen where you might find nothing or you might find a tray full of brownies. The vending machine in the employee lounge full of all the stuff she wasn't allowed to eat. The fruit swords filled her up, so food was not what she was looking for. She considered visiting the bowling alley downstairs. The last time she went to the bowling alley, she had to play three games with the Benton kids and their freak-a-ziod mother. No bowling alley. A loud roar of thunder and flickering lights reminded Ayn why she was inside the club in the first place. The ladies locker room is off limits to anyone under eighteen, but on a day like today, no one is going to notice or care. Ayn skipped down the main hall. Past the portrait of Teddy Roosevelt, the President when Presidential opened back in 1905. Past the old fashioned menus with weird foods like Welsh rarebit and oysters Rockefeller. Past all the wood and brass things honoring a bunch of dead guys. Ayn had spent so many unsupervised hours in this hall, she knew the names engraved on the brass plates the way other kids know the characters in Harry Potter novels.

Her favorite place by far at the Presidential Club was the ladies locker room. As the only girl in a set of triplets, she was always the minority, the weakling, the dumb blonde; so establishing her own turf was a substantial pursuit of Ayn's. The ladies locker was her secret hideaway. This wasn't a regular locker room like they have in gyms or schools. This was more like a fancy dressing room. The first thing she did whenever she made it past the door was to "stop and spray" at the pink marble sink. First she pilfered through the vanity tray full of toiletries. A spritz of hairspray, a spurt of deodorant, then for the grand finale, an all over dousing of this stuff that gets wrinkles out of your clothes. Ayn's clothes were never wrinkled, but she liked how it smelled. Next, she filled a small plastic cup with green mouthwash from the wall-mounted dispenser, swished it around in her mouth a few times then spit it into the sink with such force, that it ricocheted off the smooth marble and speckled her white polo shirt with small green dots.

After the stop and spray, Ayn looked through some of the open lockers to see if anyone left anything interesting behind. Once she found a bracelet. Another time she found a Vera Bradley case full of makeup. She left that because using someone else's makeup is disgusting. All the lockers looked empty today. Someone must have come through and cleaned everything out. As she rounded the corner of the last row of lockers, Ayn discovered that she didn't have the locker room to herself after all. Standing on the bench was a girl about her age, pretending she was walking along a balance beam. The girl didn't notice Ayn until she swung her tan leg behind her and twirled herself around so she was smack in front of Ayn.

"Oh!"

"Hi," said Ayn.

"Hi," said the girl, looking like she had been caught doing something wrong.

"I won't tell if you won't," said Ayn. The girl looked confused. "I mean that we're in here. What are they going to do to us anyway, arrest us?"

"Arrest us?" asked the girl seriously.

"It's no big deal. I've been in here a bunch of times. All they do is politely ask you to leave. I mean, it's not like our parents aren't paying this freak fest tons of moola."

"Huh?" asked the girl.

"Whatever. I'm Ayn Nuttin. I'm going into the third grade at the Friends Academy."

"I'm Taylor Sanchez. I go to Holy Family."

"What grade?"

"Third."

"Huh. If we went to the same school, we'd probably be in the same class. We'd probably be totally best friends and all the other girls would be so jealous. I never heard of your school."

"It's in Silver Spring."

"Is that downtown, like near the zoo?"

"I don't think so," answered Taylor.

"Have you checked out all these lockers? Because that's what I was doing. Looking for cool stuff in the lockers."

"No."

"Then I guess we should start looking. You can find totally weird stuff."

The two girls went to work opening and closing the lockers. Taylor found treasure. "Here's some stuff," she announced proudly.

"Let's see," said Ayn expertly moving closer to examine the spoils. Inside the locker was a new pair of socks, a half-filled water bottle, a pink tennis ball, a sample of Sarah Jessica Parker Lovely perfume and a pink baseball cap that said, "Run For the Cure." Ayn grabbed the sample and perfumed herself and her new friend. Taylor reached for the pink cap. She liked pink. Her mother, Arminda, was always telling her that rosado was her color. "Cool hat," said Ayn. "Let me see it, maybe it's got someone's name inside." Ayn made a cursory examination of the cap before placing it on her head.

"It's nice, but pink's not really my color. Blondes look better in blue. Brunettes in pink. Let's play store," suggested Ayn. "The bench can be the display case. I'll be the customer and you can be the checkout lady."

The two new friends carefully arranged their treasures along the wooden bench. For the next hour, Taylor and Ayn were, at times, a high-powered executive looking for the perfect gift for her housekeeper, a fashion model looking for a quick disguise from the paparazzi, a lady detective trying to act like she was just a shopper when she really suspected that the check out lady was in charge of a major hat smuggling ring. (Except for the fact that there was no murder in this story, the case was vaguely similar to a recent episode of *CSI*, one of Ayn's favorite shows.) For the remainder of the rainy afternoon, the daughter of the club's president emeritus played with the daughter of the club's cleaning lady. When it was time to leave, they divided their treasures evenly and waved goodbye as youthful optimism inspired each of them to envision a beautiful lifelong friendship ahead.

two

ACHILLES' HEEL

The aged and asthmatics were told to stay inside, the homeless were invited into air-conditioned public school gymnasiums, and everyone got to ride the bus for free. The intense combination of heat, humidity, and high ozone prompted government officials to declare the day as Code Orange, which effectively de-cluttered the streets and scenic trails of the nation's capitol. With all the wimps and slackers indoors, there was no better time for Wendy "Wenn" Mann to go for a tough twenty-two mile run along the C&O Canal. The stagnant algae-colored water in the canal smelled like sewage and swarms of thirsty gnats would be honing in on the dewy moisture of his corneas, but the trail that he loved and hated to share would be his alone.

He left the campus of Washington Prep, where he was the resident dean and a Latin teacher, at around 10:00. By 10:30, he had made it through the Disney-fied town of Bethesda and was pushing down the Capitol Crescent Trail—an old railroad line linking the formerly working class Maryland suburbs with tony Georgetown in D.C. Not long after the trains stopped running, back in the early 1980s, the line was quickly taken over by fitness-crazed suburbanites who dismantled the track, paved it over then vehemently protested any politician who suggested that reviving the train line would significantly ease the traffic blight that had settled into the area.

Any reversal of the rail-to-trail project would negatively impact the delicate ecosystem along the route is what they said, but what they meant was that converting trail back to rail would negatively impact their property values not to mention their God-given right to exercise on their beloved footpath. In time, the trail developed its own traffic issue as scores of fit parents buckled their progeny into state-of-the-art baby strollers so they could run, walk, rollerblade, or bicycle without having to ante up twenty dollars for a babysitter.

What most infuriated Wenn was that these fledgling families could not just wave hello to their neighbors as they passed them on the trail. They had to stop and compare their own pathetic lives to the pathetic lives around their neighborhood. (Is that a *new* stroller? *Where* are you going for vacation? You're having a *third* level added to your two-story house?) These pow-wows created micro traffic jams as joggers, rollerbladers, and bicyclists *sine* children attempted to pass those sport utility strollers without slowing down. The good thing about a Code Orange day was it kept the families inside. The bad thing about a Code Orange day was that it was nearly impossible to breathe and downright Herculean to keep your body temperature from soaring.

At the six-mile marker, near the water reservoir was a water fountain, at which Wenn stopped to take a drink. Wenn never stopped for a drink, preferring to tough it out most days. In fact, for Wenn, running was never anything but a lavish on-going exercise in toughing it out. Atonement for past gluttony. Two years ago, Wenn Mann was a whopping 230 pounds. Just a hair below six-feet tall, this former All-American athlete grew pudgy and bloated. It was carbs that robbed him of his once enviable physique, but it was the pursuit of goals other people had set for him that robbed him of his ability to control things like his weight, his state of mind, and his desires. A child of privilege, all he needed to do was saunter down the easy road that had been plowed, paved, and beautified by successive generations of Manns.

For over a hundred years, Mann & Mann had the honor of preparing the tax returns of presidents, senators, and other influentials. Every Mann in the family worked at the firm and there was the expectation that Wenn—or Wendy, which was his given name—would someday carry on the legacy of his great-great-grandfather, the original Wendy Mann. Family lore has it that Wenn's great-great-granddad was born in 1901 and originally named after his father, Wendell Mann, Sr. Shortly after Junior's birth, the elder Mann left his home in Ireland and sailed across the sea to America, searching for a better life or at least a better diet. He settled in Maryland with a lot of other Irish Catholics hoping to earn enough money to bring his wife and four sons to America. As Wendell toiled through a succession of menial jobs, his wife, Mary Mann, lived with her widowed mother back in Cork. Mary and her mother loved to read, and they especially enjoyed reading stories aloud to the children.

One story, in particular, captured their hearts—*Peter Pan*, the enchanting tale of the mischievous boy who refused to grow up. They read it aloud over and over again. Although she treasured her sons, Mary longed for a daughter. This longing grew stronger by the day and without a man around the house to steer her in the right direction, she began to call her infant son, Wendy after the character in the book. Soon, she grew the child's hair long and began to dress him as she would a daughter. Mary's mother, who also favored girls, encouraged her by sewing up a dainty wardrobe just for little Wendy. He was a beautiful child, with clear blue eyes, thick golden waves of hair, and skin that seemed to glow with health.

After a few years in America, Wendell, Sr. established himself—first as a maintenance man and later as an office assistant. It was a low paying job, but what it lacked in salary, it made up for in prestige. His employer was none other than Riggs Bank, the largest bank, by far, in Washington, D.C. Not too many Irishmen had the luxury of working in an office at that time. His future soon looked bright enough to bring his family over to join him.

When Mary, her mother, and the four children arrived at the Port of Baltimore, Mary was crippled with nerves; afraid the immigration officials would find some reason to prevent them from going further than the port. Stories of men in uniforms sticking hooks into people's eyes to check for trachoma and families being split up and turned back for maladies as common as nail fungus or varicose veins were well known in Cork. When they boarded the ship called

Elnora, everyone was as fit as a fiddle, but after being in close quarters with the rankest of human beings, she was certain they had been exposed to all kinds of vermin. Her worst nightmare was realized when only minutes after they got off the ship, little Wendy and her six-year-old, Desmond were pulled aside and sent down one hall while the rest of the family was herded down another. They were poked and prodded, interviewed, accessed, and evaluated in every conceivable fashion. Just as her distress became unbearable, she rounded a corner and there were her beautiful boys, bald as potatoes. Desmond looked like he was having a holiday. He kept rubbing his smooth skull and talking about all the people he had seen and the stories he had heard. Two-year-old Wendy, however, was so traumatized at being separated from his mother, he wrapped his arms around her neck and clung to her. Mary scooped him up in his little white ruffled smock and held him close, rubbing the scalp that once held his beautiful gold curls.

Their heads were shaved to rid them of head lice and now that the mites were gone, the boys were free to enter the country with the rest of the family. Relief so overwhelmed Mary that when the immigration officer asked her for the names of her children, she absent-mindedly said, Patrick, Alistair, Desmond and Wendy. No one thought to correct her, and to the immigration official, the sweet-faced child clinging to the woman looked like a girl. It wasn't until days later when Mary examined the paperwork that she realized a mistake had been made. Her husband was livid, but once he calmed down, they decided to let the mistake be for fear the immigration office would accuse them of trying to sneak an extra boy into the country.

So Wendell Mann, Jr., became Wendy Mann, who begot Wendy Mann, Jr., and so on until Wendy Mann, IV vowed to end the long succession of ridiculously named Wendy's. Even if he fathered a child, Wendy Mann, IV would never subject his son to the taunts he received throughout his youth. Kindergarten was a nightmare. First grade was a haze of ice packs and gauze bandages. By second grade, when they moved from a modest home in Chevy Chase to an immodest mansion in Chevy Chase and he transferred from Our Lady of Lourdes to Shrine of the Most Blessed Sacrament School (BS for short), he learned that introducing himself as Wenn and not Wendy kept him out of the nurse's office because guys didn't immediately feel the need to beat up a Wenn like they did a Wendy.

Though the teasing stopped, the feeling that it could happen anytime without warning did not. Were he ever to subject himself to therapy, Wendy Mann would inevitably come to the conclusion that part of his visceral reaction to being teased was the associated questioning of his manhood, something he had done himself on occasion. To compensate, Wendy Mann a.k.a. Wenn Mann became the toughest and most accomplished student ever to graduate from BS. He became the toughest and most accomplished athlete on the lacrosse field. And the toughest and most accomplished friend, son, lawn mower, dog walker, boy scout, student body president, college applicant, prom date, etc. Unlike his brothers who coasted through high school and college secure in the knowledge that no matter what, they had a job waiting at Mann & Mann, Wenn worked tirelessly to achieve.

He was the valedictorian of his high school class and MVP of Washington Prep's nationally ranked lacrosse team. He attended Georgetown University, leading their lacrosse team to three straight national titles while working his ass off to attain perfect grades. With the exception of his ancient Greek and Latin classes, he cared little for the subject matter, only the grade was important to him. After Georgetown, he enrolled in the University of North Carolina for a four-year combined JD/MBA program. His parents beamed with pride. What a son! How wonderful it will be to have him at Mann & Mann. They bought him the car of his dreams: a classic red Alfa Romeo Spider to show just how proud they were of his accomplishments. It was significant because each of his three older brothers received the same gift every college graduate in the neighborhood got: a standard-issue Jeep.

Everything was going according to plan until one day, about three and a half years into his four-year program, Wenn had an epiphany. He didn't give a fuck about torts or profit and loss. Not one bit. All the work, the drive, the pursuit would soon culminate in a degree that qualified him for the most meaningless life he could imagine. He tried pushing this revelation to the back of his mind, but it would not budge. It remained front and center as he studied for his exam on tax policy. It quietly mocked him as he wrote a paper about ethics in accounting. And then, finally, it began to taunt him, just as the schoolyard bullies had taunted him about his name. His readings about market share analysis in the communications industry never got past the first page. How could he concentrate when each sentence, each word brought him closer to the slow and painful death by ennui that awaited him at Mann and Mann?

What had been so obvious to everyone who knew him hit Wenn like the butt of a lacrosse stick to the groin. It didn't matter how hard he worked. It didn't matter what he accomplished. His job, his life, his club memberships, his future wife, and the names of his unborn children were all out there waiting for him to catch up. Whether he graduated at the top of his class or not at all, he was the next junior executive at Mann & Mann. Whether he understood product liability claims and punitive damages or not, he would still make a good income, have health insurance and be able to take great vacations to cool places like the Bahamas and Lake Tahoe. In a nutshell, he mattered very little. He was just a placeholder in the grand century-long parade of Mann & Mann.

With just a term paper and two exams between him and his MBA/JD, Wenn Mann picked up his beloved Gibson guitar, one of the two things in life that he truly loved, and walked out of the nicely appointed condo his father had purchased for him in Chapel Hill. He drove his red Spider (the other thing he loved) to the airport and charged himself a ticket to Sofia, Bulgaria with his father's credit card. In Sofia, he used the credit card for a cash advance of 1,463 Bulgarian lev, prompting the credit card company to call the bearer of the card back in Maryland. Not knowing his son had left the country, Mr. Mann, on the advice of his bank, swiftly shut down that line of credit while Pauline Mann futilely attempted to contact her son to tell him not to use his credit card. She left a chipper message on his answering machine along the lines of, "Hi Wenn, your father may be the victim of identity theft so he's canceling the Visa account. Don't want you to be embarrassed or alarmed when it's declined so don't use that card. Use the American Express. Talk to you soon. Can't wait for the big graduation day extravaganza. Love you!"

A week later, American Express called the Manns. "Have you authorized any charges in Budapest?" So Mr. Mann closed another account and Mrs. Mann made another attempt to reach her son. This time, she asked him to call her back. She wished she had been more insistent that he join the twenty-first century and get a cell phone. Each time she offered to put him on her plan, he refused, saying there was no one on the planet he needed to talk to on a cell phone no matter what the circumstances.

"What if there's an emergency?" she asked.

"Exactly," he answered before leaving the room.

When ten days had passed without a call from Wenn, Mr. and Mrs. Mann got into their classic Jaguar roadster and drove to Chapel Hill. Letting themselves into his condo, they found no evidence indicating their son had vacated the condo and even less evidence that he was there. His clothes hung neatly in the closet. A half filled coffee cup dotted with fuzzy balls of mold sat on Wenn's desk next to an open textbook. Dirty dishes, also sprouting fuzzy growths were in the sink. All of which added up to nothing. Graduate students aren't necessarily known for their housekeeping abilities.

Checking his mailbox wasn't much help either.

Since he didn't get any substantive mail (all his bills were sent to his home address in Maryland and paid by his father), it was difficult to discern how long the post cards advertising home improvement services and pizza specials had been accumulating in the box. Junk mail isn't postmarked with a date. Pauline did notice early on that his guitar was not there, and of course, a look around the parking lot did not reveal his Spider. Confused, frightened and feeling helpless, the Manns called the police. Twelve hours later, they were informed that their son's car was in a satellite parking lot near the Raleigh-Durham International Airport. They also discovered that before it was cancelled, someone had charged $1,345.00 to their Visa for a business class ticket to Sofia, Bulgaria. Both puzzled and alarmed, the Mann's next step was to visit the Dean of Students at the University of North Carolina, Chapel Hill who presented them with a letter of withdraw dated ten days prior and signed by Wendy Mann, IV.

Pauline was convinced that foul play was involved, but Wendy III wasn't so sure. He had sensed a rebellious streak in his son and was actually surprised it had taken so long to show itself. His suspicions were confirmed when he received a collect call from Belgrade the next day. It was Wenn. "Just calling to tell you that I'm taking some time off, touring the Eastern Bloc."

"That's fine," said the father to the son. "Take as much time as you need. UNC will still be here when you get back. Nothing wrong with taking a break, although it would have been nice if you had told your mother and me. We didn't know what to think."

Wenn apologized for worrying his parents then added, "Just so you know, I'm done with UNC. I'm not going back. And Dad," he said hesitating.

"What is it, son?" asked Wendy, III.

"Nothing personal, but I have no intention of working for Mann & Mann."

Mr. Mann told his son that every Mann deserved a dalliance and he hoped he would enjoy his. Hanging up the phone, he assured Pauline that there was nothing to worry about. "The boy just needs a well deserved break, that's all," he said trying to convince both himself and his wife. "He'll be back in a month or so and pick up right where he left off."

Mr. Mann re-activated his credit cards and for the next two months, Wenn moseyed through Eastern Europe, reading great literature, drinking amazing beer, and playing jazz guitar with cool Slovaks. With his good looks and American charm, he had no trouble wooing numerous pale-skinned beauties who knew their way around complex consonant clusters. Women were not the only appetite he indulged while traveling. For two months, he was like an insatiable parasite, consuming vast quantities of dumplings and kielbasa, potatoes and porridge and transforming his once All-American physique into a pudgy, double-chinned version of his father. It disgusted him and it also made him oddly homesick. Each time he caught a glimpse of himself in the mirror, his heart leapt because for one split second, he actually thought it was his father. Once he realized he was merely catching a glimpse of the fat pig that he himself had become, his heart sank.

After two months, Wenn called to say he was coming home. His parents were overjoyed and even volunteered to pick him up at the airport. (They had sensibly retrieved the Spider from the airport parking lot in Raleigh and Pauline drove it back to Maryland, talking to Wendy III on her cell phone for the entire five-hour trip.) As they circled Dulles Airport, Wendy III and Pauline each had their own list of questions they planned to gingerly ask their prodigal son. Pauline wanted to know why on earth he would choose to spend so much time in Slovenia when he could have gone to Rome or Paris or London. She wanted to know what she should do about re-scheduling the graduation party she had to cancel. A good room at the Carolina Inn took connections and months of planning. And she wanted to know what she was supposed to tell all her friends and relatives about the fact that he would not be graduating on schedule.

Mr. Mann wanted to know what his son had been doing with himself for all that time in a bunch of countries that were essentially backward hellholes. He had been a young man once and remembered how easy it is to take risks you think won't have consequences, only to find yourself knee-deep in a quagmire of consequences. He considered the possibilities, drugs, women … or men perhaps. *Could a Mann go for … men?* he wondered. It wasn't what he envisioned, but he loved his son. Period. Pauline, however, was a different story. He would let his wife ask her questions on the car ride home. He would save his curiosities for a Mann-to-Mann lunch at the Presidential Club later in the week.

The plane was due in at 3:30. The Mann's drove around and around the gigantic loop of Dulles Airport access roads, hoping each time they passed the arrivals terminal they would spot him. They did notice a bearded fat guy waving to them in the distance, but he didn't look familiar, so they kept on going. The second time they saw him wave, Pauline noticed he was carrying a guitar case.

"Oh my God!" she exclaimed. "He's fat."

The fat guy lumbered towards them and as he got closer, they recognized the Mann family nose squeezed between two fleshy cheeks. It was Wenn and they had only seconds to regain their composure. Mr. Mann put the car in park and stepped out to give his son a hug. Fat or not, he was happy to see him. Pauline could not bring herself to budge. All she could muster was a sickly smile as she fought the overwhelming need to vomit.

On the way home, they made polite chit chat before Pauline's higher than normal pitched voice casually asked, "Just curious, Wenn, why the Eastern Bloc? I mean the world is full of beautiful, amazing places." Taking a second to formulate his answer, Wenn said, "Because it's the only place I could think of that you couldn't turn into some fabulous vacation or humanitarian mission when you told your friends where I was." They drove the rest of the way home in silence.

* * * * *

In the twenty-four hours preceding his do-it-yourself Code Orange marathon, Wenn had consumed three cups of black coffee, a can of Diet

Coke, some water, a head of iceberg lettuce, and a plain egg white omelet made with twelve eggs and without butter or oil in a non-stick pan. The Diet Coke was not something he regularly indulged in, but last night he needed caffeine and the only thing available, without getting in the car, was from the machine in the basement of the empty dormitory he was living in. He had stayed up late translating a section of Catullus for his advanced Latin students. No matter how much he played with the words, the translation just wouldn't come to him. He gave up at about 4:00 a.m. Of course, there was no need to work all night since students wouldn't return for another two weeks, but once Wenn started something, it was hard for him to walk away until he was done.

Maybe it was a lack of sleep that caused his head to fog and his vision to haze … or maybe his diet, which consisted of virtually nothing. No carbs, no dairy and whenever possible, no calories. He drank a lot of coffee and tea. He consumed a lot of watery vegetables like broccoli, celery, and lettuce. And a few times a week, he enjoyed a couple of distilled alcoholic beverages. When he became weak with hunger (which was roughly every 72 hours), he would devour three rotisserie-cooked chickens purchased at the nearby supermarket. The school's kitchen staff prepared his twelve egg omelets to order whenever he awoke in a state of hypoglycemia.

As he ran down the trail, through the cool darkness of the Dale Carlia Tunnel and across the Arizona Avenue Trestle Bridge, he began to doubt his ability to continue. His energy vanished, his muscles started buckling, his mouth felt cracked and all over, he was dry to the bone. No sweat, no saliva, no tears. Like a robot, he kept moving because he lacked the mental capacity to make the decision to stop running. And besides, he was in the middle of nowhere, all by himself. No one was stupid enough to be out on a trail at high noon on a Code Orange day. He fixed his gaze downward and realized that he had left the black asphalt part of the trail and was now running along pebbly peach-colored sand. The canal was to his left, which meant he had only a short distance to go before he was in the heart of Georgetown—the half waypoint.

Perhaps before heading back to campus, he'd pop into Monty's, a bar that was wildly popular with all the jerks, whores, and nitwits he grew up with. His buddy Bric Heatherington opened Monty's to be a sort of exclusive club with a pre-approved guest list. If you weren't on the list, you didn't get into Monty's. The place was so hot that despite Monty's well-publicized strict adherence to the list, morons would line up outside and pray for a spot to open up. One rarely did, and then only if you were a tanned blonde that Bric wanted to fuck. Since he had known Bric from birth, he was permanently on the list, which was a good thing because, otherwise, he would never want to go there.

As he ran along the trail, Wenn thought about Monty's and how great it would be to stop by. He thought about the ice cube clinking around in his glass, which he imagined would probably contain bourbon and a little water. A beer would be great right now, but beer was totally off limits. As much as he enjoyed the drink, he couldn't seem to get his thoughts past the sensuously smooth ice cube. The beautiful sound it made bouncing off the side of the glass. A pair of runners loaded down with hydration belts, GPS watches, iPods, cell phones, reflective glasses and who knows what else passed him. He must be getting close to Georgetown where the runners were more interested in running accessories than they were in actual running.

For Wenn, it was a pair of shoes and sometimes a watch. No piped in music, no miles per hour calculations, no record keeping. Running consumers disgusted him. So much, that when he ran in a marathon, he started his race exactly thirty-minutes after the official start so he wouldn't have to line up with all those guys and their gizmos. If he had started with the pack, he probably would have won a few of them and placed in the top five in most of them. But what did that matter? He only did it for himself.

Lifting his gaze up from the sand, Wenn saw a bike approaching. He hated bikers. Hated how they whizzed around him leaving just inches between their bike and his skin. Hated how they dressed with those stupid nut-hugging shorts and the psychedelic colored shirts. And now he hated this one, in particular, for taking his mind out of the relative coolness of his glass of ice and back to this unbelievable heat. As the bike approached, Wenn's rage surged through his esophagus, into his throat, and with nothing in his stomach, he fell forward into a violent dry heave. Unprepared for his sudden spastic movement, the biker brushed up against his arm, lost balance, and pushed him down into the warm sand below.

He opened his eyes to see a tall woman

attempting to untangle her bike from his body. Her spandex biker's clothing left little to the imagination. Small, athletic tits. Tight toned ass. When she took off her shades and helmet, she was actually kind of pretty in a mannish kind of way. She kept repeating how sorry she was. "Truly, truly sorry," she said. She pulled a metal bottle off the bike.

"Do you want a drink?" she asked. He nodded as another vision of Monty's popped into his brain. She leaned over, brought the bottle to his lips and carefully poured some liquid into his mouth. It took a few sips before his taste buds could distinguish that what he was drinking had taste.

"What is this?" he asked.

"PowerAde," she answered.

"PowerAde Zero or regular?"

"Regular."

"Ugggghhhh!" he screamed, now in genuine pain.

"What is it? Are you allergic? Is something wrong?"

"Sugar. I don't eat sugar," he said and spit the pink swill into the air.

* * * * *

Elizabeth got the runner up onto his feet. Coated with a layer of pale grit that clung to his limbs, he was every bit as sweet and tempting as a freshly baked snicker doodle sprinkled with turbinado sugar. Longish dark waves flecked with gold fell over the kind of flinty brown eyes that never failed to make

Elizabeth melt. As a triathlete herself, men with muscle didn't usually impress her. But this guy was more than muscle. There was something about him. As she moved her attention away from his eyes, she saw blood oozing from his chin, his elbow, his palms, and his knees. It snapped her out of her momentary swoon. He could press charges. She wasn't sure it was entirely her fault, but what did that matter in a court of law? More bad publicity was not what she needed at the moment.

"I have a condo just across the canal," she said. "Why don't you come on up so you can get some water and cool off?" She helped him to his feet and he winced. His left ankle was badly bruised and already swollen. Leaving her Cannondale lying in the dirt by the side of the trail, she pulled his left arm around her shoulders and led him across the footbridge. Maybe it was his youth or maybe it was heat, dehydration, and fatigue. Whatever it was, Elizabeth felt the attraction as soon he shifted his weight off his good foot and pushed his hip against her for support.

"You look like a pretty serious runner," she said cutting the silence to make it just a little less awkward. "I mean, you're in great shape." As soon as she said it, she knew it was the wrong thing to say.

"Oh."

"Do you race? Like marathons?"

"Yep."

After asking the doorman to send someone across the bridge to pick up her bike, she led the limping, bleeding, single-syllable loving golden boy into the elevator and then to her apartment. The sparkling white pied-à-terre did nothing to loosen him up. Even Elizabeth felt uncomfortable bringing so much dirt, grit and grime into the pristine space. Technically, this wasn't actually her place. She lived in a lovely grey six-bedroom Colonial in Chevy Chase that was now mostly empty since her ex-husband married the nanny and moved his new bride and her old kids into a lovely yellow four-bedroom bungalow in Chevy Chase. She missed seeing the kids every day, but even she had to admit that they were better off with Alan. As publisher of the *Washington Tribune*, she was on call 24/7. Testament to that fact was this blindingly white apartment. Owned by the Tribune Corporation, it was here for her if she needed someplace to crash during long nights of labor negotiations or through ball-busting news cycles. She stayed there every night for three weeks when the Bovine Militia took over the U.S. Department of Agriculture. Mostly though, she used this great one-bedroom overlooking the C&O canal as a place to stop and shower after biking or running or kayaking out on the Potomac.

Here, with this injured runner, Elizabeth became the best of herself. The one part of mothering she was actually good at was managing a crisis. Day-to-day stuff overwhelmed her, but give her a broken bone or an unexcused absence from school and she knew exactly what to do. She ushered him into the bathroom, and momentarily disappeared, returning with a bottle of water.

"Drink this," she commanded twisting the cap

off the water and handing it to him. "No sugar, promise." She opened up the vanity drawers and searched for a moment before finding a box of bandages and some cotton balls. Then she pulled a brown bottle from the medicine cabinet.

"Where do I start?" she said. He had various scrapes and cuts all over. She poured a bit of the hydrogen peroxide onto a cotton ball and dabbed it on his chin. He winced.

"I'm Elizabeth," she offered.

"Wenn," he responded.

"When? Always. I'm always Elizabeth."

"No, I'm Wenn. My name is *Wenn*."

"Ah. That's unusual."

She dampened another cotton ball with the solution and rubbed it on his elbow. He was beautiful. It had been so long since she was this close to a man and even longer since she had been close to one this … incredible. It was hard to keep her focus on triaging until … she saw what any other sensible woman would have considered a deal breaker.

"You like cats?" she asked.

"Huh?"

"The tattoo on your arm, it's a cat."

"Right," he said looking into her eyes without the slightest bit of shame.

A cat. What kind of guy gets a tattoo of a cat? And not some menacing panther. Just a common house cat. She knew the likely answer but didn't want to go there just yet. The light streaming through the windows suddenly dimmed followed by a rumble of thunder. "Sounds like a storm," said Elizabeth nervously. Small talk was never her forte. It didn't seem to matter because her companion simply nodded.

She sat down on the edge of the tub to get a good look at his bruised and swollen ankle. Touching it tenderly, she asked, "Does this hurt?" He winced. "You should get it looked at. Do you have a good sports doc?"

"Uh … yeah."

"Are you sure? Because I can send you to my guy. He's genius. Really. True genius."

"I'm good," said Wenn awkwardly. She noticed that he wasn't making eye contact and wondered if he might be autistic or have Asperger's or something. She turned on the water and told him to get into the tub and chill, literally. Closing the door, she hoped he had the cognitive ability to undress and get in the tub. She listened outside the door for the sound of shoes hitting the floor or tub water being displaced by the beautifully bronzed naked body of the guy she just ran over. She heard both and felt confident that he was on the road to recovery.

"Keep drinking that water," she commanded from outside the door. She wondered if she should contact her lawyer. The guy had hardly uttered three words so it was hard to say if he might be inclined to sue her. He didn't seem like the lawsuit type. More an edgy granola-eater than a money-grubbing opportunist. At least that's what she hoped. She also hoped he would come out of the bathroom dripping wet and naked and take her right there the hallway of her white pied-à-terre.

After considering both possibilities, Elizabeth reasoned that neither was likely. Relieved and a little disappointed, she made herself busy by packing an ice bag in the kitchen, as the sound of thunder grew louder.

-three-

GENERAL
MACARTHUR

Four kids, each of whom needed sixty-four crayons, twenty-four washable markers, and twelve colored pencils meant that Pups MacArthur would be taping tiny labels that said MACARTHUR to 256 crayons, 96 washable markers, and 48 colored pencils. When she finished all that, there were calculators, glue sticks, rulers, and notebooks to brand. As tedious as the work was, Pups could think of no other way to distinguish the MacArthur crayons, markers, and pencils from all those others. With some slight variation according to grade, every student at the Holy Family Catholic School in Silver Spring, Md.— from the kindergartners to the eighth graders—had long, specific, and nearly identical lists of required school supplies.

Wearing freshly laundered uniforms and squeaky new shoes, the children would haul shopping bags brimming with three-packs of Elmer's glue sticks, red boxes of Ticonderoga #2 pencils, and marbled composition books into their classrooms on the first day of school. In a matter of days, the pristine MACARTHUR supplies would begin to mingle. Willa

MacArthur's pencils would make their way into Stephen Wong's pencil case. And Virginia MacArthur would find "SANCHEZ" crayons in her green and gold box.

Sitting at the dining room table (which was never used for dining), Pups was overwhelmed with how much stuff she needed to get four kids out the door and into their classrooms. Plastic bags filled with brightly colored spiral notebooks, serious looking white science binders, and brand-new lunch-boxes, some with characters, some without, lined the perimeter of the room. A fan of cheaper store brands, Pups didn't understand why she had to invest twice as much in Crayola when Target crayons were forty cents cheaper. And the list didn't stop at school supplies. Each child was required to bring in three boxes of Kleenex tissues, three boxes of Clorox disinfecting wipes, one case of Deer Park bottled water, and a roll of aluminum foil, any brand. Since her oldest child, Grant, had started pre-school at Holy Family, Pups sent in the required foil at the start of every year. Now she was sending in four rolls—one for each child in the school—and she still didn't know what they did with all that blasted foil.

As she cut hundreds of little MACARTHUR'S from a sheet of paper she had printed out, Pups cradled the phone between her shoulder and her ear, chit-chatting the time away with her friend Mary Ellen Packingham. Pups and Mary Ellen grew up across the street from each other in the exact same model split-level house. They both had fathers who worked and mothers who stayed home drinking coffee and smoking cigarettes all day. When they were little, the families socialized together, with the fathers bonding over frosty mugs of beer, the mom's bonding over daiquiris, while the kids—sporting red Kool-Aid mustaches—ran amuck. As youngsters, Pups and Mary Ellen were inseparable. The two friends walked to and from school together all through elementary, middle and high school, sharing their girlish dreams and their dreads. For college, Pups went to the University of Maryland and Mary Ellen, using a cousin's address to attain in-state status, went to the University of Wisconsin. Although both schools were state schools, the University of Maryland was local and therefore, the common destination for 80 percent of the graduating seniors at John F. Kennedy High. While the University of Wisconsin meant packing up and embarking on a long distance adventure. Going so far away takes guts, Mary Ellen said.

Just before heading off to their respective schools, the two friends gave each other tear-filled goodbye hugs promising to call and write as often as possible. It was all for show. Pups had already decided that she was not going to write or call someone as full of herself as Mary Ellen. And Mary Ellen seriously doubted she would have either the time or the inclination to remain close with someone who was so happily rooted in soil Mary Ellen was eager to leave behind.

Though they would never again be as close as they once were, Mary Ellen and Pups continued to lead astonishingly parallel lives. After college, Pups went to work for a bank while Mary Ellen returned to the area and went to work for a title company. Both met their future husbands in bars and both men were of similar size, shape and IQ. Mary Ellen's Kenny worked for his father in the family-owned grease disposal business. Pups's Patrick worked for his uncle in the family car dealership. Once children started arriving, both Mary Ellen and Pups left their jobs to become stay-at-home moms. On the surface, the Packinghams appeared to be ahead of the MacArthurs. They lived in a better furnished home in a slightly better neighborhood, wore nicer clothes, and whenever possible tried to fill their lives with the finer things. Thanks to her husband's job, Pups did have a leg up on Mary Ellen in the car department, sitting happily behind the wheel of a newish Chevrolet Suburban while Mary Ellen drove an older Toyota Mini Van. In every other way, Pups was firmly and proudly ensconced in the hardworking proletariat with no desire to rise above the respectable high middle of the middle class. Pups liked to brag about how tightly she ran her ship. She never bought anything that wasn't a good deal.

Sometimes she laughed and said that knowing she would always get good deals on new cars was factored into her decision to marry Patrick. It was hard to say who was better off because creating the illusion that they were landed gentry put the Packinghams deeply into debt while the MacArthurs were staunchly in the "pay cash or don't buy it" corner of the economy. And because they owed nothing to anyone, the MacArthurs carried themselves with the kind of complacency commonly found among people who believe they are in complete control.

The MacArthurs had five smug children: Grant,

thirteen; Virginia, eleven; Willa, ten; Caddy, six; and two-year-old Maddox. All of her children inherited their strong sense of moral superiority from their mother. They understood that the world was essentially an unfair place—with loads of people getting ahead based on their race or their athletic ability or who their grandma knew. The MacArthurs might not be perfect, but whatever they were, it was earned fair and square (not counting Patrick's job, a tiny slice of nepotism the family turned a blind eye to). And none of them would have wanted it any other way.

The Packinghams were a more refined version of the MacArthurs. Mary Ellen's four arrogant sons were her pride and joy. Brophy was her oldest followed by Doyle, Tanner, and Kier. Decent students and pretty good athletes, the Packingham boys grew up hearing their mother tell them they were big winners. She was right—they were winners—but more in the "free-shake-with-the-purchase-of-a-big-Mac" sense than the $500 million jackpot sense.

The MacArthurs and the Packinghams didn't travel in the same circles, they didn't shop at the same stores, and they certainly didn't enjoy the same hobbies or interests, yet every other month or so, either Mary Ellen or Pups would pick up the phone to see how the other was doing. When Mary Ellen's son made the elite travel team for his lacrosse league, she called Pups. When Cady was selected to be Mary in the annual May procession at school, Pups called Mary Ellen. On the flip side, when Mary Ellen received a phone call from Visa informing her that the interest rate on her credit card was being increased, a quick chat with Pups about everything but Visa and interest rates, was enough to remind her how much she valued all that stuff she charged because without it, she would be ... Pups.

Today, the two old friends were trading tales of their back-to-school strategies. Pups bragged about how between coupons and advertised sales, she saved at least $65 on supplies. She complained that once a polyester pleated skirt is hemmed and ironed, it forms a permanent crease, so you can never make the skirt longer, only shorter, and who has children who shrink? She was convinced it was a conspiracy to sell more skirts. "Of course, the girls prefer shorter skirts, but just try and show up to school with a shorter than regulation skirt (or any other uniform infraction) and you lose recess for three days and even worse, you are forced to sit at a special lunch table with all the miscreants."

"I guess that's what you get with a Catholic School," said Mary Ellen. Another similarity, both women—the products of the same mediocre public schools—chose to send their children to Catholic schools. For Mary Ellen, it was a choice based on entry-level exclusivity. For Pups, it was a decision born of moral snobbery. The economics of Catholic schools made St. Anthony's Mary Ellen's only choice. Unlike regular private schools, the local Catholic schools actually rewarded you for having more children. Tuition went down with each successive child enrolled in the school. That value enticed Pups as well, but the heaping dose of old-fashioned Catholicism didn't hurt either.

Pups frequently found herself at odds with the

politically correct all-inclusiveness found in the rest of society. Catholicism was all about her favorite colors—black and white. Abortion is bad. Abstinence is good. She liked the definitiveness of the church, how you always knew where you stood. She could never figure out those who called themselves Catholic, but didn't "agree" with the church on hot topic issues. The bumper sticker affixed to the back of her Suburban said it all. "You can't be Catholic and pro-abortion!" What she appreciated most about her faith was the ritual and routine of it. Every night at dinner, the MacArthur's raced through a prayer of thanks, regurgitated so many times; the words had lost their flavor long ago. Every Sunday, the MacArthur's could be found fidgeting in the third pew on the left at Mass. And every Friday during Lent, the MacArthur's could be found at the local Knights of Columbus hall, drinking cheap beer and eating peel-and-eat shrimp or fried fish.

"I guess you know that Brophy is going to Washington Prep this year?" said Mary Ellen proudly.

"Really? That huge country club they call a school?"

"Yep. He's already started football practice."

"Isn't that a boarding school?" asked Pups.

"They have boarding students but Brophy will be a day student. They say it's much harder to get in as a day student."

"Really?" asked Pups.

"Sure. Day students' tuition is $25,000 and for boarders it's $45,000."

"Good God. For one student? For one year?"

"Yep," answered Mary Ellen.

As she listened to Mary Ellen name drop about all the big shots who sent their sons to Washington Prep, Pups heard the rumble of thunder and she knew she would have to cut the conversation short.

"It's thundering!" screamed Willa, bolting down the stairs.

"There's nothing to worry about," Pups told Willa. "I'm afraid I'm going to have to jump off, Mary Ellen. Willa is not a big fan of thunder."

"So I hear!" said Mary Ellen. "We'll have to get together soon. Call me!"

Get together my ass, thought Pups. They might talk on the phone but they never got together and probably never would until people they both knew started dying. Another rumble of thunder sent Willa into hysterics.

"We're all inside and we're safe," said Pups.

"But what about Daddy? How do you know he's not sitting under a tree or in the middle of a field somewhere?"

"Because Daddy sells cars and there are no trees or fields near his dealership. Just a parking lot and a Taco Bell."

"There are too trees. They're all along the road leading up to the showroom."

"Touché, Willa. I forgot about those. But why would Daddy deliberately sit under a pathetically small tree in a thunderstorm, when he could go twenty yards further and be dry and warm inside the showroom? Your father is not an idiot." Willa's cherubic face contorted as she attempted to come up with a rebuttal, but before she could offer a counter argument, Pups said, "Go see what Maddox and Cady are doing. Make sure they're not hiding somewhere would you?"

Willa had always been highly excitable so Pups learned long ago that the best way to keep her calm was to give her a responsibility—something that demanded strong and effective leadership skills. Then, no matter how loud the thunder, she would suck it up so as not to frighten her troops, Cady and Maddox. In addition to being a drama queen, Willa was also obstinate, sneaky, manipulative, and a total control freak. Pups saw a lot of herself in Willa, which didn't necessarily help their relationship. Pups always knew where Willa was headed—even before Willa herself had figured it out. There's nothing like having your mother waiting for you around every corner to make you embrace your stealthy side. As Willa left to carry out her mission, Grant came into the dining room wearing swimming trunks and flip-flops. "Mom, is it okay if I go to the pool with Mike?"

"Absolutely not. It's thundering."

"But we're not actually going to swim during the storm. We're going to hang out in the pool house. They won't let us in the pool until after it stops anyhow."

"So tell Mike he can come here and hang out while the storm passes."

"Why would he want to do that?" asked Grant.

"Because if he doesn't, he's not going to get to see his buddy because you're not going anywhere until this storm has past." Mike was a nice enough kid, but his mother worked, leaving Mike and his brother in the care of a young and beautiful Swedish au pair girl who had yet to earn Pups's trust.

"Oh, man!" whined Grant, trouncing out of the room.

Pups counted calmly in her head. She could feel the tension level of the household edging upward. It was simply a matter of ... twelve, thirteen, fourteen-seconds before Virginia, Willa, Cady, and baby Maddox, who didn't even talk much, were in the dining room screaming. "Will you all be quiet?" Pups asked sternly. "Willa. Willa! WILLA!" The child never responded to anything that wasn't repeated at least three times and then only when you had the strength to shout over her. "Shut your mouth and sit down now." Willa followed her mother's directions but wore the crazed look of a soldier planning to go AWOL. "Virginia, Cady, sit down now." Lacking their sister's renegade nature, they instantly did what they were told. Pups reached out and caught hold of Maddox. She scooped him up and planted a giant raspberry kiss on his naked belly forcing a loud squeal of glee. There is nothing more infectious than a two-year-old's giggle, and like that, the tenor of the house had changed yet again. "What's going on with your hair this morning, ladies? You all look like 'who did it and ran.'"

Almost daily, she told her daughters they looked

like "who did it and ran," and not one of them had any inkling what she meant. As raindrops bounced off the roof, Pups pulled Virginia's straight brown hair back into a sensible French braid while Willa and Cady waited their turn. They were a handful, these children, and they had their shortcomings. Grant was conceited and obstinate. Virginia was timid, but with a deceitful streak. Willa was a conniver. Cady had a terrible temper. And Maddox had no interest in potty training, but Pups knew that deep down, they all possessed the kind of strong character and high level intelligence that made them better than their peers. No mother could ask for more, but sometimes Pups did.

* * * * *

Upstairs, Grant sat in front of his computer and logged on to one of his many Facebook accounts. George Markel, a guy whose picture he obtained on-line by morphing photos of his mother's favorite singers, Billy Joel and Barry Manilow, from their younger days. The result was a guy with spiky blonde hair and bulbous eyes. He was creepy all right. George Markel had friended this guy Cole Reardon a few days ago and so far, no response. Grant had noticed that if you friend somebody who already has a lot of friends, they almost always friend you back, even if they had no idea who you are. To prove the point, even though George Markel didn't exist, he had over seventy friends. People just want to look popular. The more friends you have, the better. Hopefully, this guy Cole Reardon would turn out to be like everyone else.

-four-

RETAIL THERAPY

Thunder in the distance meant that any minute, the phone would ring. It would be her sister, Suzanne—in a panic—begging Mary Ellen to rescue her children, again. Mary Ellen, who had four children of her own, a dog who refused to poop outside, and a dip shit husband. Mary Ellen, whose only source of reliable help was Esmelda, her every-other-week cleaning lady. Her sister Suzanne, on the other hand, had a full-time housekeeper—who unfortunately didn't drive—a part-time gardener, and a long list of babysitters, caterers, pet care experts, and the like, waiting for the phone to ring. Suzanne was loaded … with help and everything else. Her husband, Corn, only worked three half-days a week, but still employed a professional staff that included two personal assistants; one who took care of all his errands like dry cleaning, buying gifts, and securing stellar dinner reservations, and the other to manage the ever-growing list of doctors appointments, medical tests, and prescription refills. He also retained a driver who was on call 24/7. Why Suzanne felt it was reasonable to call on her big sister to retrieve the triplets, time after time, was infuriating but Mary Ellen never voiced even the meekest protest, fearing those coveted payback invitations to swim or eat or even dance the night away at the Presidential Club would dry up.

Mary Ellen belonged to a country club too, but next to Presidential, Houndstooth Club was little more than a glorified public swimming hole with a semi-decent golf course and a few tennis courts. It was the kind of club that moderately successful plumbers or flooring dealers could afford to join, not the leaders of industry, commerce, and government that Presidential had on its rolls. The Houndstooth swim team, however, kicked ass when they competed against Presidential and all the other posh clubs. Apparently swimming, unlike tennis and golf, was a more plebeian talent.

"Good Morning Suzanne," she said when her cell phone chirped.

"Hi, Mary Ellen. It's lightning so I have to make this quick. I'm out on the river, too far from the boathouse. I have to sit this storm out by the shore. Meanwhile, tennis camp is cancelled. Corn is at the podiatrist; otherwise I'd ask him. Anyway you could pick up Ayn at Presidential?"

"Gosh, umm. I was just about to … "

"You know I wouldn't ask unless I really needed you. I mean, I am literally in the middle of the freakin' Potomac and I can see the storm clouds approaching. I should not be on the phone. Can you?"

As if to verify Suzanne's story, a loud clap of thunder sounded. "Yes. Yes. Don't worry. I'll take care of it. What about the boys?"

"They're at sleep away camp, where she would be if she wasn't so fussy."

"Right. Hang up now. I'll take care of it," said Mary Ellen nervously. Imagine getting hit by lighting because you lingered on the phone dissing your eight-year-old daughter. From the start, Suzanne and her daughter Ayn were as different as Under Armor and Ungaro. With each progressive stage of development, mother and daughter moved farther apart. When Suzanne offered building blocks to her toddlers, Ayn sought a pink plastic kitchen set. When Suzanne purchased bikes for her preschoolers, Ayn begged for Barbies. And when Ayn asked for high heels, Suzanne got her a field hockey stick.

Mary Ellen, on the other hand, truly enjoyed Ayn's company. For the mother of four rough and tumble boys, it was wonderful to have a little girl in her life to share her passions of decorating, cooking, and fashion. And as much as she complained about being taken advantage of, Mary Ellen never really minded a trip to Presidential. It could take her as long as 45 minutes to locate the child in the cavernous clubhouse. While she was there, she always ran into people she knew who presumed she belonged there. It was exhilarating. That people thought she belonged. As if her husband Kenny, could not only afford but would willingly pay the $125,000 initiation and all the other outlandish fees it took to join the most exclusive club in Washington.

She took her new beige and black plaid skort from her closet and paired it with a black polo shirt. The look screamed Burberry but in a tasteful way. It was part of the Plaid-IT-tudes line of clothing for which Mary Ellen was the exclusive in-home distributor for lower Montgomery County, including Chevy Chase, Bethesda, and her own hometown of Kensington. She pulled her blonde hair back into a classic country club pony-tail, slipped her feet into gold Jack Rogers thongs (the same sandals Jackie Kennedy paired with a sheath dress on a trip to India), threw a matching beige cardigan over her shoulders, applied some watermelon pink lip gloss, and she was ready to go.

Twenty minutes later, Mary Ellen pulled onto the tree-lined drive of Presidential Club, gave the guard in the gatehouse her "$125,000 initiation fee is no problem for me" wave, then steered around the traffic circle landscaped with blue petunias encircling a big red "P" of geraniums. The valet opened her car door with a well-practiced smile. Reaching for her cardigan and purse, Mary Ellen smiled sweetly and said, "I'll be back in a flash. I'm just picking someone up."

"No problem, Ma'am," he said.

She turned to the entrance and didn't get further than the heirloom rose bushes before hearing, "Hi, Aunt Mel!"

"Hi Honey, I thought I'd have to go in and hunt around for you."

"Nope," said Ayn walking towards Mary Ellen's mini van.

"Do you have all your stuff?" asked Mary Ellen trying to mask her disappointment.

"Yep," answered Ayn holding up her tennis bag.

"Do you need to say goodbye to anyone?"

"Nope."

Mary Ellen thought for a moment. "Tell you what. I have to use the little girls' room. Do you want to come with me or wait in the car?"

"I'll wait here," said Ayn climbing into the front passenger seat.

"Okay. Back in a jiffy," said Mary Ellen. She closed the door and, catching the eye of the head valet, said, "I'll be just a second." No matter how many times Mary Ellen walked through the doors of the Presidential Club, the sheer beauty of the place never failed to overwhelm her. It was as exotic and opulent as a Moroccan palace. You would think that a place called "Presidential" would look like the White House or some classic federal style building full of white wash and moldings. Built in the 1900s, Presidential was the epitome of gauche Mediterranean Revival complete with imported Italian red tile roofs, lavish mosaic coffered ceilings and intricately carved dark wood beams. To Mary Ellen, no other place on earth was as beautiful as this.

She wandered down Heritage Hall, past all the trophies, photos and memorabilia of the four Presidents who originally founded the club and the sixteen other Presidents who were members. (Everyone in modern history but Jimmy Carter.) The walls were filled with plaques honoring club members through the ages in the same way that St. Patrick's Cathedral in New York honored saints. In fact, Presidential was a lot like St. Patrick's Cathedral—a place that evoked not only a reverence for history but for the blessed among the living who were fortunate enough to make such beauty a part of their daily routine. Just past the entrance to the formal dining room, Mary Ellen came face to face with Claudia Tellers Manfrey, a former neighbor whom Mary Ellen never really liked even if they were at one time, best friends.

A few years back, catastrophe zoomed down Sundale Drive and took a sloppy wide left into Claudia's driveway. At first, she was the pity of the neighborhood, but in time, Claudia became a suburban legend. A completely random beneficiary of that preverbal silver lining everyone always talks about, but no one really believes in. Not until Claudia, that is. It all started when Claudia's husband Vernon gave her his customary peck on her indifferent cheek, asked her to pick up razor blades at the store and left for work in his Buick LeSabre. Vernon was a bureaucrat at the Department of Labor in downtown D.C. No one knew exactly what he did and, honestly, no one cared. In Washington, career government workers were the drones who kept the big show going and it didn't matter if you were a Labor drone or a Health and Human Services drone or a Pentagon drone. Drones droned. By contrast, introducing yourself as a political appointee was a real conversation starter. People would pepper you with questions about your connections and finances trying to piece together whom you knew and what led to your appointment. Of course, elected officials were the headliners of the whole enterprise. Even the lowliest freshmen congressmen from the poorest, most indigent district in the middle of Tennessee, the butt of every other congressmen's jokes, was like a rock star in the suburbs of D.C.

On that fateful April day, Claudia's drone, Vernon, backed out of the one car garage attached to their modest split level home in Kensington, never to return because less than half a mile away, a teenager, late to morning soccer practice for the third consecutive day and fearing the wrath of his coach, ran a red light, slamming his orange Honda Element into the driver's side of Vernon's Buick.

While pouring Honey Bunches of Oats into cereal bowls, Claudia heard sirens converging nearby. It never occurred to her that those air horns could have anything to do with her, until the phone rang. It was Sandy Hendricks from across the street. She didn't want to alarm Claudia, but her husband, Fred, had come upon a horrendous accident up at the corner of Saul Road and Connecticut Ave. He was fairly certain that Vernon was involved because while the tan Buick LeSabre was unrecognizable, Vernon's personalized rear license plate "Skins Head" (commemorating both his baldness and his beloved Washington Redskins) was undamaged and in plain view.

Claudia thanked Sandy for the phone call and hung up. She was upset but not hysterical, refusing to believe that anything major had taken place that morning. She did try calling Vernon's cell phone, but it went directly to voicemail. She finished packing her three daughters' lunches, hugged them a little longer than usual, and sent them out the door to school. Then, instead of having another cup of coffee and reading the morning paper like she usually did, Claudia went upstairs, showered, put on her make up and a simple yet elegant sheath dress, and went downstairs to wait for the phone to ring … which it did just one hour and twenty-seven minutes after she sat down at the kitchen table.

The teenage boy was banged up, but he survived the accident remarkably well. Vernon never knew what hit him. Numb from shock, Claudia's mind retreated to where it was most comfortable, making up a long, sad to-do list to get herself through the rest of her life. First, she would have to identify the body. Next, she would call his boss, the rectory at St. Anthony's, Gate of Heaven Cemetery, Collins Funeral Home and finally, *The Washington Tribune* to place a death notice. What else? There must be other calls. Claudia's breath became shallow and she started to gag as another item on her list dawned on her. She would have to tell her three beautiful daughters that they no longer had a father. Only then did the enormity of the situation hit her with a force every bit as violent and unexpected as the Honda Element crashing into Vernon's Buick. Claudia ran to the powder room off the kitchen and vomited. Then she called Mary Ellen.

Once Mary Ellen was involved, everything got easier. She took over Claudia's to-do list so all Claudia had to do was mourn, which she did with the help of a steady stream of white wine given to her by well-meaning friends, and a powerful prescription tranquilizer given to her by a well-meaning doctor who lived a few doors down. Mary Ellen sent Vernon's brother to identify the body. Mary Ellen contacted the rectory and the funeral home and all the well meaning people whom Claudia didn't have the strength to talk to.

While all the other moms on the block were busy preparing casseroles the Teller gals would scrape into the garbage for the next three months, Mary Ellen set out to find appropriate funeral attire for the entire family, including Vernon's mother who was on her way from Virginia Beach. She went to Nordstrom and Bloomingdales, Lord and Taylor and Loehmann's and anything she thought would work, she bought—charging everything on her credit card. Whatever they didn't want, she would return. For the girls, Mary Ellen sought somber yet youthful dresses in navy blue and ivory. For Claudia, Mary Ellen tried channeling Nancy Reagan at her husband's funeral—frail but elegant and always beautiful. And for Vernon's mother, Mary Ellen sought out easy care polyester dresses in prints that were predominantly black with a splash of red or yellow or magenta. After an exhausting eight-hour shopping spree, Mary Ellen racked up close to $3,500 in charges. She delivered the clothes to the Teller home expecting a front row seat to the glummest fashion show ever. Instead, Claudia, her mother-in-law and the girls delighted in trying on the garments and critiquing each other as they modeled their selections. At the funeral, first everyone said what a tragedy it all was, and then they said how lovely the Teller girls looked. Mary Ellen beamed with pride. If there was one thing she was brilliant at, it was creating a look.

A few weeks after the funeral, Claudia dropped by Mary Ellen's with a check for $634 and a pound cake she had baked. "I don't know how to thank you. Buying all those beautiful clothes. And charging them on your account. That is friendship. I returned everything we didn't wear—credited to your account. And I baked this. It doesn't begin to show how enormous my gratitude is, but I wanted to do *something*," said Claudia.

"Claudia, you really didn't need to do this. I mean, you have your hands full."

"It helps to be busy. The first week or so, everyone was calling and stopping by, now, when people see me at the Safeway, they make a quick turn down the incontinence supplies aisle. It's like I've got death all over me and they're afraid they might catch it."

"They don't know what to say. It's just too awkward right now. But don't worry, it'll get better."

"In the meantime, I'm going stir crazy. God, Mary Ellen what I wouldn't give for a night out on the town with no worries. No death. No widow talk. No insurance, wills, or annuities. Just a good old fashioned whoop it up night out. Do you have anything fun planned?"

"There's the annual Leukemia ball at Presidential, but tickets are like $400. We're going as my sister, Suzanne's, guests. I'd invite you to join us but … "

"$400 for a good cause is absolutely no problem. Between the life insurance, investments and Vernon's government pension, money is not going to be a worry—at least, not for a few years."

"But, Claudia, it's so soon."

"Maybe, but the Leukemia ball only comes once a year. Do you think they have any tickets left? Ask

Suzanne if she can get me a ticket. I'll pay, of course. I can't wait. What would I do without you?"

Mary Ellen got Claudia a ticket and invited her to ride with them to the party despite Kenny's protests. "Going to this Goddamned fancy ass ball is bullshit to begin with and now we've got to entertain the fucking widow Teller all night? Christ, Mary Ellen why didn't you tell her it was all sold out?"

They were both a little surprised when they pulled into the Teller's driveway and saw Claudia practically skipping out the front door in a frothy strapless yellow chiffon mini dress and silver stiletto sandals. Mary Ellen was even more surprised when Claudia disappeared midway through cocktail hour. Worried that her friend had taken on too much, too soon, she went in search of Claudia. Was she in the ladies room trembling with fear at the prospect of navigating social functions alone? Maybe she was in the lobby dabbing her eyes as the full realization of her loss took hold. Actually, as Mary Ellen discovered on her way back to the ball, Claudia was hanging out at the Presidential Club bar, allowing a trio of hot young members to buy her mojitos.

"There you are. I was worried about you!"

"No worries about me, girlfriend. Couldn't be better! These are my new friends, Henry, Greg and Dave. Gentlemen, Mary Ellen is my bestest friend in the whole wide world."

"Nice to meet you," said Mary Ellen suspiciously. Why would these handsome twenty-somethings have any interest in Claudia? Mary Ellen was dumbfounded. Claudia never did re-join the party, and wasn't seen again until the end of the night when Kenny and Mary Ellen were waiting for the valet to bring their car around.

"Hey neighbors!" said Claudia, sashaying towards them. Her cheeks were flushed and her hair was a bit mussed, but honestly, she looked radiant.

Kenny looked down his nose at the disheveled and clearly drunk woman who lived two doors away. "Enjoy yourself tonight?" he asked her facetiously.

"Enjoy myself? You betcha! For the first time in nineteen years, I feel like a million bucks. I wasn't upset. I didn't say or do the wrong thing … or at least if I did, Henry, Grease and what's-his-face didn't feel the need to point it out. I'd say I had an excellent time."

After they dropped Claudia off that night, Kenny, with his unique charm and fondness for stating the obvious said, "Man, that poor bitch is like a fucking dog in heat."

Mary Ellen didn't disagree. But she did have an epiphany. Claudia was not all that poor. She and Vernon did not have a particularly stellar marriage. Like most couples, including the Packinghams, he was into his thing—his football, his once a week poker night, his perfectly green lawn and his addiction to Internet porn. (Unbeknown to Claudia until she opened their Visa bill for the first time ever and discovered hundreds of dollars of charges from the XXXinyerface.com site.) And she was into her thing, her shopping, her once a month girls' night out, her perfect house and daughters. They hardly ever did anything together and when they did, they usually ended up arguing. And as much as she accepted him for all that he was and wasn't, the spark had gone out of their marriage long ago, if it was ever there to begin with.

As unfortunate as Vernon's death had been—especially for his daughters—for Claudia, it was an unexpected chance to fix up her life with the same gusto and attention to detail that she put into fixing up her home. While everyone was busy feeling sorry for poor Claudia, she was busy planning her biggest renovation ever. Poor Claudia was the luckiest woman on Sundale Drive. Claudia wasn't laundering skid marked briefs in the hottest water with bleach or wiping black stubble out of the bathroom sink every morning. Claudia was given the most precious of gifts—a do-over.

Soon after that, Claudia attended a charity gala with another couple she knew where she met a widower whose wife had died of ovarian cancer. He was struggling to raise his two sons alone just as Claudia was struggling with her girls. As luck would have it, he was a rock star, or at least he was the Washington version of a rock star—a freshmen congressmen from the poorest, most indigent district in Tennessee. Despite the fact that the median household income of his district was far below the poverty line, Representative Grover Manfrey was filthy rich. They were married before the one-year anniversary of Vernon's death in a lavish yet tasteful ceremony back in Tennessee. Claudia and her girls moved out of the neighborhood and into a Neighborhood, settling into a classic Tudor in Chevy Chase with Grover and his two sons.

To Mary Ellen, Claudia was living the ultimate life. She was actually happy. She seemed to genuinely love her new husband who just happened to be as dashing as he was rich. At least that's how it looked on those personalized photo Christmas cards they sent out. As skilled as Mary Ellen was at painting a pretty picture of the Packingham family, no amount of dressing them well, enrolling them in fancy schools or keeping their modest home looking like a million dollars, could make being married to Kenny Packingham look good. Overbearing and quick-tempered, Kenny's talent for weaving profanity into everything he said rivaled that of the best rappers and hip hop artists. His boorish behavior was exaggerated tenfold by the fact that when he was with his wife, he had two volumes yelling or screaming. He was so loud, so often, Mary Ellen stopped noticing. Their conversations were like a riotous theater of the absurd production with him howling four-letter gems and her pleasantly prattling on like she was conversing with the queen of England.

"Oh my God, Mary Ellen! How are you? It's been forever," gushed Claudia.

Mary Ellen leaned in to hug and air kiss Claudia, saying, "It's so wonderful to see you here."

Claudia gave Mary Ellen a conspicuous once over then emphatically stated, "Life on Sundale Drive must be good for the Packingham clan!" She had that sort of clubby tone that people at the top use to speak to other people at the top. The "ain't the view grand from up here at the top?" tone.

"Life is good," countered Mary Ellen who knew

that Claudia believed the Packinghams had moved up in the world if they could afford Presidential.

"Those boys of yours must be growing like weeds!" said Claudia.

"Brophy is starting over at Washington Prep in a few weeks," she said hoping to impress Claudia. She left out the part about how much financial aid Brophy was receiving so he could attend the expensive school. "He's a little nervous. Doesn't know a soul there. But I told him he'd have no trouble making new friends."

"Oh. My. God. So is Salter."

Mary Ellen smiled, but she had no idea who or what a Salter was.

"My stepson, Grover's youngest. He's starting at Prep too. They. Are. In. The. Same. Class!" Claudia's pitch increased with each new word.

"Oh! Oh, of course. Salter."

"We MUST get them together. Burke, my other stepson, is about to be a senior at Prep. I can't believe how time flies. Mary Ellen, you are going to … Love. It."

"We couldn't be prouder of him," said Mary Ellen. "He's such a great student and he's an amazing lacrosse player. That's why he wanted to go there. Best lacrosse team in the nation."

Though her optimism was bottomless, not even Mary Ellen could imagine Kenny moving the family up any rungs on the social ladder. The only way the Packinghams could possibly rise above the murky middle class was on the backs of their sons, especially Brophy, who showed every sign that he was the man Mary Ellen had been waiting for all her life.

"My boys are more into football and baseball, but you're right, Prep lacrosse is totally number one. Bar none. And the school, what can I say? It. Is. Phenomenal. Boy, things really are good on Sundale Drive."

"Yep. They sure are. And you know, I'm working now. Selling Plaid-IT-tudes. 'A label to watch' according the Harper's Bazaar. This is their latest," she said waving her hand down the length of her body.

"I love it. I thought it was Burberry."

"You may have seen their ads, it's a great line of preppy clothes for kids and moms. Lots of mommy and me matchy-matchy things. Adorable stuff. Ashley and Bea would look fabulous in it. I'll send you an invitation to my next trunk show. We'll have a blast. You don't have to buy anything. It's really just an excuse for a ladies' night full of Chardonnay and shopping! And if you can't make it to the trunk show, we always have a super fun Christmas event called Chix-mas. Just the girls. Tons. Of. Fun," said Mary Ellen echoing Claudia's distinctive cadence.

"God knows, you are a whiz with fashion," said Claudia knowingly. "Of course it helps when you look great in everything. You never gain an ounce. I'd love to know your secret."

Whenever someone asked her about her slender figure, Mary Ellen would typically smile and credit a sound diet and yoga. In truth, Mary Ellen's physique was the result of a highly personalized plan known only to her as "The Kenny Diet." One of the side effects of being married to a man who made you feel hollow inside is that your entire digestive track becomes so conditioned to clench down at the mere sound of his voice, eventually, it doesn't unclench. More than a few bites and she was full, so Mary Ellen kept herself nourished a few nibbles at a time.

"I so want to catch up, but I'm late for a change. We're having the kitchen re-done. Again! This time I've got Marko Phipps designing so I know I'm going to love it. We're supposed to finalize the drawer pulls today. Maybe I'll see you here at the Labor Day Dance?"

"Maybe," said Mary Ellen, unable to quickly come up with a plausible excuse.

"Can you believe all that's happened since the first time you and Kenny brought me here? Where on earth did the time go? It's funny because I was just thinking about Kenny the other day. Grover told me that a friend of his is opening a donut shop and I said 'Donuts are nothing but grease. Make sure you get him Kenny Packingham's number.' Anyhow, Labor Day will be great. We're sitting with the Tabbs. I'd ask you to join us but I think our table is already too full."

"That's okay," bluffed Mary Ellen. Mary Ellen hated it when people brought up Kenny's line of work. It was so … unrefined. Sure, ever since he bought the franchise from his father, he owned his own business, but unfortunately, the business was The Grease Police, servicing almost every fast food joint in the area. Of course, Kenny didn't actually go out in the trucks anymore. He wore a suit and tie to work each day and appeared to be a successful businessman. But to Mary Ellen, the nature of his business was such an embarrassment, he may as well have been wearing smelly, oil stained coveralls. "I'll mention it. He's been pretty busy lately," said Mary Ellen.

"Gotta run," said Claudia who made it about twenty-five feet down the hall before bumping into another friend she had to stop and chat with.

Just seeing Claudia made Mary Ellen feel like a loser. Still in the same house. Still married to the same asshole. Still not the person she deserved to be.

"How about we stop at the mall?" Mary Ellen asked as she climbed back into her car. Ayn beamed.

"I need a little retail therapy and there's a pair of darling shoes I saw in the Bloomingdales catalogue that I want to try on. And there's lunch. You didn't eat yet?"

"Nope. Just snacks," said Ayn placing her hand on the wrapped mints in her pocket. The storm blew over quickly and by the time they got to the mall, the sun was shining and a layer of steam rose over the asphalt parking lot.

"It looks like an enchanted palace in the clouds," said Ayn.

"It sure does," said Mary Ellen. "It's heavenly."

Inside Bloomingdales, they went directly to the ladies shoe department to try on a pair of Tory Burch flats Mary Ellen could not afford. She followed many top designers, but there was something special about Tory. It spoke to her in a way other lines didn't. She especially liked the shoes with the shiny gold medallions on the toes.

"Adorable!" declared Mary Ellen. "Will they go on sale anytime soon?" she asked the sales clerk.

"I doubt it. We literally just got them in yesterday and we've already sold four pairs."

$325 was about $275 more than she liked to pay for shoes. By watching items like a hawk, she almost always got the things she wanted on sale but this time it wouldn't be that easy. She weighed her options. Wait for the shoes to go on sale and or go for it? She needed these shoes too much. Technically, she was working. Her Plaid-IT-tudes business hadn't actually turned a profit yet but she did have an image to maintain.

"They are just too cute, don't you think?" she asked Ayn.

"Yep. They look like they have crosses on them."

"I never noticed it, but you're right. It's actually two T's end to end, but now that you mention it, it does look like a cross."

"I'll take them." Mary Ellen handed her credit card to the salesperson. She was glad it was her card alone and that Kenny didn't see or even know about the bills. He'd lose it if he found out she bought $325 shoes. When she started her Plaid-IT-tudes business, she needed start up capital, so she got her own American Express card and opened a separate bank account. She had to pay for all those "Pl-add it to your calendar" invitations, colorful catalogues, flyers, and postcards she sent out to her clients. She also had to buy samples up front, to the tune of about $3,000 a season. Putting herself on the line for that much money was a little scary at first, but once people saw the clothes, like Tory Burch flats, they had to have them. And with each of the three seasons she had sold so far, her profits steadily increased. She still wasn't bringing in more than it cost her, but she was close and fully expected to be in the black by Christmas. Especially since the Burberry-inspired fall line was sure to be a big seller. A twinge of guilt made her neck muscles tense, but she chased it with a deep cleansing breath. Those shoes were necessary, especially to Brophy. The mother of a scholarship student would never have brand new Tory Burch flats that hadn't even gone on sale yet. Wearing those shoes would protect Brophy from being labeled a charity case. Feeling more like a great mom than a status obsessed poser, Mary Ellen gave Ayn a bright look. "Hey sweetie, you must be starving. What do you say we get take out for lunch then go back home and play hair salon?" Ayn scratched the back of her head and gave Mary Ellen and enthusiastic nod.

five

L O V E L Y

BY SARAH JESSICA PARKER

They say that movie stars have a certain something, an indefinable quality that makes people look at them, like them, and want to be them. It's called the "It factor" and "It" is what separates true movie stars from the pack of ordinary working actors. Other professions have their share of "Its"—CEO's, athletes, politicians. "It" is something you're born with, so there are "Its" of all ages. Cole Reardon had "It," in spades. Guys wanted to be him. Girls wanted to date him. Parents wanted their own children to be just like him. He was smart, pulling in mostly A's with an odd B+ from a pent-up old shrew of a religion teacher. He was handsome in that casual, preppy, unaware way. And he was a beast on the lacrosse field, which gave him a fierce demeanor not to mention a fierce body. Those qualities contributed to Cole's aura, but there were many smart, good-looking beasts in the jungles of Potomac. Cole was Cole because he possessed "It."

What made Cole unique among "its" was the fact that he was also a genuinely nice guy. Unpretentious, caring, committed, it seemed as though Cole Reardon could do no wrong. People watched with great interest as he moved through each stage of life. If they were waiting for disaster or a comeuppance or a moral correction, they were disappointed because with each new chapter of Cole's dazzling life, he enjoyed the best the world had to offer. Despite all his brilliance, there wasn't the slightest bit of jealousy from his peers. If you lost the race for student body president to Cole Reardon, well then, it wasn't so much a loss as an opportunity to be a part of the Cole Reardon legend. His presence on the ticket actually increased the caliber of students running for lower positions such as vice president, treasurer, or secretary because a win meant you would get to work with Cole.

So sure was his success, that Cole could relax and enjoy life. All he had to do was check the master schedule every now and then so as not to miss some accolade or achievement coming his way. But Cole didn't relax. He worked hard to brighten the already blinding glow he emitted, hoping that one day the two people who seemed neither awed nor impressed by his accomplishments would take a step off their own fabulous life paths and notice his. His parents meant well, and he knew they loved him, but they were just too darned busy to make much fuss about him or his siblings.

His mother was too consumed with the family business—publishing *The Washington Tribune*—to have any time leftover for her actual family. She had always worked at the paper but when she was named publisher five years ago, she effectively quit her side job as mom and wife, two things she was never any good at anyhow. Her own childhood—filled with nannies, babysitters, boarding schools, and sleep away camps—left her lacking the basic knowledge of what a good mother does or even how a normal husband and wife are supposed to behave. She loved her children. She was proud of their accomplishments, but she was never the one to comfort or cheer them, guide them or push them, reprimand or scold them. She simply got briefed on them, the way she was briefed on the newspaper's stock value or advertising revenues. She used to clear her schedule for birthday dinners or parent teacher conferences, but when she became publisher, she couldn't … or at least she didn't. Between her rigorous triathlon training and her job, there wasn't much time left for mothering. It was bad for Cole, but he knew it was worse for his younger brother, Lewis, and it was downright tragic for his little sister, Dagny.

In one of the weirdest turn of events of Cole's short life, his dad, a workaholic in his own right, became the go-to parent for the Reardon kids. This was pretty insane because his dad was a crusader— fighting for the rights of any and every kind of downtrodden person in America. Native Americans, migrant workers, illegal aliens, you name it—if you lived in the kind of place that left your shoes covered with red clay dust, Alan Reardon was probably your hero. Cole was proud of his dad because at least he was doing something good for people. And he knew his father had good intentions in the father-son department. He tried to be there, but unfortunately, saving every poor wretch in America took a lot of time.

When his parents split up, his mother stayed in her house, the only home Cole had ever known, the one that had been in her family for generations. Cole, Lewis and Dagny moved with their dad to a somewhat smaller house around the corner. They stayed in the same neighborhood because his dad thought it would be easier on them if they could drop by and see their mother from time to time, which was great, except she was never home.

Determined to do things his way, his dad fired the bossy old Jamaican woman who had been taking care of them, replacing her with a bossy, young Ecuadorian grad student from Georgetown. She got them off to school in the morning, picked them up after soccer or lacrosse in the afternoon, and helped them with their homework if they needed it. After about a year, his dad married the grad student. When Inez Aguirre became Inez Aguirre Reardon, she followed in the footsteps of the first Mrs. Reardon and retired from the job of caring for any other Reardon. She replaced herself with another grad student, a weird dude named Pete. He had greasy hair and BO and he was always asking Cole about baseball teams because he thought that's what guys like Cole talked about.

At fifteen, Cole was tall for his age and could easily pass for seventeen, maybe even eighteen; but all appearances to the contrary, he wasn't even officially in high school yet. When he showed promise as a lacrosse attack man in the third grade, his coach suggested that his parents hold him back a year in school. An extra year to grow taller, stronger and develop his skills would make him a beast on the field when he got to high school. It worked, because tomorrow he would move into his room at his new school: Washington Prep, home of the best high school lacrosse program in the country. Excited as he was about moving out of his dad's house and into the dorm, he was also a little nervous about the absence of female diversions on campus. He lived for popped buttons on female classmate's oxford shirts and gusts of wind that blew their plaid pleated skirts upward.

To get himself through the long dry days without women that lie ahead, Cole planned a romantic day with the girl he had been lusting after all summer. Brittany was the summer helper at The Ninth Hole, the mid-course snack bar at Presidential Club. Whenever Cole had an idle moment, like when he was waiting for Pete to pick him up, he passed the time dreaming of a hook-up with Brittany. He first noticed her on Memorial Day when he and his dad were out for a rare day of bonding, playing in the father-son golf tournament. (His father's presence at Presidential club was even more rare than his presence at the dinner table, but since the tournament was a fundraiser for inner city youth, he made an exception.)

They stopped by The Ninth Hole and instead of Gus, the usual counter guy, there was Brittany. With her long, black, silky hair, and her dark brown eyes, she looked like a young Eva Mendes—without the mole. She was everything the girls he normally hung around with weren't, which is exactly why he liked her. And at thirteen, she was still developing, but what was there already was spectacular. Although golf was never really his thing, he started playing regularly and made a point to stop at The Ninth Hole every time he passed it. He would saunter over to the counter acting thirsty and disinterested.

"Can I get you something?" she asked.

"Uhh. Yeah. A Coke, lots of ice." In less than thirty seconds, there was his Coke. After few more instantaneously filled orders, he learned to ask for a slushy. The dispenser was finicky so there was a fifty-fifty chance he could spend more than a few seconds with her while they waited for the machine to work.

"It's not cold enough yet. Come back in fifteen minutes," she said.

"Sure." He returned in ten minutes so he could spend five minutes chatting. "Hey, do you live around here?" he asked.

"No," she answered.

"Oh."

As the summer wore on, they slowly struck up a friendship, but it took until the beginning of August to get her away from The Ninth Hole. It was complicated because of her work schedule, the fact that they were both too young to drive and where she lived. A couple of times, she was able to quit work a little early so they could take the bus two stops up the road to McDonalds and get back to the club before her mother, a year-round part of the housekeeping staff at Presidential, finished her shift.

Brittany arrived at 8:00 a.m. with her mother and instead of heading to The Ninth Hole, she met Cole by the entrance to the pool. Gus had given her the day off so she was free until six when her mother got off work. Cole and Brittany took the bus all the way from the gates of Presidential, ten miles south to the heart of Georgetown. The bus was empty, because in Potomac, the only people who took the bus were gardeners and cooks and housekeepers who worked for all the lawyers and lobbyists and politicians; and in the morning, all those people were traveling into Potomac, not out of it.

Though the trip was long and the air in the bus was both over-chilled and humid, he liked just being with her. They didn't have much in common and they didn't even talk much, but when he was with her, he felt comfortable. At ease. She didn't judge him. She didn't try to get him to do something he didn't want to do. And most of all, she wasn't a non-stop chatterbox like all the other girls he knew. The girls who wanted to know about his family. Where they lived. Where they vacationed. Did they really own a yacht? What was it like at Presidential? Was he leaning more towards Harvard like his mom or Princeton like his dad?

Brittany was quiet and when she spoke, she did not express the least bit of interest in his family, his house, his country club, or his college plans. She did seem nervous, however. She kept squirming around in her seat and scratching her head. He read on a web site that weird twitches, scratches, and tics could mean a girl wasn't interested. It could also mean she was itchy or nervous. He wanted to calm her so he used the same technique that helped settle his black lab, Wexley whenever he got excited. He stroked her long silky hair and held her hand until she relaxed. Adrenaline shot through his system every time the bus went over a bump and forced his hand to fall from her hair to her neck or from her hand to her leg.

After an endless bus ride, they walked around Georgetown. She couldn't have been less interested in all the little shops and boutiques that made most girls drool. She did show some excitement at the sight of the new Chipotle, but when she realized that it wasn't the one her cousin worked at, she returned to her regular, composed demeanor. For lunch, they stopped at the most venerable of Georgetown restaurant/bars: Clyde's. Cole ate at Clyde's all the time. It was no big deal for him, but Brittany seemed pretty excited to be at a place with tablecloths and waiters. He had a bacon burger and she had a cheeseburger. He liked that she actually ate real food like burgers and fries. The girls he had been out with before had ordered salad, taking a few tiny nibbles before announcing that they were full.

Cole was pretty experienced for a fifteen-year-old. Being tall and good-looking didn't hurt. Two summers ago, when his parents were battling out their final divorce settlement, they sent him, his brother and sister to East Hampton to stay with their aunt for the season. He hung out with Scott, his slightly older cousin who introduced him to a bunch of thin, blonde girls who weren't shy about being with boys and seemed to find his inexperience a big turn-on.

After splitting a brownie sundae for dessert, Cole paid the bill with the credit card his dad got him. That's when Brittany started scratching again so he suggested a walk along the Potomac River, hoping the fresh air would help her relax. He held her right hand, which seemed to calm her somewhat because after that, she scratched less and only with her left hand.

"See those kayaks out there?" he asked.

"The little boats?"

"Yeah. We have those. Man, I love paddling around the water. Have you ever kayaked?"

"No."

"When I get my license I'll take you out for the day. You'll love it. We have a two-man so we can go out together. It's fun."

"Sounds fun," she said. "When do you get your license?"

"I don't know. Not for a while. Officially, I can get it in a few months but who knows when my dad will have the time to actually take me."

"What about your mom?"

"She's not exactly around."

"Oh. Sorry."

"It's not like she's dead or anything. She's just not around much. They're divorced. No big deal." They walked around a little more and in the middle of the waterfront park, he could wait no longer. He wrapped his arms around her and gave her a kiss. When she kissed him back, he knew the day would live up to his expectations.

"Man, you smell good," he said. She blushed and opened her purse. She took out a bottle of Lovely by Sarah Jessica Parker perfume and gave herself, and for fun, Cole, a good spritz. "Let's go," he said, pulling her arm. They walked under the Whitehurst Freeway, up a steep hill and turned into a narrow cobblestoned alley. Brittany looked unsure so he said, "Don't worry, my Mom has a place in this building." He pushed a heavy metal door that looked like it led to a dark warehouse or even a dungeon but instead, it opened into a very modern and very fancy lobby. Cole said hello to the doorman and waved to the security guard.

"Can I help you?" asked the guard.

"We're just going up to my Mom's place. Elizabeth Sherwood, number 302." The guard gave Cole a look that showed he knew exactly what they were up to, but only said, "Have a lovely day."

"You too," Cole answered as he led Brittany towards the elevators. Once the door closed, he kissed her again—this time with a little more force—which she didn't seem to mind. He led her off the elevator. As long as his mom hadn't changed the code on the electronic door lock, he was golden. 3-5-4-6, the lock clicked. *Now, let it all begin*, he thought except, as she walked through the door suddenly Brittany was completely caught up in the apartment.

"I thought you said your mom wasn't around," said Brittany.

"She's not. Like this condo is hers but she never comes here."

"This place is so white. Doesn't she worry about stains and stuff?"

"Nah, she doesn't really live here or anything. I bet that sofa hasn't been sat on by more than three people tops."

"Why does she have a place she doesn't use?"

"She uses it. But mostly just to shower or change before she goes to some big party or something. I think she sleeps here in the winter when the roads are icy or snowy and she can't be late for work." Talking about his mom was a major turn off, so he led her to the bedroom and started to tug on her shirt.

"Is this your mom's room?" she asked.

"Yeah," he said indifferently, trying to let her know that he wasn't interested in his mother.

"Don't you feel a little creepy? Doing it in your mom's bed?"

The only thing Cole felt was Brittany's body and that was not at all creepy. "This isn't her regular bed. That's in Chevy Chase," he said. Moving his hands under her shirt, he started to kiss her neck. "Stop worrying about my mother. She won't be using this bed for months." He guided Brittany down onto his mother's bed, laid her head on his mother's pillow and without knowing why or how, proceeded to screw Brittany, his mother, himself, and his soon-to-be Latin teacher.

six

HOLIDAY IN SWAKOPMUND

Mary Ellen had never been much of an athlete. She couldn't catch or throw, running made her too sweaty, and getting her foot caught in the sprocket of Nelson Dinsmore's front tire when she was twelve marked the end of her bike riding days. Then, at the age of thirty-eight, Mary Ellen found something physical that appealed to her. Yoga. It was expensive, so it gave her the kind of elite status she tried to attain in all facets of her life. What you wore was critically important. And most of all, she liked the fact that yoga was exercise, but there was a lot of relaxation, deep breathing and rest built into every ninety-minute session and no one would ever push you to exceed your edge, even if your edge happened to be halfway. There were benefits. She was more flexible and at least a little stronger. When she started, a backbend or "wheel" was completely out of the realm of possibilities, but now, after ninety minutes, five days a week, every week for a year, she was starting to think about attempting the move.

Her arm muscles hinted at definition. Her abs, well her abs were about the same as they always were, but she had given birth to four children, so there was a limit and Mary Ellen was perfectly fine with that.

But the one truly tangible thing she got out of all that yoga was that each day her butt inched closer to a perfect yoga butt. Firm, round and strong. If she was honest with herself, Mary Ellen would have to admit that the pants she wore to yoga were more responsible for the magnificent new shape of her ass than the toning effect of the yoga. These insanely expensive stretch pants which incorporated every advance in fiber technology, design, light refraction, sports medicine, muscle compression, and even odor control had the power to turn any old fat ass into a near perfect posterior; junk in the trunk into a voluptuous derriere; a loose caboose into a glorious gluteus maximus. The manufacturer of those magic ass-lifters knew they had something special. Confident that women would pay any price for an instantly buoyant bottom, the company offered free yoga lessons in their stores three times a week with a carefully selected instructor who didn't need magic ass pants but who looked so ethereal in them, it was impossible for any mortal woman to get out of the store without buying a pair of the $200 wonders.

Not only did these pants become ubiquitous in certain neighborhoods, people started to call them "Butt Crack" because they were every bit as addictive as crack cocaine. Like most nicknames this one was not too far off the mark. Within seconds of pulling on the pants, the wearer experienced total euphoria. Checking out her shape in the mirror, supreme confidence edged out insecurity. These initial effects of Butt Crack were followed by loss of appetite (because suddenly it was possible to imagine how even more fabulous your butt would look if you somehow managed to drop a few pounds), insomnia, alertness, increased energy, paranoia (*Does my butt really look good or am I delusional?*) and finally, a seemingly insatiable craving for ... more pants. Shrewd observers likened the company's marketing plan to the "free sample" drug dealers offer to new clientele. That small free taste of yoga spawned not just an addiction to expensive spandex, but once those pants were in your closet, your habit grew exponentially. When the addiction took hold, the new addict started mixing with a new crowd at the junkies' hangout of choice—the yoga studio. Which studio depended on whatever corrupt, under-the-table scheme the retailer managed to arrange.

The days of the happy-go-lucky hippie chick yogi dressed in saggy leggings and homemade tie-dyed t-shirts were gone. Today's yogis are expertly outfitted in all the latest versions of Butt Crack which they received free of charge—a way to market new products to a hungry horde. And of course, once you started going to the studio, you couldn't very well show up in the same pants every day. You needed a few different colors and a few different lengths. Add a few pretty tops, a serenely colored yoga mat and carrying case, a matching towel with little rubber nibs on it so it doesn't slip around on the mat and ... in the end, the investment these ladies made in yoga, a centuries old physical discipline that eschews material possessions and was originally intended to be practiced alone in your home, rivaled what people pay to send their children to college.

So Mary Ellen followed scores of upper middle class women into the yoga studio. She had three pairs of Butt Cracks, one black, one dark grey, and one brown. She also had a collection of tops that showed off her emerging biceps and held in her unbudging abs. She got her money's worth though, because unless she was had a trunk show or a doctor's appointment, she wore her yoga gear all day long—to the grocery store, to pick up the kids from school, to the lacrosse game. How else would people see how great her ass looked? Mary Ellen fully embraced yoga when it came to fashion, but she would never come close to the yoga tenants of living in the moment and staying focused and mindful of yourself. Your inhale and your exhale. Your down dog and your vinyasa. Mary Ellen liked yoga because it gave her an opportunity to observe people who were more attractive, better connected, richer, and thus happier than she was but yet, here they were, flipping their dog right next to her. Whenever her gaze was supposed to be focused on her Drishti—a tiny spot on the floor—Mary Ellen would subtly scan the room. She quickly learned that the most accomplished and best looking yogis looked even better in their heinie hammocks because they didn't wear underpants to ruin the smooth lines. She discovered that the spoiled college-aged yogis who flooded the studio over the summer and liked to practice in the skimpiest boy shorts version of butt crack, were diligent waxers. And Mary Ellen could not believe how many elegant, well-coifed, society women had feet gnarled by bunions, hammertoes, and foot fungus.

Most of the regulars at Humble Warrior Studio were stay-at-home moms like Mary Ellen. Women who dropped the kids at school (private, parochial, or impossible to get into public magnet programs), then swung by Starbucks for a tall skim latte before heading to the 9:30 a.m. yoga class. After class, many of them stopped for lunch at Lean & Green, the big-ticket salad place across the street, or perhaps they'd pick up some fruit at the organic market, or go to the mall to shop. As the most expensive yoga studio in the area, Humble Warrior had its share of minor celebrities (like the weather lady from Channel 6). That part of the equation really appealed to Mary Ellen, who felt it was worth the extra money to be in the company of people who were a lot more interesting than she was. Kenny would die if he ever found out how much money she spent on yoga, and for that matter a lot of other stuff too, but since she charged everything on her own personal Plaid-IT-tudes business charge card, so far, he was miserably unaware. Mary Ellen always made it a point to arrive early enough to claim the best space in the studio for herself. She liked to be in the front of the room because it afforded her the best view of the class when she was bent over with her head between her ankles. She unrolled her burgundy yoga mat, folded her special yoga towel, and placed it at the front of her mat next to her bottle of water. Then she went to the open shelves on the side of the room and selected her props: two hard foam blocks that made it easier to reach the floor from certain poses and a Navaho blanket she used to wedge under her tight hip muscles in half-pigeon pose or to cushion her head during Shavasana.

As she arranged her space, a woman she didn't recognize unrolled her mat beside her. Her non-existent panty line announced that she was young, hip and cool and the sheen on the black fabric enveloping her lower half announced it was expensive and brand spanking new. As any devotee of magic ass pants knew, if you dared to wash them in the washing machine with other laundry, the pants would sprout little pilly balls. In no time, they looked like the bottom half of a four-year-old's bikini after a summer of being dragged across the cement edge of the pool. When Mary Ellen first discovered the pilly balls, she took her pants back to the store to exchange her obviously defective merchandise—only to be told by a perky young sales associate that in order to retain the integrity of the product, they recommend hand washing and air drying only. If you must use the washing machine, wash the pants and only the pants. Do not include any other items in that load, especially anything cotton like a towel.

Those pilly balls are what separated "the haves" from the "have-nots" in yoga class. The "haves" had help doing the laundry, the dry cleaner or a housekeeper … or at least, they had the time to run an entire load for a single spandex item. To the "haves," special needs garments were not a problem. The "have-nots," on the other hand, did their own laundry and a million other things. They didn't have time for single-item loads. They stuffed their washing machines to capacity and their precious booty braces were thrown into the machine with everything else: socks, t-shirts and yes, even towels—pilly balls be damned.

"Let's all take a comfortable seat and close our eyes," said Suki, the yoga teacher, closing the door behind her. "Think about your breath. Fill your lungs with air," she said. Mary Ellen inhaled deeply. "Empty your mind and concentrate on being present. In this moment. What are you feeling?"

Mary Ellen tried focusing on herself but as always, this first moment of stillness was like a starter's pistol going off in her mind, sending her thoughts on a wild ride through her mundane to-do list, her stifling worries and her fantastic aspirations, creating such trompe l'oeil mish mash of fantasy and reality, it would be impossible to take a step without walking into a wall.

"Let's start with three ohms."

As Mary Ellen chanted with the rest of the class, she heard the studio door open and sensed a latecomer situating herself fairly close to her mat. It was a struggle, but she forced herself to keep her eyes closed and her thoughts focused.

"Now, set an intention for today's practice. Maybe you wish for less judgment. Kindness. Compassion ... for yourself or someone else. Or perhaps you simply hope to tune into your breath. Go ahead and recognize it and when you are ready, open your eyes and find your way to down dog."

Mary Ellen set the same intention every day. To feel connected. She opened her eyes and took the down dog pose; hands on the floor in front of her, feet planted about four feet behind her hands, and her butt sticking up, high in the air. She pedaled her feet, moved her head back and forth and twisted her spine. Then she settled herself, trying to focus on her breath but actually focusing on everything but. The Asian woman two rows over was fidgeting. "No underpants" behind her was exaggerating her breath so much, she sounded like an iron lung. Looking through her legs, Mary Ellen noticed that the latecomer set herself up behind her and to the right. A tan muscled forearm, slightly on the hairy side and marked prominently with some kind of a tattoo was all Mary Ellen could see.

"Hop or jump to the front of your mat. Standing forward bend."

From this position, her view improved and Mary Ellen discovered that the latecomer was not a she, but the rare exotic bird of weekday morning yoga classes: a gorgeous younger man. "Just rock back and forth and work out all those kinks."

Bronzed body with the kind of muscles Mary Ellen had only seen pictures of, topped by waves that glimmered where they had been kissed by the sun. His face was a perfect blend of strength and softness with thick bushy brows to counter those permanently amused brown eyes. Powerful jaw and rugged unshaven skin countered by the slightest bit of a smirk common among men who know they have received more than their fair share of God's gifts. His only obvious physical defect was below his ankles were the rugged bronze glow stopped abruptly and became a sickly bluish white. His blistered feet were a mangled mess of black, crusty toenails, purple, bruised digits and yellowish, calloused heels offset by two shriveled nail less big toes that looked like her son Doyle's newborn hamsters.

"With a flat back, let's come up to standing."

While the front of her mind followed Suki's commands, the back of her mind was one row behind and to the right. The front of her mind, a strictly black and white entity handled everything from grocery lists to dental appointments while the back of her mind, profuse with color, whooshed her off to her favorite destination: endless possibility.

On that particular day and for many days afterward, the story began just a few hours into the future when, in between picking up her Plaid-IT-tudes invitation order at Kinkos and stopping at the Safeway to buy dinner, she treats herself to a Starbucks chai latte and who does she overhear ordering a double espresso? Him. He complements her on her form and tells her it was his first yoga class ever. She smiles and tells him that he was impressive for a beginner. That's as far as it goes but then they start to see each other regularly at yoga. Since he is a ... deciding what he does for a living momentarily interrupts her flow. Something that affords him the time to take a morning yoga class. Something that pays well, definitely not some wimpy office job ...

The class moved through warrior one's and warrior two's with Suki moving around the room adjusting peoples' poses. A correction here or a deeper stretch there. And constantly, Suki reminded the class to breathe. Inhale deeply and exhale slowly. The room sounded like a giant ventilator with all that air rasping in and out of people's lungs. Mary Ellen's breath did not match the intensity of her classmates. She was too busy planning to visit *him* in the Kalahari Desert where he would be on assignment for a month. There were a million things to do: fill her prescription for anti-malaria medicine, make sure Suzanne had the boy's schedules straight, and call

Verizon to get her cell phone service switched to world. His tanned and toned physique along with the presence of additional tattoos on his back and shoulders and the bruised gash on his ankle pointed her imagination outdoors leading her to settle on National Geographic as his employer. He was one of those filmmakers who goes out in the wild for a long span of time and while he's there, his hair grows long and he doesn't shower much since the only company he has are the lions he's tracking and two local guides with crooked teeth and even less inclination for grooming.

Mary Ellen and ... Heath, that was his name for the moment but she left open the possibility that she might change it to Steele ... went from casual yoga acquaintances to lovers faster than moving from triangle pose to half moon. He planned to take a week off from the wild so he could meet her in Swakopmund, a city on the northwestern coast of Namibia, a place she never heard of until Angelina Jolie decided to give birth there. Who knows, maybe they would run into the Jolie-Pitts in the lobby of their hotel. Maybe they would invite Heath and Mary Ellen to dinner so they could learn about lions. Anything was possible, especially since they were staying at the top hotel in Swakopmund and wasn't she always saying that proximity to greatness was the fastest way to your own success?

Because she would never accept herself as an adulteress, she had to deal with Kenny before going any further with Heath. She settled on a horrific grease removal accident that took him swiftly and painlessly, leaving her alone and debt-free thanks to his hefty life insurance policy and the extra rider for industrial accidents. The boys were understandably devastated, but a week at Suzanne's would help. Though Corn was as old as Father Time, he was a father, and being with him should be a nice change for the boys.

"Ukatasina. Chair," said Suki.

Mary Ellen extended her arms upward while sitting back in an imaginary chair. She held her stomach in, tucked her tailbone under and took a long controlled inhale. Her pose was so well executed no one would ever guess that she had no consciousness of her own body for at that moment she was consumed by the wonders of Heath. It was hard to tell, but it looked like his tattoos were cats. Common ordinary house cats. The tattoos and the earrings excited her. They made him so exotic, so out of her realm, that she didn't dwell on the oddity of permanently inking yourself with something as mundane as an ordinary Tabby—no more than she would dwell on Tom Cruise's height or Brad Pitt's acne scars. Unlike Kenny, Heath was fun. He enjoyed her company and he told her so. When he was silent, it was a contemplative silence not a furious one. His smiles were laced with mischief or joy or kindness, never mockery or disgust or cruelty. He never smelled weird. His kisses were always firm and passionate. And he never once tried to turn the TV on so he could follow the Redskins game while they were making love (which nowadays happened about as often as the Redskins won Super Bowls).

"Vinyasa," said Suki. "Now slowly and with grace, down dog."

Mary Ellen started to move back into a down dog position, but she was so consumed with the long playing story going on her mind, she lost all sense of herself doing yoga and let her guard down. As she reached the apex of her down dog, she let one rip. And not just any old one, but a thunderously loud stinker, the likes of which she hadn't produced since giving up dairy. Yoga bombs are a common phenomenon; perfectly natural given all those positions that have your butt over your head. Mary Ellen had witnessed plenty of them over the past year, but never, never, ever, ever had she been the triggerman.

"Chaturunga all the way down to the mat," said Suki. "Inhale deeply and raise your head, arms and legs. Exhale."

Did they know it was her gas they were inhaling and exhaling? What did Heath think? Mary Ellen scanned the room for any indication of someone breathing in noxious fumes, but only saw people transfixed by their Drishtis and their breathing. Could it be? Was it possible that her panty burp had gone unnoticed? Could these people be so deep into their own meditation that something as unmistakable as a fart wafting through the class went completely ignored? It dawned on her that maybe she was the only one who didn't experience the sweet, mind freeing somnambulance that yoga is supposed to induce. For an instant, Mary Ellen wondered what she was missing.

"There is a time for effort and a time for ease," said Suki. "Whatever effort you put forth was all you could put forth. Be happy with that simple truth. Lie back, place a blanket under your head, clear your mind and just be."

After eighty minutes of monkey brain, Mary Ellen finally let go. She gave her head a good scratch, placed it on the Navajo blanket and closed her eyes.

-seven-

THE PHEROMONE
TRAIL

On the Sunday before Labor Day, SUV's and minivans packed with stuff, pulled out of their driveways and followed the well-worn pheromone trail leading them to Roland Hall, the main building of Washington Prep. That trail began in 1890 when the school was built on one hundred square acres of pristine farmland. Its closest neighbor, a sprawling tobacco plantation, was about two miles down the pebbled road. In time, streetcars brought city dwellers who built summer homes nearby. The gentry had needs, so businesses bloomed—a market, a soda fountain, a tailor and a furniture maker. When automobiles started rolling down that pebbled road, development surged, generating new homes and businesses and lots and lots of people. Like an innocent sprout of Kudzu, rampant development overtook the once bucolic land. Chain restaurants, gourmet ice cream shops, giant electronics stores, bedding marts, multiplex movie theaters and office buildings so lacking in personality they were covered in mirrored glass, disguising their own dullness by reflecting the even more lackluster buildings around them. The dusty pebbled road had become eight lanes of asphalt bordered by an overgrown forest of signs.

In the midst of all that was an unexpected clearing: four long blocks of perfectly maintained and very tall boxwood hedge. At the end of the hedge was an unassuming drive with a small, understated sign that said "Washington Preparatory School, Est. 1890." Vehicles following the trail turned onto that drive and into an unlikely oasis. Most passersby had no idea that beyond those bushes was a nine-hole golf course, a state-of-the art athletic center with indoor track, weight room, swimming pool, basketball gymnasium, a snack bar with a wood burning pizza oven, padded wrestling room and a film room, a theater with an orchestra pit and plush upholstered seats, and a cluster of stately red brick Federal style buildings with beautiful stained glass windows that functioned as dormitories, classrooms, art studios, and science labs. Nicer than many college campuses and more exclusive than most country clubs, the one-hundred rolling acres of Washington Prep had it all.

By noon, the campus was swarming with young men and their parents hauling designer comforters, high-end laptop computers, tiny television sets, trunks, and suitcases up the old staircase leading to the dormitory rooms. They dumped their belongings on top of bare mattresses, greeted the roommates, and then followed another trail leading to the local mall where they bought even more crap to cram into the austere dorm rooms of Washington Prep.

The arrival of this scourge wasn't a surprise to Wenn because he certainly knew the students would return, but it was a shock—a visceral assault to his delicately balanced system. Gone were the days of not speaking to a soul. Days when he could lose himself in ancient texts or between the tones of a well crafted jazz composition then go for a long solitary run where he could ruminate over the nuances of what was written. It also reminded him that he would have to figure out what to do with his cat before someone discovered that the residential dean was breaking one of the cardinal rules of dormitory life.

Walking across the quad, he saw Dr. Brennan, a squirrelly old man who had been headmaster of Prep long enough to remember serving up JUG—Judgment Under God (the school's moniker for punishment)—to Wenn, his brothers, his father, and his uncles. At other schools, run-of-the-mill disobedience warranted detention or a basic sentence such as exclusion from a field trip with more serious infractions incurring suspension or even expulsion. At Prep, common adolescent missteps were handled in much the same way the Church handled sin before the Reformation. For venial offences, like talking back or cutting class, JUG would suffice. JUG was physical labor. It was a remarkably effective punishment because the powers that be at Prep knew for sure that these boys did not grow up mowing the lawn or shoveling snow at home. JUG was the school's way of subtly teaching the coddled ones what might happen to them if they don't behave—namely, they won't be able to afford to pay some poor bastard to mow their lawn or shovel their snow.

In JUG, the offender might have to pick up trash after a big football game or rake leaves before

Parents' Weekend. As a student, Wenn believed that the teachers went JUG crazy whenever the school grounds department had too much on its plate. As a teacher, he found out he was right. For mortal offences, like cheating, stealing or violent behavior, parents were called into Father Bills's office. As President of the school, Father Bills handled issues relating to finances and moral character while Dr. Brennan dealt with the school administration and academics. Having your parents called into Father Bills's office was never a good thing. After a discussion of the nature of the crime, the motivation and the reason why a perfectly good kid can end up a perfectly bad kid, the sweet, red-cheeked priest would suggest that perhaps Prep wasn't a good fit for their little troublemaker.

If the boy was there on a scholarship or came from the kind of family where both parents had to work two jobs so they could afford to send their son to Prep, Father Bills took pity and usually gave them a free pass. (Meaning, the criminal would remain at the school, but would essentially become an indentured servant until graduation.) However, for the typical filthy rich Prep parents, Father Bills gave them a shake down that would impress the Goodfellas. The parents would grovel and tell him how sorry they were and about how much stress Junior was under. What they wouldn't say, Father Bills already knew: if Junior got kicked out of school, there was no way in hell he would get into a top tier university.

At some point in the conversation, the dad would discreetly slide a blank check made out to the school across the desk. Just as discreetly, Father Bills would slide that blank check into his desk drawer and soon, his opinion of the delinquent would begin to soften. It was the Prep version of a Plenary Indulgence. Supposedly, Father Bills has some kind of a rate card taped inside his desk drawer. Cheating cost $10,000 because if you get thrown out of school for cheating, you won't even get into a second tier school. Other offences, like being caught with a controlled substance, giving the new kids a swirly or getting caught toilet papering the crosstown rival the night before a big game could run your parents anywhere from $2,000 to $8,000, depending. Wenn wondered what kind of punishment would get handed out for harboring a cat in the dorm.

"Morning, Mr. Mann. What a splendid day. I never realize how much I miss all the hub-bub until it returns."

"Yes, sir. A splendid day," said Wenn stupidly. He hated Dr. Brennan and his propensity for chitchat. Hated it back when he was a student and hated it even more as resident dean. Though he came off as friendly and kind, Wenn felt like Dr. Brennan was always looking for clues in their meaningless chatter. Little nuggets that he would store up and use against him, like recording a conversation then selectively playing back only certain words to make it seem like he was insane or violent or who knows what else.

"I understand the incoming freshmen class is one of the most accomplished we've seen in years," said Dr. Brennan. "And more than a few VIP's in this class, including the Secretary of Education's son, who, by the way, should be addressed as Madame

Secretary."

"Yes," answered Wenn. "I'm on my way over to greet the new residents and their families now. See if they need any help."

"Don't let me hold you up, Mr. Mann." Wenn didn't get more than a few steps away before Dr. Brennan added, "My, my, it looks as if your limp is completely gone."

"Yes. Just a bruised ankle. No big deal."

"Terrific news. I have high hopes for our runners this fall," said Dr. Brennan referring to the cross-country team Wenn coached, or rather babysat. Required to direct one extra-curricular activity, he chose cross-country because it demanded so little of him. He met the team in front of the gym every day at 3:30 and told them to run around the perimeter of the campus for an hour. That was the extent of his "coaching." He did have to escort them to meets, but all things considered, it was the least taxing activity on campus. Cross-country was the only team in the school's athletic program that no one, including Dr. Brennan, ever paid any attention to. Why would they with championship caliber football, soccer, and basketball teams to hold everyone's interest until the spring rolled around and the lacrosse gods charged onto the playing field? The cross-country team was pretty good, but they weren't filling up the trophy cases like the other teams.

His ankle was better thanks to Carleton, the school's athletic trainer who bandaged him up and told him that yoga would help get the kinks out. Like most runners, he lacked flexibility. Five minutes into his first (and only) yoga class, however, he knew it wasn't for him. There was no way in hell he would ever be able to loosen up in a room full of moms with camel toes. *What's up with yoga pants and camel toes anyhow? Why don't they just wear sweats?* It was a relief when the swelling finally subsided enough for him to resume running. The only trace of the whole incident was a little scab on his elbow and the spectacular biker woman who kept showing up in his daydreams.

"Looking forward to a great season, sir," said Wenn before turning towards the long procession of blow hard dads and type-A moms. As much as he detested meeting parents, it was part of his job to welcome them and assure them that boarding school would not traumatize their babies. That was the truth; it wasn't the boarding that wrecked these guys. It was the academics and the fierce competition and the constant pursuit of trying, in some way, to stand out and be impressive among this school full of guys who had a million chances to either fuck up or be brilliant.

Wenn moved into the teeming crowd of bickering families, extended his hand, smiled, and began introducing himself. The parents didn't realize it, but this was the only day on the academic calendar that he would shake their hands, make eye contact or have anything whatsoever to do with them. On the first day of class, Wenn outlined his parent policy to his students. "If you have the kind of parents who are going to come and see me when you start to fuck up, I highly advise you not to fuck up." That this sentence could accomplish so much was a source of great pride. It was certainly the first time these hothouse flowers ever heard a teacher use the word "fuck" in the classroom. While lots of teachers cursed when they were outside coaching, no one cursed in any private middle school classroom that he ever heard about. The novelty of this word would wear thin as the academic year progressed, which is why it thrilled him to be the first to let it drop.

Confronted with their first in-class f-bomb, boys would smirk and chuckle, thinking they were all a part of a special club—the men's club. *We are in the company of men! Bring on the cursing!* At some point, the students would look up to the macho man who had deflowered their virgin ears to see that he was not smirking and realize he was not only serious, he would never belong to the same club as them. "If your parents take it upon themselves to come and see me, prepare for the worst, because if I have to deal with your parents, you're going to have to deal with me. The thing is, it's hard to find a good Latin teacher. We're a rare commodity, like true love or a giant with an extra eye in the middle of his forehead, so I would literally have to murder someone to get fired … and I've actually come close to losing this job a few times. Make of that what you will."

When he was done, there was no smirking. The only kids who weren't worried were the lazy ones whose parents didn't care, but parents who shell out $45,000 and don't care are more rare than Latin teachers. He loved hearing second hand the stories of what great lengths students took to prevent their parents from making that dreaded appointment with him. They would beg and plead, of course. One student even willed his appendix to burst an hour before his mother was due to see him, forcing her to choose between keeping the appointment or taking her son to the emergency room.

"Hi there. Al Sutton, Senior, and this is my son, who is also Al," said one of the more aggressive dads as he extended his hand toward Wenn. Years of translating ancient texts had trained his brain to quickly manipulate words and letters searching for meaning, intent and subtext. He was great at jumbled word puzzles. So, the man squeezing his hand was instantly catalogued in his brain as ASS. His Presidential Club logoed shirt, sunburned neck and bloated belly told Wenn that Big ASS was hoping to drop off Little ASS (just a small, under-developed version of the big guy), then head over to the club for eighteen holes and a round of mint juleps. There was even a fifty-fifty chance he'd get paired with Wenn's dad, Big Mann.

"Wenn Mann. Resident Dean and I teach Latin. Welcome to Prep," he said. He was good at playing the role of strong yet caring administrator. He had his lines down perfectly. He affected a friendly, approachable expression. He was exactly the kind of guy they were happy to leave their boys with. Even his name was sort of reassuring to parents who had heard too many horror stories about what happens to young men at boarding school. "Let me know if you need anything, Al," he said to Little ASS. "My room is at the end of the hall in front of the elevator."

"Elevator, great. We were wondering if we were going to have to carry all this crap up the stairs," said

Big ASS.

"On move-in day, you're free to use the elevator, but I have to warn you that the wait is long. It's really old and slow. Most people give up and use the stairs. The rest of the time, the elevator is just for guys on crutches or faculty."

"Guys on crutches?" asked the mother a tiny bird of a woman with a pinched face whom Wenn christened Tight ASS.

"Our teams play pretty hard. Injuries go with the territory," said Wenn.

"I've been telling Al that the athletics here are phenomenal. Part of the reason we thought this was a good place for him. I'm trying to talk him into giving football a try."

"He's never played football in his life," chirped Tight ASS. "And even if he did make the team, he'd be the one on crutches forced to use the elevator."

"Freshmen football is a great program," said Wenn ignoring her. "You don't have to tryout to make the team. It's more of a bonding thing. Great way to meet the other guys and get involved."

"And what about sophomore football?" asked Tight ASS, knowingly.

"It's JV at that point," said Wenn.

"And is that a bonding experience?"

"No. JV is competitive. They cut."

Tight ASS tightened her already pinched face as she imagined her Little ASS getting the shit kicked out of him on the field, or worse, being cut from the team.

"At that point, a guy pretty much knows whether he's suited for football or not. If not, there are plenty of other activities. Cross country, if you like running. I'm the coach of that and we don't cut. If sports don't interest you, there's drama, the newspaper, the debate team."

When he was through with the Suttons, he had the same conversation with the Barkleys, the Giffords, the Sullivans, and the reigning Secretary of Education Grace Nelson—whom he did not address as Madame Secretary—and a bunch more who were all exactly the same. Bullheaded dads, manipulative moms, and sullen sons. Conversations were always the same bullshit. How happy they were to have their son at Prep. What a great campus it is. Blah, blah, blah. Without exception, the Dad's looked like they wanted to get going and the moms looked like it would take two double martinis to take the clench out of their jaws. For some reason, these people felt the need to blather on incessantly. Most of the time, he simply tuned them out and if the mom was halfway decent looking, he'd think about re-enacting *The Decameron* with her. As he stood there imagining himself with Mrs. So and So, he considered the fact that he hadn't had sex in ages and that lead to Elizabeth, again. She was about the same age as these women, but in an all-together different league.

He considered calling her, but couldn't figure out

a plausible reason. When she dropped him off at the random address he gave her after the accident, she pressed a piece of paper into his hand and told him to call her in a few days to let her know how he felt. That was more than a week ago. Too much time had elapsed to call with a "Hi! Just wanted you to know that my ankle is better." There was a good chance she'd forgotten the whole ordeal by now, so what was the point? Anyway, as resident dean he was stuck on campus for the next 72 hours. He smiled politely at the generic parents in front of him, said something about what a great four years their son had to look forward to then quietly slipped in the side door of Roland Hall. He took the back stairs to avoid having to smile at anyone else and unlocked the door to his room.

He loved his room. It was a "double wide" meaning twice as big as the rooms the students had to share with a roommate. But size was beside the point. Here, hidden in the confines of the esteemed academy resident dean's room, was pretty much everything that could get a kid expelled. The alcohol was stored in wholesome brand name beverage containers. Mott's Apple Juice was actually Dewar's Scotch. Arizona Iced Tea was Captain Jack's Dark Rum. And Smart Water was Absolut Vodka. He had his cigarettes stashed away in a box of Ritz Crackers. Though he hardly ever indulged anymore, he hid a few joints at the bottom of a box of Lipton tea bags, next to the box of Band-Aids where he kept his stash of condoms, something else he hardly ever used anymore. And his emergency pharmaceuticals were stored in the false bottom of a box of hemorrhoid suppositories. No way would someone open that sucker up to look for anything suspicious. Of course, unlike the students' rooms, the resident dean's room was not subject to random searches, but he liked to keep his vices hidden just the same. The thing he could not hide was the very thing that could put his position in serious jeopardy: Galenthias, the black cat he found over the summer.

He closed the door and locked it, then pulled Galenthias from her favorite spot on top of his dresser and placed her next to him on his bed. He scratched her head while she stretched her long spine against his torso.

"How's it going?" he asked her.

Inspired, he reached for the old fashioned phone on his night table and dialed.

"Thanks for calling Monty's."

"Hey Bric—it's Wenn."

"Wenn Mann, the beast! You coming to Shots for Shots tonight?"

"What is that?"

"Junior League Fundraiser. Every time you buy a shot of something, we make a donation to some immunization program for homeless kids or something. I don't know all the details, but I do know there's going to be lots of free pie. You should come check it out."

"Sounds great but I'm in for the weekend. Today's move in day."

"Already? Summer went by too fucking fast."

"Listen, I need a favor. I found a cat over the summer and it's a long story, but now that the students are back, I can't keep her at Prep. Some kids are allergic … that kind of thing. I was wondering if you might take her for me?"

"Gee, I'm actually allergic myself. Never really liked cats, so it wasn't an issue until I started dating this girl with a cat. Every time we went to her place, my entire face blew up. I mean my eyelids were like, hugely swollen. I looked like a bullfrog after a crying jag. Sorry, dude. I'd help you out if it were a dog."

"Sure," said Wenn. "Just thought I'd give it a try. You don't know anyone who does like cats?"

"Not off the top of my head, but hey, come to Shots for Shots, or better yet post something on Socials."

"That's an idea," said Wenn. Socials was an invitation only form of Facebook for the hip, young Georgetown crowd. He had received his share of invites and ignored them all.

"Alright, later, man," said Bric. "See you for jazz Wednesday."

"Yeah," said Wenn, hanging up.

The sorry consequence of a life unburdened by

attachments was that, in a time of need, there was no one to watch your cat. As if she understood that he was trying to get rid of her, Galenthias hopped off the bed and made her way back to her favorite spot on the dresser. She flicked her tail against a tin box in which he kept receipts, business cards and other bits of paper that he didn't know what to do with. The tin crashed to the ground, scattering its contents all over the floor. As he picked up the papers, he sorted through what was trash and what wasn't. His brother's business card, Assistant Vice President of Mergers at Mann & Mann. What a joke. He didn't need that. A few lines of ancient poetry from Juvivial that were particularly meaningful to him, save. A Presidential Club valet ticket from the last time he saw his parents, two years ago, save. A coupon for Wingo's, trash. A water-stained piece of paper torn from a small notebook that read Elizabeth 202-555-0099. Galenthias meowed.

"Think so?" he asked. She meowed again.

eight

UNDER SIEGE

The children hadn't been in school two weeks before Pups found the letter in Willa's folder. Printed on the special goldenrod-colored paper Holy Family used to alert parents that this was required reading, the letter was official notification that Pediculosis was making its way through the school. As the mother of five, she knew the letter by heart, so she didn't have to read the part that told her that Pediculosis is the medical term for head lice. Or that because the condition is highly contagious, any child who comes in contact with active lice or viable nits (the tiny eggs mother lice attach to hair shafts) requires treatment. And most of all, she didn't have to read the last paragraph with the politically correct verbiage about how head lice afflictions cut across all socio-economic, racial, and geographic groups, because while just about everything in this letter was ridiculously watered down PC rubbish, that part about race was pure hogwash. Everyone, including the Center for Disease Control, knew that Black people hardly ever got lice, but to say so would deem the school or the local public health officials as having a bias. And in the same vein, Pups believed what the Center for Disease Control refused to acknowledge, that it was the children of oblivious non-English speakers, crazed working moms and dumb as dirt idiots who kept showing up at school with critters in their caps.

"Great," said Pups. "We're starting early this year." She balled the letter up and threw it in the garbage. "Willa come downstairs and let me check your head," she shouted.

"Awwww," Willa shouted back.

"Let's go, young lady."

"But I have homework."

"So do I, and it starts on your head," said Pups. Willa stomped down the stairs. The MacArthur children were masters of technically obeying their parents, while simultaneously expressing their complete disgust. Standing in front of the kitchen window to get the best light possible, Pups dug through Willa's wispy blonde hair searching for signs of life. She found a lot of dandruff, but no head lice. Cleared of harboring pestilence, Willa stomped back upstairs. The scene was repeated three more times as each of the elder MacArthur children angrily stomped down the stairs to get checked then triumphantly stomped up the stairs to gloat. Back in the safety of their rooms, they prayed that none of their siblings showed any signs of alien life either, because all it took was one louse to louse up the entire day.

In fact, as many times as that letter made it's way home in one backpack or another, Pups had only found one louse on Willa's head one time, two years ago. Upon discovering the tiny critter, she did what any smart, proactive parent would do to contain an epidemic. She rushed off to the local drug store and bought a few boxes of something called GitsDemNits. "Recommended by Pediatricians," boasted the package. Pups went home and poured the sweet smelling shampoo from the cheerful yellow bottle onto her children's heads. The package said nothing about treating children who did not show any signs of infestation, but Pups was the kind of mom who took no chances.

The next morning, she sent her children to school secure in the knowledge that none of them posed even the slightest risk to public heath so she was flabbergasted when Mrs. Digby, the mother who volunteered as the school nurse, called and asked her to come pick Willa up at school. "As you know, we are in the throws of an active head lice outbreak. We were conducting random inspections of all the second graders," said Mrs. Digby. "And I'm afraid one of our volunteers found a nit on Willa's head."

"But that's impossible," blurted Pups. "Willa and the rest of my children were all treated for lice last night. The MacArthur kids are clean as a whistle."

"I'm sorry, Mrs. MacArthur, but one of our screeners found a live nit on Willa's head and the school does have a no nit policy."

"Screener? Who is the screener?" asked Pups indignantly.

"Our screeners are volunteers who give their time to ensure that Holy Family is a healthy environment where children can learn. And believe me, we understand how insidious this affliction is. It's a nightmare. That's why we volunteer."

"Is it just mothers?" demanded Pups. "Who was the volunteer?"

"I'm sorry Mrs. MacArthur, we don't reveal the names of our volunteers. Some parents tend to harbor a grudge."

"Did Willa sign a confidentially agreement? Because you know that's the first thing I'm going to ask her."

"Mrs. MacArthur, please don't make this personal."

Personal? Some mother/volunteer told another mother/volunteer that her kid had cooties and she's the one who's making it personal? Still sweaty from her morning power walk, Pups didn't even bother to freshen up. If they think the MacArthurs are bug-infested dirt balls—to hell with them! She grabbed her keys, jumped in her Suburban and floored it.

When she arrived at school, she found a sign taped to the front door. "All parents picking up their children due to the 'outbreak,' please report to the back of the church." *The church,* thought Pups. *Maybe they're performing an exorcism on the lice.* She found Willa sitting on a folding chair next to a handful of other kids. Mrs. Digby was seated behind a wobbly card table with about six different clipboards and a large plastic filing bin on it. Pups waved and smiled at Willa.

"I'm here for Willa MacArthur," she said to Mrs. Digby who gave her the once over, like she was applying for a job or a loan. "May I take my daughter now?" asked Pups quickly losing her resolve to stay calm for Willa's sake.

"This is the sign out sheet," said Mrs. Digby handing Pups a clipboard. "And this is the form that says you understand that our no nit policy means we cannot allow Willa back into the classroom until she has been thoroughly checked by two different volunteers. Sign the bottom, if you will." After Pups had signed the forms on both clipboards, Mrs. Digby peeled a handful of multi-colored papers from two more clipboards and handed them to her. "Here's some information you might find helpful. It's from the Center for Disease Control."

"Can I take my daughter now?"

"Of course," said Mrs. Digby. Pups motioned to Willa, who looked miserable. She picked up her ladybug backpack and her matching lunch box and slumped over to her mom.

Putting her arm around Willa's shoulder, Pups said, "Let's go, sweetie. How about hitting the drive thru for some lunch?"

They were almost to the door when Mrs. Digby shouted, "Oh, Mrs. MacArthur, wait a minute!" Pups turned around and saw the ferret-faced woman pulling a large zip lock bag out of the plastic file bin. "I almost forgot," she said, extending the bag towards Pups.

"What is it?" asked Pups walking back to get it.

"It's the nit found in Willa's head."

"Seriously?" asked Pups.

"Yep," said Mrs. Digby holding the bag up to the light. "See it?"

Pups squinted. Once her eyes focused, she did see the tiniest little whitish gray speck resting on a single strand of Willa's hair. "What am I supposed to do with this?" she asked.

"We suggest you burn it," said Mrs. Digby. "Not the bag of course. Plastic is toxic. Just the strand of hair. That's the only way to be sure the little troublemaker is dead."

"Huh," said Pups taking the bag. "So I guess if all else fails, I can always set my kids' hair on fire! Come on Willa, I'm hungry."

After getting Willa a burger and a shake from the drive thru, Pups stopped by the drug store and had a thirty-minute consult with Mr. Tran, the pharmacist. A brilliant man who had at various times turned Pups on to all kinds of great stuff you don't need a prescription for that's kept behind the pharmacy counter. Emitrol, re-christened in the MacArthur household as "magic medicine" worked wonders when a virulent stomach flu had the children spouting like cherubs in a fountain. Real Sudafed, which, unfortunately, contains a key ingredient for making crystal meth and is the only thing that effectively clears clogged sinuses. And that other stuff, the what-chama-call-it granules that helped quell the kids' squirts when that flu traveled south. At least so far, Mr. Tran never failed to have some fantastic potion that would cure whatever ailed the MacArthur family. So Pups pumped him for every bit of his expertise on head lice. Initially, Mr. Tran tried to steer her towards a mild organic product with an efficacy rate of 75 percent but that remaining 25 percent was too much for Pups. She wanted foolproof.

"Basically, I want the strongest stuff you can legally apply to a child's head," she said. "Something that will definitely kill the bugs, and won't cause any permanent harm to the child." Mr. Tran disappeared behind the counter. Fifteen minutes later, he emerged with four containers of something he had whipped up and poured into generic pharmacy bottles. She paid $19.99 per bottle (not covered by insurance), but she would have happily paid twice that. Pups had her poison! And Mr. Tran had a loyal customer who was sure to come back with another $79.96 the next time she found a goldenrod-colored letter in someone's backpack.

It didn't take long for Pups to realize that whatever was in those bottles worked wonders. First, she applied it to her children's heads starting with the oldest and working her way down. After Grant's application, Pups ran downstairs to retrieve a pair of rubber gloves from under the kitchen sink. The brown goo burned her skin. When the kids complained that their head was on fire, she told them that's how you know the tonic is working. By the time she got to Willa, the noxious fumes started to take her breath away. But when she treated Cady, she hardly smelled it any more. In fact, she hardly smelled anything on account of the chemical burn to her nasal passages. "This stuff is better than Sudafed for clearing your sinuses," she said to Cady, who had no idea what a sinus was. Once both the hair and scalp were totally saturated, you let it sit for twenty minutes.

This was the hardest part of the process, because inevitably, a brown drip would travel very slowly down the forehead and before it even got past the eyebrow, the eye would start to burn and tear up. It happened often so every few minutes, one of the kids would let out a shriek. Pups solved the problem by giving each of them a white washcloth to hold above their eyes.

Next, she rinsed their heads under the hottest water they could stand. And finally, she took the tiny hair rake Mr. Tran had given her and combed through their heads to remove anything strong enough to withstand chemical Armageddon. When she was finally through, she was buzzed from a day of inhaling caustic fumes.

Later, when Patrick came home from work, he sniffed the air and asked her if she finally started to paint the upstairs bathroom.

"No. Why?" she asked.

"Because it smells like turpentine. I thought you were cleaning the brushes or something."

That was the downside. The house was probably a contender for a federal bio-remediation grant. In subsequent outbreaks, she learned to open the windows and turn on the attic fan before treatment. Patrick took the kids out for pizza while Pups, coasting on her noxious high, proceeded to wash all the sheets in scalding hot water, spray the upholstery with lice killing disinfectant and seal up all the children's beloved stuffed animals in garbage bags—where they would be quarantined for 48 hours. When she had done all that, she thought she would go ahead and treat the dog, but noticed that the label carried a bold warning, "Not safe for use on pets," so Winfield got a reprieve. As she lathered him up with his regular dog shampoo, Pups wondered what kind of product was safe for little kids but not for pets?

Since then, Pups had become a veritable expert in the extermination of head lice. In fact, the whole family knew way more about head lice than any of them cared to admit. It became such a touchy subject that certain words were eliminated from their normal vocabulary. A person who criticized was never a nitpicker; rain didn't make them feel lousy; if you did something stupid, you were not a nitwit; all to avoid sending Pups into another fume induced mania that could only be eased by scalding hot water, noxious goo, and tiny blue rakes. All of that and there had only been that one louse and the zip lock bag that may or may not have contained an actual live nit. Since then, the school had seen it's fair share of lice outbreaks, and Pups had diligently battled them all. In the process, she became a staunch supporter of the no-nit policy; seeing it as the only way to contain an epidemic.

But last year, Pups and Holy Family were presented with a game-changer. Sister Mary Faith, the school's beloved principal for thirty-six years, retired. Replacing her was Ms. Krista Gagner, a woman whose outlook was a mixture of old-fashioned Catholicism and new age bullshit. Ms. Gagner instituted many, unwelcome changes at the school but none were as contentious as her latest reform; abolishment of the no-nit policy as outlined in the latest goldenrod letter. "Is she nuts?" asked Pups when Ginger Garity called to see if she read the letter. "Without a no-nit policy, not even Moses could fight the plague that's coming."

Well aware of her family's sensitivity to the subject, Pups casually brought up the dreaded letter she found in Willa's folder. First in a general way. "So, any of your classmates fidgeting with their hair a lot?" All four of the older children adamantly shook their heads no.

"Willa, how about in your class?"

"I don't think so," said Willa shoveling more spaghetti into her mouth so she wouldn't have to talk.

"Is it Angelo?" Pups asked Willa, who continued to chew while shaking her head back and forth. "Sun Ya?" Again, Willa shook her head no.

"Can we cool it with the lice business, Pups?" said Patrick.

The two adults exchanged looks. "Fine by me. As long as you agree to deal with the next outbreak." To the world, Patrick was a tough-minded macho-man with a good old-boy personality. Inside the house at 45 Peachpit Lane, however, Pups ran the show, especially on the subject of head lice. Defeated, he got up to get himself another beer, his third since arriving home from work. Pups looked at Willa and said, "We have chocolate chip ice cream this evening. But only for those who don't keep secrets."

Willa was miserable. She continued to chew as if her life depended on it while the dinner conversation moved on to a new topic. They talked about the new PE teacher and what an idiot she was. They talked about how Anthony Mangia got detention for putting a cricket into Rebecca Hallow's lunchbox. Willa knew what they were doing. They were pretending that no one was thinking about her, but they weren't doing a very good job because Willa could feel their thoughts traveling around the table and landing smack in her head. It made her feel like scratching every time one of those thoughts landed, but she sat on her hand and concentrated on not feeling itchy.

"It was Taylor. Taylor was scratching a lot," Willa blurted as her hand reached up and gave her own head a good scratch. Every time they talked about lice, she always got itchy.

"Taylor? Taylor Sanchez?" asked Grant suddenly fascinated by the conversation.

"Yep," said Willa.

"Does that mean you're going to invite Taylor over? Does it, Mom?" demanded Grant.

"It's possible," said Pups.

"And her sister?" Grant looked panicked.

"Brit–tan–ee!" Virginia chimed in.

"Shut up, Virginia," said Grant angrily.

"Grant likes Brittany," said Virginia.

"Shut up. Mom, will you make her shut up?"

"Virginia! Enough," said Pups.

"Tell me you're not going to invite Taylor and her sister over to do their heads," said Grant.

"What difference does it make?" asked Pups

getting up to clear the table.

"How about I'm sick of being the kid whose mom is like the Orkin man for people's heads."

"You're being ridiculous."

"No, Mom, you're being ridiculous. Thinking you can just pour that ... that ... crap all over everybody's head. That's ridiculous." Grant got up from the table and stormed up the stairs. The rest of the table was momentarily shocked at his use of profanity. Four-letter words were not acceptable in the MacArthur house.

"Who wants ice cream?" asked Pups.

Willa felt the same way Grant did. Terrible. She didn't really care if her mother knew who started the lice invasion; it was what her mother would do with that information that bothered her. First she would get on the phone and start blabbing to Mrs. Adams and Mrs. Hardy. Then, depending on her mood and if the head-scratcher was a boy or a girl, she would probably call their mother and in the most fake nice voice ever, invite that kid over for a play-date. Tomorrow. Did she ever stop to think that Willa might not want to hang out with the geeks and goobers that were always the ones to get lice first? This happened a few times a year and Willa was pretty darned sick of it because even when the outbreak started in Virginia's class or Cady's class, this was something the whole family had to endure. She would pick them up from school. The lucky guest probably never noticed what Willa and her siblings saw immediately. The car headrests would be covered with plastic grocery bags. They also knew that their mother would be so super nice to the kid that before they got home, the kid would think she was either nuts or trying to con them out of their gum. She would say something about how the kid seemed to be scratching her head. "I'd better check that for you, honey," she would say. "With that outbreak at school and all." When they got home, the MacArthur kids would bolt inside like a storm was coming, leaving the unsuspecting guest still out in the car with the crazy woman.

Pups would say she had read somewhere that sunlight is much better for checking heads. What she wouldn't say was that she read it in her own diary since it was the millionth time she had pulled this stunt. They would stand out in the front yard with Pups parting the kid's hair with a pencil she just happened to have in her pocket, looking for critters. It never took long to spot one since she already knew they were there. And if she didn't find anything, she probably lied and said she had just to be safe. Then, she'd tell the kid to sit on the front porch while she went to call their mother. Inside, she'd order Willa to take her friend a Popsicle or something while she made an urgent phone call. This was the part Willa liked second to worst. Sitting on the step with a kid she didn't like.

In a few minutes, Pups would come to the door with a sense of purpose exhibited by people on special military missions and tell the kid that her mother said it was okay to go ahead and take care of the problem since she was experienced and had all the stuff anyhow. She would announce, as if this was the first time it ever happened, that it would be for the best if she treated everyone, just to be on the safe side.

One at a time, they would lean over the tub so she could wet their heads and apply Mr. Tran's disgusting shampoo/bug killer. (Which he now sold her for only $7.50 a bottle since she was such a great repeat customer.) The children would sit on green plastic lawn bags spread out on the floor of the family room and watch TV while poison seeped into their scalps. Once, some of it dripped onto the blue carpet. It took the color right out leaving a permanent white stain. Next, was the rinse. Each kid took a turn leaning over the bathtub while Pups poured 7-Eleven Big Gulp cups full of scalding hot water over their heads. At this point, there was an excellent chance that poison would drip down your face and burn your eyeball out of its socket. Then came the worst. The absolute worst. The tiny blue rake with the sharp teeth.

After delousing all four of her older kids and their special guest—baby Maddox was thankfully spared—Pups would be so exhausted that she'd treat them all to a pizza dinner. It got to the point that every time any one of the MacArthur children so much as smelled pizza, their scalp would start to tingle. As Willa dug her spoon into the frosty mound of ice cream, she heard Pups talking to Taylor's mother on the phone.

"Hola, Arminda! How are you?"

nine

A BED OF LIES

Over the years, more than a few Prep men were caught trying to sneak pussy into the dorms. As far as Wenn knew, he was the only one who had ever attempted to sneak a pussy out of the dorms. He snuggled Galenthias close to his abdomen and zipped up his jacket. It wasn't cold enough to wear a jacket but hopefully, no one would notice. He moved stealthily down the long hall lined by heavy wooden doors with engraved brass nameplates identifying which students lived in which rooms. At this time of the day, they were busy running themselves ragged on the athletic fields so Wenn didn't anticipate seeing anyone. As he neared the last wooden door, the one to the back staircase, he heard the familiar click, whine and creak of the aged hardware.

"Hey, Mr. Mann!"

There was Cole Reardon, sweaty, grimy and slightly out of breath from darting up the stairs. The tall, lanky freshmen flashed Wenn a brilliant, easy-going smile. Damn, if that kid didn't glow.

"Hey, how's it going?" He stood as straight and as tall as possible, doing his best to keep the boy's eyes on his—lest he look down and notice the feline bulge emanating from his midsection.

"Pretty good, sir. I left my playbook in my room."

"Right. The quarterback needs his playbook."

"Yep."

"Well, don't let me hold you up."

"Sure. See you Mr. Mann."

"Yeah, see you. And hey, great job on that Latin test. Keep it up," said Wenn trying to sound casual. Wenn was relieved when Cole was finally behind him. The boy probably didn't notice anything. And even if he did, he was a kid. What was he going to do? Report him? Wenn made it down the stairs and out the back door unnoticed. He plowed ahead but in the wide-open expanse of the campus, he felt like a target—an easy one at that.

He kept his head down but just as he reached the center of the quad, the most vulnerable place on campus as any experienced sniper would attest to, he heard the familiar, "Mr. Mann!" There was Dr. Brennan heading directly for him. Wenn waved to Dr. Brennan nonchalantly with the hand that was not holding Galenthias. His jumpiness must have rattled the black cat who squirmed and meowed so loudly, he feared that Dr. Brennan could hear her. He reached his hand into his jacket to calm her.

"How's the cross country team coming along?" shouted Dr. Brennan.

Galenthias dug her claws into Wenn's flesh as the

old goat made a beeline towards him. In a flash of inspiration, Wenn reached into the back pocket of his jeans and pulled out his wallet. He looked at it with intense interest, before pushing his finger into the black leather. He raised the wallet to his ear and prayed that Galenthias would behave.

"Hello?" he said into the wallet. "Hold on."

Dr. Brennan was now less than a hundred feet from him. "I need to take this Sir. It's ... a parent," he said with deference.

"Of course," said Dr. Brennan who waved him on. Wenn inhaled deeply. Finally, he understood the value of a cell phone.

* * * * *

Re-directed, Dr. Brennan turned to see Cole Reardon coming out of the same door from which Wenn Mann had just emerged. That was curious.

"Mr. Reardon?"

"Hey, Dr. Brennan."

"Everything ... all right?"

"Yes, sir. Just forgot my playbook," said Cole, holding up the binder as proof.

"Of course," said Dr. Brennan. "Carry on."

He watched the boy run towards the football field. Plenty of Cole Reardons had passed through Prep during Dr. Brennan's reign. Those glorious creatures touched by the gods. The boys who won all the accolades and honors. Made all the memorable plays on the fields and went on to achieve greatness beyond Dr. Brennan's wildest dreams. Dr. Brennan was not one to fawn over these golden boys. He didn't like Cole Reardon now any more than he liked Wenn Mann ten years ago. These guys were all the same; polite and hard working, with a sinister quality under the surface.

Wenn Mann was as golden as they came when he was a student here. Look at him now; the pierced ears, the tattoos peeking out from under his rolled up sleeves and those ridiculous moccasin bedroom slippers he wore to class ... all red flags for Dr. Brennan. There was no denying his brilliance as a Latin teacher, so even Dr. Brennan had to suppress his concerns for the good of the students, who seemed to revere the young teacher. In fact, that was another thing that made Dr. Brennan wonder. Why would these boys be so fond of such a tough-minded teacher who thought nothing of bullying his students? A man who has a reputation for physical violence if the rumors were true. A few parents had complained about Mr. Mann's strong-arm tactics, but there was nothing they could prove because there were never any witnesses. At least not any witnesses willing to speak out against Wenn Mann. All of this unsettled Dr. Brennan. It was quite clear to him that the fellow was hiding something because whenever their paths crossed, he always seemed hurried and nervous. Even his body language was odd, like right now. Hunched over, talking on the phone while gripping his stomach and wearing a jacket in this heat. Something about Wenn Mann just wasn't right.

* * * * *

On the outskirts of Georgetown, Wenn started

to have regrets. It had been stupid to contact Elizabeth. She was nice on the phone, easy to talk to, warm and funny, but in person. Ugh! She's going to apologize again, and then what? Here's a cat for you. Take good care of her and I'll pick her up over Christmas break. And by the way, don't try to contact me because not one thing I've told you about myself is true.

He found a parking space on K Street, filled the meter up to the two-hour maximum and walked up the hill. With a private covered bridge over the canal, this had to be the coolest apartment building in the city. "Galenthias, you're moving up," he told his companion. Inside the heavy metal door was a modern, upscale lobby full of shiny white marble and chrome. From behind the front desk, the security guard asked, "May I help you, Sir?"

Wenn realized that he didn't even know her last name. "I'm here to see Elizabeth in apartment 302." The guard nodded towards the entrance behind him. It took him a second, but Wenn finally turned to see her coming through the door.

"Hey there! Here I am, late as usual," said Elizabeth. Whoa! The last time he saw her, she was covered in bike grease and canal sand and he was in a state of near delirium. He knew she was attractive, but never in his wildest fantasies did she come close to the woman before him. A tad older than he remembered, she nevertheless evoked such a visceral stirring, he felt like Tarzan the first time he saw Jane. She was his biological equal.

As if giving up carbs wasn't enough of a test, for

the past six months, Wenn had waged a fierce wrestling match with the vile lizard that lurked on the edge of his psyche, to smother his baser urges. He thought he had succeeded, but the mere sight of Elizabeth in a prim but alluring business suit, silky white blouse with the first two buttons unbuttoned and high heels, not only revived the lizard, but had him back in command; sending lewd messages to his brain and releasing potent hormones into his blood stream. He was powerless as instinct took over and the beastly lacrosse player he thought he had so deftly transformed into a stoic Latin scholar returned to claim his prize.

"Hello there," she said leaning down to look inside the cat carrier.

"Hey," said Wenn transfixed by Elizabeth's ass.

In the elevator, they made small talk. She asked about his ankle. He asked if she suffered any injuries. She answered, but he wasn't listening. All he could think about was the last time he had sex. Six months ago. A post-Monty's hook up with a girl he had known since high school named Cullen Carson. She too, was the kind of girl he was born and bred to mate with. Dare he say, a younger version of Elizabeth? The sex was good, but he could not get over the disgust he felt afterward. It was as if carrying out the act was the equivalent of endorsing a set of core values he found repugnant. Rolling out of Cullen's bed, bumping into one of her hung over housemates on the way to the bathroom, hearing a bunch of weird girl shrieks and chortles come from the room he just left while he splashed cold water on his face; all of it made him feel loathsome. That's when he decided to give celibacy a try. He had come so far in the past two years. He'd given up his cushy future, carbs, a bunch of other food groups, and contact with his family. It only stood to reason that he give up sex too. And so he did. As he followed his siren down a short corridor and waited while she unlocked the door to her oddly impersonal and glaringly white apartment he asked himself, *what's so great about celibacy?*

"Here we go. Welcome home … " Elizabeth said to the cat.

"Are you sure you don't mind keeping her for a while?" he asked.

"Absolutely not. Like I told you, I don't get here every day. As long as that's not a problem, it's fine," she said holding the door for him to pass through.

"Not a problem at all," he said. "She's used to being alone." He set the carrier down in the middle of the living room and opened it. Galenthias stayed where she was. "Come on out, Gay."

"Gay? That's sort of unusual," said Elizabeth. "For a name I mean."

"Her full name is Galenthias. I call her Gay for short."

"Galenthias?" she asked.

"She was an ancient Greek woman who turned into a black cat and then became the priestess of Hecate. Goddess of darkness."

"Sounds ominous," said Elizabeth.

"Not really. Just a good name for a black cat. I

have more cat stuff in the car. I'll go get it."

"Wait. I'm dying of thirst. How about you?" She went into the kitchen and took two tumblers from a cabinet. "Can you stay for a drink?"

"Sure," he said. "I filled the meter up." The lizard wondered if she understood that "filled the meter up" was code for I have almost two full hours in case you feel like a good fuck. He was starting to repulse himself again. He challenged that goddamned lizard to a winner take all match, while Elizabeth went to the kitchen and surveyed what the housekeeper had stocked the bar with.

"Let's see," she said. "Vodka, gin, rum, or scotch? I'm sure there's beer and wine in the refrigerator too. And look, there's even tequila."

He was surprised she was offering alcohol. "Vodka sounds good."

She opened the refrigerator, "With cranberry juice or OJ?"

"No thanks," he said.

"Right—no sugar. Do you have diabetes? Did I already ask that when you were here? It's just a blur. God that day was so unbelievably hot wasn't it?"

"Nothing like that. Just try not to eat many carbs," he said.

"Are you on Atkins? Doesn't vodka have carbs? It's made from potatoes, right?"

"Atkins? No, I just don't eat carbs. Distilled alcohol has no sugar or carbs. But fermented beverages like beer and wine do have some sugar."

"Huh!" she said. "I never knew that. Do you want it with Diet Coke?"

"No thanks."

"Ice?"

"One," he answered.

"One?"

"Yeah, one cube. If you have it."

She came into the living room with his one-cube vodka and a vodka cranberry for herself. "Are you hungry? Do you want something to eat?"

"No thanks. This is good."

She reached out and placed her finger softly on his forearm, just above his tattoo. "So you're really fond of cats?"

He started with the truth, about how he found Gay as a kitten in a box along the C&O Canal. He told her how he believed cats were really mystical. How as far as he was concerned, the only truly honest relationship he's ever known was with a cat. Not Gay, but one he had a few years ago. A cat he spent a considerable amount of (his father's) money nursing through a long bout of feline AIDS.

"Cats don't make judgments," he said. "They don't care about all the stuff—the tons and tons of bullshit that cloud human heads. They are never impressed or disappointed. That's what separates them from dogs. Dogs are easily disappointed. Also, dogs pretend to be your best friend when you're eating, but otherwise, they couldn't care less. With cats it's nothing but honesty." From honesty, he moved to dishonesty, proceeding to set his pants afire by telling one lie after another. He was a professor at Georgetown University. He lived in Bethesda with his new roommate, a sales associate with a computer firm, who was allergic to cats. Two lies he would classify as practical. The kind of lies that made his presence here in her white apartment, logical. The next group of lies came directly from the lizard and were pure sport. His parents were retired. They lived in Florida. He was an only child. And, he had recently broken up with his girlfriend of two years. That's why he moved in with his buddy in Bethesda. A well-crafted tale designed to highlight both his availability and his enthusiasm for long-term commitment.

Ace as he was at hitting whoppers out of the park, he was up against a seasoned pro. She said she was a vice president of a small publishing endeavor. (Some people might consider *The Washington Tribune* small. It was smaller, if just by a hair than *The New York Times*.) She told him that she was a divorced mother of three, which was true. But she also told him that her children were young, ages five, seven and nine when, in fact, they were eleven, thirteen and fifteen. Her oldest had just started high school which made her feel very old and she didn't want this very young and very attractive professor to think of her as very old. She told him that she went to Boston University and then GW Law, when, in fact, she graduated from Harvard and Yale Law. Ivy League girls learn early that while their alma mater may impress employers and condo boards, it does not attract interesting, good-looking and mentally well-adjusted men. Even male Ivy grads don't want to associate with their female schoolmates fearing they might not always be the smartest person in the room.

As the lies continued to roll back and forth, each better crafted than the one before, the pair began to sense they were nearing the edge of a bottomless canyon into which they would plummet, if they dared to push their falsehoods any further. So the conversation hit a lull. Ordinarily, this silence might be felt as awkward, but they were both buzzing from the rush of adrenaline that comes from spinning tales and the warm bliss of alcohol before it starts to make you silly. To cut the silence, Elizabeth asked, "Where's Gay?"

"I forgot all about her," said Wenn.

They got up and looked around. She wasn't in the kitchen or the bathroom. The next door was to the bedroom, and sure enough, there she was, on the corner of the mahogany dresser, soaking in the last few rays of golden light before sunset. Elizabeth saw the cat, but her attention went to the bed.

"What's wrong?" asked Wenn.

"The bed. It's not made right."

"No big deal. I never make my bed."

"No, it's not that. I just don't know why it would be rumpled if no one has slept in it."

"Maybe Gay rolled around."

"Yeah, I guess," she said, looking disturbed and reluctant to embrace his cat theory.

Elizabeth leaned over to smooth the bedspread as if brushing away her lingering doubts as Wenn stepped up behind her. The vodka synergized with the testosterone the lizard was now mainlining into his blood stream; driving him to place his hands gently on her ass and lean into her. She was unbelievably warm and soft, like what he remembered of doughnuts.

"Hey!" she said as she turned towards him. She was now so close she had to puff out her chest to stand straight. He pulled her gaze into him holding it, just holding it. Like all golden boys, Wenn had lived a life full of yeses. He never kissed a girl who didn't happily kiss him back so it was a shock when doubt flashed through his mind. *Elizabeth isn't like those other girls,* he thought. Leaning in, he kissed her tentatively at first but when her lips met his he felt her answer in the affirmative.

He cupped his hand behind her head and pulled her closer. His other hand deftly moved down her blouse, undoing the buttons. "Do you have any idea how old I am?" she asked, pulling away as her blouse fell to the ground.

"Why?" he whispered into her ear. Before she could answer he unhooked her bra and moved his hands across her sleek back. It was strong, with rippled muscles under her unbelievably smooth skin. Not until he allowed his hands to wander around to the front of her body did he feel anything distinctly feminine.

She tugged his shirt over his head and ran her hands over his shoulders and down to his chest. Never mind sex, her touch alone was mind blowing. She pulled him towards her and together they fell backwards onto the rumpled bed. Positioning himself over her, he caught a whiff of flowers or perfume or something. It was nice.

The lizard wanted to pounce on her and be done with it, but he fought back. His eyes stayed fixed on hers and for once, he thought about what was happening to her. Not about pleasing her. Not about making her come. About what she was feeling. What it felt like to be her. At that moment. He knew how to please the ladies but it was always about crossing the finish line. Now, when it really counted, he overcame the lizard and allowed himself to be driven by passion not lust. It was carnal; fiery, purposeful, and like nothing else. Ever.

* * * * *

Elizabeth's hair fanned out around the pillow. She tried to concentrate on the man who was now delicately kissing her neck. Tried to because a perfumey smell, a decidedly *feminine* perfumey smell would not leave her alone. It was lavender mixed with … paper whites and a bit of … musk. It was definitely womanly. Could he be wearing woman's perfume? Because, even though he was clearly a master of the female anatomy, he was also sort of weirdly into cats which was not the most masculine of pursuits. As she turned her head slightly towards him, she was relieved to discover that what she smelled was not him. It was her pillow. As publisher of the esteemed *Washington Tribune*, Elizabeth read three daily newspapers, a host of newsweeklies and to keep herself up-to-date on current trends and cultural matters, a large pile of fashion and entertainment magazines. She had ripped out so many of those darned fragrance sample cards; she could make her way around a department store perfume counter blindfolded. This wasn't an altogether foul smell. Actually, it was sort of lovely. That's it, she thought. Lovely by Sarah Jessica Parker perfume was on her pillowcase. The only perfume she ever wore was Acqua Di Parma, an Italian fragrance once favored by Audrey Hepburn and available only at high-end retailers ... so why did her pillow smell like Macy's?

ten

WHITE WHITE

"How rich could these fuckers be if they have to live out in Tim-fuck-tu?"

"Oh they're rich alright," answered Mary Ellen ignoring the expletives. Better to let him get it out of his system now so he's COA—calm on arrival. "They own a fleet of trucks. How many is a fleet anyhow?"

"How the fuck should I know? More than three? At least."

"I think we should turn around and go back the other way," she said. "This doesn't seem right."

"You think? Goddamn it, Mel, why didn't you bring the GPS? How fucking stupid can you be? Wait, let me answer that. Completely fucking stupid. Route 93 to 102 west and left on Meridian Way is not directions. Not when you don't know where the fuck 102 West is. And for what? A pricey potluck with a bunch of rich cocksuckers. So fucking typical."

Driving through horse country on a curvy, poorly lit road, without a GPS, without accurate directions and without a trace of refinement, Kenny continued to curse, hurling obscenities so fancy that even Mary Ellen who thought she had heard it all, was impressed. For her part, Mary Ellen summoned all her strength to remain civil to the lout she once said "I do" to. There was a time when a scene such as this would elicit a steady stream of tears, threats and insults from her, but now her insides were as tough and leathery as her athletic sister's neglected feet. Tonight, she bottled up her disgust at the ruinous decision she made seventeen years ago, determined not to allow Kenny's foul mood to spoil her night out. She took a deep breath and gave her head a good scratch. Kenny had a way of making her skin crawl.

"I see some lights over there. Turn onto this street," she commanded.

Kenny turned down the mystery road without a street sign. As they neared the one developed parcel in the otherwise barren landscape, Kenny exhaled in utter frustration. At the top of the winding driveway was an expansive French Colonial clubhouse, a few small groundskeepers' sheds and a magnificent two-story horse stable.

"That's some kind of a cunt-tree club or a whores farm … "

"Saddle club. Pull up. I'll run in and ask for directions," she offered.

"No way. One look at this place and you'll have a bug up your ass about why we need to join a saddle club, just like you think we need to belong to the fucking Presidential Club."

"Don't be ridiculous. Horses are not my thing, although I do like the look of jodhpurs tucked into tall boots. Come on, it's getting late. You don't want to miss cocktail hour."

These were the only lights they had seen for miles so rather than admit that Mary Ellen was right, he silently pulled past the open gate and the carved wood sign that said, "Welcome to Merry Land" and up the long, winding driveway which ended at a circle with a fountain in the middle. How odd that the valets were parking cars in the open field next to the building. Mary Ellen looked around and even in the darkness, she could see there wasn't a parking lot.

"This is it," she said in disbelief. "All the cars have WP stickers on the back window." About ten years ago, cryptic initial stickers started appearing on the rear windows of minivans and SUV's in the upscale suburbs surrounding Washington. There was the red "SJC," the purple "AHC," the green "GV," and the navy blue "GP". Like gang hats or tattoos, these ubiquitous stickers identified the occupants of the vehicle as belonging to certain elite private academies in the region. After four years, the high school sticker would be joined by a more serious decal; one with a fancy collegiate font spelling out the name of the institute of higher education the child who had attended SJC or GV had matriculated to. Given the horrendous traffic issues of the region, the presence of these stickers turned some streets into a no mans' land during the afterschool rush hour. Woe betide the mother driving the GV stickered vehicle through the AHC neighborhood. She needed to pick a lane and stay in it because no one was going to let her cut in.

"Well, fuck me," said Kenny as a valet approached the car.

Mary Ellen whispered, "Try to stick with G-rated language, dear. For Brophy's sake." The valet, who Mary Ellen assumed was the oldest Johnson boy, opened the door of their Honda Accord.

"Good evening, Ma'am."

"Hi there! We're the Packinghams," said Mary Ellen unaware that eighteen-year-old boys don't care who you are unless you're famous, sexy or giving away free food.

Leaving his key in the ignition, Kenny smirked and said, "She's all yours, buddy. Highlight of your night, parking a Honda."

The Johnson boy smiled politely and said, "Go on in. Enjoy the party."

Mary Ellen intended to do just that. The Freshmen Parents Social was a longstanding tradition at Prep. Hosted by a family with both an incoming freshmen and at least one older son at the school, its purpose was to give all the parents an opportunity meet, mingle and schmooze. It would be a milestone for the Packinghams; A star studded social event they were actually invited to not just brought along as "guests of" Suzanne and Corn. There would be elected officials, captains of industry, and power players of all stripes. Except for the daunting financial chasm that separated the Packinghams from the rest of the crowd, they were just like everyone else; Parents who were thrilled to see their sons join the esteemed WP class of 2016. Such mingling and schmoozing came with a price tag of $98 per couple. Mary Ellen paid for it out of her own account, because Kenny refused to. And the only reason he was at this pricey potluck, as he called it, was because Mary Ellen convinced him that their presence would squelch any notion that Brophy was a scholarship student. A kind of reverse psychology. "I don't want my son stigmatized," she said. As much as Kenny didn't mind accepting greatly reduced tuition so that his son could attend Washington Prep, he did mind accepting the humility of knowing that the generous donations of a bunch of snobs and pricks made that attendance possible.

Brophy's scholarship status was not the only thing subject to evaluation by the social powers that be. By accepting the invitation to the Freshmen Parent Social, the first of many such dinners over the next four years, Mary Ellen believed that the Packinghams themselves were being scrutinized; aspects of their lives fed into a complex algorithm to calculate their relative importance. Those on the top of the scale might be asked to chair the annual gala or collect money for special causes like the new building fund. Low scoring Prep families were almost always charity cases. Where you live and what you do for a living carried the most weight, but there were fractional values given for the brand of handbag or golf clubs you had, size of the family matriarch's diamond engagement ring, and the breed, name and pedigree of the family dog (cats garnered a negative value). A savvy bottom feeder, Mary Ellen's knowledge of knockoffs, fakes, seconds and outlet mall specials put the Packinghams a few notches higher on that scale than they rightfully deserved as did the pedigree of their beloved pooch Winston, a Springer spaniel from the same lineage as President Bush's Millie. The umbilical hernia he was born with made him the doggie equivalent of a "second" or an irregular which, in turn, made him a bargain.

"Behave yourself. Show people where Brophy gets his good looks and his athletic ability from," she said giving Kenny a peck on the cheek. She left out intellect because that would be taking things too far. The compliment was a grown up version of the tootsie pops she handed the kids in the grocery store, it would keep him quiet, content and out of her hair for a while. She smoothed the wrinkles out of her beige skirt and ran her fingers through her blonde hair. That sulfate free shampoo she switched to must be drying out her scalp because it sure was itchy. She popped a mint into her mouth and took a deep, calming breath.

Through the massive reproduction antique double doors of the Johnson's house, Mary Ellen expected to see Dianne Keaton or Meg Ryan waiting to greet her. Fresh, spacious, tastefully appointed, this was the kind of fabulous house that average American movie characters live in without regard for the fact that actual average, everyday Americans can't afford four million dollar homes stuffed with two million dollars worth of stuff. Suzanne had this kind of house, but it was ruined by her busy Victorian decor—with so many darned prints and patterns, it was like stepping into a Magic Eye poster. Mary Ellen could never figure out why her sister went so crazy over Victoriana—the fussy wallpaper, the uncomfortable upholstered furniture, the fringed lampshades and that ridiculous antique harp that no one knew how to play—until she had an epiphany. While riding down Disney's Main Street USA in a horse drawn wagon during one of the few family vacations Kenny ever took them on, it dawned on her. Cornelius was so old; he had actually lived in a Victorian when Victorians were considered modern. Her sister's choice of decor paid homage to her ancient husband's boyhood home. What the Johnson's home paid homage to was ... the Johnsons. Everywhere she looked there was something reminding Mary Ellen whose house she was in; from the six rocking chairs painted different colors and personalized with the name of each Johnson on the front porch, to the large custom made doormat with a lavish script "Johnson" on it and the interlocking J's door knocker.

In the center of the grand foyer was a round table with an easel holding a cut out photo of the Johnson family mounted on cardboard. A cartoon bubble above their heads said, "The Johnson family welcomes you!" In front of the cardboard welcoming committee, pre-printed nametags embellished with gold "J's" in the upper left corner were lined up in alphabetical order. Mary Ellen found the two Packinghams, peeled off the paper backings and placed one on the lapel of Kenny's navy blue blazer and another on the right side of her new Burberry-ish blouse from the fall Plaid-IT-tudes line. The crowd was well dressed, but this being suburban Washington, no one veered too far off the well-worn preppy path. The universally appropriate navy blazer, khaki pants combo was the male uniform of choice, while the women's fashions ranged from sherbet colored Capris with paisley printed tops to sherbet colored mini-dresses or skirts that showed off their tan legs.

To Mary Ellen, soaking in the splendor of the Johnson's home was like a dunk in the baptismal font; instantly washing away the char of Kenny's hellfire and renewing her own innate optimism. After all, there were so many possibilities ahead. A few good years for the Grease Police and polished dark walnut floors could be hers. Or, if hard work and good business practices fell short, a cataclysmic event like a death in the family or well chosen lottery numbers could allow the Packinghams to live within sumptuous matte white walls embellished with layer upon layer of high gloss white molding.

"This is my dream white," she whispered to Kenny.

"What?"

"The walls. The color of the walls, it's my dream white."

"Jesus fucking Christ, Mel. You know what my dream white is?"

"What?"

"Chardonnay. Want one?"

"Please." He headed towards the bar in the living room. Kenny didn't understand, but this white paint was as personal a statement as the doorknocker or the rocking chairs. Instead of choosing some trendy mushroom hue or an outdated grape hyacinth with slate grey accents, Jackie Johnson chose pure, classic white. A white so refined it practically shouted, "As rich as this white is, the Johnsons are richer!" Mary Ellen had a longstanding fantasy about white like this. An old fashioned white you can't get any more, like the white of a country club membership directory before the lawsuits. A full-fat white so thick it enveloped the walls the way Cool-Whip coats the back of a spoon. Although it was only paint, and therefore, presumably affordable, she instinctually understood that it was some kind of very special, ultra-expensive paint. The only kind of white paint she could afford was bland blah white. The kind of "keep it neutral" white decorating magazines recommend for quick and easy real estate sales. A white so washed out, it practically screamed, "as transparent as this white is, the Packinghams are nearly invisible."

Set against the stately alabaster walls were six large oil paintings in elaborate gold frames, each depicting a member of the Johnson family astride one of six different magnificent horses. The paintings were exquisite, but as she went from the parents to the sons, Mary Ellen could not help but notice that with each successive Johnson, the gene pool seemed to get a little more common. Jack Jr., their parking valet and the eldest Johnson brother, was the physical ideal with a strong jaw, broad shoulders and well developed muscles built up by athletics. The next brother was nice looking, followed by the next who was average. The youngest Johnson, identified as Ryder A. Johnson on the small brass tag at the bottom of the painting, possessed the same slightly upturned nose, the same hazel eyes, the same full upper lip over a thin bottom lip as his brothers, but the haphazard way his features were set into his portly face produced a decidedly homely child; Like a beautiful photograph copied too many times so the lines start to blur and the colors become dull.

Captivated by the paintings, Mary Ellen was startled when she heard a voice over her left shoulder. "Beautiful, aren't they? I understand the artist paints presidential portraits." There was Claudia in a wild turquoise and melon paisley print tunic.

"Hi stranger!" said Mary Ellen giving Claudia a polite air kiss.

"I've been hearing a lot about Brophy. Salter says he's a beast on the football field. How's he like Prep?"

"Wow, so far, it's wonderful. Brophy is so happy. He's meeting such wonderful boys and his teachers are just so ... wonderful. How about Salter?"

"Not totally happy about no girls, but he'll survive. His brother did."

"I can't imagine. You must be thinking about college already."

"Ha! Thinking about college. Honey, we are eating, sleeping, breathing college. Wait until it's your turn."

Kenny came up beside Mary Ellen and handed her a glass of Chardonnay.

"Oh my God, Kenny!" Claudia wrapped her arms around Kenny.

"Hello Claudia," said Kenny awkwardly sipping his beer.

"Grover's son, Salter is in Brophy's class," explained Mary Ellen.

"Grover?"

"My husband. Representative Grover Manfrey."

"Right. The Congressman," said Kenny skirting the line between dick and asshole.

"Her older stepson, Burke, is a senior."

"Doing the college drill? Where does he want to go?" asked Kenny. "Some place that plays good football, I hope."

"He thinks he wants Brown, but our college counselor says, at this stage in the game, they all do. The perceived lack of structure there is a big draw for kids. Anyhow, we're hoping he'll follow the family tradition and choose Yale."

"Impressive," said Kenny.

"All the Manfreys are Yalies. Grover's even in their football hall of fame."

"Sounds like it's in the bag," said Kenny, raising his beer as if making a toast.

"His legacy status will help, but you can never really count on it, so we've made sure he has what it takes to stand out in a sea of applications."

"Like grades and SAT's?" chirped Mary Ellen.

"God, no! A C student probably has a better chance of admissions than one with straight A's because the C student will stand out. They'd probably give him bonus points for having the balls to apply. I mean life experiences for the all-important essay. The right topic is a golden ticket. Charity work was hot for a while but overnight, everyone and his brother hauled ass to the barrios of the DR to build huts or dig ditches or just generally de-slumify the place. And poof, no more service work distinctions."

"DR?" asked Kenny.

"Dominican Republic. Good thing that fad is over. My nephew spent a summer teaching English down there. Came back with worms in his feet. Actually, it was a worm. One, big, long one."

"Ugh!" said Mary Ellen.

"I know. Literally. Worm. In. His. Foot. Can you imagine? When Grover's sister called, I wanted to throw up. Anyhow, there was none of that for Burke. What's the good of spending all that time and money for great volunteer opportunities if they're not going to pay off?"

Mary Ellen ran her fingers through her hair and took a sip of Chardonnay. "Gosh, I never realized …"

"I know. Who would think? Lucky for us, Grover pulled some strings and got Burke a summer position with the county."

"Intern at town hall?" asked Kenny with a smug "fat cats get all the breaks" smirk.

"Definitely not. Prestige internships are the kiss of death. He worked for the Division of Solid Waste Services. Made $11.66 an hour—same as all the other Job Corps kids."

"You mean he … "

"Yep. He was the right rear man on truck number 84. Collected trash all summer long. God, did that kid stink when he came home. I made him take his coveralls off in the backyard so Yolanda, our housekeeper, could take them to the laundromat. No way were those filthy things going into my Maytag."

Mary Ellen and Kenny were dumbfounded. Never in a million years would it occur to them to get their kids lousy jobs so they could get into a good college.

"He was assigned to a neighborhood on the other side of town." Claudia lowered her voice to a whisper. "H–I–S–P–A–N–I–C. But now, summer is over, and he's going to have a knock 'em dead essay about what it's like for a rich white boy to collect poor people's trash and, as a bonus, he was the only Caucasian on an all African American crew. Brilliant, huh?"

"Yes. It really is," said Mary Ellen in awe.

"I'll tell you what. All that manual labor got him in shape for football too. By the end of the summer, he was ripped, cut and tan. Some marketing genius could promote the Trash Truck Workout and make millions." As if toasting her good fortune, and her stepson's trash toned abs, Claudia took an exuberant sip of wine. "For Gawdsakes, there's Grover heading for the bar. I better go catch him before he orders himself another scotch. One of us needs to drive home, and it's not going to be me! And we don't need a mug shot of Tennessee's most esteemed member of Congress plastered all over the news for a DUI." Claudia leaned in to air kiss Mary Ellen. "See you soon. Hey, I volunteered to run the football boosters—are you interested in helping?"

"Sure, I'd love to help," said Mary Ellen.

"Great. I'll give you a call next week. Take care."

In a flash of turquoise and pink, Claudia was gone.

"Oh my God. What is Brophy going to write about?" wondered Mary Ellen aloud.

"I need a refill," said Kenny. "You?"

"Sure."

While Kenny was looking for alcohol, Mary Ellen made her way into the dining room where an elaborate display of food was arranged around the king-sized table. A chef was carving ruby red slices of roast beef and silver chafing dishes warmed vegetables, salmon and rice. This is no potluck. Everything looked delicious. Mary Ellen circled the buffet, filling her gold rimmed plate with a little of everything. She wasn't going to eat much, but she wanted to taste it all.

"Doesn't all this look yummy!" said a Black woman with close-cropped hair, bright red lipstick and large gold hoop earrings.

"Delicious! And I'm sure it's all low calorie too!" said Mary Ellen.

"If only that were true! I'm Ebony Tilford."

"Oh you're Remington's mom aren't you?"

"Guilty."

"My Brophy talks about Remington all the time. Says he's an amazing running back."

"He is! Great point guard and first baseman too. He's also got it going on in soccer and around the track but I put my foot down. Now that he's in high school, it's time to specialize. Just one sport per season. I said, 'Remy, it's no use spreading yourself so thin. You get injured, and you won't be playing anything in college.'"

"Of course," said Mary Ellen as her mind raced towards the horrifying realization that Brophy was not the best athlete in the class of 2016. Football was more or less a social activity. He was only great at lacrosse.

"I sure do miss him, though," said Ebony.

"Oh, he's a border?"

"Yep. He's roomies with Cole Reardon. Nice boy. Handsome, smart, good at sports. And having a family that's richer than God doesn't hurt either. I'm hoping some of his aura will rub off on Remy. There's his mom. Elizabeth! How you doing, girl?"

Elizabeth came up beside Ebony and gave her a warm embrace.

"Elizabeth, this is Mary Ellen … " Ebony's eyes darted to the sticker on Mary Ellen's chest. "Packingham."

"Nice to meet you," said Elizabeth.

Mary Ellen extended her hand saying, "Same here." Elizabeth looked familiar, but not in a personal way. Like she'd seen her picture somewhere.

"So you made it after all," said Ebony.

"By a hair. And I'm headed back to the office later," said Elizabeth.

As Ebony and Elizabeth chatted, Mary Ellen's mind raced. All she wanted to do was scratch her head—both because it itched and because she could not believe she was so ridiculously unprepared—for Prep, for Brophy's future, and if she really wanted to create an itch fest, for everything else down the road too. Keeping up with this crowd was going to take muscle.

Mary Ellen excused herself and went looking for the powder room. She found it at the end of a long hallway off the living room. Like the rest of the Johnson home, it was impeccably decorated, covered in custom wallpaper with a repetitive pattern of J's. It's funny how similar her taste was to Jackie Johnson's. She hiked her skirt up and squatted over the commode. She always squatted unless she was in her own home. This is exactly the color combo I would pick thought Mary Ellen admiring the burgundy script J's over a tan background. Someone knocked at the door, and Mary Ellen called out a clubby, "Just a minute!" When she was done, she rearranged her skirt and reached over to flush the beige commode. Horror enveloped every cell in her body. There, as plain as day on the back of the toilet seat, was a poop smear. A substantial one at that. One that would be impossible not to notice. Whoever was waiting out in the hall would see her leave, enter the room, see the poop smear and would automatically think she did it.

For the next four years, that person would see her as the woman who left a poop smear on the Johnson's toilet. There were a million possibilities. What if it was the senator from Nebraska Claudia had mentioned, or that reporter from CNN? Or the Secretary of Education? She opened the cabinet under the sink looking for some kind of cleaning product but found only tissue boxes, extra toilet paper and a fancy box of lavender guest soap. She knew that the longer she stayed in there, the more likely the person on the other side of the door was putting her down for a number two. God. She pulled an enormous wad of toilet paper off the roller, balled it up, wet it slightly in the sink and gave the smear a wipe. It must have been on there a while because it was dried and did not come off easily. It took her many wads worth of toilet paper to get that seat clean. To avoid the possibility of clogging the toilet, she put the paper into the trashcan then scrubbed her hands with hot water and lavender soap for at least 3 minutes.

When she finally opened the door, she was horrified to find Kenny. "It figures," she said.

"What?" asked Kenny pushing past her into the powder room. "Took you long enough."

Another glass of wine was needed. Rounding the corner into the living room, she came face to face with her hostess. "Welcome. I'm Jackie Johnson. The night's half over and I'm still trying to make the rounds." Whatever vast amount of money Jackie and her husband Thom paid the talented artist who captured her likeness on canvas, it was not nearly enough because the dowdy, oversized woman standing before her resembled the beauty depicted in the portrait, the way grandma's mushy homemade green bean casserole resembles the luscious crispy onion-topped dish depicted in the November women's magazines.

"Nice to meet you, Jackie. I'm Brophy's mom.

It's so sweet of you host all of us. You have a beautiful home," said Mary Ellen extending her hand.

"Thanks, we like it here," said Jackie, adding, "My, your hand sure is warm."

"It's just so beautifully done. Every detail. I love the foyer—especially the color of the walls. It's the exact color I've been trying to get my painters to mix, but they never get it quite right. Do you mind if I ask you what paint you used?"

"For the foyer?"

"Yes. That lovely … "

"You mean white?"

"Yes, but it's not just any white, it's … "

"No, it is. Off the shelf Home Depot white white."

"Really?"

"The decorator was pushing for some kind of glitzy textured stuff, but honestly, with four boys who ride horses and play football and … well, you know. I wanted something that wasn't going to be a hassle to touch up. White white."

A wave of disgust washed over Mary Ellen. How could someone who could choose anything, choose something so … common? So attainable? Mary Ellen felt stricken.

"Jackie, it was so wonderful to meet you. Thank you for your hospitality. I see my husband by the bar, and I need to get him home. Early tee time tomorrow and all."

"Oh sure. Nice meeting you," said Jackie. "I'm sure we'll be seeing a lot of each other." Kenny was out of the bathroom and was now wandering aimlessly in front of the Johnson gallery of Johnson paintings. Mary Ellen rushed over to him. "I'm ready when you are."

"Then let's go." He leaned over and whispered in her ear, "Man, we had this place pegged right when we called it a saddle club. What a load of horse shit I had to wade through all night. Jesus."

Mary Ellen grimaced as she considered the shit she had to deal with. "Oh my God, Kenny. We haven't given any thought whatsoever to Brophy's college application. What are we going to do?"

"I was thinking the same thing. But look, if it makes you feel better, he can tag along on the grease truck next summer. Not much difference between collecting poor people's trash and pumping used lard from Chinese restaurants. And if my plans for expansion pan out, I'll assign him to the new port a potty pumper. Man, that's so fucking awful, he'll get a full ride to Harvard."

-eleven-

OUTBREAK

Heat and humidity still ruled the daytime, but with each successive September night, Brookstone wireless remote weather stations from Alexandria to Wheaton were recording incrementally lower temperatures. The minuscule chill, barely perceptible to those still locked in air conditioning, prompted millions of tiny brown shields to prepare for home invasions. Thousands of them congregated on the sunny side of buildings, giving cheerful yellow siding a putrid brown mustard cast. As cool shade edged out warm light, the shields clustered around windows and doors looking for missing caulking or a hole in a screen big enough to allow their rigid exoskeletons to pass through.

They hitchhiked inside on the backs of dogs and cats, scurried across door thresholds when children ran out to play, and made a slow deliberative march down chimneys. In living rooms up and down the East Coast, the first fire of the season would be punctuated by intermittent popping as their scorched bodies exploded, filling houses with the repugnant odor of toasted brown marmorated stinkbug. Native to Asian countries, this particular species of stinkbug was unknown to Americans until about fifteen years ago when it was first spotted in Allentown, Pa. Since then, the roughly one inch by one inch pests had decimated fruit and vegetable crops along the mid-Atlantic coast, driving grocery prices up. But when it came to stinkbugs, economics were beside the point. Their stout, awkwardly shaped bodies created such a buzz as they bumped into lampshades and furniture, it sounded as if a humming bird was loose in the living room. And although they didn't bite or spread disease, they were so ugly, that when you discovered that one had landed in your hair or on your shoulder, you jumped and swatted with a fury usually reserved for scary things like spiders or threatening ones like bees or mosquitoes.

Despite their warrior-like facade, they were an easily excitable species; with the slightest scare triggering the release of a noxious odor hence their common name, the stinkbug. Squish one and that distinctive rotten cilantro smell would linger for hours. Each year, the stinkbug situation got worse, and experts said this year would be biblical. With no natural predators in the United States, and an ungodly tolerance for the harshest of pesticides, the only way to battle stinkbugs was to very gently (so as not to scare them) wrap them in tissue and flush them down the toilet. Some people took to vacuuming them, but over time, the vacuum became coated in their scent, making it like one gigantic electric stinkbug spewing rotten cilantro fumes out its exhaust.

As Pups swung her Suburban into the parking lot of Holy Family, her thoughts raced from stinkbugs to another, smaller and more insidious pest. Despite her best efforts, she was loosing her battle against Pediculosis. Mr. Tran's magic solution had proven effective too many times to count so clearly, her methods were not the issue. The issue was other parents. Parents who were too busy or too stupid or too lazy to treat their own children so no matter how pure the MacArthur's heads were when they were dropped off at school in the morning, by the time Pups picked them up at 3:00 there was a darned good chance that those heads had been corrupted. It was simply inevitable.

When Willa and her friend Amber stopped fighting over who was first in line at the pencil sharpener, they agreed to let bygones be bygones and gave each other a hug to show the seriousness of their truce. As peace loving as any mother, Pups was nonetheless horrified that her daughter had compromised the health of the entire family when she allowed her temple to graze Amber's. She was just as disturbed about Virginia's whispered conversations with Corrine about how much they both despised that stupid Johnny Zingo. While Pups fully agreed that Johnny Zingo was indeed, stupid, she deemed the whispering "high risk behavior" and banned her eldest daughter from getting too close to Corrine's head. "Write her a note for Pete's sake!" said Pups.

As she made her way through the orderly rows of vehicles parked nose to tail in the parking lot—a formation that allowed the maximum number of vehicles onto the lot and theoretically ensured a safe and efficient dismissal—Pups surveyed the enemy. There was Señora Alvarez, the seventy-year-old matriarch of a large, extended Peruvian family. Her grandchildren spanned every grade in the school so if Señora didn't get the lice business right, everyone was doomed. There was Alice Kim, a sweet-natured Korean mom whose children were adorable. Pups knew the school sent home Spanish versions of the goldenrod alerts, but she wasn't sure they had a Korean version. There was Mike's Swedish babysitter, Sigrid, talking on her phone for a change. Mike was a special case, since his father was Black and his mother was White. Not wispy thin like his mom's, but not anywhere near the kinkiness of his dad's, Mike's hair seemed to be an even split genetically. Therefore, he had to be viewed as a potential threat, especially since his parents seemed too busy to read the goldenrod notifications. Unless they found a way to send the goldenrod alert via text message, there was no way Sigrid would know about the problem.

Pups wondered what happened to all the Americans who lived in the neighborhood and had sent their children to Holy Family. When Grant started going there, it was about 75 percent white and 20 percent African American. The remaining five percent was a mix of Hispanic Americans and Asian Americans. They had their differences, but still, all of them were Americans. They were born here. They spoke English. They didn't require special versions of school notices. But in recent years, non-English speaking students had overrun the nearby public elementary school. These students were legally entitled to the extra help and attention they needed to succeed so some classes had as many as four different translators in the room. Conversely, those kids who arrived at school fully fluent in English were not legally entitled to anything but a chair and a desk.

Limited by budget and resources, Catholic schools could not afford to kowtow to every variety of childhood shortcoming ... until kowtowing to those shortcomings became a survival strategy. When the economy soured, many Catholic schools that once had long waiting lists suddenly had empty seats instead, prompting the archdiocese to find a way to increase their enrollment. They didn't need to look further than the people who showed up for Saturday confessions. The Mexicans and the Africans and the Guatemalans and the Haitians were far better Catholics than most natural-born Americans, and they would pay for the privilege of giving their children a faith-based education, even if it meant taking on a second or third job. Soon, the Archdiocese unveiled a new policy. They slashed the budget for art and music instruction to pay for teachers' aids whose singular responsibility was to help non-English speaking students in Catholic classrooms. Now eight years later, all the seats were filled again, and so were the Archdiocese's coffers.

Holy Family was now at least 60% minority and the vast majority of those people did not originate here. They were immigrants from Ghana and Vietnam and Honduras. They celebrated different holidays. They enjoyed different TV programs. They didn't get their news from *The Washington Tribune*. They got it from a local foreign language newspaper. The smell of their spices and their cooking techniques permeated the cheap polyester uniforms their children wore to school each day, giving some homerooms the aroma of a shopping center food court.

And there were so many of them, they no longer

felt the need to try and assimilate into the school. Rather, they boldly expected Holy Family to accommodate not only their language difficulties, but their cultural proclivities and their particular point of view as well. These new immigrants started from the idea that their heritage was not only equal to any other, it was actually superior to others, an attitude that didn't sit well with Holy Family's old timers. "If your homeland was so great, why the hell did you pack up and move here?" was murmured within the tight circles of mothers in the parking lot. These jabs were never louder than a whisper and spoken only after a good scan of who was within earshot because the women doing the jabbing were educated, patriotic, God-loving, human beings who were known for their sensitivity to needs of the under privileged. They knew better than to judge, they just wished the underprivileged knew that too. It would make helping them so much easier. These ladies who had always sided with the needy, given to charity, and were regulars at Sunday Mass, suddenly found themselves at a crossroads when the school, or rather, Ms. Gagner called the no-nit policy discriminatory, ineffective and politically incorrect, and with a sweep of her pen, killed the no-nit policy. There were many shrieking phone calls with establishment moms threatening to pull their children out of St. Anthony's altogether. All they wanted was to make the school safe for everyone, no matter what overwhelming spice they favored ... at least, that's what the moms kept telling themselves.

"Hola Señora Alvarez!" said Pups cheerfully as she approached the older woman.

"Hola, Pups."

Having exhausted her knowledge of Spanish, Pups proceeded to speak to Señora Alavarez, compensating for the language barrier through modulation and volume.

"Have you seen ... the ... notices ... about ... the ... lice?"

"Lice?" asked Señora Alvarez furrowing her brow.

Pups nodded. "Yes. Lice. You know ... " she wiggled her fingers over her scalp.

"Ahh. Los piojos! Sí." The old woman nodded enthusiastically.

"Yes. Piojos."

Señora took off on a lengthy rant about piojos and possibly about other things as well, but since the entire litany was in Spanish, she could have been analyzing the President's new immigration policy or the latest Miami Dolphins New York Jets blow out. When Pups saw her friend Angie Watson on the other side of the pick up line, she gave her a big important wave. "Hey Angie!" Pups smiled deferentially to the elder woman. "Señora, I'm sorry, but I have to talk to Angie about something. Call me if you need help with the piojos." Señora scowled. Even with the language barrier, she knew a blow off when she saw one.

Before July, Pups knew Angie only as the sweater lady—the mother who had a themed sweater for every occasion. When Angie's oldest child was in preschool, she arrived at the class Halloween party wearing a sweater with jack-o-lantern buttons and scenes of witches silhouetted against sparkly silver moons. People were quick to compliment her festive attire, though behind her back, there were snickers. A month later, Angie wore a Thanksgiving sweater with gold, orange and brown embroidered leaves floating over a repetitive pattern of pilgrims and Indians. More compliments. More snickers. All that positive feedback led Angie to fill her closet with fun garments of every theme imaginable. There were snowman sweaters and Christmas tree sweaters, heart sweaters, bunny sweaters. She even had a super bowl sweater. As her children grew older, they begged her to stop wearing all those crazy sweaters, but there she was, wearing a lightweight cotton cardigan with soccer balls all over it.

Pups had her share of giggles at Angie's expense, but a few months back, Angie's husband, an army captain, was deployed to Afghanistan, putting an end to all the snickers as the do-good brigade sprang into action. Suddenly people were giving Angie's children rides to birthday parties and inviting the family over for dinner. And while Pups had never been particularly close to Angie, she was the most prodigious do-gooder in the Holy Family community, so in a very short amount of time she and Angie became the best of friends, and their children became best friends too.

It wasn't the first time Pups found herself a new "project" as her family called it. Angie just happened to be the latest. The women who found themselves in her crosshairs shared a few common traits. First of all, they were needy in some significant way. Like they had a terminally ill family member or they were going through a brutal divorce. They had to be available to be helped, meaning some other do-gooder hadn't gotten there first. And they had to be gullible enough not to realize that everything Pups did was for Pups no matter how much it seemed otherwise.

Every one of her projects followed the same precise pattern:

Phase I – Pups goes from being a modest acquaintance to the subject's very best friend in a matter of a few weeks though when necessary, she has been known to ramp it up and complete phase one in a matter of days. It starts with random phone calls. Do you know a good dry cleaner because hers is closing? Do you have the recipe for those delicious brownies your daughter brought to school because Willa can't stop raving about them? Pups would get her answer, but then she'd linger on the phone long enough to let the person know how interesting she found her.

Phase II – More calls, perhaps a few per day. And when the woman picked up her phone, she didn't hear a routine "hello." She heard a bright and cheery sounding Pups asking her, "How's your day going?" A simple question that most stay home moms never get asked. It made the person on the other end of the phone giddy with joy—someone actually cared!

Phase III – She starts to include the family. Her kids are forced to fall in love with the project's kids, no matter how incompatible they might be. Not even a vast age difference could excuse a MacArthur child from this duty. The project family would be invited over for dinner on a Saturday with the routine excuse of, "I bought way too much pork, why don't you guys come on over and help us eat this monstrosity?"

Phase IV–The longest phase, sometimes it went on for years, other times just months. It all depended on the person's neediness, attention span, and tolerance for mind control. Pups and her new best friend did everything together. They would confide in each other and snicker about other mothers at the school. "My God did you see that hair?" Or "Did you see those sorry looking cupcakes she sent in for the bake sale?" Like two peas in a pod, the project realizes that in Pups, she had found the sister she never had.

Phase V–The honeymoon was over. The project said or did something to show how little she really cared for Pups. The slight would sting Pups. And the words "after all I've done for her" would be bandied about as Pups discussed the problem with her old friends like Mary Ellen or people she knew in college. People far enough away they couldn't get wind of what the other moms in the parking lot were saying about Pups and her project. The project would be totally unaware that she had inadvertently insulted Pups, so the sudden and near complete withdraw of her once besotted admirer would leave the poor woman completely dazed. And the words, "I don't know what I did" would be bandied about by her as she told the long lamentable tale to her other friends (with whom she had fallen out of touch).

Pups and Angie were still in Phase III. Pups drove the Watson kids to soccer and brownie meetings. Pups picked up industrial sized boxes of laundry detergent at Costco then gave them to Angie saying, "Patrick got this by accident and I can't use it because Virginia is allergic to everything but Tide. Could you guys use it?" Pups invited all three of the Watson kids to sleep over a few times a month just to give Angie a break.

Without giving Señora another thought, Pups rushed across the black top towards her new project. "How's it going?" Pups asked. "Cute sweater!"

"Thanks. I'm on top of the world as usual!" said Angie sarcastically.

"Did something happen?" Pups asked. Angie rolled her eyes. "What is it? Do you need help?"

"No, Pups. I wouldn't dream of asking you … "

"I've said it before. You can ask me for anything. I'm here for you. Whatever you need."

"But this is … embarrassing."

A wave of recognition washed over Pups. "Is it the … you know … " she said as she silently mouthed a word. Angie nodded. She knew that if Pups had pushed tone through those mouth movements, she would have heard the word dreaded by every single person in the parking lot. Lice.

The rest of the afternoon was a blur of activity. When the bell finally sounded, Pups loaded her kids into her Suburban, dashed them home and started dinner. While that was cooking, she dunked Willa, Cady and Maddox, one at a time in descending order of age, into the bathtub. After that, she went downstairs to put the noodles on and helped Virginia with her homework. At 4:30, they all flash-crossed themselves and speed-recited grace. Then she served the children their dinner, a stew she just threw together. No one was hungry at that early hour and they all hated stew, but she promised them ice cream later if they ate their supper without complaint. She cleaned the dishes and put a covered plate of stew in the refrigerator for Patrick to warm up when he came home, changed Maddox's diaper and finally read Grant the riot act about being responsible and keeping the household humming until 6:30 when Patrick would come through the door. Pups headed to the garage to retrieve her big brown bottle of Mr. T's solution.

Driving up to Angie's house, Pups noticed the overgrown bushes lining the driveway and the weeds in the flowerbeds. She made a mental note to ask Patrick to stop by with his electric hedge clippers.

"Hey Pups! Come on in," said Angie. "I don't know what I'd do without you."

"It's no big deal," said Pups. "Really, it's the least I can do. You and Billy and the kids too for that matter are giving up so much for us. For the country. It's my patriotic duty."

Angie led Pups to the children's bathroom in the upstairs hall. The tub was coated with soap scum and a reddish mold ring encircled the toilet bowl. The room smelled of soapy urine. "Here you go. How should we work this?" asked Angie.

"One at a time. I'll shampoo the first one. This stuff needs to sit on their heads for about twenty minutes so I'll do the next one while the first one is sitting. I always have mine sit on plastic trash bags.

This stuff will take the color out of your carpets."

"What should I do? Do you want me to help?"

"No, just keep an eye on whoever is sitting. Make sure they don't get it in their eyes. We'll need some washcloths for them to hold on their foreheads."

Then Pups—the patriot—conducted chemical warfare on the Watsons' heads while Angie sat and watched TV with her kids. When the night was over, Angie's children were lice free, their bed linens and stuffed animals were sealed in plastic bags and thanks to Pups, their upstairs bathroom was sparkling clean and it smelled like bleach, not urine.

Back home, Grant had barricaded himself in his room without the least bit of interest in what his siblings were up to. He had work to do. He logged onto George Markel's Facebook account. Bingo. Cole Reardon had friended George Markel. *Bad move dude. George is going to do some damage* thought Grant who had never met Cole Reardon. Didn't know a thing about him, other than what was on Facebook. But he did know that Brittany was totally enthralled with the guy. So enthralled, that she no longer gave Grant the time of day. Now that Cole had friended his alter ego, George Markel, he ... or rather, George ... would post a few suspicious things on Cole's wall ... which Brittany will see. Hopefully, she will be so creeped out by his postings, she will un-friend Cole both on Facebook and in real life.

-twelve-

THE TOMBS

Living in a chip driven, satellite transponded, WiFi enabled world makes stealing someone's identity a snap, but it makes fabricating a false identity tough as hell. Between caller id, organizationally linked email addresses, cell phone GPS and who knew what else, passing yourself off as someone you're not requires tremendous effort. As much as Wenn wanted to call Elizabeth, he knew he couldn't use another pay phone because when he did, her caller id would say "pay phone," and she might wonder why a gainfully employed college professor with both an office and an apartment relied so heavily on germy pay phones. He got himself a new generic email address, scoped out a real address in Bethesda where he could plausibly have an apartment with his cat allergic roommate, memorized the academic calendar at Georgetown and after years of refusing to join the cell phone revolution, he got himself an unlocked, used phone with two features; voicemail and an alarm clock, all for Elizabeth. She was the only person he would call and the only person who would have his number. Given the responsibilities of his job, his aversion to the Internet and the fact that he had absolutely no established credit history, it took almost three days to accomplish all this. As soon as the phone had service, he left her a message with his new number, switched the phone to vibrate, put it in his pocket, and waited.

The first time it went off, so nearly did he. He was in the middle of a class re-teaching sophomores what they should have learned as freshmen. "Translate 'The Rape of Lucretia.' I'll be right back," he said stepping out of the basement lair under the chapel that was his classroom.

"Hey," he answered tenderly as he sat down on the cement stairs.

"Hello, this is Verizon calling to confirm that your new Verizon number is operational ... " A recording. "If you have any questions or concerns press one. Thank you for being a Verizon customer. We appreciate your business. Good bye." Denied the sound of his lover's voice, his spirits plummeted.

During his next class, he wondered if she even got the message. He kept taking the phone out, checking to see if he missed her call. As far as he could tell, he hadn't. This waiting sent his normally demanding and impatient demeanor in the classroom to a whole new level of nasty. By third period, Wenn Mann was giving his freshmen students a reaming.

"Sutton, what do you have for line thirteen?

Little ASS stood up, as is the protocol in Mr. Mann's class and stammered, "Umm. Did the ... "

"Sit the fuck down." Wenn barked. "Remy?" Remy timidly rose to his feet.

"Does ... " said Remy. Wenn banged his arm on

the table with such force, his textbook jumped off the table and landed with a thud on the linoleum floor.

"Fuck, no."

Remy sat down and shook his head.

"Packingham can you save us?"

Brophy was already sweating, but as he stood, beads of perspiration started rolling down his temple. "Will the kind boy … "

"Go on," said Wenn.

"That's as far as I got." As if in a vacuum, all sound of the outside world disappeared as they waited for the eruption. It came in the form of a chair being thrown in the general direction of Packingham, but landing far short of his actual location. Being freshmen, none of them knew if the inaccuracy was a calculated attention getter or the work of a lame marksman.

"Get out."

"Sir?"

"You dare come to this class without doing the work?" whispered Wenn, doing his best Christopher Walken impression.

Packingham stared at the table in front of him trying to summon the courage to move. "Yes, Sir." He appeared to be the odds on favorite to be the first freshmen to get "Mann-handled" as it was called in the locker room. Anticipating the kind of scene that would fuel great stories for the rest of their lives, the class fixated on the opponents. While rooting for Brophy—their David, to Mr. Mann's Goliath—the twisted monsters lurking in the hypothalamus of every adolescent boy wanted to see Goliath pushed to his edge. (Conveniently, when none of them were the object of his wrath.) *Would there be blood? Would David survive? How great would it be if David actually beat Goliath like the story?* Finally able to lift his gaze, Brophy met his opponent's eyes. A moment of stillness as the two sides held their ground. "Get the fuck out of here. And fair warning, if you ever show up unprepared again, you'll be up against it, pal." Brophy scrambled to gather his books and get out the door before Mr. Mann changed his mind. He was no match for Wenn Mann. None of them were.

Invigorating. Nothing like a little brute force to take the edge off of waiting for that Goddamned phone to buzz. Packingham was an easy mark, but what the fuck. They would each have their turn, eventually. "Cole? Redeem these fucking pussies."

Cole scratched his head and stood up. "Will the kind boy dare to give roses … "

Wenn nodded his approval. "Continue," he said calmly. There was something about this kid, Cole. He's smarter. More self assured, but also more sympathetic. And something about the way he looked. Oddly familiar especially the shape of his eyes which stirred something in Wenn. It was making him feel kind of …

Cole studied the ragged paper in his right hand as his left hand reached up to scratch the back of his head. He closed his eyes as if expecting a blow, then blurted, "… give away the nice roses and letters of the pretty girl?"

Wenn smiled slightly. It wasn't Cole specifically that aroused him. Just something about him. About his eyes. "Nice try. Still wrong, but you were closer. Keep at it." Secure in his manhood, he scanned the remaining eight students who were clearly struggling to control their bowels. The Cole break was over, and he changed his tone back to draconian taskmaster. "You guys are fucking pathetic."

Fucking pathetic was an apt description of many things besides this class. It described his other classes too. And his job. His life. And for that matter, the rest of that particular day which was a blur of checking his comatose cell phone, haranguing his nitwit students and scratching his raging scalp. Poison ivy of the head? He had seen Cole scratching too. Maybe the water in the dorm showers is messed up. Too hard or something. Maybe it is just a case of jitters. Maybe if he actually had a life like other people with real responsibilities, goals, relationships, there would be no room for serious doubt about Elizabeth what's-her-name to fester like this. He waited all day for that cell phone to buzz, growing itchier, meaner and more intolerant with each passing class. The seniors in his seventh period class, hearing tales of his invective, all skipped, which was fine by him. Fuck them. They'd get their due tomorrow.

Before he went up to his room to sulk and wait, he stopped in the school kitchen for a plastic tub of ice. Upstairs, he put on his favorite Charlie Parker album, dropped an ice cube into a glass, got his bottle of Smartwater off the shelf and poured himself a glass of vodka. Lying back on his bed, he took the cell phone out of his pocket, and stared at it while sipping his drink.

Willing it to buzz. Willing her voice to seep out of the black plastic and caress his wounded psyche. Since he kissed her goodbye early Sunday morning he could think of nothing but running back into her blinding whiteness. And since then, anything overly bright gave him a charge. Brought back the memory of her. And what she alone was capable of bringing out in him. Two pink pieces of paper lay next to the clock on his night table. Parking tickets he had found tucked under the windshield wiper of his car Sunday morning. $25 souvenirs of the best night of his life. Proof that what he had been reliving all week in his mind was not a dream.

He fell asleep with the phone in one hand and the tickets in another. Shortly after 7:00, the phone buzzed. Groggy from sleep and vodka, he awoke in a confused state to the unfamiliar sound. Not until the third buzz did he figure it out.

"Hello?"

"I was beginning to wonder if you were going to call."

"I've been … really busy," he said, running his fingers through his hair. Already, he sounded like an asshole. "Actually, I've been having some phone trouble. But now, it's all good. New phone. New number."

"I was in meetings all day. I got your message, but I honestly didn't have a minute to spare."

"I figured it was something like that." He took a breath preparing to ask her out.

"Do you want to meet for lunch?" she asked. "I can cab over to Georgetown and meet you or whatever."

"Definitely. Lunch is good." Actually, lunch sucked. Lunch was short. Lunch meant you had to go back to wherever you came from when it was over. His lunch was only forty-minutes long, and Georgetown was a good twenty-minute drive with traffic.

"Let's see. Tomorrow, I'm meeting with a new ...um, client. Wednesday, I'm in New York. But Thursday...Thursday is wide open. How about you?"

"Thursday?" Thursday he was doing the same thing he was doing Monday, Tuesday, Wednesday, and Friday. Teaching adolescent boys about ancient sex rituals. Of the most deviant kind. That was Latin. Sure it was a dead language, but what was written was brimming with life. The great dramas of Euripides, the adventure stories of Homer and Virgil. The love poems of Catullus and Ovid—they were a *Kama Sutra* for poets. This was what made Latin a subject high school boys did not entirely hate. The freshmen busied themselves with tales of roses and love letters and the more advanced students were learning about various positions, techniques and details of the female sexual response. Of course, it wasn't all sex, but there was enough of it to keep them interested. To enjoy translating a poem about patriotism you have to love the language it was written in. But when the poem you're translating is about a threesome, the language becomes secondary.

"Thursday's fine," he lied.

"Great. What time do you get out of class?"

"Uh. Let's see ... 11:30?"

"Do you have an afternoon class, because we can just meet at the Tombs if that's easy."

"Actually, I've got another class at 1:50. So the Tombs would be great." He wanted to seem busy. And as he recalled from his own undergraduate days at Georgetown, nearly everyone had classes on Tuesdays and Thursdays.

"Well then. I'll see you at the Tombs."

* * * * *

Thursday arrived like any other day. He woke up at 6:00. Ran south for one hour then challenged himself to make it back to Prep in fifty minutes. By 8:20, he was on his way to class dressed in faded jeans, cowboy boots, a blue striped button down shirt and in deference to his pretend position as a university professor, a tie. He would feint a stomachache at the end of third period and his students would enjoy the unexpected pleasure of his absence.

When the third period bell rang, only six of his eleven students were there. "Where is everyone?" he asked.

"Utley puked in Biology so they sent him home," said Sutton.

"What about Rogers?" he asked.

"Sick. Same with Anderson," said Sutton.

"Zullings is getting his cast off today," said

Packingham.

"And Reardon?"

"Cole went to the infirmary. Something's wrong with his head," said Remy. The boys snickered and guffawed.

"What does that mean? Did he take a hit at football practice?"

"Nahh. Nothing like that. More like a scratching," said Remy.

"What kind of scratch?"

"Not a scratch. Scratch *ing*. Like the dude couldn't stop itching his head. He was like doing it all the time," said Remy. "Kinda freaky if you ask me."

"Man, I had that kind of scratching once," said Sutton. "Thought my head was going to explode."

"What was it?" asked Packingham.

"Lice. It was like, the most disgusting thing I've ever had. Little tiny bugs crawling around in your head. Worse than chicken pox."

Lice? Did he have lice? Could he possibly have … thought Wenn.

"Oh man, that's some nasty business," said Remy. "Cole better not have lice. And he doubly better not give me lice."

The students chattered on about lice which segued into a conversation about crabs, which segued into bed bugs and, of course, back to their favorite topic, sex, in the guise of disgusting symptoms of sexually transmitted diseases. Wenn ignored all of it.

He was wedged into his corner of the large u-shaped table frantically searching the Internet for information about lice. He found what he was looking for on the Center for Disease Control website. "… second only to the common cold among communicable diseases affecting school children. Head lice are tiny, wingless, parasitic insects that live and feed on blood from your scalp. This itchy infestation, also called Pediculosis capitis, most commonly spreads through close personal contact."

* * * * *

In his twenty plus years as the headmaster of Prep, Dr. Brennan had witnessed his share of outbreaks. One year, a virulent strain of flu had wiped out half of the student body, forcing the school to shut down for ten days. Another year, impetigo, a contagious skin disorder decimated the sophomore class. There were diarrhea bursts, strep throat flare-ups, chicken pox waves. Troublesome as all those infections were, none were as insidious as head lice. Once those damn creepy crawlies had their hooks in the school, it could be months before they were eradicated. The key, he had learned, was to go heavy on the offensive at the first hint of an infestation. A firm no-nit policy and an aggressive hunt for new cases, contained the damage.

Frustrating as the condition was, Dr. Brennan could not deny an interesting bright side to the affliction. It offered him a unique opportunity to see connections that had heretofore been unknown. Sometimes, there was a perfectly logical explanation why one Prep Panther might pass lice to another Panther. They had accidentally switched lacrosse helmets, or they wore the wrong fedora rehearsing the drama department's production of *Guys and Dolls*. Other times, the transmission from one person to the next revealed a potentially more titillating relationship Dr. Brennan had never … considered. Like when the lead trumpet player in the school band and the center on the football team were simultaneously diagnosed. The latest outbreak was no different. When Mrs. Rockowski, the school nurse called to tell him that Cole Reardon had visited the infirmary during second period and left with a diagnosis of Pediculosis capitis, Dr. Brennan took it in stride, fully expecting the next phone call he received from her to add another football player to the list. However, it was a shock when she called a short time later to tell him that Wenn Mann claimed second in the diagnosis of Pediculosis capitis. Experience had proven that the first two cases were always linked, and Dr. Brennan's mind did not have to work very hard to construe a plausible explanation.

* * * * *

Every university has a tavern that reflects the character and culture of the school. The kind of place that remains in alum's hearts far longer than any of the lecture halls or laboratories parents pay so royally for their offspring to gain access to. For Georgetown, that place was The Tombs, the gritty underbelly of 1789, a posh restaurant frequented by those who could afford fine dining; namely elected officials, lobbyists and parents. It was like an on-going, grown-up dinner party upstairs at 1789, while the kids ran amok at The Tombs in the basement.

Upstairs, the social elite dined on quail eggs and

tuna carpaccio, downstairs students were throwing back Natty Bo's and wolfing down cheeseburgers. Because it was Georgetown's version of a dive bar, the Tombs was naturally more virtuous than every other college dive bar in the country. It was especially more virtuous than the dive bars of the Ivy League as well as Stanford, Duke and UVA. Since the kitchen was connected to 1789, the Tombs' food was actually good; mostly sandwiches, but there were more substantial entrees available. The decor was without pretense, basement chic. The kind of place your sporty, preppy, old uncle might have if he loved crew and had won a bunch of regattas. In the center of the dining room was an enormous brick hearth decorated with a gigantic fan of championship oars. There were other oars around the room, from Yale, and Harvard and other universities the Hoyas had beaten. On the walls were various prints, photos and other memorabilia of Georgetown's crew team and to a lesser degree, their perennially unspectacular football team and the always top-rated basketball team.

Wenn descended the narrow stairs leading to the entrance. As he walked through the door, the familiar smells of spilled beer, fry oil and Axe body spray brought on an unexpected wave of nausea. This had been his place, once. The beast man's cave. He would party with his lacrosse buddies until the wee hours and never leave without a petite longhaired beauty under his arm. Just the thought of his old self made him sick.

He approached the hostess stand and scanned the room for Elizabeth. It was the same crowd as always. There was the group of dapper boys wearing bowties and wool blazers at a long table scarfing down fries and cokes. There was a table of the Georgetown fashionistas; wearing black cashmere sweaters, no make up and their trademark scowls. They all had large Caesar salads in front of them, which they poked at, but never ate. He spotted Elizabeth sitting at a booth against the back wall. Dressed in a dark brown business suit with a silky white blouse, she looked like an off course 1789 patron.

"Hey!" he said leaning over her. Though passion was welling up inside of him, a chaste peck on the cheek was all she got. He took a seat across from her.

"God, it's been ages since I've been here. Still the same, I see," said Elizabeth.

"Yeah, I don't think this place ever changes. Only the customers change. Every year, a new class of the same people. How's Galenthias?"

"Good. She's good."

"Busy day?"

"Yeah. I was in meetings all morning. Just like this place . . . the faces change, but nothing else does. Not really."

A fresh-faced waiter wearing a blue pinpoint shirt, blue and grey bow tie and suspenders handed them menus. "Our special today is fish and chips. Can I get you something to drink?"

"I'll have an unsweetened iced tea," said Elizabeth.

"Same," said Wenn. The waiter left and they

both cast their eyes down to the menu. Menus were a problem for Wenn, especially when he was with someone. The list of foods he would eat was impossibly short, but at the same time, he hated appearing fussy. Hated to seem too concerned about his diet. Hated that word "manorexic."

"I know what I'm getting," said Elizabeth folding her menu and placing it on the laminated wood tabletop. "Mussels!"

"Mussels?"

"Gosh, I love them. I ate them all the time when I lived in Paris. Mussels and French fries, and the most wonderful bread. And of course wine. Plenty of that," she mused smiling.

"You lived in Paris?"

"Junior year abroad. How about you?"

"Rome," he said wistfully.

"How fabulous? All that spectacular art. You probably studied all the ancient Latin texts?"

"Not exactly. I studied international trade, which I never understood and have completely forgotten. But in my spare time, I traveled around on my own. Went to Venice. And Ponza, the most beautiful place in the world. It's where Circe's cave is."

"Circe? Like the goddess who turns Odysseus' men to pigs?"

"That's her," he said impressed with her knowledge of ancient literature. "And Florence was great too—where Dante lived and Boccaccio." He looked down at the iced tea the waiter had placed in front of him waiting for her to respond to his test. It was expecting too much to believe that she would know even one of the poets he mentioned.

"Dante! And Boccaccio? *The Decameron*. Wow."

"You know it?"

"Well, not intimately. I read it years ago. And some parts I still remember," she said with a twinkle in her eye. Wenn was speechless. *The Decameron* was the world's first erotic novel. It made *Fifty Shades of Grey* seem tame by comparison ... not that he read *Fifty Shades of Grey*.

"What can I get you?" asked the waiter.

"The mussels. Do those come with fries?" she asked.

"I believe they do."

"Great. And can you bring some bread with that?"

"Sure thing." He said turning towards Wenn.

"You know," said Elizabeth interrupting. "I think I'd like a glass of Chardonnay."

"Sure. Sir?"

"I'll have the roast chicken and steamed broccoli. No butter or oil. Just plain," said Wenn handing the waiter his menu. Every synapse in his body was firing. His head was sending out desperate scratch me messages while the lizard was busy pumping up the volume down below. His heart was thumping, his stomach was flipping, and his lungs were gasping. Even his throat was involved, trying to stay clear so his voice would come out smooth and in control even though he was anything but. The source of all this activity was a colossal struggle between him and the lizard who wanted to forget the food and retire back to her place. His logical mind reminded him that he was infected. Contagious even. A diagnosed carrier of head lice. A suicide bomber of public health.

"So are you in a rush to get back ... or what?" he asked, trying to sound casual.

"Not in a rush exactly, but I do have to get back."

Elizabeth reached up and scratched her head. It was about the fifth time she had done that since the waiter took their order. Completely unaware of her actions she looked perfectly content and carefree. There was no battle of the wills going on inside that brain. She was the poster child of living in the moment. When their food arrived, she dug in with gusto. It was the first time he had been on a date with a woman who actually ate the food she ordered. And relished it.

"My God, these are wonderful. You have to try them."

"I don't think ... "

"Come on. Don't tell me you only ate chicken in Italy. Not that this compares to Italian shellfish, but I must say, pretty good for Georgetown. Just have a taste." She poked her fork between the two identical blue-black shells and opened them revealing a peachy nub nestled inside. Carefully, she separated the meat from the pearly walls and pushed the succulent flesh-colored bivalve towards him. How could he deny her? He took a bite. Soft. Unbelievably soft, with a bit of saltiness chastened by the tartness of the wine and the richness of the butter it was steamed in.

"Good."

"I told you. Here," she said reaching for a slice of warm crusty bread. "You have to taste it with the broth." She dipped the bread into the golden broth until it was sopping wet then pulled another naked mussel from the shell and placed it atop the bread.

"I can't. I don't … "

"Oh come on. Just try it." She held the food out waving it back and forth in front of his face. Tempting him. He hated bread. He hated buttery golden broth. But he could not refuse this seductress offering him her treasures. He opened his mouth and into it, she placed the first starch, the first bit of butter, the first thing that tasted really good in over two years. It was heavenly. And when he was finished chewing she reached across the table with her napkin and wiped a bit of the broth that remained on his face.

He scratched his head. It was the first time he allowed himself to do so and it felt almost as good as the food tasted. She scratched her head too. She held out her glass of wine, offering it to him and he took it without even thinking.

"Can I interest you in dessert?" asked the waiter. Elizabeth took the small menu from his hand and studied it. There had been times when he was weak and trembling, and still he denied himself anything but water. And here he was sucking down her mussels and accepting sips of her Chardonnay. All those single runner marathon races he challenged himself to. Those grueling two long runs a day, and ... *did he really just agree to split a peach cobbler with her? What was happening to him and what kind of woman orders dessert? At lunch?*

"Does your head itch?" he asked, watching her run her nails over her scalp for the umpteenth time.

"It really does," she said. "It's driving me crazy."

He smiled as he realized that did not have to jeopardize her health to scratch his itch. All he had to do was jeopardize her dignity. "So what was the best thing about Paris?"

While she recounted her Parisian adventure, he considered his options. *Should he tell her?* Stuck between a rock and a hard place, he waited until the peach cobbler was finished then grabbed her hand. "I have to tell you something, and it's not an easy thing to say." The carefree expression melted off her face in a flash. "I went to the ... uh ... university health service today and ... "

She looked stricken. "Oh God, not herpes?"

"No. Nothing like that."

"Phew. Because I've never just done it. Like that. That was a new one for me. And of course afterward, that's all I thought about. How irresponsible I was."

"Don't worry. It's not a disease, not really. The thing is. I've noticed you've been scratching a lot." He paused to assess how she was taking this because some women ... in fact, all of the women he knew would hear what he had to say, and stomp out in a huff. If anything, Elizabeth looked a little confused.

"And while I haven't been scratching, I have been itching."

Still nothing. No reaction from her, whatsoever. "I think I know why you feel so itchy. I think it's possible that you might have ... head lice."

There was no huff. No disgust even. She burst out laughing. "What? Are you serious? Head lice? Grown ups don't get head lice."

"Actually, they must. Because I did."

"You? You have lice?"

"Shhh," he said, suddenly aware of how easy it was for other people to hear her. "And you think you gave them to me?" she whispered.

"I don't know their origins. But I went to the ... eh university health center today, just before lunch because my head was itching and that's what I have. Lice. I wasn't going to say anything, but you're scratching. I could be totally wrong, but then again, I could be totally right."

He paid the check and together they walked across the street and descended the steep Exorcist steps, so named because they filmed a scene for the movie there. At the bottom, they turned left and at Elizabeth's urging stopped in Dixie Liquors for a bottle of Bulleit Bourbon. After that, they walked a few blocks down M Street to CVS where they bought two boxes of Nix Lice remover. As they waited to cross the street on the way to her beautiful white apartment, he took her hand in his.

"Just wondering," she said. "If I wasn't scratching were you going to tell me?"

"What do you mean?"

"Were you going to tell me you had lice or were you just going to let me catch them from you?"

He lifted her hand to his mouth and kissed it. "I would never do anything to harm you. Ever," he said.

thirteen

PLAID·IT·TUDES

It wasn't the sulfate free shampoo or nerves that was irritating Mary Ellen. It was head lice. That's what you get for playing beauty salon with an eight-year-old. Ewwwe. Ewwwe. Ewwwe. Suzanne, an avowed homeopath, recommended a specialty tonic made by her acupuncturist. "It's got tea tree oil, lavender oil, peppermint oil and eucalyptus oil. We slathered their heads with it, put those old fashioned plastic shower caps on them and they are watching all the Harry Potter movies as we speak," said Suzanne when she called to tell Mary Ellen the news.

"All of them? In one sitting?"

"Yep. The only way something that non-toxic can work is with time. It takes at least fifteen hours. You're supposed to do it overnight, but they would never sleep with those caps on. Imagine the mess. And with Ella on vacation…"

The next day, Mary Ellen picked up her own bottle of $150 essential oils from Suzanne's acupuncturist, and when all of her men had gone to bed, Mary Ellen applied the oil, donned a shower cap and conducted a sort of death vigil for the mites by staying up all night while the potion did its magic. She treated the linens and the upholstery, she read the newspaper, and when she could think of nothing else to do, she went online. With the Washington Prep student directory by her side, Mary Ellen Googled the parents of Brophy's classmates. It was an impressive list. Secretary of Education Nelson, two senators, two congressmen, an Under Secretary of State, a columnist for the *Wall Street Journal*, that ubiquitous ultra conservative radio pundit, Trey Collins, and Elizabeth Sherwood. As Ebony had alluded to at the Johnson's party, she was, in fact, richer than God. And when she saw her photo on a society blog, she remembered the story that made Elizabeth Sherwood a minor celebrity a few years back. When she was going through that nasty divorce, the competing paper, the *Washington News*, took great delight in reporting every tawdry detail of the whole ugly affair—from the hot young nanny who stole her husband's heart to Elizabeth's dalliances with that gorgeous young senator. There were pages of hits when Googling Elizabeth and lots of photos of her on the red carpet at the big charity events like the Kennedy Center Honors or the Corcoran Ball. Her face was too plain to be called pretty, but she was in great shape and she wore lovely dresses that emphasized her toned arms and back.

The parents who weren't notable were boring, but rich—lawyers or stockbrokers mostly. People who must be way too busy spending money to spend their time Googling names out of the school directory. She smiled as she thought of someone Googling Mr. and Mrs. Kenneth Packingham only to land on the homepage of the East County Grease Police. They'd see Kenny dressed like a cop with the tall boots, tight pants, and mirrored glasses astride a motorcycle in front of one of his grease trucks. The photo was taken at least ten years ago, but Kenny hadn't changed much.

Still had all his hair, he might have gained a few pounds, but he was still in good shape. What changed about Kenny wasn't how he looked. It was his outlook. He used to have a sense of humor. He enjoyed doing things ... with her, even. But now, he was miserable. Loud, overbearing, belligerent. But only towards her. To the boys, he was the same good-natured doofus dad he had always been. Something had spooked him and every time she tried to talk about it, he blew up and told her to leave him the fuck alone. So she did.

Tired of Googling, Mary Ellen moved on to her second favorite pastime, Facebook. Specifically, Brophy's Facebook, which she had easy access to. As bright as he was, he was also lazy so every on-line account that required a password, from Facebook to Gmail to sports junkie sites and even free porn sites, he used the exact same user name, "laxplaya" and password, "#1Beast." Mary Ellen signed on to his Facebook and scanned his recent posts. Dumb as ever. He had joined two new groups, "Prep football rocks!" and "Chester Cheeto for Mayor!" His status was listed as "There is no "I" in team." Mary Ellen had no interest in Brophy's moronic posts, but she was very interested in keeping up with his friends and especially, his friends' families. He had recently friended a lot of new and very interesting faces. There was Trent Collins' son Kirby, who, despite his father's teetotaler image was clearly a party animal and there was Cole Reardon who seemed surprisingly normal. She was struck by how handsome he was. Even in a crappy photo taken with somebody's cell phone, he radiated success. According to his profile, he had a girlfriend named Brittany who looks Latino, he loves *South Park* and *Star Wars*, he's a liberal, and he believes in God. Except for the liberal part, nothing out of the ordinary.

What's so great about him she wondered? Wait until people really have a chance to know Brophy. Before the semester is over, they'll be asking "Cole Reardon who?"

The first rays of light peeked through the kitchen window. Her head tingled, but it did not itch. They were gone. She tiptoed upstairs and showered, washing her hair three times to get the oil out.

Two days later, Mary Ellen was friending a whole new group of people herself. Suzanne had agreed to host Mary Ellen's first annual Fall-into-Fall Plaid-IT-tudes trunk show at her home, which was apparently a not-to-be-missed destination. Not only did everyone accept her invitation, they all brought their nosey friends with them. Even Jackie Johnson, who's home far outshone Suzanne's Victorian monstrosity, couldn't resist.

"I want to invite you to a little get together I'm having," Mary Ellen told Jackie when she called to invite her. "I'm the area's only rep for Plaid-IT-tudes. Maybe you've seen their ads in Glamour Magazine?" She paused for a second then plowed on. "Well, anyway, it's a fab-u-lous line of sporty yet ultra feminine fashions. You're going to flip over this season's look, which can be summed up with two words. Burberry E-ques-tri-an! Let me tell you, these clothes are ... BE. YOND. Amazing. I'm hosting my first annual "Fall-into-Fall" trunk show. A great way to get acquainted with a line that everyone's talking about. Harpers Bazaar actually said, 'Everyone's talking about it.' So please come. Bring some friends if you want. It's next Thursday."

"Thursday, I'll have to check ... " said Jackie, sounding like she was trying to fabricate a plausible conflict. Ignoring Jackie entirely, Mary Ellen went in for the kill. "My house is such a mess. We're having our kitchen remodeled. You know what that means? Disaster zone! So, I'm having our super fun girls night out at my sister's house. Suzanne Nuttin… "

"Suzanne Nuttin is your sister?" said Jackie. "I hear her house is amazing. Wasn't it featured in *Victoriana Magazine* a few years back?"

"As a matter of fact, it was."

She never expected Jackie to accept the invitation, but there she was, sitting on Suzanne's ridiculously hard Victorian settee with a few of her horsey friends pouring through the Plaid-IT-tudes book.

"Suzanne, your home is amazing," gushed Jackie when Mary Ellen introduced them.

"It's all Corn," said Suzanne. "Most of the furniture has been in his family for decades. I just had it re-upholstered."

"You can tell," said Jackie forlornly. "There is something so special about an old house filled with antiques. You can't buy that kind of authenticity."

"Look who's talking," said Mary Ellen. "Jackie's home is extraordinary."

"Nothing like this, though," said Jackie looking like the former Miss America just moments after crowning her successor. Mary Ellen almost felt sorry for her, but then, she remembered that this was the woman who willingly selected off the shelf white when she could have an entire color-wheel of customized whites.

Jackie and her friends ordered the entire assortment of silk blouses commemorating the Triple Crown winners. Claudia brought some friends and they too placed hefty orders. Every single guest ordered something except for Pups who said she liked the clothes well enough, but felt that $200 was far too much to spend on a blouse. This group of trendsetters will wear their new Burberry-ish apparel and garner compliments from their friends who will, in turn, want to have the showy plaids for themselves.

The chimera of all stay home moms—to make it big on your own terms, from the comfort of your own home, without the hassle of daycare or commuting or having to grocery shop on Saturdays— wrapped its serpent tail around Mary Ellen's heart. She had the magic formula—the right combination of a piping hot product and a hungry consumer. Anything really is possible. Not only did she sell enough merchandise to cover her investment in samples and catalogues, she was about to make a profit—and a sizable one at that. At the end of the night, Mary Ellen hugged each of her guests and reminded them to get their special goodie bag on the way out the door. It was just a bunch of junk, really. Leftover promotional items from the many charitable events Suzanne and Corn had hosted. Inside the pink Breast Cancer Awareness bags were Leukemia Society pedometers, Juvenile Diabetes Association sugar free mints, Live Strong rubber bracelets, Prevention of Blindness LED flashlights, and baseball caps of all sorts. After Mary Ellen's party, Suzanne's closet was cleaned out and the triplets had a blast putting the bags together. Being eight, Ayn and her brothers, Ryan and Bryan approached the task creatively. They sampled some of the mints; they turned on the flashlights and they tried on every single hat before placing them in the bags. The three adorable children stood by the front door smiling as they presented each guest with a special memento of the night.

As Mary Ellen saw the last of her guests to the door, Pups did what she usually did at parties, she cleaned up. While Claudia did what she usually did at parties, she poured herself another glass of wine. "So Pups is it? Where on earth did you get that name of yours?" asked Claudia.

"Oh it's actually kind of a funny story. My older brother was ... "

Before she got any further, Mary Ellen, buzzed on Chardonnay and the prospect of success, came into the living room. "Phew!" she exclaimed. "What a night!"

"Mary Ellen, you really out did yourself. This was amazing. I don't think I've ever gone to a shopping party as nice as this one," said Claudia who was so moved she stood up and applauded.

Mary Ellen smiled triumphantly. "It did all come together didn't it?"

"It was first class all the way," said Pups collecting dirtied plaid paper plates from the coffee table, not bothering to finish her story.

"Don't worry about that, Pups. Ella will get it," said Suzanne.

"It's no big deal," said Pups who wouldn't feel comfortable just sitting.

"Speaking of big deals, have I got a tidbit for you," said Claudia with the kind of lilting tone reserved for snarky gossip. "I've been dying to tell you all night, but I didn't want to look like a bitchy gossip in front of Jackie Johnson."

"What?" asked Mary Ellen mimicking the tone.

"I heard they found cooties on a certain newspaper publisher's son last week!"

Mary Ellen, Suzanne and Pups all cringed. They were all intimately familiar with what Claudia was talking about, but nevertheless, they all stared blankly ahead as if they had no idea.

"Head lice! They found head lice on Cole Reardon. Can you believe it?"

"Who's Cole Reardon?" asked Pups.

"He's the golden boy of Washington Prep," said Mary Ellen. "His mother is Elizabeth Sherwood, publisher of *The Tribune*."

"I know Elizabeth. She's a great triathlete," said

Suzanne.

"The woman who went through that divorce?" asked Pups. "Was that pathetic or what? She's better off without that dirt bag, but man, he got the house and the kids and half of all that newspaper money."

"Well, now he can add head lice to the list of things he's got. I hear they sent the boy home to get treated," said Claudia.

Mary Ellen tried to maintain her composure. "Really?"

"You should be getting one of those politically correct semi-government official letters in the mail in the next few days. From what I hear, it's only affecting the residents so far. And one odd faculty member, but I don't know who."

"We had an outbreak at my kids school," said Pups. "My kids didn't get it, thank God, but I treated them anyhow. Preventatively you know?"

"Huh," said Mary Ellen.

"My pharmacist, Mr. Tran whipped me up some magic solution that ... well all I can say is that it really is magic." Mary Ellen wanted to ask Pups how to contact Mr. Tran, but decided wait until Claudia wasn't around.

"Let's hope the job gets done so it doesn't spread to the rest of the school," said Claudia. "From what I understand, Elizabeth's not really in the picture where the kids are concerned. At. All. So, it's in the hands of his new honey who's about seventeen and Ecuadorian. Did someone say Pan-dem-ic?"

-fourteen-

COTILLION

Glancing down at the odometer, Pups realized that she had put close to a hundred miles on her Suburban in the past twelve hours. She could have gone to Philadelphia for a cheese steak or traveled to Richmond to watch Patrick don a dark blue frock coat and sky blue trousers to reenact the Siege of Petersburg. Every weekend from Labor Day to Veteran's Day, Patrick, an avowed Civil War buff, joined hundreds of equally obsessed buffs to play a gigantic game of soldier in some remote field. She didn't begrudge him these little excursions. He worked hard selling big expensive American vehicles that no one really wanted any more. He was good at his job; good enough to afford the luxury of having Pups stay home and raise their children properly, which these days, meant driving her big expensive American vehicle that no one wanted, all over town.

So instead of a scenic drive along country byways, Pups spent over three hours in the worst kind of meandering Saturday traffic; scurrying ten miles to a soccer game, fifteen miles to a birthday party, and eight miles to a special craft store that sold the Martha Stewart brand glitter she needed for her Brownie troop. Now that the sun had set, Pups was making her last seven-mile run of the day with Willa riding shotgun.

"Who did it and ran?" she asked, assessing Willa's flyaway hair. They were on their way to fetch Grant and his buddies from their first cotillion, an event about which there was a great deal of speculation and curiosity in the MacArthur house. All week, Virginia and Willa battled it out, earning points for small acts of kindness in a contest to decide who would get to accompany Pups on the cotillion carpool. It was neck and neck until Grant's incessant taunting of Virginia caused her to have a meltdown, which in turn, caused her to lose the character contest to Willa.

As eighth-graders, Grant and his classmates had risen to the highest summit of the Catholic school mountain. These lionhearted thirteen-years-olds were honored with prestigious posts like safety patrol, wined and dined at the once monthly eighth-grade pizza social afterschool and given special privileges like using the computer room during recess. Glamorous as those entitlements were, what truly announced your place at the top of the Catholic school ladder was the invitation the archdiocese extended to every eighth grader enrolled in one of their schools. Cotillion.

From October to December, 870 eighth graders congregated in the gymnasium of Our Lady of Mercy High School for instruction on how to gracefully make the transition from socially awkward children to polite young ladies and gentlemen. They had all received embossed invitations, stating the time, days and location of the cotillion and requesting that attendees dress in "appropriate attire." Printed on the back of those ivory cards was non-embossed type stipulating that "appropriate" meant jackets, ties, khaki pants and non-scuffed dress shoes for the boys. For the girls, it meant party dresses that were not low-cut, strapless, too short or too revealing. Young ladies' heels could be no higher than two inches, and both pantyhose and white gloves were required. Anyone who dared ignore what was printed on the back of the invitation would be asked to wait outside the gym until pick up.

Boys and girls learned different things at the cotillion. Boys learned to find their dates a chair, fetch them punch and cookies and ask them to dance. Girls learned how to be pleasant to all the gentlemen, not just the cool ones. Cotillion was run by Mrs. P, the seventy-five-year-old doyenne of the Catholic school social scene such that it was. At the start of each gathering, Mrs. B and her husband Vincent would demonstrate some antique dance moves like the foxtrot, the waltz, or the hustle then give the students a chance to practice those moves with a partner. With the exception of Mr. and Mrs. B, everyone, all the students, their parents, their teachers and anyone else who ever heard about cotillion knew that outside of this particular event, they would never again waltz or foxtrot or hustle, but no one dared to tell Mrs. B for fear that she would abruptly end the nearly forty-five-year old tradition.

In fact, Mrs. B would be horrified to see her young charges in little more than a year's time at a high school dance in this very gymnasium. The boys would never think of getting the girls punch unless it was spiked and the girls would never dream of talking to any guy unless he was cool. And when the thumping beat of the music compelled them to move, it wouldn't be a foxtrot or waltz they would be dancing. Instead, they would substitute their own generation's signature dance, known variously as freaking, grinding or twerking. No matter what they called it, the moves were the same. A boy would bounce his hips a little and extend a leg in a semi-lunge position while the girl straddled his out-stretched thigh and proceed to rub her pelvis back and forth over him ... to the beat, of course. Alternately, the girl could rock her hips while sticking her rear end out so the boy could place his hands on her hips while pushing his pelvis into her backside. The all-girls Catholic schools in the area forbade such rug cutting, but the boys' schools and the coed schools turned a blind eye, thankful that at least the dance partners were still fully clothed.

Pups and Willa stood on the second floor of the athletic center, looking down through a window at the hundreds of eighth-graders learning how to be proper 1950s teenagers. A large circle of girls faced an equally large circle of boys who introduced themselves to the girls and asked them to dance. Extending their arms towards each other, the couples waited until the PA system blared a scratchy version of Kermit the Frog singing his big hit, *Rainbow Connection*. As the music played, hundreds of randomly made couples did their best to execute a decent waltz. They had about 90 seconds to get it right before the music stopped. The young men took the young ladies' hands, gave them a shake and thanked them for the dance. And like a giant caterpillar, the navy blue side of the circle took a giant step to the right; placing the young men in front of their next dance partners. The process repeated until the song was over.

"What do you think? You'll be down there in a few years!" exclaimed Pups. "Looks like you're going to need a fancy dress." Wearing a fancy dress didn't make much of an impression on Willa. Being the recipient of Virginia's hand-me-downs extinguished any interest she may have had in fashion. She knew that even though the dress didn't even exist yet, by the time she was invited to cotillion, that dress would have something just a little bit wrong with it; like an almost imperceptible stain or a minuscule tear along the hemline inexpertly mended by Pups. It's true that no one but Willa would even know the tiny defect existed, but the fact that she did know, was enough to take the joy out of wearing the dress in the first place. "There's a lot of really short boys," said Willa. She was right. Watching Grant navigate through the line, Pups couldn't help but feel proud.

He wasn't one of the undersized boys who craned their necks to make eye contact with their partners. He wasn't pimply-faced or overweight or bespectacled or burdened with a smile full of orthodontia. Grant was everything any mother could want, and everything a respectable young lady could desire; a serious student, a fine athlete, and a boy whose strong moral character distinguished him from all the average boys and girls now parading arm and arm around the gym.

Mrs. B lifted her wireless microphone to her mouth and after a few false starts punctuated by ear numbing feedback, announced, "Ladies and gentlemen, thank you very much for your exquisite behavior tonight. May you have a blessed evening. I look forward to your enchanting, mannerly and well-dressed presence back here in two weeks!"

The orderly line of twosomes marched regally towards the double doors. But the well-mannered children from the 1950s remained in the gym, while on the other side of the threshold, loud obnoxious modern teenagers whipped off their ties and white gloves while their cackles and screams bounced off the glossy cinder block walls. Pups and Willa stood on the stairs scanning the pack of young time travelers for Grant.

"Hey, Buddy" shouted Pups as Grant bound through the doors jerking his arm away from his partner and yanking at his tie.

"Aww Jeeze. Why'd you have to bring HER?" asked Grant meeting them at the stairs.

"Where are your friends?" asked Pups.

"Around here somewhere. I saw Bennett with a ginger a minute ago."

"Ginger?"

"Never mind. I'll go find them."

As Grant went off to find his friends, Willa confided, "A ginger is a girl with red hair and freckles."

"Really? Good thing you're here to help me translate."

"Yep," said Willa proud to prove herself useful.

When he returned, Bennett, Joey, Stephen and Ward were with him.

"Hey boys! Have fun tonight?" asked Pups.

"It was okay," said Bennett.

"Yeah. I'd say it was less than okay," said Ward.

"Basically, it sucked. Unless you're like Grant here; a huge fan of Kermit the Frog," said Joey.

"All the girls sure looked pretty," said Pups.

"Yeah, pretty stuck up. They're all into high school boys now," countered Grant.

The guys chuckled with Pups as they walked through the parking lot. "I'm over there at the end of that row," said Pups. Even though she was practically invisible, Willa was glad to be there. She idolized Grant and his friends, and it was nice to have her mother to herself for at least a little bit. Inside the car, Grant asked Pups if they could stop off at McDonalds. They were starving, and all the kids from the cotillion would be there. Pups agreed only after drilling each boy about whether or not his mother would mind if they were a little later than she promised to have them home. They all adamantly said their mothers were fine with it even though none of them actually knew ... until confronted by a crazy woman seething with rage and ranting about how irresponsible they had been. That's when they knew their mothers weren't fine with something.

Pups pulled into the normally sleepy McDonalds. It was 9:00 on a Saturday night, by all measures, a slow time for the restaurant. However, tonight, the parking lot was crawling with minivans and SUV's dropping off barelegged girls in party dresses and flip flops and boys in white undershirts, khaki pants and non-scuffed dress shoes.

"The lot is full. I'm going to have to park somewhere on the street," said Pups as the boys climbed out of her truck. She handed Grant a ten dollar bill.

"Willa, do you want a chocolate shake?" Willa nodded. "Get her a shake and wait for us outside when you're done."

Pups parked on the street behind the McDonalds and she and Willa trudged up the hill towards the glowing restaurant. Inside the McDonalds, the front counter looked like the stage at a One Direction concert; with a throng of giddy teens vying for the attention of the overwhelmed superstars who would get them their burgers and fries. "Good Lord, I feel sorry for the people who work there," Pups said to Willa.

"It looks like a beehive," said Willa.

"You're right, that's exactly what it looks like," said Pups. The outside of the restaurant was almost as crowded as the inside. Parents huddled on the brightly lit sidewalk trading war stories about what it took to get their daughters to wear pantyhose and white gloves and their sons to wear ties. One of those huddles was made up of a group of mothers from Holy Family. Pups gave them a friendly wave, but there was no expectation that anyone of them would actually talk to her. She wasn't a part of the in crowd. Never had been. Never would be. She was startled when she heard a voice behind her. "Everybody's dying to know what your secret is?" It was Judy Pillson, mother of Courtney, William and David. She had broken away from the mom's huddle and was now beside Pups and Willa.

"Oh hey, Judy. What secret?" asked Pups.

"Oh, you know," said Judy swinging her pointer finger around her head.

Pups smiled. "No secret. Just diligence."

"Diligence? That's putting it mildly. People are calling you the Rambo of head lice."

"Rambo? I'm just trying to help. I mean abolishing the no-nits rule is … well, it's killing us."

"I couldn't agree more. We all know that as long as certain *individuals* keep showing up … untreated … we'll never get this thing licked."

"What can you do but hope for the best?" asked Pups who had no desire to get into a deep conversation about certain *individuals* with Judy Pillson.

"You know, we all think you should go see Ms. Gagner. Let her know how we feel. I mean, it's interfering with the quality of education. What are we paying tuition for? Who can learn with all that scratching going on?"

"Me?" asked Pups feeling both honored and bamboozled.

"Frankly, most of us have worn out our welcome. You've heard of the do not call list? Most of us are on Ms. Gagner's "do not listen to" list. We've been too vocal, and she's locked us out. To the best of our knowledge, yours is one of the few names not on that list. Besides, you have such a great reputation for helping ... like really helping. Doing the dirty work. A real knight for social justice. She'll respect you." Pups was flattered by this sudden attention from Judy, but like the ugly girl who is suddenly the object of the star quarterback's attention, she played it cool and kept her defenses up.

While Pups played footsie with Judy Pillson, Willa grew antsy. She expected to have her mother all to herself for the night, but now, here she was, losing out to dumb Mrs. Pillson. She wandered over towards the restaurant to get a closer look at all the teenage fizz that was fogging the windows. The line was still ten deep at the counter, and every seat at every table was full. Girls stood on the bench seats as boys threw French fries at them. And boys swung their ties around like lassos trying to "rope" the girl's sodas. The brown puddles on the floor were a testament to their good aim. Willa had a hard time locating Grant, but when she did, she couldn't believe it. He was not in the line waiting to get her chocolate shake; he was in the deserted side hall leading to the restrooms with Brittany Sanchez. Brittany was leaning against the wall with Grant pushed up against her. And he was kissing her. KISSING HER! Running his hands through her hair and kissing her. After what seemed to Willa like an awfully long time for a kiss, Grant stepped back and pulled something out of his pocket. It was the ten-dollar bill. *My chocolate shake money*, thought Willa.

She watched as Brittany looked at the money curiously. Grant said something, which must have ticked her off because Brittany scowled and plucked the money from Grant's fingers. She then proceeded to tear Willa's shake money to shreds.

Grant looked like he always did when he was in trouble but he just shrugged, ambled out into the main restaurant and gave Bennett a high five.

Disgusted, Willa moved back alongside her mother who was still busy chattering with Mrs. Pillson.

"You know, if parents would just pay a little more attention to their kids, we could all avoid a whole mess of trouble," said Pups.

"You're singing to the choir, Pups. How many mothers are blind to what's going on right in front of them? The parents who don't know what's on top of their kids' heads certainly don't know what's going on inside their kids' heads. Enough of this heady stuff. How's Patrick doing? We have to get together sometime."

"He's good. He's down in Richmond for a re-enactment."

"Re-enactment?"

"Yeah. Civil War. It's kind of a nerd fest, but he enjoys it. There are worse things for a husband to be involved with I guess."

Through the glass, Willa watched as Grant picked up a handful of Courtney Pillson's fries and, despite her smiley protests, stuffed them into his mouth all at once. "I'm hungry," she said with disgust.

Pups looked down, surprised to hear Willa who

had been so quiet, she had forgotten she was even there. "Grant will be out in a minute with your shake. Kids are starting to leave," she said putting her arm around Willa's shoulder.

"I'd better round up Courtney and the gang. Good talking to you Pups. Give it some thought. You're the gal for the job!"

The kids swarmed out the door and soon, the quiet parking lot was humming with the sound of engines starting. Pups and Willa trudged back down the hill to get the Suburban and when they returned to the lot, Grant and his friends were waiting on the sidewalk.

"Where's my shake?" demanded Willa as the boys climbed in.

"Oh Jeeze, I forgot all about the shake. Sorry Willa."

"But I'm hungry!"

"We've got plenty of stuff to eat at home. Don't worry," said Pups. "Hey buddy, any change for me?"

"Oh … uh … no. I had some, but then … I had to lend a few bucks to Otito. Can't guarantee she's going to pay me back either," said Grant with a Cheshire cat grin for the benefit of his friends.

"That's alright honey. You did the right thing. A few dollars aren't going to make much difference," said Pups radiating her approval for her son's benevolence.

Willa glared at Grant. "What about Brittany? Did you lend her money too?"

The entire group of boys squirmed. "I don't know what you're talking about," said Grant. "Brittany wasn't even there, was she?"

A chorus of nopes resounded through the car.

"But, I saw her," said Willa glaring at Grant.

"You must have seen her at the cotillion. She was at the cotillion, but she wasn't at McDonalds. At least I didn't see her there. Any of you guys see her?"

Another chorus of nopes. The rest of the ride was silent except for the radio.

fifteen

MONTY'S

People walking past the chapel were mystified by the odd sounds emanating from its depths. Some were so alarmed they crouched down to look through the small windows at the top of the chapel dungeon Mr. Mann used as a classroom. They were shocked by what they saw. Mr. Mann's third period class was having fun. They were smiling and chuckling. In Wenn Mann's class! Freshmen were actually enjoying Latin. The fact that they were reading the text in English first might have had something to do with their joy. By the following week, when they would be plodding through one ponderous Latin line at a time, the fun would be a distant memory.

"So what is an Autumnal beauty?" asked Wenn.

"Someone who was born in the fall?" said Sutton.

"No."

"An older woman?" offered Packingham.

"Yep. And what does Ovid say about older women?"

"An age that knows to give and take delight," said Packingham.

"Right. He alludes to this a few times. Anywhere else?"

"Courts the juicy joys of riper growth?" The boys stifled their snickers.

"Yes."

"Juicy joy? I thought they dry up when they get old!" said Remy.

"Older, not ancient," said Wenn. "He's not suggesting you go out and fuck a corpse." They all laughed. Mr. Mann sure was a lot looser lately.

"So good old Ovid was a cougar hunter?" said Cole.

"I guess so."

"Damn!" said Remy.

The bell rang and the students were up and almost out the door before he caught them.

"Packingham, Bardo, Sutton, Johnson, Rogers, I need a few minutes of your time."

The fun was over. Like all teenage boys, they looked guilty as hell. They didn't know exactly what he thought they were guilty of, but because they spent 97% of their time thinking about, talking about or actually engaging in sex, they knew the odds were not on their side. Guilt owned them.

"So interims go out in a few days, and yours aren't going to be something your parents will open and celebrate. That's not surprising to any of you is it?"

In unison, the boys stared at the floor and shook

their heads.

"Right. So, I just wanted to re-iterate my policy of parental intervention, just in case you forgot. If I so much as get a whiff of your parent on the premises thinking they're going to see me, you're dead meat. If there's a voicemail or an email or a snail mail or any other type of fucking mail with your parent's name on it, life as you now know it will cease to exist. And if your mother is here to water the fucking flowers or whatever the fuck they come here to do, and she decides to fucking ambush me, hell will be a place you go to for vacation. That's how bad it will be. Any questions? Anybody not understand? Don't even whisper my name in your prayers. Get it? Because if I have to deal with any fucking parent. Your. Ass. Is. Mine. Understand?" In unison, the boys shook their heads up and down. "Work harder and bring up those abysmal grades." As the accused scrambled out the door he walked back over to his Ovid text, and read a little further.

"With them, pleasure comes naturally, without provocation, the pleasure which is sweeter than all, the pleasure which is shared equally by the man and the woman. How sweet it is to hear her voice quaver as she tells me the joy she feels, and to hear her imploring me to slacken my speed so as to prolong her bliss. How I love to see her, drunk with delight, gazing with swooning eyes upon me, or, languishing with love, keeping me a long while at arms' length. But these accomplishments are not vouchsafed by nature to young girls. They are reserved for women who have passed the age of thirty-five."

So what if this particular passage wasn't originally

on the syllabus. It was one lesson they won't forget.

* * * * *

Every Wednesday evening, Wenn walked out of Roland Hall with his guitar case in hand to become the man he wanted to be. As the permanent Wednesday night player at Monty's, he performed a repertoire of songs that fed his famished soul. Besides his time with Elizabeth, playing at Monty's was the only time he felt alive. The rest of his time was shit. Countless hours of meaningless shit. Teaching a bunch of thickheaded, disinterested, dullards was ruining his love of Latin. If he could figure out a way to support himself doing something else, he would, but until then, he was relegated to small puffs of joy on Wednesday night and whenever he was with Elizabeth.

Monty's was located Glover Park, the sketchy part of upper Georgetown best known for the handful of titty bars that lined its streets. The kinds of places that generated enough trouble that late night newscasters knew all the managers by name, having interviewed them repeatedly for live on-the-scene crime reports. There was a city run aid office for Spanish speaking immigrants where they could go for information about social services, jobs and other useful things. There was a liquor store that stocked both $2,000 1961 Chateau Latour for the wealthy of the neighborhood and Night Train for the Georgetowners who preferred park benches to park views. The Whole Foods was a favorite of the Georgetown medical students who stopped by, in their scrubs, for fruit salads and organic pizzas. There were some high-end antiques stores, the kind that kept their doors locked just in case some titty bar customer or Spanish aid patron developed an interest in mid century modern. The best Sushi place in the city was wedged between Isabel's Pupusas and the Roi du Soleil French restaurant. There was a burger joint, a hardware store, and Monty's.

From the outside, it looked like a run of the mill Georgetown restaurant, with a flickering gas lamp and too many coats of drab colonial blue paint slapped onto 250-year-old bricks. There was a menu posted outside in an illuminated glass display case, but anyone stupid enough to look it over and attempt to get a table inside was either a tourist or an idiot. Monty's was open to neither. To make it through the door, you had to be on the list. Most everyone on the list graduated from one of a small handful of elite Washington, D.C private schools. They all swam together on the Presidential Club swim team as children. They all had jobs in finance or real estate or law except for Bric, whose father gave him the money to open Monty's after he failed at finance, real estate and law. As soon as Wenn stopped being an up and comer and started fucking away all that life had in store for him, his status should have plummeted, but thanks to his lifelong friendship with Bric, he not only stayed on top, he got himself a standing gig for every Wednesday night, from 7:00 until 10:00. Quiet hours for Monty's which didn't really get hopping until later.

By midnight, the place was always teeming with young Republicans chatting up blonde socialites with their long legs, their fuck me heels, and their adorable little dresses that showed off their "weekend in the Bahamas" tans. Bored as he was with that particular breed, Wenn didn't mind playing jazz for them. Jazz made everything tolerable. Something about it spoke to him in the same way ancient languages did. It had its own conventions, its own rhythms—as free flowing and ephemeral as the wind, as precise as anything Virgil ever wrote. Notes on lines were as meaningless as words on a page until you applied yourself to the equation. But unlike math, what you brought to the work; how you filtered those markings could produce infinite outcomes. Some almost as brilliant as their creator intended. He was an intermediary. A humble servant to Gods named Coltrane and Bird and Porter; channeling their intentions and, in the process, feeling the warmth of their reflected glow. The first thing he did when he got to Monty's was to find the keeper of the list, a big barrel-chested, jarhead named Phinn. "Elizabeth what?" asked Phinn officiously holding his pen at the ready to record her last name.

"Just Elizabeth," said Wenn. "Shortish hair. Older than everyone else on the list." He set himself up in the corner of the dining room, which was beginning to fill up. There were a few people he knew. Some he didn't. Whether he knew them or not, everyone was familiar. They were all just variations on the same model. Some taller, some heavier.

Nerves were creeping up on him, something he never had to wrestle with before. He got himself his new favorite drink, bourbon on the rock from the bartender who told him that Bric would be in later. His head was sort of itchy. *Could he possibly have lice again? A bad case of nerves?* While he waited for the bourbon to announce itself, Cullen, his old friend and sometimes fuck buddy, arrived with a group of girls, every bit as pretty as she was. She gave him an awkward wave. He returned the gesture with an awkward smile. Cullen was nice enough. She was fun, and good in bed, but after the third date, things got kind of weird. Like all she saw when she looked at him were rings and dish designs and flower girls.

Elizabeth was different. When she looked at him, there was nothing. No expectations, no demands. She was the perfect woman. Wenn kept his eyes fixed on the door, expecting to see her sweep in. She still wasn't there at 7:00, when he started his set with *Moonglow*. Or when he played *Moon River*. Or when he rounded out the moon tunes with *Paper Moon*, a personal favorite by Harold Arlen. Three crowd pleasers thematically linked; always a good opener. He segued into a collection of Cole Porter songs and he finished the first set with Charlie Parker, then looked up expecting to see her, but all he saw were cheerful faces smiling and clapping. She missed the entire first set.

They had been seeing each other about three times a week which was a lot given the fact that Wenn was supposed to be on duty six nights out of seven, had class every day and cross country after school with meets on weekends. Thank God for Dave Haber, the Junior Resident Dean who never minded covering for him. Elizabeth was chronically late, so this wasn't unexpected, but tonight was different. He had asked her to be on time. He swigged down the rest of his drink then went through the kitchen and out the back door. In the ally, he pulled a pack of Marlboros from his pocket. He loved smoking. Loved everything about it and hated the fact that you couldn't do it anywhere. He only smoked on Wednesday nights, in the ally behind Monty's. He didn't hide it, but most people would never take him for a smoker given his intense running schedule. What they didn't realize is that, in addition to all his other blessings, he had a ridiculous lung capacity, so smoking didn't slow him down in the least. Besides, smoking and drinking while playing music made him feel more authentic. She still wasn't there when he went inside, but Bric was now behind the bar.

"Nice set, Dude. Love the moon tunes. Vodka?" said Bric.

"Bourbon. Thanks. Hey, I'm expecting someone. Elizabeth. Pretty, short hair. Kind of older. She's on my tab."

"Sure. See Cullen's here?"

"Yeah." Wenn gave him a look that ended the conversation.

"Just saying … " said Bric defensively.

He took his drink and avoiding Cullen's table, he went to the door to see if Phinn could have possibly turned her away. Phinn assured him he had not. No messages on his phone. She just wasn't there.

On his way back, he ran into Todd Baylor, a friend of his oldest brother, Mike.

"Wenn Mann. How the fuck are you?"

"Good." He despised Todd Baylor.

"How's Mikey doing? Haven't seen that dude in ages."

"Me neither," he said. "Gotta get back to playing, Todd. See you around."

"You bet." As much as he wanted to stall, he wasn't going to do it with fucking Todd Baylor. He took his time tuning his guitar, but finally, he gave up and started playing. He had to do some calculations. Which song he could afford to lose? *The Way You Look Tonight* was expendable, especially since he didn't know how she looked since she wasn't fucking there. Usually, when he performed, he never looked up until the song was over and the audience was politely applauding. But tonight, he found himself looking up—a lot—to see if Elizabeth was there yet. She wasn't, but what he saw was sickening.

A vulgar bacchanal of eating, drinking and merriment, with people satisfying their every urge. Shoveling garbage into their mouths. Baked potatoes and steak, pasta primavera and shrimp cocktail into their gaping open fat fucking pie holes. People laughing and drinking without the slightest regard for the fact that he was performing. People with spinach dip on their teeth. People who talked with their mouth open spraying bits of black forest cake on their companions. A sea of plaid blazers and bare shoulders laughing it up in their ritualized pre-hook up way. He didn't expect a concert hall, just a little respect. A little attention, maybe. What a repugnant bunch. Other than Cullen, not a single person was paying attention. As he neared the end of his song, they quieted down, stopped chewing, stopped drinking, smiled and politely applauded. That is what he was used to. Christ, no wonder he never looked up. What went on while his head was down was best left unseen. While he was deciding what his next song should be, she arrived … a whirlwind as usual. Phinn pointed her in the direction of the bar. The sight of her made his head itch and ever since that day at the Tombs, itchiness triggered a semi. For the rest of his life, itching would be his secret aphrodisiac with poison ivy, mosquito bites and like producing incredibly intense sensations.

Safe in the knowledge that she was there, he cast his eyes down upon his instrument and proceeded to strum his love to her. *I've Got a Crush on You, Nice and Easy* and *For Once in My Life*. He looked up and like clockwork; there were the nice reliable smiling faces, including Elizabeth's and polite applause. He adjusted the mic in front of his face.

"Good evening. I'm going to try something a little different tonight. Hope you like it." He stared at Elizabeth who smiled warmly. He cleared his throat and began to play. He kept his eyes downward, too afraid the grotesque scene in front of him would throw him off key. He leaned into the microphone and sang a heartfelt rendition of *Out of Nowhere*.

Between verses, he looked up to see her expression. She was smiling. But she was smiling at Todd Baylor. Fucking Todd Baylor.

Another verse. Another look. Another smile for Todd Baylor. What the fuck? Todd Baylor? Why was his hand resting on her shoulder? How did they know each other and most importantly, why the fuck wasn't she fixated on him? While he presented her with an earnest gift of song, she was ogling Todd Baylor? Baylor went to Prep, and Georgetown and got married right out of college. He had a few kids. His dad pulled a few strings and got him a job on the corporate side of *The Washington Tribune*. Baylor was living the life. Great house, great wife, great car. And in true douche bag style, he never let his vows stop him from trolling around places like Monty's looking for a good time.

The only problem is that the other part of Monty's, the part Wenn refused to have anything to do with, was Socials—a kind of secret society that met and intermingled on a members only website. It started small, but like anything exclusive, it grew. Once people entered the domain, the rules of decorum were gone. They shared the most intimate of details about their most intimate of hook ups with the entire club. They used avatars to cloak their identity, but it was pretty easy to tell who was who. A lot of it was meaningless. Comments about how hot some girl was or what a creep some guy was. But it soon turned into a pornographic play-by-play of socially well-connected youth. Who liked anal, who had herpes, who didn't know his way around a woman's anatomy, who did. When Todd's avatar started showing up on Socials it was just a matter of time before his wife got wind of it. Now that he was in the final stages of his first divorce, his trolling at Monty's had intensified.

Wenn finished the song and the audience applauded, but Elizabeth was apparently too caught up with Todd to notice. He wanted to run back outside to the ally and have a smoke and think it over, but who knows how far Todd would go if left unchecked. He had to go over there and get his woman back.

"Thank you," he said with disgust into the microphone. Setting his guitar on a stand, he walked to the bar.

"That was a–MAZE-ing, Wenn," said Cullen as he passed her by.

"Thanks." He approached Elizabeth from behind, so she didn't see him coming. Baylor saw him, but didn't react until Wenn put his hands on Elizabeth's shoulders, and leaned in to give her a good one on lips, but she moved and all he got was her cheek.

"Hey!" he said trying to sound casual.

Elizabeth turned to give him a hug. "Wow, you are full of surprises! I had no idea you were so talented."

"Wenn Mann, stellar show," said Todd.

"You know each other?" she asked.

"I could ask you the same thing," he said.

"Todd and I used to work together."

"Yep. We're battle buddies having been in the trenches of contract negotiation warfare. God, I don't know how we managed with so little sleep."

"A lot of coffee and a lot of sugar," she said.

Ignoring their chitchat he said, "I wasn't sure you were going to make it."

"I know, I got held up with a last minute emergency. I couldn't help it. But you sounded great. Really wonderful."

"Yeah, dude. You're talented," said Todd. "Never knew you could sing like that."

"I need to get some air," he took Elizabeth's hand and pulled her with him as he headed for the front door.

"Todd Baylor?" he said stepping out into the cold.

"What's wrong?"

"Todd Baylor is the biggest douche bag I know. That's all. And why weren't you listening to me in there?"

"I was listening, but he came up and started talking and I couldn't be rude," she said.

"But you were. You were rude to me."

"Don't be angry. I didn't purposely try to hurt you." She wrapped her arms around him. "Whew, you smell like an ashtray." She stepped back and looked at him. "You don't smoke do you?" She had a peculiar expression, like suddenly he disgusted her. Like suddenly, despite all the kismet they had going, this one incidental thing about him so repulsed her, she could barely stand him. That must have been it because during his next break, she told him that she wasn't feeling well. She was going home. Her Chevy Chase home. Where she kept her migraine medication. So don't think you're going to drop by when you're finished your set.

It was a classic mid-date dump—something he had heard about, but never experienced. Before she left, she gave him a peck on the cheek and said, "Oh yeah. The condo association sent out a notice. They're fumigating the building for roaches, and we have to keep pets out for about a week. I forget when it is, but you'll have to take Gay back." With that, she left. He could not have felt worse if she had stomped her stiletto heel through the top of his foot. The rest of the night was a big, bourbon fueled blur. There was more jazz. But now the playlist was made up of songs about having your still beating heart savagely ripped out of your chest. There were many more drinks. There may have been French fries or onion rings. Something fried was definitely consumed. And there was a long drunken stagger back to the apartment Cullen shared with two other girls. He woke up with the sun, naked in her bed.

His head was pounding from the bourbon, and it itched like a motherfucker. It was no longer a question why. He got dressed and sat down on the edge of Cullen's bed. He softly brushed her hair off her face and gave her a tender kiss on her cheek. He hoped she wouldn't hate him too much. She was a nice girl. They got along well, had pretty good sex together, but then she would start talking and he would realize they just didn't share the same interests. He hoped she wouldn't hate him for skipping out before she woke up or for not calling her later. Of for leaving her with some teeny tiny souvenirs of their tryst.

sixteen

TROUBLE

"The divine light in me bows to the divine light in you. Namaste."

"Namaste," said the class before bowing. They sat in silence for an instant before allowing mania to resume its grip on their spirits. As Mary Ellen was rolling up her mat, Suki tapped her on the shoulder. "James needs to see you at the desk before you leave. Have a joyous day."

James had never asked to see her before. "Hi, James," she said approaching the tall reception desk crafted entirely from outdated yellow pages phonebooks. "You wanted to see me?"

"Mary Ellen! We ran the monthly charges this morning and ... American Express declined the charge." He handed over a thin strip of curled thermal paper.

"Declined the charge? I don't see why, I mean …"

James smiled politely. "Do you have another card perhaps?"

"Sure. Of course." Mary Ellen rifled through her

purse pulled her Visa out of her wallet.

She was flabbergasted. Her other cards, the ones she shared with Kenny were declined all the time. Sometimes bills went unpaid, which Mary Ellen credited to Kenny's adult on-set ADD (a malady she diagnosed without the help of a doctor). His disorder had gotten markedly worse in recent months, but Kenny didn't have anything to do with paying this card. It was hers alone. She sent her payment in two weeks ago because, thanks to her wonderfully successful Plaid-IT-tudes event, she actually had money in the bank. The afterglow of her successful trunk show left her with such a high that she hit the stores the next day and spent most or perhaps all of her profit on a new purse, another pair of Tory Burch flats, and some other stuff she had to have.

James ran the Visa through his card reader. He tore off another thin strip of curly thermal paper from the printer and presented it to her like a prize, saying, "Namaste."

On the way home, she stopped at the Safeway and while pushing her cart through the aisles, her cell phone buzzed. "Hello Suzanne."

"I'm freaking out! The triplets were sent home from school today. Three guesses why?"

"I don't know. Cheating?" she said steering her cart to the twelve items or less lane. She had thirteen items, but that toilet paper bargain was too good to pass up.

"Cheating! My children don't cheat. Since when …"

"You told me to guess. I did. And based on your reaction, I'm forfeiting my other two guesses so you may as well go ahead and tell me."

"THE LICE ARE BACK! Or maybe they never left. Who knows? Ayn was scratching a lot so they sent her to the nurse, and sure enough, the little fuckers are back. No surprise, the boys have them too. And everyone knows."

"Who knows?"

"Everybody. I know what they're all saying. That I'm a rotten mom."

"Who cares what anyone says? And what about that special formula from your acupuncturist?" asked Mary Ellen as she loaded her groceries onto the belt.

"Right. Do you have the name of a good acupuncturist? Because I'm done with her. I called and told her that they're back and do you know what she said?" Mary Ellen's patience for Suzanne's question heavy syntax was wearing thin. "She said, 'Oh well, nothing's perfect.' Like 'Oh, well your back is messed up, and no matter how many whisper thin needles I stick in your ear, you're going to be living with back pain forever. But, oh well.'"

"I didn't know you were having trouble with your back."

"I'm just saying ... how freaking unwilling she is to take responsibility. Why doesn't it say that on her business card, 'Oh well?'" Mary Ellen kept a close eye on the cashier, a girl of about seventeen with four piercings through her face. She had seen cashiers double or even triple scan things when a customer talked on the cell phone while checking out. "Suzanne, I think you have more important things to worry about. Like how to get rid of those ... undesirables."

While Mary Ellen spoke like the calm and in control big sister Suzanne knew her to be, internally she was clenching. She probably still had lice too. And by now, so did Kenny and the boys, and the linens and the upholstery. Another round of treatment meant another all-nighter. She was tired. She swiped her debit card and punched in her PIN while Suzanne prattled on. "I called the pediatrician and he was ready to write a prescription for some toxic muck. Sure it kills lice, it probably kills humans too, if you leave it on long enough. Anyhow, when I questioned him, he told me to try an all natural over the counter product. It's not as effective as the muck, so you have to do more combing, UGH. But anyhow, I sent Ricardo, our gardener, out to get it for me."

Mary Ellen glanced down the electronic card reader screaming NOT APPROVED in red LED's. "Hold on Suzanne. Did that not go through?" she asked the cashier.

"Says 'not approved' so I guess not."

Mary Ellen reached for her Visa and ran that through the scanner. She tried to remain calm, like it was no big deal, but the more it happened, the bigger a deal it became.

"Hello? You still there?"

"Oh, sorry," said Mary Ellen. "What's it called? Because I'm probably going to need it too. I don't think my nerves can take another round of this."

"Nerves? Mary Ellen you're the rock," said Suzanne. She was the rock. She had always been the rock. And even when she was about to crumble, she was still the rock to Suzanne. This time a happy LED "APPROVED" came up on the display.

"It's called Scuttle Bug," said Suzanne. "I'll let you know how it works because we're slathering that stuff on their heads as soon as Ricardo gets back. Wish me luck. Bye."

Suzanne already had good luck. She hit the jackpot again and again while Mary Ellen was the perennial loser, always one number away from a big win. If Suzanne had contracted lice when she was little, Mary Ellen would have been the one to deal with it, just like she dealt with everything the family needed. Starting in 8th grade, Mary Ellen would get home from school, fix dinner, straighten the house, help Suzanne with her homework, do a load of laundry and somehow manage to do her own homework well enough to achieve straight A's. When Suzanne needed something for a school project, Mary Ellen made sure Daddy stopped to get it, or when she was older and could drive, she went to the store and got it herself. When Suzanne was too sick to go to school, Mary Ellen stayed home to take care of her.

Their mother, Betty had done all of those things for Mary Ellen; dressing her in the cutest, most stylish outfits the 1970s had to offer, planning extravagant birthday parties to which she invited all the neighborhood children and showing up at school parades and pageants looking far better than any other mother in the school. But by the time Suzanne was nine and Mary Ellen was thirteen, Betty had planted herself on the family room couch and stayed there, watching soap operas on TV until Mary Ellen left for college. She couldn't even get up to see Mary Ellen graduate as the valedictorian of her class.

While she was away at the University of Wisconsin, Suzanne entered high school, joined the crew team and rowed her way to the 1984 Olympic trials. So phenomenon was her talent that Betty got herself off that couch and made it out the door so she could attend Suzanne's regattas and the many award ceremony's and dinners they were invited to.

And so it was, Mary Ellen was the unlucky sister whose mother checked out when she needed her most. The one who wasn't special enough to bother with. And Suzanne was the lucky sister who never once doubted the love of either her mother or her sister or anyone else. She harbored no resentment or guilt while Mary Ellen always felt partially to blame for Betty's withdraw. Perhaps if she had been less ordinary Betty would have loved her more.

Originally from Wisconsin, Bob and Betty O'Donnell moved to Washington when their daughters were small. A staffer for Ted Riccan, the Republican Congressman from a suburban district outside of Madison, Bob settled his family into a four bedroom colonial in the modest neighborhood of Silver Spring, Md., believing that once it looked like Riccan was keeping the voters happy, they would move up to something bigger and nicer in a better neighborhood. They never did. In the middle of his third term, scandal forced Riccan to resign which forced Bob and the rest of his staff into the unemployment line. Being the former communications chief for a crook wasn't a real door opener when Bob was looking for work. He was untouchable–so untouchable that just before his unemployment benefits ran out, he enrolled in real estate school and started selling houses … just until something better came along. His timing was good because he entered the field when people were buying, but it meant that he was never home in the evenings or on weekends. At about the same time, Betty took to the couch. Maybe going from being a Washington insider to a Washington outsider was simply too much. She did seem to enjoy all those Congressional cocktail parties and formal dinners and once the invitations stopped coming, she lost interest.

Sometimes Bob took Mary Ellen with him to his open houses on Sundays. She loved getting an inside look at the elegant old homes in Chevy Chase and the modern new homes in Potomac. Since the people who were selling these homes were never around during open houses, Mary Ellen imagined the perfectly happy families who were leaving one fabulous home to move to an even more fabulous home. Moving up was the only possibility for Mary Ellen's imaginary mothers, fathers and children. They never moved into something smaller or less grand. And they certainly never moved out of one big house and into two smaller homes because of a divorce or separation.

Living in one of those houses soon became the sum total of Mary Ellen's ambition. While some of her friends started to think about professions like nursing or teaching or even being a housewife, all Mary Ellen wanted was to live in a beautiful home. Whom she lived with and what she did outside of the home was of little concern, just as long as she could come home to something lovely. To a front door that hadn't been slammed while the deadbolt was out leaving the trim banged up. To floors covered with hard wood not vinyl that was curling at the edges. To a kitchen set where none of the chairs was deemed "the bad chair" so you never had to graciously direct a guest not to sit in it. To bathrooms where the sink, toilet and tub were all the same color. To a mud room full of great stuff like tennis racquets and ice skates instead of mildewed rags and abandoned socks. To a family room sofa you could sit on without having someone's feet or head in your lap. To carpets that were neither darker nor lighter than the color they started out as. To monogrammed towels and custom made draperies, to accent pillows and hassocks, to bookshelves lined with real books not board games with missing pieces. To a home that was as welcoming and cheerful as any place on earth.

She pictured herself hosting fun barbeques and dinner parties for neighborhood friends. In those daydreams, she was always wearing the latest fashion—like cool stretchy pantsuits with chunky heels or short tunic dresses with thong sandals. Her hair and her make up were always just right, and her family was just right too. Her handsome husband had a fabulous job that allowed them to live the life families in those kinds of neighborhoods typically lived. The club membership, the parties, the schools, the inside knowledge of upscale living. What an idiot she was to have ever believed Kenny could be that husband. At twenty-five, however, Kenny had all the markings of success—his own branch of the family business, a cool bachelor pad in Bethesda, a Mazda 280ZX. Mary Ellen was single minded enough to overlook his courser qualities and even forgo true love if it meant she would finally get her dream house. Eighteen years later there was no dream house and certainly no true love and overlooking Kenny's coarser qualities was about as easy as overlooking a giant pustule on the tip of someone's nose.

Mary Ellen put her groceries away then she sat down at the kitchen table and proceeded to punch digits into the keypad of the phone. When she finally got through to a person at the credit card company, he informed her that she had exceeded her $10,000 limit by $54.00. Once her balance fell below $10,000, she could go ahead and use the card again. A review of her charges reminded her that Plaid-IT-tudes charged her $5,789. With a previous balance of $2,822 and some recent charges from Bloomingdales, Nordstrom and Sammy's Beverages, where she purchased a few cases of wine for her Plaid-IT-tudes trunk show, $10,000 made sense. She took a deep breath and persuaded herself that there was nothing to worry about. The big box of Plaid-IT-tudes merchandise would arrive any day now. And once it did, she would collect the remaining 85% her customers owed her then write American Express a giant check.

She needed a time out. Grabbing a yogurt from the fridge, she went into the office for some computer time. There wasn't a student, teacher or administrator listed in the Prep directory that she hadn't already Googled, so she logged onto Brophy's Facebook page to see what was new in the world of spoiled high school students.

Someone named Kara was now in a relationship with someone named Allison. Mark Kawalichek invited Brophy to join the group "My bulimic sister ate my homework then threw it up. Still want it?" and Brophy's photo was tagged in a few albums—mostly from football. He looked happy in the photos. She smiled, knowing that if it weren't for her, he never would have applied to Prep. She hopped from one tagged friend to another until she landed on Cole Reardon's page. Girls from all the finest schools in the area had left cute yet suggestive messages like, "Ha-ha, you still owe me!" or "Call me when you need some down time."

The next one was kind of puzzling. It was from someone named George Markel. It said, "You rocked my world. Let's have a repeat performance." From the looks of it, George was older—definitely gay— with spiky blonde hair, tan skin and blue twinkly eyes. He actually looked kind of like Barry Manilow. *What do you know?* thought Mary Ellen, *God's gift is gay? Or at least bi? Maybe he's just playing the girls in an effort to hide his true identity.* Checking in on a few more of Brophy's friends, she discovered that Salter had a new girlfriend and the Johnson boy had a new horse. Briefly immersing herself in the social lives of over-privileged teens had helped. She felt better. Calmer. The American Express thing was no big deal. The yoga studio didn't care. And the Safeway girl ... forgotten just like Kenny forgot to pay the bills. Once he got back on track, everything would get better.

Later that night, while Kenny was in the family room watching football on TV, Mary Ellen poured herself a glass of Chardonnay and finally sat down to open the mail; a couple of flyers, some insurance stuff she put in Kenny's pile, and two things that actually interested her, something from Plaid-IT-tudes and a hand-addressed envelope from Prep. Ever since Brophy received his acceptance letter, there had been a steady stream of communication from the school. Invitations to social events, appeals for donations, notice of upcoming parents meetings. She figured this was just more of the same.

"The transition from middle school to high school is a difficult one which is why we are sending a very preliminary report on your son's progress ... " said the first page and there were a bunch of pages behind it; one from each of Brophy's teachers. Mary Ellen shuffled through the pages with excitement, anticipating a stack of aces. Physical Education, A.

English, B. Biology, B+. Latin, D-. Her heart sank. "Brophy, get down here," she yelled from the bottom of the stairs. "Kenny, you too."

Neither her son nor her husband so much as flinched at the sound of her voice so the next time she called them she was angry, and the third time, she was furious. Furious worked because despite his loud, "Can't even let me watch the fucking game can you?" Kenny got up from his recliner and Brophy, just out of the shower, emerged from his room and trotted down the stairs.

"What's going on with Latin?" she demanded, handing the report to Brophy.

"Nothing."

"You're right because nothing is exactly what I'd call a D-."

"Whoa! D-?" said Brophy giving a convincing performance of a boy who has no idea he's barely passing.

"Who the fuck cares if you can speak Latin? I'd drop that class if I were you," was Kenny's fatherly advice.

"You can't drop it. It's required," countered Mary Ellen. "So what's going on?"

"I don't know mom. That guy, Mr. Mann, he, like ... hates me."

"Nobody has ever hated you. Especially not a teacher."

"This dude isn't like anyone else. He's insane. No joke. Certifiable."

"I need to go in and talk to him."

"NO!"

"Why not?"

"Look, he hates parents, alright? You go into see him, and I'm dead. Like, literally dead. He will throw a desk at me or something."

"He will not."

"Mom, I'm not kidding. He already threw a chair at me."

"He threw a chair at you and you didn't tell me?"

"He missed. He told us if our parents go see him, he *will* kill us. Look, I'll talk to him. I'll work harder. I promise."

"Am I the only one who thinks this is ridiculous? D-? From a teacher you're not allowed to talk to. Who throws furniture? And the rest of these grades aren't going to wow any colleges either. Look at this," she said continuing through the pages. "B in math? That used to be your best subject."

"Jeeze, Brophy, you've been there a little over a month, and you're not on the dean's list. What the fuck?" said Kenny. "Give the kid a break for Christ sakes." Mary Ellen bit her lower lip, something she did a lot when she felt like exploding. "If that's all, I'm going back to my game." Kenny went over to the refrigerator and got himself another beer. "Son, study hard. Bring those grades up. Understand?"

When Kenny was gone, Brophy wrapped his arms around her and gave her a hug. He smelled like soap, and his wet hair tickled her neck. "Don't worry, Mom. I'll get it right," he said, kissing her cheek.

"I'm counting on you. Don't let me down."

"I won't," he said as he ran up the stairs.

Mary Ellen sat down to open the second letter of interest, the one from Plaid-IT-tudes. She expected good news.

"We regret to inform you … " the letter began. "That due to an on-going legal dispute regarding intellectual property infringement with a major fashion house, the fall line of Plaid-IT-tudes will not be released. Your account will be credited in the manner in which you paid your deposit. We look forward to working with you on our resort collection coming in mid-December." Mary Ellen knew what she had in her hands was bad, but she couldn't exactly grasp what it all meant.

"Kenny, I need you. Could you come in here?"

"I'm watching the game."

"But, I really need you to help me."

"Can't it wait 'til halftime?"

"NO! IT ABSOLUTELY CANNOT WAIT. COME IN HERE NOW."

Mary Ellen's tone left little room for interpretation, so Kenny sauntered like usual, but he sauntered quickly. Mary Ellen handed him the letter. "So what's the big deal? No Plaid-IT-tudes this fall. Guess the ladies will have to squeeze their fat asses into some other fake designer shit for those rockin' girls' nights out."

"You don't understand. I sold over $6,000 worth of stuff. And people put down like fifteen percent. Now I have to give that fifteen percent back because I can't fulfill their order."

"Right. So give it the fuck back and let me go watch my game."

"But see, I don't have it. I fully expected to take delivery any day now, and collect the balance they owe me … so I sort of spent a lot of it."

"Like how much?"

"I don't know … maybe most of it."

"And how much is that?"

"Like $900."

"So what, you want me to give you the money?"

"Umm," Mary Ellen took a deep gulp of breath. "That's the other thing. Um. When I was out today, a couple of the cards were declined and then I used the debit card, and it didn't go through either."

Kenny glared at her for a long time before asking, "So what's your Goddamned point?" he asked.

"My point? My Goddamned point? How about you tell me what is going on? Why aren't you paying our bills and what happened to our checking account?"

He started walking out of the kitchen. "We are not going to have this fucking conversation now."

"What fucking conversation? Where are you going?"

"I'm going to watch the game."

"Answer me! I have a right to know what's going on with our money."

"Nothing. That's what." He started to walk out, but then he turned around and practically spewed, "Because we don't have any fucking money. You spent it all."

"What do you mean?"

"Let me say it in your language. We. Don't. Have. Any. Money," he said emphasizing the breaks between each word.

"But … "

"We're going to have to wait until I can cut myself a paycheck. Business sucks, and you and your fancy schools and your fancy fucking country clubs have tapped us out. That school gives Brophy a lot, but it's not free. Three boys at St. Anthony's aren't free either. And piano lessons, and lacrosse camp, and you fuckin' name it. We're tapped out. And it's not likely to improve anytime soon. Get used to it. The economy is in the crapper. Maybe not for all those fat cats at Brophy's school, but for regular businesses, it's a fucking double scoop shit sundae."

"But … how am I going to pay American Express? And what about the other card? Do we have cash?"

"Not unless you count the ten dollars we keep in the hall drawer for emergencies. Satisfied? We're down to fucking nothing."

"What about our investments? Could you sell some stock or something?"

"Done. Started cashing out last April when I had to come up with money to pay our taxes. Pulled a little out here and there over the summer. We're fucking broke."

He got himself another beer from the refrigerator and went back to his game.

"What are you going to do about it?" demanded Mary Ellen, but he was gone. She reached up and ran her fingers through her hair. "OH FUCK!" she shouted suddenly remembering her conversation about the return of the lice with Suzanne.

* * * * *

Mary Ellen stalled as long as she could before telling her customers she wouldn't be delivering their Plaid-IT-tudes order. When she finally did call them, she lied and said that once the Plaid-IT-tudes company cut her a check, she would immediately reimburse them. *It's not like any one of them needed their money back to make ends meet* she thought. She took a calming breath and reminded herself to play it cool if she ran into Claudia or Jackie Johnson later that evening at back to school night. *You are not a thief. You are not a thief,* she chanted.

Dressed in a black pencil skirt paired with a beige cardigan, her new Tory Burch shoes and Marc Jacobs purse, Mary Ellen looked amazing. No one would believe the Packinghams were a few bucks away from flat broke based on her appearance. Kenny, on the other hand, was another story. He refused to wear his blue blazer with a tie for back to school night, and she didn't have the strength to challenge him to a wardrobe duel, so he wore his regular khaki pants with his scuffed up loafers and a reasonably decent polo shirt. He did give in and untuck his polo shirt at her request.

Back-to-school night started in the Neale Theater. Parents packed into the blue and grey bucket seats and exchanged expertly crafted war stories of their sons' first weeks of school. Every single tall tale was shaped around the universal theme of ... no matter what hardship this place throws his way, my son is a resourceful genius who can meet any challenge and will continue on to rule the universe. The crowing continued until the lights dimmed and

Father Bills stepped out on the bare stage. He blessed the parents and then he blessed their sons—men he said, who would go on to lead the nation with the courage and conviction they learned here at Prep. He paused briefly, then added, "Of course what they learn in their own homes is important too," as a polite afterthought.

For the freshmen parents especially, his words set off a euphoric buzz that would last for weeks. He verbalized their innermost suspicions and here they were, elbow to elbow, with the parents of all the men who would hold cabinet positions in their son's administration.

Next, Dr. Brennan took the stage. "This school is a dream destination for many more boys than we have room for. This year we received five hundred applications for one hundred spots. We took a fine toothcomb to those applications and chose only the best and the brightest. Proof of this was in evidence today when the school was informed that one our freshmen has been selected to represent the United States in an international model U.N. summit to be held in Germany over Christmas break. "Let's have a round of applause for Cole Reardon. Are Cole's parents here this evening?"

A man sitting a few rows up from the Packinghams waved while the theater erupted in cheers. *So that's God the Father*, thought Mary Ellen. *His tie doesn't match his shirt.* When the applause died down, Dr. Brennan thanked the parents for the job they had done raising such exceptional young men then, more or less, implied it was now time to let go and allow the school to guide them from here on out.

They were experts after all, and if you had any doubt, just look at the tax bracket 97% of the schools graduates fall into. To justify his rather crude allusion to money, Dr. Brennan drew attention to the fact that successful alumni make substantial donations to the school's annual fund, which allows the school to offer scholarships and financial aid to boys who would not otherwise have the opportunity to attend Prep. Those boys, in particular, enrich the school tremendously.

When Dr. Brennan was through, the lights of the Neale Theater came up, and parents set off on a ridiculous version of beat the clock. Armed with their sons' schedules and a campus map, they had five minutes to find their son's classes spread out on multiple floors of multiple buildings around the campus. The dads saw it as a test of their navigational ability. The moms saw it as a test of their fitness level. As a result, when the five minutes were up, the teachers looked out on a class of breathless moms as the dad's, who were too proud to ask for directions, straggled in late.

Brophy's English teacher started his talk by directing parents' attention to the list of names he had scrawled on the white board at the front of the classroom. Mary Ellen didn't recognize all the names, but the ones she did were actors; Edward Burns, David Duchovney, and Matt Damon. "What do the names on this list have in common?" asked Mr. Gibley. When not one parent raised their hand, he smirked and said, "Every person on this list was an English major in college." The room chuckled because to these parents, the thought of putting a boy through the rigors and expense of Prep and then a top-tier university, only to have him major in English, was a joke.

Literally, a joke. With one or two exceptions, eight years from now, these parents would be watching their sons graduate from college with degrees in engineering, economics, business, biology/pre-med or American history in preparation for law school. Kenny leaned forward and whispered, "He left Jason Martindale off that list."

"Who is Jason Martindale?" asked Mary Ellen.

"The kid who serves me my Egg McMuffin every morning. He was an English major and look how fucking far he went."

The rest of the night was, more or less, variations on a theme. There was the hippie religion teacher with an arm full of rubber bracelets commemorating various causes, the fuddy-duddy biology teacher with a face full of moles, the lesbian math teacher sporting one hell of a chip on her shoulder (perhaps an all-boys Catholic school was not the ideal place of employment for her).

With more or less grace depending on the individual, they all delivered the exact same message, both spoken and unspoken:

1. I'm looking forward to working with your son this year. This seems like a really great class. (But then again, so did all the other classes and, in the end, they all turned out to be arrogant assholes.)

2. If you ever need to get in touch with me, the preferred mode of communication is email because I never check my voicemail (but as you will find out if

you actually do email me, I don't really check that either … or if I do, I don't respond to it.)

3. Here's the formula I use to calculate grades. 12 (grade on the first quiz + 78) x 1/2 (grade on the first test) − 6 (grade on the midterm) = final grade. Homework and class participation will be added to help boost a grade that might be borderline. (In other words, your child will receive the grade I believe he deserves. Period. And no parent conference or record keeping is going to make an iota of difference if you choose to challenge my assessment.)

So went all but the one class Mary Ellen was most interested in, Latin. She couldn't wait to see the evil Mr. Mann. He was probably not as bad as Brophy said. He was probably some grumpy old guy who was just set in his ways. A little charm goes a long way with people like that. Unlike the rest of Brophy's classes, which were held in regular school buildings, his Latin class was located in the chapel basement—accessible by a set of poorly lit concrete stairs outside the building. Descending the cracked stairs in the dark, Mary Ellen felt like she was entering a secret crypt.

Inside, the room was chilly and dank, and the ceiling was stained various shades of brown from a succession of leaks over the years. There were four or five other couples awkwardly squeezed behind a large U-shaped table that was ridiculously close to the walls. One of the more rotund fathers stood by the door—no doubt well aware that he would not fit between the cinderblock wall and the table. Claudia and Grover entered the room just as the bell sounded. Squeezing into the seat beside Mary Ellen, Claudia leaned over and whispered, "Wait till you get a load of Mr. Mann."

While the room full of parents sat awkwardly waiting for Mr. Mann, in walked … Heath. Her Heath. The bronze, muscled, National Geographic photographer she was planning to meet in Namibia. Those gold highlights in his hair lost some of their luster in the flat florescent lighting. He looked less like a renaissance painting and more like an ad for Wrangler jeans, but it was him all right. He had on a retro printed shirt opened a little at the collar and rolled up at the sleeves.

His faded blue jeans were as well worn as his scuffed up cowboy boots. Small gold hoops adorned both ears and there it was, the cat tattoo on his forearm. He remained the most gorgeous man Mary Ellen had ever seen.

"Hello. Thank you all for coming. I'm Wenn Mann, and I'll be teaching your sons' Latin class this year."

Claudia leaned over and whispered in Mary Ellen's ear, "How do you say hunk in Latin?"

Mary Ellen smiled, but inside she was still too stunned and confused to focus.

"This is a challenge," said Mr. Mann. "Latin is really hard. Most of them will struggle for a while. I do things a little differently. They need to learn this stuff the correct way, so no Internet help. No memorizing. They have to get it organically, by reading Latin. Other than *Cassell's Latin Dictionary*, almost everything they read is in Latin. By

Thanksgiving, it starts to click … *if* they put in the time *and* do the work. I'm expecting at least an hour every night but Saturday. That's six hours a week minimum. As long as your son does that, I have no doubt he will master Latin."

He didn't seem mean. Or tough or aggressive. He seemed wonderful. Soft spoken, smart. How could that be the face of evil?

"If he does have trouble, the best thing for him to do is to reach out to one of the upper classmen for help. The sooner these guys learn to rely on each other, the better." Eight minutes were left in this class, but apparently Wenn Mann was finished. "If you'll excuse me, I'm also the residential dean and I really should get back to the dorms." He was gone. No answering questions. No here's how to contact me. No here's how I determine grades. Nothing.

"Hardest class Brophy will ever have," said Claudia. "From what I hear, they're all failing at this point. Except of course, for Cole Reardon, but he doesn't count. All the regular mortals, D's. But don't worry; it was the same story for Burke's class. By Christmas, most of them were doing fine. Or at least getting C's."

Mary Ellen was dumbfounded. This man is failing Brophy? He's the one who hates parents? The same man who also loves the way her eyes twinkle in the moonlight and wants to have her name tattooed over his heart? How could one man be both of those very different people? Both the person she wanted to fuck and the person she wanted to FUCK.

-seventeen-

CLARA BARTON

On the cusp of a deep sleep, Pups heard pipes rumble in protest as hot water was summoned to the washing machine. Who was doing the laundry at 11:30 p.m.? On a Sunday? Who, besides her would do laundry period? The answer tiptoed into the bedroom. He didn't come over and kiss her cheek like he usually did when he got in late, so she sat up in bed. "I could have done the laundry tomorrow."

"I didn't want to bother you."

"How was the Battle of Petersburg?"

"Siege," said Patrick turning on the lamp. What a vision. With his white fleshy gut sagging over the blue striped elastic waistband of his underpants, he looked like Homer Simpson's brother; same body type, only Patrick still had most of his hair.

"Huh?"

"Siege. It was the Siege of Petersburg, not the battle."

"Oh. Who won?"

"We did. But it took like nine months. We just re-enacted the Battle of the Crater. It was pretty cool.

Lots of explosions and stuff. But man, did we suffer."

"So you lost the Battle of the Crater?"

"Yep. I was among the wounded. Needed both legs amputated."

"Wow. Is that why you're in your underwear?"

"Yeah. My uniform is filthy. Sweats were too so I'm washing them." He looked uncomfortable, like a student explaining to his teacher why his homework was late again.

"Thanks for doing laundry. Glad you're healed. Come give me a goodnight kiss so I can go to sleep."

"Uh. My throat is kind of scratchy. Probably just a reaction to all that battlefield dust, but to be safe, I better not kiss you. I'm going to jump in the shower. They had us digging trenches and man am I ripe."

"Put your officer's coat on the bench in the hall. I'll take it to the cleaners tomorrow." Happy to know her husband was home safe and sound and her children were tucked into their beds, Pups allowed herself to sleep.

She didn't stir until the alarm woke her at 6:00. She got up, made coffee, packed four lunches, let the dog out and got herself dressed. At 6:30, she started to rouse the kids and Patrick who needed at least three warnings before he even thought about getting out of bed. By 7:00, the kids were up and fighting over the bathroom, searching for parts of their uniforms and remembering books or homework or permission slips they needed for the day ahead. Pups got Maddox up, changed his diaper then locked him in his high chair with a bowl of dry Cheerios while she made breakfast.

By 7:30, Patrick was downstairs so he could watch Maddox while she loaded the other four kids into her Suburban and set out for the first run of the day. Their school was only three miles from home, but during the morning rush it could take as long as half an hour to inch their way there. In the rear view mirror, she could see Willa bouncing her head back and forth to music, but … there was no music. She had a strict no radio policy for the morning commute.

"What are you doing, Willa?"

Willa ignored her.

"Willa, answer me!" Again, nothing.

"She can't hear you. She's listening to her iPod," said Virginia who reached over and pulled an ear bud out of Willa's ear.

"Where did you get an iPod?" asked Pups.

"Grant gave it to me," said Willa proudly.

"He did?"

"Yep."

"Well, that was nice of you," said Pups. Grant glowered. "Have an amazing day!" said Pups pulling into the school drop off zone. When she pulled back into her own driveway, Patrick was standing in front of the glass storm door waiting for her. He said his throat was still iffy, so he opted for a brisk peck on Pups's cheek instead or their normal, firm, almost-not-touching-lips kiss.

Once he was gone, she plopped Maddox in front

of the TV, poured herself another cup of coffee and spent fifteen minutes perusing the newspaper. She paid little attention to the actual news. In fact, the front-page went entirely unread most days. Like just about everything in Pups's life, her interest in the printed word was highly practical and very specific. Her serious reading consisted of consumer news—the kind of reports that warned against the heretofore-unknown dangers of things like sweatshirt hoods, plastic water bottles and microwave bacon cookers. For light reading, Pups was a gossip hound. In the morning, she liked the Style section of the newspaper, home to feature stories about TV, movies and pop culture. She always turned to page B2 first to see what new kind of trouble Hollywood stars and Beltway bigwigs had gotten themselves into. To a woman who had only one semi-serious boyfriend before she found the man of her dreams, the endless supply of new couplings, uncouplings and subsequent re-couplings the column focused on fascinated her.

While most people worshiped the bold-faced names that appeared in the paper, Pups eschewed pop culture, believing that movies and TV shows were embedded with messages validating every lewd, immoral and unnatural lifestyle while openly mocking and repudiating old-fashioned nuclear families like hers. But instead of simply ignoring the thing she found so distasteful, Pups consumed it. She followed the tabloid scandals the way other people followed sports teams or elections or significant international news. She allowed herself to purchase one tabloid a week, usually *US Magazine* or *In Touch*, but she kept up with all of them. She regularly chose the longest line at the Safeway so she could scan the glossies. She especially liked the photos showing the extensive plastic surgery stars underwent. It somehow made her feel better about herself; reasoning that if she had the time, money and inclination she would look more like a movie star and conversely, without the time, money and inclination on her end, Jennifer Aniston would look more like her. Pups couldn't read enough about the misfortunes people who seemed to have it all. The combination of pity and moral superiority she felt when reading this news was enough to keep her own sense of self worth soaring. There was nothing very compelling in today's edition. Country singer Austin Cross, in town to promote breast cancer awareness, was seen dining at Café Milano, and Redskins star JoJo Malone had drinks at J. Paul's.

After her fifteen-minute break, Pups plunged back into her day, washing dirty breakfast dishes, dressing Maddox, and letting the dog out before buckling Maddox into his car seat. Like everything Maddox had, it was a hand-me-down. When they bought it for Grant, it was a top of the line model covered in a fuzzy caramel colored fabric. Four babyhoods worth of spilled juice and smashed French fries had turned fuzzy to crusty and warm caramel to scary mottled brown. Some days, Maddox could spend hours harnessed to that seat. It's where he took his nap, ate his snack, played with his action figures, watched his favorite videos and sang along with educational CD's.

Over the next several hours, Pups took care of family business, dropping Patrick's fake blood and real mud encrusted Civil War coat at the dry cleaners, picking up Cady's allergy medicine from Mr. Tran, and filling a large Costco shopping cart with industrial-sized detergents, mega-packs of toilet paper and king-sized packages of the bread, cereal and snack foods the MacArthur family lived on. She loaded the back of the Suburban with boxes brimming with stuff and strapped Maddox back into his seat. He was snoozing before they made it out of the parking lot.

Pulling into her driveway, Pups was met with a surprise. Patrick's car was there. He was home. In the middle of the day. That scratchy throat must be more than just a reaction to Civil War dust. He must have strep or some other kind of infection. She unbuckled Maddox who was still sleeping and carried him gently inside. One of the good things about being the youngest of five is that you learned to sleep anywhere. And nothing, not noise or motion or anything else could interrupt your sweet rest. She laid him down on the family room carpet and went upstairs. Patrick was in their bathroom, sitting on the closed toilet wearing the suit he had worn to work cradling his face in his hands.

"What's wrong? Is it your throat?" she asked.

"No." He said through his hands.

"What is it? What's going on?" An enormity of possibilities assaulted Pups. *Patrick is home in the middle of the day. And it's not his throat.*

"Your stomach bothering you again?"

"No. I'm not sick."

More possibilities. He's upset. Someone died.

"Patrick, what is it? Please tell me."

Lifting his face out of his hands, she could see he had been crying. Actual tears. "Patrick?"

"Pups. God, I'm ... just ... "

Pups had a flash of clairvoyance. *Patrick had been accosted in some way. His wallet was stolen or he was ... carjacked.*

"Are you alright?" she asked, rushing over to him and rubbing his hunched over back. She had just read about a car salesman who was attacked and left for dead by the side of the road during a test drive gone bad.

Without looking her in the eye, he said, "Pups. I was ... unfaithful." Then he buried his face back in his hands and resumed crying. It didn't sink in. She was still playing out the carjacking scene where some thug pretends to want to buy a Tahoe then aims a revolver at Patrick's head.

"It's going to be okay," she said reassuringly.

"Pups. Did you hear me? I was unfaithful. To you."

The "to you" did it. It helped her refocus her thoughts of Patrick being a victim to ... to ... her being the victim. But even with her husband's tear stained face looking her directly in the eye, she could not grasp that such a thing could really happen ... to her. This particular form of doom had never made it to her mental list of possible calamities.

"I don't understand," she said.

"It was at the Battle of the Crater."

"You were with ... another re-enactor?"

God. He was a homo. How could she not have known? Did she miss the clues? Sex was not a frequent occurrence, but when it happened, it was fine. Good even. She didn't have much experience to compare him to, but he seemed to function properly. There were never any issues. On the other hand, that bold printed shirt he liked to wear on vacation always did strike her as kind of gay.

"Yes. A re-enactor."

"Oh my God. It's not enough to crap all over everything. Everything we stand for. But you have to do it with … with … ugh! … I mean, never mind me. What about Grant and Maddox? And the girls?"

"I know." Patrick put his head back down into his hands leaving Pups to sort everything out by herself.

She was flabbergasted. Too angry to cry, too shocked to scream, too overwhelmed to move. Patrick's sink caught her attention. As usual, he hadn't cleaned it out after shaving, so it was covered in with grey soap scum and jet black whiskers. She pulled a long tail of toilet paper from the roll and wiped it around the sink.

"Couldn't resist a man in uniform, huh?" Up until now, Pups had done an excellent job of compressing all the thoughts and emotions surging through her. But now she took the dirty dripping wad of toilet paper and hurled it at Patrick; an easy mark, as his face was still resting in his hands. He jumped when the sopping mess smacked against the crown of his head.

"What? Pups! It wasn't another soldier."

"It wasn't?"

"No. It was a battlefield nurse," he said, picking bits of Charmin out of his hair.

"A battlefield nurse? Like a woman?"

"Yeah. I told you I was wounded."

"Oh." Pups wasn't sure if this was good news or not.

"Mommmmyyyyyyyyy!" called Maddox from downstairs.

"Maddox is up," said Pups. She whooshed out of the bathroom, leaving Patrick sitting on the closed toilet; the disintegrating clump of mushy toilet paper now dripping off his knee.

"Aren't you going to get mad? Like scream or something?" he called out. She popped her head back into the bathroom and calmly said, "I am mad. But after seventeen years, you should know that it's going to take a little while for me to process all this. Give me time. I feel a lot of yelling on the way."

Stone faced, Pups stomped downstairs to change Maddox's diaper, tugging and pulling on the child's pants like they were challenging her authority. She forced a cup of yogurt in front of him and went back upstairs where Patrick was still sitting exactly where she left him, toilet paper and all.

"So how did it happen?" she demanded.

"I don't know. I was injured. Both legs were basically torn to shreds. Full of shrapnel, so they carried me off the battlefield on a stretcher and took me to the hospital tent. It was packed with wounded soldiers. Never in my life have I seen so much blood."

"It was fake blood, Patrick. Fake."

"Well, it seemed real at the time. Next thing I know this guy comes around with a bottle of whisky to help with the pain."

"Whiskey? They were just giving out whiskey?"

"No. You had to pay for it,"

"I see. And you did?"

"Yeah. I paid for whiskey."

"Like a lot?"

"Ten bucks."

"I mean a lot of whiskey. Did you drink a lot of whiskey?"

"Yes. I had to considering I was about to have both my legs amputated."

"Of course."

"And so this gruff old doc comes over and says they're going to have to amputate both my legs. Let me tell you, that's something. Hearing those words."

Refusing to be swayed by the theatrics, Pups let out a long, loud sigh and crossed her arms.

"So alongside this old doc is a nurse."

"I didn't know they had nurse re-enactors."

"There were a few, but it turns out, this one was

none other than Clara Barton. Do you know who Clara Barton is?"

Pups thought for a second. "I know Clara Barton Parkway. I know Clara Barton Rest Stop on the New Jersey Turnpike," she said impatiently.

"Yes. That's her. She was this great nurse in the Civil War. She actually founded the Red Cross."

Pups rolled her eyes, unwilling to concede even the most minor point to Patrick.

"So the doc says he'll be back later and well, Miss Clara stays by my bed just trying to keep me calm. She had her own bottle of whiskey which she generously offered me in my miserable state."

"Oh brother, spare me."

"No, really, it sounds stupid I know, but these things, these reenactments are just so real. Really real."

"Blah, blah, blah. Cut the history lesson, what happened?"

"Well, the thing ended and it turns out, Clara and I were both staying at the same Courtyard Marriott …"

"Go on."

"Look, I don't think we have to go into every single detail. I mean, I'm telling you something … bad … happened, and I'm not sure I'll ever be able to live with myself again."

"Good Lord!" Pups turned and left the room. She would need to know the details. Every last one, but she was incapable of taking in too much information at one time so, she went downstairs to the kitchen and unpacked all her groceries. Shoving, wedging, heaving and otherwise manhandling the innocent supersized foodstuffs into her pantry. She checked her email so hard she cracked her mouse. She plopped Maddox on her lap, picked up *Fluffy Bunny*, his favorite book, and proceeded to read so fast and so angrily she sounded like a contender at the Def Jam Poetry Slam. Before she left to get the children from school, she went back upstairs. Patrick hadn't moved an inch. "What did she look like?" she demanded.

"Um. I don't know. She was tiny."

"Tiny?"

"Yeah."

"And did you take down her name or her phone number? Does she know how to contact you?"

"No. I don't think so."

"Do you know her name?"

"Why do you need … "

"Do you?"

"It was um … Thu."

"Thu? What the hell kind of a name is Thu?"

"Asian. Maybe Vietnamese."

"Vietnamese?" Pups didn't wait for an answer before storming out of the bathroom. In a voice that was slightly less than a full on yell called out, "I may not know what the fuck Clara Barton did to get a

Goddamned rest stop named after her, but I sure as hell know it wasn't for her prizewinning Pho. For Christ's sake, Patrick." She scooped Maddox up from the floor of the family room and marched to the car. It was pick up time.

Ten minutes later, the Suburban was packed with kids who stunk of fresh pencil shavings mixed with fart. Normally disgusted by their foul odor, today it helped her feel normal. When they got home, Patrick's car was gone. She opened up the new tub of peanut butter she got at Costco and spread it on crackers and got the kids started on their homework. When the phone rang, she answered it in an edgy version of her regular singsong voice. "Hello? Hi, Angie, how's your day going?"

Angie never asked her how her day was going. Not ever. And if she did, Pups would never offer anything more than a "not too bad" or a "just fine," but still, it would be nice to be asked; especially on a day like today. Angie was calling to see if Pups could drive Maddie to Brownies, one line item on her agenda Pups completely forgot about. "Sure. No problem," she said confidently, tabulating all the things she needed to do before the Bridge Ceremony that she, as the co-troop leader, was responsible for. "I need to get there early so I'll swing by around 6:00. Okay, gotta run. See you later!"

"Crap!" she exclaimed hanging up the phone.

"What's wrong, Mom?" asked Willa.

"Nothing. I just forgot about this stupid Bridge Ceremony tonight. I can't imagine why it totally slipped my mind."

"It's not stupid," said Willa quietly.

"Aww man. Does that mean you're not going to be home to help me with my religion paper?" whined Grant.

"Sorry, chief. I guess not," said Pups looking in the refrigerator for a quick solution to dinner. The chicken nuggets she bought at Costco and a big can of green beans should suffice.

"Did you get the cupcakes?" asked Willa.

"Damn it. I forgot the cupcakes." She was supposed to stop at the bakery before she picked the kids up from school. "I'm so sorry. It's after 3:00. Bakery's closed," said Pups going to the pantry to see what her cake mix situation was.

"But you promised. You promised we could have special cupcakes with pink flowers on them!" said Willa urgently.

"Calm down. You'll have them. Look, I've got two boxes of mix right here."

"And what about icing?"

"Icing too," said Pups pulling a container of icing from the back of the top shelf.

"And pink flowers? You promised pink flowers."

"Yes. Yes. Pink flowers. Pink flowers." The pantry was brimming with rice and pasta, tomato sauce, applesauce, ketchup, breadcrumbs, tuna fish, and other staples, but nothing that could make a pink flower.

"What if we have plain cupcakes tonight and the

next time we meet, I'll have the pink flowers for you?"

"Nooooo. You promised!"

"You're right." She scanned the shelves, holding on to the possibility that a wayward package of pink flowers might be lurking behind the baking soda. "Oh look what I found!" she said with the enthusiasm of a Lotto winner. "Sprinkles!"

"I don't want stupid sprinkles. You always do everything single solitary thing for everybody else and you promised me pink flowers."

A minor constricting of her throat made Pups breath just a bit harder. Willa's face was serious; challenging her mother to step up to the plate and show how much she cared by producing the promised pink flowers. She knew this was a definitive thing, just like every promise she made to Willa was definitive. Not delivering meant she was less than the mother she wanted to be just like not picking up Angie's children would make her less than the friend she wanted to be or not taking Patrick's uniform to the cleaners would make her less than the wife she wanted to be.

"Grant, I need you to watch everyone while I run to the store. Virginia, can you please follow the directions on the cake mix package and start to make the batter? Don't go any further than the mixing part. Alright? Do not. I repeat, DO NOT pour the batter into the pans and especially, DO NOT put anything in the oven. Do you understand me?" Virginia nodded. "Willa, get out the cupcake pans and start putting the liners into them. Cady, can you read a book to Maddox? He's had virtually no human interaction all day." Pups grabbed her keys and dashed out the door.

When she returned home, she had four packages of blue sugar flowers affixed to cardboard and a promise to take Willa to lunch at Burger King next weekend, the heavily negotiated result of the empty place on the store shelf that normally held pink sugar flowers. Having to search and negotiate was a good thing actually, because in the food store, Pups realized she was alone for the first time all day, and the magnitude of Patrick's words started to bubble up from the bottom of her esophagus. But then her cell phone rang, and it was as if she had never left home, talking to one or another of her children for the duration of her short trip. Grant had a religion question. Then Cady wanted to know if she could stop reading to Maddox since he wasn't paying any attention. And then there was Willa, and the delicate back and forth over what would be an adequate substitution for pink flowers.

Virginia had managed to get quite a few eggshells in the mix, but other than an unusual crunch, the cupcakes turned out fine and they looked beautiful topped with blue flowers. She warmed up dinner. While the kids were eating, ran upstairs, showered, dressed in the brownie leader uniform—a navy cardigan, white shirt and regulation imitation silk scarf over khaki pants—fixed her hair, and put on lipstick. In between getting dressed and putting on lipstick, she sat down on the closed toilet that Patrick had occupied a few hours ago. She prided herself on being prepared. And she was ... for anything but this.

Hurricanes, tornados, terrorist assaults, bee stings, strep throat, burglars, ants marching across Virginia's first holy communion cake, a leaky roof, flat tires, fender benders, chronic illness preferably one that is not life threatening, broken bones, bumps and bruises, attention deficit disorder, calls from the principal saying Grant behaved inappropriately by including the lyrics, "underpants around your ankles" for a song he was assigned to write for music class, termites, clogged gutters, overflowing toilets, power failures, head lice, leaky diapers, middle child syndrome, identity theft, spam, e coli, alcoholism, drug abuse, bullying, eating undercooked food, huffing.

Any reasonable human being understood that unpleasant things were bound to happen, and Pups was extremely reasonable. In fact, preparing for this elementary certainty was how Pups spent a considerable amount of time; trouble-shooting problems she would never have. How ironic, that one of the most obvious and common crisis's in modern times had completely escaped her attention—despite the fact that she watched all the *Real Housewives* shows and read tabloids and scoured the internet for any and all potential threats to her family's well-being. For all her mockery of Hollywood values, here they were, in Silver Spring. In her own home. No more immune to humiliation than anyone else.

As much as she wanted to wallow in self-pity, she couldn't be late. The ceremony was too important to Willa, so she combed her hair, re-applied her lipstick and went downstairs. Willa had her brownie vest on over her school uniform, and was guarding the cupcakes from the fingers of Cady and Maddox.

"Mom, they're going to mess them up!" she wailed.

"Guys, keep away. You'll get one after the Bridge Ceremony. I promise." She picked up Maddox and smelled his pants. "Let's get you changed, buddy. Cady, go to the bathroom. Willa, fix your hair, you look like who did it and ran." Pups took Maddox upstairs, and after five minutes, she instinctually yelled, "Now, Cady. Move it!"

Pups, Willa, Cady and Maddox climbed back into the Suburban. On the way to school, Willa unleashed a doozy. "Oh yeah. I forgot to tell you. Daddy called. He's going to meet us there."

"Where?"

"The Bridge Ceremony, silly."

Pups winced. "Why is he coming? I mean, I don't remember um, discussing it with him."

"When he called, I reminded him. I told him to bring his camera because that's what you told us at the last meeting. To tell our parents to bring their cameras."

Pups didn't say anything. Seeing Patrick in public was not in her game plan.

"Hey! Aren't we picking up Maddie?" demanded Willa.

"Shit. Sorry, yes. I forgot." Pups made an illegal U turn and backtracked down Randolph Road. When she pulled up to the house, Angie waved from the doorway as Maddie ran towards the truck. Pups waved back. She felt a glimmer of need. Maybe she would feel better if she could talk to Angie about all of this.

"Hey Maddie! How's your mom?" she asked as the child climbed into the back seat.

"She's all mad at John for dropping the entire thing of milk all over the floor. We needed like ten whole towels to soak it all up."

Pups reconsidered. Angie's a good friend, but she's got plenty of her own problems. When they arrived at school, Mindy Crosby, the other troop leader was dragging a heavy wooden bridge across the old linoleum floor. A husky woman, Mindy had no trouble with the 6'x3' bridge. It was the kind of thing you'd put on your lawn for ornamental purposes. Too small to actually span anything, it worked great for Brownie ceremonies. When she had it where she wanted it, Mindy positioned a long shiny aluminum foil and cardboard stream underneath the bridge.

"Hi Mindy. Can I help?"

"Hi Pups. Sure. Why don't you set up our refreshments? There's a bag with cups and Juicy Juice in it over by the door." Activity, even mindless, mundane activity like pouring juice always helped and soon Pups felt more like her old self. More in control. Meanwhile, Willa acted like she was the belle of the ball, greeting Brownies as they arrived with their parents and siblings with trays of baked goods or jugs of punch in tow, while Maddox and Cady played with the other younger siblings along for the night.

"Hey, Pups. Need a hand with anything?" Trish

Baker asked when she arrived.

"Hey there, Trish. Thanks, but I think we've got it all under control." Whenever someone told Pups that they didn't need help, she knew better and helped anyhow, but apparently, she was the only one who operated like that because Trish was already gone.

"Hello Mrs. Pups!" exclaimed Señora Alvarez.

"Buenos Noches, Señora!"

"Mrs. Pups. How you say … uh, los piojos?"

"Lice?"

"Sí. Um." Señora seemed to search for words that Pups knew would never in a million years come to her … at least not in English.

"Do you need help? With the piojos?"

Sí!" said Señora. Pups looked over towards Señora's granddaughter Cynthia.

"Where's Juanita?"

"Oh, she's working."

"Have Juanita call me tomorrow. She speaks English, right?"

"Sí."

"Good, then have her call me. I'll see if I can help."

"Okay, Mrs. Pups. Juanita call you tomorrow!"

As Pups was talking to Señora, Mindy walked to the center of the room and silently lifted her arm in the air, making the two-fingered peace sign with her raised hand and holding the index finger of her other hand to her lips. It was the universal sign for "be quiet." A few Brownies followed her example and raised their arms. Others did the same and soon, everyone in the room held the same pose. Pups scanned the crowd of people with their arms in the air. Patrick was not among them.

"Welcome Brownies, parents and friends. Tonight, we celebrate the passage from the world of Brownies into the world of … what?" asked Mindy playfully. Pups was a Brownie leader because no one else stepped forward to fill the job while Mindy was a Brownie leader because it was her calling. She loved everything about scouts and took particular joy in ceremonial occasions like the Friendship Circle, Investitures, and this, the Bridge Ceremony.

"JUNIOR GIRL SCOUTS!" shouted the Brownies.

"That's right! Junior Girl Scouts. Tonight, we bear witness to this important rite of passage as fifteen remarkable young ladies make their way across the great stream of life. This is a transition that allows them to look back on all they have accomplished as Brownies and look ahead to all they will accomplish as Junior Girl Scouts. Before we go any further, lets honor these past accomplishments. Who can name something we have accomplished?"

Fifteen pairs of eyes stared blankly at Mindy until little redheaded Megan offered, "We learned how to say the Brownie Pledge."

As more hands went up, Patrick came through the door. He met the sour look on Pups's face with a conciliatory smile. She pursed her lips and looked away.

"Now I'm going to hand this microphone over to Mrs. MacArthur who will announce the name of each Brownie. Parents, we ask you to accompany your daughter across the bridge to symbolize your presence on this path alongside her."

Mindy handed the battery-powered Karaoke microphone to Pups and Pups began reading the names of the Brownies in alphabetical order. "Dakota Abbott." One by one, the Brownies stepped solemnly across the wooden bridge followed by their mother and in some cases their father.

"Stella Baker." Different as they all were ... "Mary Margaret Butta." And as much as she disliked them for any number of reasons ... "Sue Choi." She knew that they were basically good people. "Katherine Crosby." She had helped all of them at one time or another.

"Maria Crosina."

She drove Maria to school for three weeks when her baby brother was born. "Christina Diez." How many casseroles had she dropped off at the Diez house when Christina's mother broke her leg?

"Samena Doman." The Doman household had Pups to thank for their lice-free status. There wasn't a family crossing that bridge that hadn't benefitted from Pups's largess. Yet here she was, miserable and alone and bottled up and unable to reach out to a soul, because what she had, her own terrible misfortune, wasn't a problem to share.

"Phillipa Farrar."

Despite all the time she spent on the phone talking to her friends, or her mother or her sister-in-law or any needy parent, grandparent, aunt or uncle, she never so much as hinted at her own troubles. Not that she had any up till now, at least nothing significant. And now that a full-blown demon had arrived in a beautifully wrapped gift box hand delivered by Patrick, what was she supposed to do? "Gina Gomez." Who could she unburden herself to? For the past eighteen years, she never had to look further than Patrick when she wanted to get something off her chest. "Tiffani Lei." Pups looked up from her list to see Willa anxiously waiting to cross the bridge. Holding Patrick's hand, she looked both proud and vulnerable. Who but the most innocent child would think that by simply walking across a dusty old ornamental lawn bridge spanning an aluminum foil river she was actually crossing over to something new; putting a part of her life entirely behind her and embarking on some exciting new adventure. No one but a child, or a fool. Willa waved frantically for Pups to join them. Handing the list and the microphone to Mindy and gingerly stepping over the aluminum foil, Pups reached for Willa's other hand. It was soft and warm, like risen bread dough.

"Willa MacArthur," announced Mindy.

The tiny bridge was barely big enough to hold the three of them. Willa smiled with glee. "I can't believe it," she said. "I'm finally a Junior."

Pups gave Willa's hand a squeeze. "I'm so proud of you!" she said.

"Way to go Willa," said Patrick trying his best to sound enthusiastic, but only managing to sound like an insincere cornball. *Had he always been a jerk and she just never realized it?*

On one side of the bridge, deep within the crinkled foil were her marriage, her confidence and all sense of security. She didn't know what was lurking in the creases of the foil in front of her. She only knew that whatever it was, she would have to make her own way through it. If it was death, or cancer or an overseas deployment, the people in the room would rally around her, offering casseroles, nights out with the girls, free babysitting. But she was not lucky enough to have that kind of calamity. Her curse was insidious; one she would have to bear alone because to do otherwise would cause her children to suffer. That would never happen.

Willa smiled with pride as a flurry of flashes went off. Every parent in the troop was eager to do the MacArthur's a favor by photographing them. There were so many flashes, Pups was nearly blinded. Blinking against the flashes, Pups felt tears well up in her eyes. She tried to dab them indiscreetly, but it was no use, the first tear had jumped her eyelid and was streaming down her face, followed closely by a few others. "Look at you, getting all emotional," said Mindy, giving Pups a hug as the MacArthurs stepped off the bridge. "Don't worry there, Mom. It's only Junior Girl Scouts. Most of us wait till they graduate to Cadet's before we're pulling out the Kleenex."

After the ceremony, Willa, Patrick, Maddox and Cady darted to the snacks while Pups, dutifully posed for photos with members of her troop. Her smile, which was normally a little forced, now looked like something that could have been painted on. She was fine she kept telling herself. Absolutely fine. Until she saw Patrick about to bite into one of her crunchy cupcakes with the blue sugar flowers.

"Excuse me," she said to the Choi family as she hurried over to Patrick.

Still smiling that mean, tense smile, she placed her hand gently over Patrick's and whispered, "*You* are not allowed to eat these cupcakes."

"What do you mean?"

"I mean," she said sternly, "that *you* are not allowed to eat these cupcakes." He looked like she had just kicked him in the teeth, which was exactly how she wanted him to feel, but for good measure she added, "These cupcakes are for good people. Not degenerates." Patrick handed the cupcake to Pups who took it, wrapped it in a napkin, then savagely smashed it and threw it in the trash so hard, the grey plastic bin almost tipped over.

"That was a perfectly good cupcake. At least you could have eaten it," said Patrick, appealing to her frugal nature.

"I'd be crazy to eat anything you handled. Who knows what kind of germs I'd be exposing myself to." Pups stormed off and busied herself by wiping up spilled punch and disposing of abandoned cups. The event was over and little by little the room emptied. Patrick took Willa and Maddie home while Pups helped Mindy wrestle that big unwieldy bridge back into the storage shed. When she was done, she looked around for Cady and Maddox, who had thoroughly enjoyed a night of running amok with the other restless and bored younger siblings. They weren't in the main auditorium, so she went out into the hall to look for them. Past the restrooms and the water fountain, was a desk where Mrs. Hill, the school secretary, sat during the day. On the far side of that desk, Pups could see movement. As she neared the desk, she witnessed as horrifying a sight as she had ever seen. Maddox and Cady, in the hall outside the auditorium, dressed in a rag tag collection of scarves, coats, and yes, even hats, pilfered from the disgusting old box labeled "lost and found."

-eighteen-

THE CUPCAKE WAR

Everything went on the credit cards. Everything. Food, camps, uniforms, Christmas' and birthdays, dental check ups, pizza nights, movie tickets and all those trips to McDonald's drive thru, all of it went on the credit card. And Mary Ellen just assumed that Kenny was paying the bills when in reality, he was paying just the bare minimum. It all added up to colossal debt, with their credit limit hovering mere inches over their lice infested heads.

And if money problems weren't enough of an affliction, the Packingham family suffered the greatest of humiliations when Brophy was sent home from school with a full-blown case of head lice. It was hard to say what was worse, Brophy having lice or having everyone know he had lice. Washington Prep's no-nit policy made everything so public they may as well have printed a list of the condemned in the school paper. Soon after Brophy contracted lice, so did the Secretary of Education's son, and the son of CNN reporter Dino Salone, and Trent Collins' son, Parker. Trent even talked about it on his radio show. As awful as it was, Mary Ellen couldn't help but feel the slightest bit of pride; the caliber of people Brophy had contaminated was impressive.

Doyle, Tanner and Kier also came home with a letter from their school nurse about what she found crawling around in their heads. Everyone was invited to return to school once the situation was under control. What the letter didn't say was how any sensible modern day warrior mother could exterminate one life form without compromising another.

While her family took all of this in stride, Mary Ellen felt like a phantom observer, passively watching as all that she had worked so hard to construct began to unravel. Her mind was a catalogue of what ifs. What if the car breaks down or the dryer stops working? What if that gap between Kier's two front teeth doesn't close up like Dr. Rutters predicts and he actually needs orthodontics? What if Kenny can't figure this out? What if they can't make the car payments or the mortgage?

Eating became impossible and breathing was done with great difficulty. And when she spoke to her husband, which was not very often, she spoke in a quiet voice very slowly. Anything more than that could trigger a spike in emotion and that would unleash a torrent of tears and accusations that would be so exhausting, she would have to spend the entire next day in bed.

Alcohol helped. Kenny had discovered its tonic properties long ago; probably about the same time he started having trouble keeping up with their expenses. He claimed he told her they were in trouble. She said he didn't. Sure, he complained about how much money she spent, but he never put it into specific terms. He never said, *if we don't cut our expenses, we're going to go under.* She would have remembered if he said that. Instead, he said things like, "can you do anything besides fucking spend money?" or "who do you think you're married to? Donald fuckin' Trump?" Just regular Kenny-speak as far as she was concerned. She cut costs wherever she could. The first thing to go was Humble Warrior Yoga. "Sick mother," she whispered to James. She was terrified that they would have to pull the kids out of their tuition heavy schools. That would be devastating. For everyone.

Giving up yoga left a huge hole in her daily schedule, a hole she decided to fill by doing what other upwardly mobile mothers do to fill their time, she volunteered. For its students, the Prep campus was a place they returned to again and again, long after they graduated. There were football games, homecomings and reunions; alumni bull roasts, smokers and hall of fame inductions. Countless alumni weddings were held in the magnificent bronze and marble chapel. By the same token, not a week went by without the mournful procession of an alumnus funeral. While the men of Prep had a lifetime of opportunities to visit their alma mater, it was quite a different story for the women of Prep.

The wives and mothers of Prep loved the gentlemanly campus every bit as much as their men, but until very recently, opportunity for ladies to spend any substantial time on campus was limited to special occasions such as graduation and the annual Mother's Day tea. All that changed soon after Father Bills moved into the President's office. A keen observer of the upper class, Father Bills noticed that well-heeled stay-home moms suddenly had a tremendous amount of free time once their children entered high school. Some went back to work, others took up new hobbies, but the vast majority of these mothers exercised an inner need to increase their social footprint. In other words, they dedicated their lives to charity. For the uber-ambitious, there were the marquee causes like breast cancer, leukemia and autism. Second tier charitarians had to settle for lesser causes, like the library fund, animal welfare or arts education.

Not one to let a resource go untapped, Father Bills set out to harness the power of these high energy women by inventing volunteer jobs for them on campus. He created committees and duties that appealed to a wide variety of moms; from the high society bell ringers to the bottom feeding climbers, there was a place at Father Bills's volunteer table for all of them. For these underappreciated but highly skilled women, volunteering was as habit forming as Purell, and once bitten with the volunteer bug, many sought out greater and greater positions. Prep called upon its mothers to take on a long list of irrelevant and ridiculous projects. There was the gardening club to plant pansies, mums, kale, daffodils, tulips, and their triumphant end of the school year blanket of blue and white petunias. Because it is a well-known fact that a handwritten envelope is one that screams to be opened, there was the mailing committee to hand address social invitations, Christmas cards, and the all-important solicitations for the endowment fund. There was the welcoming committee, the Thursday meditation and prayer group, and the school store committee. There was the decorating committee which fashioned pumpkin and Indian corn arrangements in the fall and wrapped miles of pine boughs around every rail and column on campus at Christmas. Beyond the school-wide volunteer opportunities, there were also specialty groups—the theater boosters, the golf boosters. There were boosters for every club and interest in the school.

Once the ladies had a taste of Prep-style volunteerism, the more ambitious among them started jockeying for a coveted co-chairmanship in school's triple crown of volunteerism, The Annual Dinner Dance and Auction, the Annual Phone-a-thon or the Annual Christmas Ball. Father Bills personally selected the chairs of those events, and as everyone knew, the easiest way to get Father Bills's attention was to back up their generous donations of time with even more generous donations of money. A few more zeros on their annual fund donation would benefit the entire family, or so they told their husbands.

As hard as this brigade of women worked, not a single student cared about or even noticed the flowers lining the driveway or the decorations in the entrance hall. And while some of the faculty and administration enjoyed the beautification of the campus, they also dreaded the possibility of impromptu meetings with the guardians of those they had recently flunked, punished or ignored. If anyone asked, which they didn't, the faculty would have preferred to keep the mothers at bay. However, these ladies operated with impunity having the full blessing of Father Bills who saw them as foot soldiers in his never ending quest to fill his coffers.

Unfortunately, the one thing there was no volunteer for was someone to coordinate all the volunteers. Committee chairs were supposed to submit their plans to the secretary of the Parents' Association, so she could maintain a master calendar of volunteer activity. But like many things in the volunteer world, it didn't always happen the way it should.

On an unseasonably warm October day, the football boosters, headed by Claudia who was assisted by Mary Ellen, arrived at the Prep dining hall just before lunch to unpack two hundred chocolate cupcakes topped with blue fondant panthers sitting on thick ivory swirls of buttercream. Two hundred more were stored in Mr. Harkin's office for the second wave of lunch. It was their first fundraiser, selling S'up Cakes, cupcakes from the area's hottest new cupcake establishment. Given the popularity of S'up cupcakes, and the fact that you would normally have to wait in a substantial line to get one, the football boosters had every expectation of selling all four hundred, which would more than cover the cost of chrysanthemum corsages the senior mothers wore to the last home football game.

"Whatever we have left over, we can use as starter money for the coaches' gifts," said Claudia. "Last year we gave all the assistants $250 gift certificates to Sports Authority. We gave Coach Dudley $2,500 cash and a weekend stay at one of the parents beach house in Rehoboth."

"Wow!"

"I know. It's a lot, but those guys are won-der-ful. Truly. The things they do with those boys … "

The large room was empty except for a handful

of workers; one servicing the milk machine, another refilling the silverware bins and a few planting pots of salad dressing in the ice over at the salad bar. A large erasable white board by the entrance announced "Today's Menu" as hot turkey sandwiches with mashed potatoes and cranberry sauce. The door to the kitchen was closed, but the briny smell of turkey gravy wafted through the entire first floor of the building, like a fetid invitation to lunch.

As Mary Ellen and Claudia unpacked, the door to the Ketchum Dining Hall swung open with a bang and in came two women carrying towers of distinctive turquoise boxes from Bethesda Cupcake, last year's hottest cupcake establishment. Aside from the fact that they were both carrying the same type of box, no one would ever logically link the two women. They were as far apart in style as Raggedy Ann is from Barbie.

"Splendid," muttered Claudia under her breath.

"Oh. My. God!" exclaimed the Barbie when she saw the football boosters. "Don't tell me you guys are selling cupcakes?" Shaking her well-designed mop top with its chunks of butter highlights and chocolate low lights she waited for an answer to her obvious question.

"How'd you guess?" asked Claudia pointing to the brightly colored handmade sign taped to the front of their table. The one that said, "Support your Football Panthers! $2.50 for a S'up Cake!"

"Sissy Peterschmidt and Helene Waller, this is Mary Ellen Packingham. She's helping with football boosters this year."

"Oh wow. That's fabulous!" said Sissy extending one French manicured hand towards Mary Ellen and using the other to sweep the butter chunks out of her eyes. "What year is your son?"

"Freshman," said Mary Ellen.

"Oh my God, you are sooooooo lucky. You have four years of the ... greatest ... no kidding, the greatest years of your life ahead of you." Maybe it was the unseasonably warm weather, or the effects of the turkey gravy fumes, or maybe, it was just raw emotion welling up inside of her, but Sissy suddenly became teary eyed.

"Do you have other sons?" she asked.

"Actually, I do. Three more—a seventh grader, a fifth grader and a third grader."

"I am sooooo jealous! My baby is a senior. God, I can't believe it. A few more months and I'm out of here! What am I going to do? Really guys, like what am I going to do?" Anticipating the twilight of active motherhood caused tears to roll down her perfectly made up cheek. A stay home mom who split her time between getting ready to go to Prep, and being at Prep, she was, without a doubt, the hottest mom ever to have a son in the school. She was such a MILF that even those teachers who shuddered at the thought of parental confrontations felt a pang of melancholy at her impending departure.

"Jeeze, Sissy, it's only October. You've got the whole year left. I have a sophomore and a senior," said Helene, the Raggedy Anne to Sissy's Barbie, extending her hand to Mary Ellen. "You know, I put our bake sale on the master calendar two weeks ago, and we were the only entry." Every ounce of Sissy's hotness was countered by the glacial Helene, a no-nonsense, reliable get-things-done type mom. The kind who approached every challenge with a grimace and a belief that the only thing between her and greatness were the dolts she was forced to collaborate with.

"You guys got S'up Cakes? Wow! How'd you manage that?" asked Helene.

"Turns out one of the owners is originally from Tennessee. Loves Gro. Loves football. All I had to do was ask. They donated the whole bunch."

"That's great," said Helene. "I hear their cupcakes are to die for even if I don't at all get their name."

"S'up cakes? It's like Wasss–up cakes?" said Claudia doing her best impression of a ghetto youth. Helene stared blankly no closer to understanding the meaning than she was before.

"You know like, 'what's up'? The kids kind of slur it so it's more like wasssss–up? And then they slurred it even more, so it became 's'up'?"

Helene remained unimpressed. "I'm sure they taste better than they sound," she said curtly.

Claudia smiled and shrugged her shoulders. There was an awkward silence as each booster team waited for the other booster team to volunteer to return the next day. When that didn't happen, Helene commandeered another lunch table and started unpacking their 200 blue panther topped confections, while Mary Ellen and Claudia busied themselves re-arranging their cupcakes so they wouldn't have to stand idle and watch their adversaries open up shop.

"I didn't know about that calendar," whispered Mary Ellen.

"Who cares? We were here first and besides, football trumps soccer any day."

"Better team?"

"Bigger team. Strength in numbers. And how about that do? I'm told she spends half the day fixing all those random pieces. And I don't even want to think about the money she throws at that rat's nest. Really, two bottles of Miss Clairol and a weedwhacker is all she needs."

Mary Ellen watched as Helene unpacked cupcakes which appeared to have been frosted with wet cement as Sissy unrolled their hand written sign.

"Gawd. That grey icing looks like sludge. Just because the school colors are grey and blue doesn't mean we have to eat sludge colored frosting for four years," said Claudia. "Sometimes you just have to take a little artistic license."

"Hey girls, do you have any extra tape with you?" asked Sissy from across the room.

"Oh, sorry. We just ran out. I'm sure the front office will lend you theirs," said Claudia. Lowering her voice back to a whisper, she said, "And check out the rock around her neck. It might not look like much, but it's insured for $20,000. "

Mary Ellen tried to get a glimpse of Sissy's

necklace without seeming obvious, but Sissy was on her way out the door. "I guess I'll go for a walk," she said flapping the lapels of her chic purple blazer to create a little ventilation. "Gawd, it's like a sauna in here, isn't it? Maybe it's hormones, but I feel like I'm wilting."

Seconds after Sissy teetered out of the room, the school bell rang, and the heavy mahogany doors of the cafeteria swung open with another loud bang. In came a throng of young men who, with their blue crested blazers and grey striped ties appeared every bit the future leaders of America that Dr. Brennan purported them to be. Closer inspection, however, revealed scuffed shoes, frayed cuffs on their khakis, buttonless blazers and stained shirts, giving the future leaders a far more scrappy presence. Mary Ellen was surprised, and even a little relieved to see these boys who were so ... so normal. Not at all like the impeccably tailored blue bloods they always showed in movies about prep school. She felt a small sense of smug satisfaction knowing that she would never let Brophy leave the house with buttons missing, scuffed shoes or stained pants. Even up close, her son looked good.

It would horrify Mary Ellen to learn that the only students who consistently showed up for school in clean, pressed and mended clothes were the scholarship students. In the same way the movies got the prep look wrong by making the students look well-tailored, so did Mary Ellen. The kids with the worst looking, tattered up old Burberry blazers with torn linings and gaping holes where the buttons used to be, the ones their fathers' were too fat to fit into anymore, those kids were the real deal. The old line preps. The kids with shiny gold buttons on the sleeves of their new stain repellent blazers and their freshly shined shoes, those kids were the "others." The enrichers. The guys who were invited to Prep because they were great athletes or super smart projected perfect SAT scorers or represented some under represented minority. The teachers knew it. The administration knew it. Even some of the boys knew it. The only ones who didn't know it were moms, like Mary Ellen, who were too busy trying to look like they belonged to this stuffy old men's club to realized they'd be better off sending their sons to school in wrinkled shirts and ill-fitting pants.

As boys passed by the bake sale table to get their hot turkey sandwiches, Claudia called out, "Hi guys! When you're finished eating, come buy a S'up Cake and support the football team."

Most smiled politely and said nothing. Those who knew her, offered well-rehearsed "Hello Mrs. Manfreys." In accordance with the school dress code, there was not a piercing, tattoo, wild hairstyle, mustache, beard or overly grown side burn among them. At least none that were visible. As Mary Ellen scanned the crowd for Brophy, she was impressed with how presentable these boys were. Even in their scuffed up shoes, they were every parent's dream children, except ...

"They don't seem very happy," said Mary Ellen. Though they were sitting in a grand mahogany paneled dining room with shiny brass chandeliers eating premium quality turkey, the room was full of glum faces, downcast eyes and purposeful eating.

Take away the fancy clothes and the plush surroundings and the boys in Ketchum hall could be inmates at a juvenile detention center.

"Oh they're happy alright. They just don't know it yet," said Claudia. "Once they leave for college, they realize just how good *this* is. That's why they always come back. Year after year. Even the ones who despise the place now will show up for reunions and games for the rest of their lives. Look at Gil, to hear him talk, he was all but abused when he was here, but would he miss the annual alumni Turkey Bowl? Not on your life."

The tables started to fill up and Mary Ellen began to worry about Brophy who still wasn't there. "Get a load of Mr. Wonderful," said Claudia, practically salivating over Wenn Mann who was standing by the hot water dispenser. "Such a shame all that sinewy muscle for ... what? A Latin teacher? *Paaaalllleeease*. By the way, from what I hear, Adonis is the mystery faculty member."

Mary Ellen gave Claudia a blank smile that Claudia took as an invitation to elaborate.

"Wenn Mann is the faculty member with lice. Like the same day they found lice on boy wonder, they found them on him."

"Huh."

"Don't you think it's just a little suspicious? Cole is a resident. Wenn Mann is the resident dean."

"You don't mean ... "

"All boys boarding school ... stranger things have happened."

Mary Ellen was horrified. "A teacher and a student?" she said, silently praying that the object of her lust wasn't gay. Realistically, it didn't matter in the least what his sexual preferences were, but if she actually knew for a fact that he wasn't into women, she just couldn't feel the same way about him.

"Don't be so shocked. I could tell you stories about this place that could get me arrested in some states just for saying it out loud."

There was that weird post on Cole's Facebook. Maybe it wasn't so implausible. What did she know? It's not like she's ever been around an all-boys school. She knew what people said. Especially petty jealous people who would never in a million years have the mental, physical or financial stamina for a place like Washington Prep.

"Well, it's spreading like wildfire. They're sending more kids home every day."

"For being gay?"

"For having lice. Brophy had it, didn't he?

"Yes, but it was a very mild case."

"We've been lucky so far. I've been spraying that stuff you spray on the upholstery on their heads."

"Really? Isn't that toxic?"

"It says 'safe for pets,' so I guess not. Did you hear that Alex Malony had it?"

"Who's Alex Malony?"

"Son of JoJo Malony; the Redskins' running back?"

"I didn't know he went here."

"He transferred in like the second day of school. They're not in the directory. Now the entire offensive line of the Washington Redskins has it."

"No kidding! Wow."

"Oh yeah. This is one massive outbreak. And it doesn't help that some of these boys have caught on. They are actually planting those little buggers in their own heads. Fantastic way to be excused from a test. Imagine. I told mine that if they dare come home with lice, I'm shaving their heads. It's so unfortunate that the whole school and beyond has to suffer just because *some* people can't get things right."

Which *somes* was Claudia talking about? Were the Packinghams *somes*?

"Hey there handsome, how about a cupcake?" purred Claudia as Salter came through the doors with a couple of buddies.

"Hey," he said nonchalantly. "What's all this?"

"I told you. We're selling S'up Cakes for the football team. Go get all your friends to buy them." She leaned in to whisper, "and not those dreadful sludge cakes they're selling for the soccer team."

When Brophy came through the door of the cafeteria, he was red faced, sweaty and alone. He glanced over towards Mary Ellen, but when she smiled and waved he looked away. She watched him make his way through the lunch line without talking to a soul. He walked over to an empty table, sat down with his back towards her and ate his lunch. A few seconds later, Cole Reardon placed his tray across from Brophy and sat down. Mary Ellen breathed a sigh of relief. They must be friends if they're eating lunch together. Probably like two peas in a pod. Before she could move Brophy through an extended friendship with Cole (which would have included a joint graduation party and four years of being roommates at Princeton), Cole abruptly stood up and left. Just like that. And he wasn't done eating because he took his tray with him and sat down at another table on the other side of the room, leaving poor Brophy alone again.

"Everything all right?" asked Claudia.

"I don't know. I hope Brophy is alright."

"You know, they got their Latin tests back."

Latin. That would explain it. And being dissed by Cole Reardon probably didn't help elevate his mood either. *Who does that little fuck Cole Reardon think he is anyway? He's not such a prize. He's actually kind of gawky looking, in a handsome kind of way.* The next time she looked over, some of the seats at his table had been filled, which momentarily eased her worry until she got a glimpse of Brophy's new companions; a pimple faced kid with hollow eyes, a fat kid with greasy hair and a large white stain on the shoulder of his blazer and a four-eyed brace face who looked like the kind of kid who can make milk come out of his nose on command. Brophy was sitting with the rejects. The sudden realization that her Brophy might not be the toast of the town was like a dose of ipecac— producing such a strong urge to vomit, she had to bite down on the inside of her cheek and dig her long fingernails into the skin of her hands to ward off anything that might embarrass her son.

For boys looking for a sweet conclusion to an otherwise forgettable lunch, the football table was the overwhelming favorite. Claudia and Mary Ellen filled up their cash box as their S'up Cakes disappeared. Flush with the thrill of popularity, they didn't notice Sissy come through the door carrying a tape dispenser in one hand and her cute purple jacket in the other. The deep cut V-neck of her tissue cotton designer t-shirt left little to the imagination. Around her tanned neck, was a slim leather cord with what looked like a common grayish black rock swinging from it.

"How do you like the rock of Gibraltar?" asked Claudia.

"What is that?" asked Mary Ellen.

"I can't believe that you, the fashionista, don't know about raw diamonds. That's how they look right out of the ground, before they are cut and polished."

"Really? They're ugly."

"No, they are hot! Almost as hot as Sissy," said Claudia who like everyone else in the room was watching Sissy toddle across Ketchem on her platforms. She looked like a girl in a Pepsi commercial; moving in slow motion, so every jiggle was exaggerated, damp and dewy from the heat, with that boulder bouncing between her ample cleavage, and her blonde butter chunks swinging alongside her brown chocolate chunks. Though she was in the twilight of active motherhood, she was as ripe and luscious as a peach on the July cover of *Martha Stewart*

Living Magazine. Silence descended as hundreds of eyes fixated on one hot mamma who was, at that moment, the object of lust for every single person in the room. The boys plain out wanted to fuck her. So what if she was someone's mom? The teachers and the cafeteria workers, they wanted to be her or at least they wanted the kind of comfortable idleness that allowed you to hang around a school lunchroom in the middle of a Tuesday selling cupcakes. And the mothers in the room, they wanted the rock.

As Sissy bent over the soccer booster table and carefully taped her homemade sign advertising cupcakes for $3.00, she gave the boys in the room a rare after lunch treat not often found in the dining room of an all boys school. All at once, the place to go for a happy ending to a forgettable meal was the soccer booster stand. The more Sissy leaned over to scoop up the sludge cupcakes, the longer the line for them became.

Meanwhile, the football boosters were standing in front of 150 premium cupcakes they couldn't give away. As the chaos that only a spectacular set of boobs can incite swirled through Ketchum, Brophy remained seated and almost motionless with his back to Mary Ellen. The sad hunch of his shoulders broke her heart. Mary Ellen was frozen. Her ears buzzed, and her throat constricted. As Sissy and Helene adeptly took in cash and doled out sweets, Claudia barked even louder enticements to customers who couldn't care less about cupcakes. Their sole fascination lie in the pendulous confections hanging inches above the cupcakes and on that front, there was no contest.

Mary Ellen and Claudia were so engrossed in the spectacle before them they didn't even notice the one brave soul who bucked what was popular in favor of what was right. "Excuse me, how much are the cupcakes?"

It was Cole Reardon smiling sweetly. "Oh Cole honey, how are you?" asked Claudia.

"I'm good, thank you. These look awesome. How much are they?"

"For you Cole, nothing. Just take one," said Claudia.

Mary Ellen was shocked. Cole Reardon, the recipient of every conceivable gift known to man including wealth beyond belief and he doesn't have to pay for a cupcake? Like $3.00 would make a difference someone like him?

"Wow! Thank you."

"Cole, this is Mrs. Packingham. She's Brophy's mother."

"Nice to meet you," said Cole barely looking at Mary Ellen. "Hey, Mrs. Manfrey. My dad should be giving you a call about the reservation trip. He just needs to work out a few of the details."

"He knows my number. It's going to be fabulous. All you boys pow-wowing around. Salter is psyched."

"Yeah. Definitely. Thanks for the cupcakes," he said taking another one for the road. Outrage seeped from Mary Ellen's gut. *What trip? For who? Not one, but two free cupcakes?*

"What's a reservation trip?" she asked in a lilting singsong voice to camouflage her disgust.

"Oh, some of the boys are going to South Dakota with Cole's dad to do a service project on a Native American reservation."

Some boys, as in … not Brophy. Mary Ellen could think of nothing to say.

"They've been planning this since, I don't know, forever. Cole, Salter and a bunch of the BS boys. They've been friends since kindergarten and … this will be something special for *them* to do."

Mary Ellen had been waiting for snub like this for months and here it was, a bold, italicized, quotation marked *"them."* A "them" that used punctuation and tone to convey what a mere four letters could not. Regular "them" referred to Brophy and the other students who had gone to average schools and somehow landed here at Boys Wonderland through the good graces of people like Claudia and Sissy. The other *"them."* The fancy one, referred to boys like Salter and Cole and everyone else for whom this spacious campus was a birthright—and an under-appreciated one at that. Since the day Brophy's acceptance arrived, she had anticipated being shut out by certain snobby mothers, but she never expected it would be her old friend Claudia— who technically, was just as much a trespasser on this rarified landscape as she was—to be the gatekeeper. Even her innate optimism didn't blind her to the cold realities of social climbing. Mary Ellen knew as well as anyone that unless you are a Kennedy or a Sherwood or a member of a similar dynasty, you would never be welcomed into anyone's circle with open arms. They might play nice for the cameras and pretend they were happy to hold the door open for all the wonderfully brilliant and diverse people coming through, but in private, they still viewed anyone who wasn't one of *"them"* as one of them. Getting sent home for harboring lice probably didn't help elevate Brophy on the social strata. In fact, Brophy and the other "thems" were probably responsible for the whole miserable outbreak as far as Claudia and her friends were concerned.

"How wonderful," said Mary Ellen, who could think of nothing else to say. "When are they going?"

"It's all still up in the air, but probably second half of Christmas break, when Cole gets back from Germany. A lot of it depends on Remy's basketball practice."

"Remy? I didn't know he went to BS."

"Oh he didn't … but, he is Cole's roommate."

Of course, Remy. Mary Ellen started to wonder if Remy wasn't actually the luckiest boy on earth. Not Cole. Everything Cole got was set-aside for him at birth. Remy, on the other hand, seemed to be enjoying the opportunities previously reserved for the few industrious mavericks whose desire to succeed was surpassed only by their desire to prove themselves worthy through good old-fashioned hard work and butt kissing. Someone like Brophy, if he was motivated, hardworking and obsequious.

"Here he comes again. Is he gorgeous or is he *gorgeous?*"

"What?" snapped Mary Ellen. Now that their bond had been broken by Claudia's ill timed "them," the desire to be agreeable to this catty bitch disappeared.

"Mr. Mann. Is he a man's Mann or a ladies' Mann? What do you think?"

Mary Ellen looked over at the drink dispensers where Mr. Mann getting himself another cup of hot water. It was the fourth time he had been in the cafeteria, yet all he ever got was hot water and lemons.

"What is it with the water and the lemons?"

Mary Ellen watched as Wenn Mann squeezed the juice out of two lemon wedges into his steaming hot cup of water. Then he took the cup and instead of heading out the big double door as he had done all the other times, he walked over to the tables and directly towards ... Brophy and his table full of freaks. He stopped beside Brophy and said something. Since Brophy's back was to her, there were no clues as to how he was reacting.

Mr. Mann finished by putting his right hand down on Brophy's shoulder and giving it a little squeeze. At least that's what appeared to happen. Is that allowed? Why was he touching Brophy? And Brophy's back was as still as stiff as ever so it certainly wasn't any kind of reassuring, "relax kid" kind of exchange. Mr. Mann patted Brophy's back a few times, then took his hot lemon water and left. No sooner was he out the door than Brophy was getting up to clear his tray. To cut him off at the pass, Mary Ellen headed to the dirty dish area.

"Mom, what are you doing? You're embarrassing me."

"Embarrassing you?"

"Yes," he twisted himself around her so that he could get close to the dirty tray cart.

"I don't think I'm any more or less embarrassing than any other mother."

"Right. Because you are all embarrassing. Can't you just leave me alone? Why do you have to get involved in everything?"

He slid his tray onto the aluminum cart and left without even looking at her. This was not the happy-go-lucky Brophy who was king of the castle at St. Anthony's. She was in and out of that lunchroom all the time, and he never cared a bit. This was an altogether different animal. One she wasn't sure she liked or knew how to care for. Claudia stood idle while the soccer moms continued to rake in the bucks. She looked like she could handle things alone for a few minutes. Mary Ellen stepped out of the cafeteria where she felt like she could breathe again. The silence of the long, empty hallway was a welcome respite from the loud clanking lunchroom. To her left, were windows looking out onto the quad. To her right, was a long row of old dark wood doors inset with grooved glass and painted gold letters identifying whose office it was. She passed the main office and the school business office. She stopped near the college counseling office to look at a bulletin board with the school honor roll stapled to it. It was from last spring—the last time report cards were sent out. There were very few names on the Dean's List. A moderate number of names on the first honors list and a relative crowd on the second honors list. As she scanned the lists for any recognizable names, she heard a door shut from the other end of the hall followed by the sound of heavy boots against the smooth marble floor. It was him, Mr. Mann. He was coming right towards her. For the first time, they were alone. Should she say something to him? Tell him who she was? Put in a good word for Brophy? Tell him how much time he spent studying Latin?

As she stood there thinking of her options and trying to make a good decision, her eyes met his and, for a Nano second, they connected. Her stomach flipped like it did in high school whenever she passed her secret crush in the hallway. But … it was not to be. Mr. Mann took an abrupt turn into the men's room, which was right next door to the ladies' room.

When Roland Hall was built, it was used exclusively by men. When they finally started employing women in the school offices, they realized they were going to need a ladies room. Just as Eve was fashioned out of Adam's rib, the ladies room at Prep was fashioned out of a part of the original men's room. They built a wall to divide the space, but since there were a lot of pipes and fixtures in the ceiling, the partition only went up about ten feet and the ceiling was at least fifteen feet high. There was no chance that anyone's privacy would be compromised as long as they didn't make any noise.

Mary Ellen entered the deserted ladies' room and went into a stall. As she was unbuttoning her pants, she heard voices coming from the men's room. At first it was just noise muffled by running water and a flushing toilet. When the water quieted, Mary Ellen recognized the distinctive voice of Mr. Mann. She remembered it from his brief chat at back to school night.

She heard heavy footsteps followed by bit of silence.

"Bend over," said Mr. Mann. Followed by a prolonged silence. Followed by a very loud, very guttural, "Ugh!"

Followed by a boyish sounding, "Ewww!" Mary Ellen was horrified. Surely she was jumping to conclusions. She was doing an excellent job of convincing herself of that until she heard Mr. Mann say, "Look, if you know what's good for you, you won't tell anyone. Once they find out, you're out of here, and so am I for that matter."

"But … "

"I'm just telling you for your own good. Come by my room after dinner and we'll figure this out."

They continued their conversation, but someone turned on the water again and everything was muffled. Mary Ellen finished her business quickly so she could get a glimpse of who the other person in the bathroom was. Without even stopping to wash her hands, she rushed out into the hall just in time to see Wenn Mann and Cole Reardon emerge from the men's room. Suddenly, it all made sense.

nineteen

MY FAVORITE
THINGS

Treating yourself for lice was not nearly as fun as doing it with a partner as Wenn learned soon after his night with Cullen. He also learned, when he took the time to read through the entire booklet of directions included in the box of lice remover that you are supposed to re-treat head lice ten to fourteen days after the first treatment, and possibly once more, just in case you don't manage to comb out all those fucking nits. So he spent Friday night, alone in his room with a plastic shower cap over his head. It was his first Friday night without Elizabeth since summer. He hadn't seen her since she left Monty's that night. She called a few days later to say he needed to pick up Galenthias because she was going out of town and the condo was being fumigated. When he went by, Gay in her carrier and a big Dean & Deluca shopping bag with the rest of her stuff were waiting for him at the security guard's desk. A note taped to the cat carrier promised to call when she returned so they could "figure out what to do about the cat."

Since then, all his free time was spent in his room reading and playing guitar. Gay had been known to go on meowing jags and sometimes her tail sent things crashing to the floor as she hopped on and off the furniture. It was easier to claim the noise as his own in case anyone wondered what was going on in the resident dean's room. He didn't mind. He liked his room. His own little cave that he didn't have to share with anyone or fix up for anyone. Just his. The way he liked it. He missed Elizabeth more than he expected. The firmness of her skin. The strength and the softness in her body. The web of fine silvery lines that covered her belly and the permanent welt she had above her pubic bone, from her Caesarians. The way she smelled like his landlady's backyard garden in Rome. And how perfectly she could fit herself around him. She was the antithesis of every other woman he had known. Like a unique species, one lacking that insatiable female curiosity. That ridiculous compulsion to know everything. And the ridiculous counter compulsion to share everything in return.

He thought about how much time he had spent with her, yet how little he actually knew about her. It was miraculous. He knew virtually nothing. Only the most random and irrelevant things. She knew even less about him, and it didn't bother her a bit. This was Elizabeth's singular distinction among women. She was a goddess.

Below her were mortal women. Nags, like Cullen who hunted him down by leaving so many messages on his school voicemail that his inbox filled up, prompting Mrs. Pringle, the school secretary to tape a nasty form letter about the importance of checking voice mails on his door. When he finally called Cullen back, she was cold and distant. As though she had neither the desire, nor the time, to take his call. Which begged the question, if you don't want to talk to someone, why the fuck are you filling up his voice mailbox? The only reason he called her back was guilt about sharing his lice with her, but she made no mention of an infestation of any kind. She did say that she hoped he would take her out on a proper date. That he owed her that much. He said he'd think about it, which was a lie. When he wasn't in class or in his room, he was out on the trails training for the Washington Marathon, which was just around the corner. On an unseasonably warm October day, a long morning run had left him wiped out. To re-hydrate, he trotted in and out of the dining hall between classes for hot water and lemon. At one point, he entered the quiet dining hall and saw Sissy Peterschmidt and some other moms selling some noxious cupcakes and after that, he started going in by the side door to avoid any eye contact. By lunch, he had consumed eight cups of piping hot brew. All that liquid kept him running to the faculty men's room just outside Dr. Brennan's office. Sometime in the mid-morning, he came out of that restroom and found Dr. Brennan standing in the hall waiting for him.

"Everything alright, Mr. Mann?"

"Yes, Sir," said Wenn, surprised to be called out for too much pissing.

"Because I've been counting and you've been in and out of the men's room seven times. And it's not even noon." Dr. Brennan delivered this report as if it were some kind of revelation. An undercover investigation. He said it like he was expecting Wenn to confess to something.

"I'm sorry. I guess I've been drinking too much hot lemon water. Trying to stay hydrated."

"Yes. If that's all it is," said Dr. Brennan giving him the evil eye. He could tell Dr. Brennan suspected something. Did he know about Galenthias? What would that have to do with pissing? To avoid another confrontation, the next time he had to pee, he skipped the faculty restroom and went to the regular men's room near the college counseling office. Those guys were too busy to keep track of how many times people used the bathroom. On one of his trips to the men's room, he felt the hair on the back of his neck prickle and sensed a predator approaching. She was blonde, with the ubiquitous style and attitude combo that identified her as ... a mother. The conflicted expression on her face when she looked at him identified her specifically as a mother of one of his students. He had seen the look many times.

The one that broadcast both her indignation at a teacher with such a strong anti-parent stance and her inherent need to protect her son. Nine times out of ten, the kid won, and the mom backed down. But there were exceptions. The moms who just plowed ahead and confronted him anyway. Sissy Peterschmidt, that poodle haired woman with the big tits was a classic example. Sissy never missed an opportunity to corner him. She was harmless; without a threatening bone in her tight little body and too stupid to remember that she wasn't supposed to talk to him. He kind of enjoyed looking at her while she spoke about whatever it was she spoke to him about. He never listened. Just nodded with a serious look while he considered her from all angles. Evidently, she believed her boys were close to failing, but that would never happen. As long as a kid passes, no one at the school gives you any shit about the grade you give. But just try and flunk someone, and Dr. Brennan is up your ass, poking around, asking to see your grade book. None of Wenn's students ever failed. There had been D's but a D is passing. Most of them end up with C's, maybe a C+. The smart kids, they'll pull a B, B-. And one or two per year manage to eek out a precious A from Wenn Mann.

Seeing mothers of his students always threw him because genetics made these women he had never seen before, seem familiar. Like the way Grandpa Irving, who has Alzheimer's, instinctually recognizes Wenn's face, yet he never has a clue who he is. Such was the case with the woman who was looking directly at him. He was certain he taught her son, but who he was, how badly he was doing, he couldn't say. Before she summoned the strength to speak to him, he turned into the men's room.

"Hey Mr. Mann, how's it going?" asked Cole who was standing in front of a urinal.

"I've had better days. How about you?" Wenn approached the urinal on the opposite side of the room.

"Not that good."

"What's up?" Cole finished peeing. He looked around to be sure there wasn't anyone else in the room then he went over to the sink and turned on the water. Wenn did the same at the next sink over.

"Mr. Mann, I think the lice are back. I've got a huge history exam tomorrow, and we have a game tomorrow after school. Against Landon. If they send me home like they did the last time, I won't make either."

"Fuck." Wenn's heart went out for the kid. He knew exactly what he was going through.

"My stupid step-mother didn't know what she was doing when she treated me. She wouldn't have done it at all except my dad was out of town and she couldn't get a hold of my mom. If she has to do it again, she'll kill me."

"Do you want me to check for you?"

"That would be so great. Thanks." They turned off the water, pulled paper towels from the metal dispenser and dried their hands. Standing in front of Cole, Wenn tried to see his scalp but the kid was too tall to see anything above the ears.

"Bend over," said Wenn. He expertly picked through Cole's sandy colored hair looking for …

"Ugh!" he found one.

"Ewwwe," answered Cole.

"Look, if you know what's good for you, you won't tell anyone. Once they find out, you're out of here and so am I for that matter," he said imagining Dr. Brennan's glare.

"But … "

"Come by my room after dinner," he said as he walked back to the sink and turned the water on. "We'll figure this out." Disturbed by his proximity to lice, Wenn was compelled to wash his hands a second time. When he was done, he and Cole went back out into the hall as if nothing happened. The mother he had seen a few minutes before emerged from the ladies room looking spooked. She gave him a strange look then hurried down the hallway.

* * * * *

By afternoon, the temperature was up to 90 degrees. The boarding students cranked open the old casement windows and switched on their portable fans. Using the heat as an excuse, Wenn called cross-country practice early. He jumped into his car and drove a few miles into D.C. to a CVS in a crummy neighborhood. There, he bought their entire stock of lice remover; five boxes at $24.99 a piece. One for Cole, one for himself and three more to save himself another trip, because the stores on the Maryland side of the line were cleaned out of their lice supplies. At about 7:30, he was laying on his bed staring at the ceiling when there was a tentative knock on his door. "Yeah?" he answered gruffly. He had been mulling over how to handle things.

"Mr. Mann? It's Cole." He went to the door opening it a crack.

"Listen. Before we do this, I need to know if I can trust you."

"Yeah, sure. You can trust me … but I don't get it."

"Like really trust you? Like you won't share anything with anyone … even if you fuck up an exam. No one. Especially Dr. Brennan. Because I will beat the shit out of you, if you so much as think about sharing. Got it?"

"Word."

Wenn opened the door and watched as Cole entered looked around and finally spotted Gay who was in her favorite spot on his dresser.

"Whoa!" He was like a little kid when he saw Gay. He went over and started scratching her head. Gay appreciated the attention and stretched her neck around.

"You get it now?"

Cole nodded. "No worries, Mr. Mann. That's so cool. What's her name?"

"I call her Gay."

Cole looked uncomfortable. "Gay?"

"Short for Galenthias. Come on. Have a seat. We've got a job to do."

He picked up his heavy wooden desk chair like it was made of plastic and placed it in the center of the room. Cole sat down and Wenn put on the latex gloves included in the box of poison. As he was breaking the safety seal on the brown bottle, Cole's cell phone rang. "It's my mom. Is it alright?"

"Go ahead," he said.

"Hey Mom." Cole said. "Nothing. Just uh, doing Latin ... Good ... Yeah. No, I don't think I need help ... Wow, that's awesome! ... Alright. Yeah, it's tomorrow ... Hopefully ... Nope. Absolutely nothing to worry about. It's all good ... All right. Love you too. Bye." He hung up. "Sorry."

"It's cool," said Wenn proceeding with the treatment.

"She's kind of sick."

"That sucks."

"Yeah. She says she's fine, but it's hard to tell if that's the truth or if that's what she's telling us, my brother and sister and me, so we don't worry."

"Sure," said Wenn trying to imagine how he might have turned out if his mother ever kept anything from him. Probably a lot better. He poured the de-louser onto Cole's head and worked it into a lather. Then he unwrapped the balled up plastic shower cap that came in the box and carefully placed it over Cole's head.

"Alright, my turn," he said. Cole looked at him with confusion. "Get up. You're going to put a bottle of that crap on me."

"You have lice?"

"Probably not. But given the fact that you do, I'm not taking any chances."

They switched places and Cole administered the treatment to Wenn, pouring another brown bottle of potion onto his head, scrubbing until it frothed then finishing with a matching plastic shower cap.

"Twenty minutes and we can rinse this shit off," said Wenn. Cole sat down on the only other chair in the room, a folding chair Wenn used when he played guitar. "So what's happening, Cole?"

"Nothing. Really."

"How's school treating you?" Despite the fact that he had been teaching for over two years, he still couldn't relate to his students outside of the classroom. It's not like he disliked them. At least, not all of them and he certainly didn't dislike Cole. He just wasn't all that interested.

"Good. Classes are good. Football is good."

Since Cole took the initiative and answered both "How is school treating you?" and his normal follow up of "How's football (or baseball or basketball, etc.)?" his entire repertoire of stock questions for students was exhausted. He looked at the clock, eighteen minutes left. "You want a book or something?"

"No. Thanks." Cole got up to give Gay some attention.

"Where did you get her?" he asked.

"Found her. Out on a running trail and she was just this little thing in a shoebox. Meowing. I didn't have the heart to leave her there."

"Wow, so she's been here like the whole time. Since she was a kitten?"

"No. A friend was watching her for me."

"So what happened? Why'd you get her back?"

Wenn got up and switched on his record player. "You like jazz?"

"Don't really know jazz. I mean, it seems cool and all but I mostly listen to rap, a little hip-hop, even a little country. I'm pretty open-minded."

"Listen to this." He clicked his turntable on, set the needle down on the black vinyl, and watched Cole's face as he took in John Coltrane. Cole was a nice looking kid. Familiar in that same weird way that most of the faces at Prep were familiar. Cole kind of bopped his head a little to the beat. Eager to please even if it meant jamming to something he wasn't into.

"You have an older brother?" Wenn asked.

"Nope. A younger one. And a sister. This jazz is all right. I like it."

Cole's green eyes fluttered as a drip of brown goo seeped out from under his shower cap and started to roll down his temple. He wiped it away with his palm leaving a shiny sepia trail. Wenn studied the kid, the shape of his hands, the nose that was a little too small for the face, his strong chin with just a hint of fuzz on it. He had a strange feeling that he had seen him before. That more than third period Latin and head lice connected them.

"You went to Prep didn't you?" Cole asked.

"Yeah."

"Everybody says you were a beast at lacrosse."

"Yep."

"I've seen your picture in the athletic center hall of fame. Tewaarton winner. That's so awesome."

"Yep."

"So you probably work with Coach Don?"

"Not at all."

"Really? I would think you would be … "

"It's not my thing anymore. Hasn't been for a long time."

"What'd you play? Attack?" Wenn nodded indifferently. "I play attack," said Cole. There was a pause, as if Cole was getting his nerve up.

"People say you, like killed some dude in a game, once. That they called the paramedics, but the kid bled to death."

"He didn't die," said Wenn. "But it looked like he was going to die."

"What happened?"

"His helmet failed. They probably weren't as good as the helmets you guys have now. The butt of my stick broke through the face guard. Crushed his entire nose and the bone around his eye."

"Whoa."

"Yeah. It was gruesome. There was a crack in his helmet and the whole fucking thing split in half. It was like a goddamned blood bomb going off. Like his whole fucking head exploded or something. It looked like I had just slaughtered a cow. That's how much blood there was."

"What happened?"

"The kid had to have surgery. A couple actually. And no more contact sports, ever, but in the end, I guess he was fine."

"Intense!"

"Yeah."

Wenn didn't mention that the reason the back of his stick was anywhere near that guy's face was because Wenn wanted to get that motherfucker away from him. The kid was in his face the entire game. Fucking non-stop body checking him like he had something to prove. Illegal moves and the ref never called it. When he sensed the guy coming around on his right side, he lifted his stick so the kid ran into it at full speed. Who ever heard of a helmet splitting in two? Jesus, there was a lot of blood. Massive. And it haunted him. The sight of blood never fails to make him nauseous. They ruled the play an accident. The helmet shouldn't have broken. But in his heart, he knew the stick shouldn't have been there either. He was responsible and it terrified him. What terrified him even more was knowing that the same ugly beast that ruled over the first 24 years of his life was still in there. He was reined in, but under the right circumstances, Wenn knew he would surface in a flash.

"You must love it here. To come back and be a teacher and all."

"Not really."

"Huh? Then why do you stay?"

Youth and all its promise, here in the middle of his room, with a head full of brown goo under a cheap ass plastic shower cap, was asking him why he was here. Why indeed? What a ridiculously obvious question. One that until now, it had never even occurred to him to ask himself much less ponder the answer to. He sat there for a moment. Half stunned, half irritated. Then without a word, he got up and started rifling around the one shelf in his bookcase that wasn't crammed full of books. The one where he kept his shampoo and deodorant and the stuff he used instead of food.

"What are you looking for?"

"Tea."

"I'm boiling. Don't you think it's way too hot for tea?" said Cole.

There wasn't much actual food on the shelf. Some powdered protein mix. Zero calorie powdered sports beverage. An old jar of peanut butter in case he needed a quick protein fix. There had been a couple of nights that he had to scoop a handful of that shit out of the jar and try to swallow it so he'd have enough energy to make it down to the kitchen for some real food.

"Ah ha!" he said as he pulled out his box of Lipton tea. Cole looked befuddled as Wenn removed the top layer of white paper wrapped tea bags and pulled out a small zip lock bag of weed.

-twenty-

MAD DOG

They say that vigilantes are made not born. That some miscarriage of justice, either calculated or completely random, pushes a normal psyche over the edge of reason and into the deep dark ravine of believing that it alone can prevail against the forces of evil. For Batman, it was a trip to the movie theater. For Bernard Goetz, it was a subway ride. For Pups MacArthur, it was a twelve-hour span of time that started with Patrick's horrific account of the Battle of Crater, circa 2012, and ended with Brownie troop 251's Bridge ceremony. Both events caused considerable head scratching, one cerebral—why would Patrick do such a thing? The other, completely corporeal, until Pups plucked Maddox and Cady out of the school lost and found, tied plastic grocery bags around their heads and gave them "the treatment" within minutes of returning home that night. For the moment, the lice were under control, but Patrick ...

Of all the questions percolating in her mind, the one that bubbled its way to the top was, why did he feel compelled to share this indiscretion with her? When asked, he could think of nothing more than "I don't know." After twenty-four hours of non-stop grilling he came up with, "I've always told you everything. I couldn't live with myself if I didn't tell you."

"That makes two of us," said Pups. The non-stop grilling stopped and gelid silence began. In her gut, she wanted to throw him out, but Pups was practical and a mother first. She understood that any such action would devastate her children as much as Patrick's pillaging of their marriage had devastated her. So instead, she stewed; mulling over the fundamental unfairness of her situation and letting her responsibilities go. She spent considerable time on the sofa staring up at the ceiling light whose luminance was dimmed by a collection of dead stinkbugs piled inside the glass cover. There must have been fifty dead bugs in that thing. She had asked Patrick about a million times to take care of it, but it never got done. She would have done it herself if she knew how to get the cover off, but she didn't so all she could do was wait for Patrick to find the time to take care of it. That light, those stinkbugs, her dependence on that procrastinating cheat of a husband, together they added up to something.

That's when a light bulb went off in her head. A clear brilliant illumination unobstructed by stinkbugs. At that very moment, lice were feasting upon the scalps of half the student body of Holy Family, but lice were not the problem. The problem was the parents of Holy Family who couldn't do the job themselves. They were too foolish or too busy or too afraid or too non-English speaking; these people were waiting around, doing nothing, living with a problem they were incapable of solving and in the process, they were unfairly inflicting the problem right back on the good citizens who thought they had conquered the infestation once and for all.

When she wasn't thinking about head lice, she tried to wrap her head around the fact that the man who promised her his undying fidelity had fallen prey to a Vietnamese Clara Barton impersonator and in the mock hysteria of a simulated battle, inflicted such genuine hurt, such gnawing disgust, such complete and utter disillusionment, that Pups felt like a rabid raccoon, ready to attack anything that happened by. All the petty grievances she resisted getting emotionally involved in; dumb rules, drivers who cut her off, children who didn't listen, husbands who let her down and people who asked for more than their fair share, blended into one thick slurry of outrage. She became a warrior ready to fight. And hers was a genuine battle, not a stupid simulated re-enactment. All she needed was a target.

Given her circumstances and frame of mind, it didn't take long before her seething rage was channeled into fighting the scourge of the community; not wayward husbands, or comic book criminals or opportunistic Civil War sluts. Under the non-threatening guise of a simple suburban mom named Pups MacArthur, "Mad Dog" set out to conquer injustice. Her campaign started innocently enough. Pretending to drop off Girl Scout information or collect money for a class gift to a teacher, Pups dropped by a few "high probability" houses. While there, she casually mentioned that, as the mother of five little heads, she had done her share of lice hunting and considered herself a bit of an expert. Would you like me to check your child/grandchild/niece/nephew or person you were employed to babysit? No one ever turned her down. She was a well-respected leader of the community. A person who was genuinely concerned about people. If Pups found what she was looking for, an active case of Pediculosis, she volunteered to treat the problem on the spot, and when she left, everyone was happy.

With Pups off crusading, her family had to fend for themselves. Although there wasn't an aspect of their lives she didn't have complete control over, her sudden absence was far less traumatic than she or they would have imagined. Dinners were less nutritious, but nobody seemed to mind. On Mondays, they ate store-baked rotisserie chicken because the Safeway offered two for the price of one. The rest of the week they ate sandwiches, giant foil trays of frozen casseroles from Costco and Virginia's new specialty, Kraft mac and cheese.

Pups regretted leaving her kids to pursue her cause, but she didn't regret for a minute being away from Patrick. They barely spoke—and then only to exchange important information like when to pick the kids up from soccer practice or what to do about the constantly running toilet in the downstairs bathroom. She found herself thinking about his transgression more often than she would have liked. Wondering about the few details she had yet to extract from him. The saddest part of all of it was that her marriage was one thing in her life that was exactly how she wanted it. Functional and low maintenance. They always had sex on Father's Day and Patrick's birthday. There were attempts at sex on Mother's Day and her birthday, but Pups was always too tired and asked for a rain check she never cashed in. On the odd occasion that Pups was in the mood, Patrick wasn't around. Sometimes she fantasized about being with someone like the Roger Cabot, one of the younger dads at the school and the coach of Willa's soccer team. It was exciting at first, but soon Pups would realize that wildest part of her fantasy wasn't the sex, it was the fact that she was actually relaxed and enjoying the moment, instead of calculating how much time she had before she had to move on to the next item on her to do list. The notion of letting go that much was too much of a fantasy, like imagining she could fly—too far out to be much fun.

Two weeks of casually calculated "drop by's" left Pups exhausted and disheartened. She had treated more little heads than she could count. The entire inside lining of her nose was denuded by chemical fumes. And even though she was getting a steep volume discount from Mr. Tran, all those brown bottles were costing her plenty. To top it all off, four of the sixteen families she treated had already been re-infected. Pups needed a plan so Judy Pillson's phone call couldn't have come at a better time.

After some small talk, Judy got down to business. "So how on earth can we defend ourselves?"

Flattered to be asked, Pups laid out her two-point plan. First and foremost, they needed to re-instate the no-nit policy. Without it, there was no hope. Second, she wanted to outfit all of the children with kerchiefs or do-rags, once they were deemed "clean."

"Great concept, but what about when they take

those things off and start sharing them?" asked Judy, playing the devil's advocate.

Instantly recognizing a kindred soul, Pups felt a surge of adrenaline. "I've thought about that. We need an official policy that makes any attempt to remove a head covering during school hour as grounds for early dismissal. With that in place, I think we might have a shot. Also, the children could personalize their head coverings so it would be fairly easy to spot any borrowing."

"I love it!" screamed Judy. "Pups you think of everything!"

They had a plan, but they couldn't do it alone. They needed a battalion of moms to fan out into the community for impromptu head checks. She was sure a group could prevail where she alone could not. When she hung up the phone, Pups felt more optimistic than she had in weeks. Recruiting foot soldiers in their war against head lice was easy. All they needed to do was ask. Even Angie who never got involved in anything, was among twenty mothers gathered in Judy's knotty pine paneled family room sipping pink zinfandel and listening to Pups reveal the secrets of lice busting. These were not just regular mothers; these were the movers and the shakers of Holy Family. The head of the parents' association, scout leaders, soccer coaches, room mothers, lunchroom volunteers, playground helpers, and even the volunteer nurse, Mrs. Digby who had seen first hand the ravages of Ms. Gagner's no no-nit policy. At 9:45 p.m., the ladies scurried out to their station wagons, minivans and SUV's to deal with laundry, lunches, and little ones at home. On subsequent nights, there were lessons on treatment strategies, (a two-parter due to the complexity of the material), bedding and upholstery, and stuffed animals. The ladies agreed it was best to keep their plans secret during the training phase. They didn't want to look like a bunch of schemers trying to overthrow Ms. Gagner's policy.

"What could happen?" asked Judy boldly. "I mean if the entire school signs a petition requesting head coverings and reinstatement of the no-nit policy, is she really going to challenge it?" To answer that question, you had to know Ms. Gagner.

Some things never change. That's what people used to say about Holy Family before Ms. Krista Gagner became the principal. Young and hip, from the minute Ms. Gagner entered the building, almost everything about the 63-year-old institution changed. Lunches had to be nutritious. Sugary drinks were not allowed on the premises during school hours. The front table in the cafeteria used to be reserved for all the misbehavers. Now, it's the lunchroom Siberia for the children who bring peanut butter sandwiches for lunch. Ms. Gagner did not believe in subjecting the three peanut allergic children enrolled in the school to any kind of ostracism, preferring instead, to give the regular kids a hard time for being uncaring enough to eat peanut butter. People grumbled, but no one did anything about it. Who's going to take a stand for junk food? Or peanuts for that matter?

When her sweeping modernization extended beyond lunch, she really started to rub parents the wrong way. First, she modified the science program, outlawing any lab experiment involving living creatures. No earthworms, no frogs and no bug collections. For a while, she also banned the growing of mold fearing it would lead classes down the slippery slope of investigating bigger and more complex organisms but Mr. Newton the science teacher had a chat with her and in that case at least, reason prevailed. Next, she banned all student elections, essay contests, and even team sports in gym class because competition sent the "wrong message." Instead, she promoted "team building" with everyone, the entire school, on one big team. Next, she abolished any kind of skill level grouping in the classroom. She would have eliminated grade levels too, but such a bold move would have brought in the archdiocese. There were no high reading groups or low reading groups—just reading chairs like musical chairs. If there was an open chair, you could discuss the assigned book with your peers. If all the chairs were filled, you'd have to wait for the next discussion.

Then, Ms. Gagner, with her hand knit sweaters and earrings carved out of recycled phone cards by villagers in Kenya, did the unthinkable. She started messing around with school traditions. The Halloween party was no more; long live the new Pumpkin Festival. That pissed off a lot of parents. The next thing to be "Gagner-ized" was the venerable Thanksgiving feast. It started out as it had for decades, with the kindergarteners filing onto the small wooden stage, half of them outfitted in fake suede ponchos, feather headdresses, and moccasins and the other half wearing buckled shoes, starched white collared shirts, black hats and puritan bonnets. Pups dressed Cady in the same Pocahontas dress that Virginia and Willa had worn. They sang "Five Little

Turkey's" and "Thank you Lord for this Food." And then Ms. Gagner took the mic.

"I want to thank our many supporters for your presence here today and for all those generous contributions of turkey, to-furky, cranberry sauce and pumpkin pie both vegan and regular that our students will enjoy at the conclusion of this presentation. Before we end, I would like to introduce a new tradition into the annual Holy Family Thanksgiving feast. Giving thanks is not uniquely American. It's universal. So in the spirit of the universe, we will conclude this year's presentation with a performance of a Swahili song and dance of thanksgiving that is performed at the annual yam festival in Swaziland. Of course, yams are an integral part of most Thanksgiving feasts, so I thought this would be an appropriate way to end our celebration."

With that, 25 pilgrims and 23 Indians started chanting Swahili and hopping around the stage while raising their arms in the air. They were having a blast. The audience, however, was horrified. They weren't even speaking English. On Thanksgiving. The most American of holidays! She heard from a lot of parents the next day, but Ms. Gagner did not back down and even insinuated that to challenge her re-tooling of the age old Thanksgiving program was as good as coming out and admitting you were a racist. In fact, once Ms. Gagner made a change whether it was the Christmas pageant or the playground policy; it stuck no matter who complained. Reversing the no no-nit policy and revising the uniform policy wouldn't be easy, but Pups and her cohorts were determined to take her on.

"What if someone doesn't sign the petition?"

asked Mrs. Digby.

"Look around," said Alice Roarback, the head of the parents association. "If someone doesn't feel like signing our petition, well then, their kid doesn't play on Cathy's soccer team, or get into Nancy's cub scout troop, or any of the millions of things the people in this very room run and control."

In the evenings, the "Pink Zin Girls" as they now called themselves brought sharp scissors, straight pins and sewing machines to Judy's house and made 250 red kerchiefs and 250 black do-rags while sipping more pink zin. During the day, they fanned out into the neighborhoods. Traveling in pairs, they would roll up to an unsuspecting house, knock on the door and explain that they were working with the parents association to get the head lice problem under control.

"We believe the best way to reduce the transmission rate is to cover the children's' heads while they are at school. We also want the no-nit policy re-instated."

If the mother looked like she wasn't sure about signing for some reason, Pink Zin Girls were instructed to jump in with some upbeat observation like "Sammy sure is a wonder out on the baseball diamond. Coach Filbert's one of our biggest supporters what with those batting helmets and all."

Once the signature had been obtained, the Pink Zin Girls would casually say, "Before we go, do you want us to check your kids? We're sort of experts and honestly, we don't mind." Without exception, the parents agreed. If they found "an active case," they would call it in to Mrs. Digby back at headquarters who would schedule a follow up by a treatment team in the next twelve to twenty-four hours. Exhausted parents happily accepted the help and most offered to pay for the luxury. When they had 498 signatures, Pups made an appointment with Ms. Gagner. Should Gagner refuse either demand, Pups and the Pink Zin Girls had their petition to back them up. On the fateful morning, Pups pulled her Suburban into the lot and parked alongside Judy's green minivan. Judy hopped into the back seat of the Suburban.

"Good morning fearless leader!" she chirped. "All ready?"

"I don't know," said Pups starting to think this was all a very bad idea.

"You're going to be great. We all believe in you, Pups. And don't worry about a thing. Maddox and I will be here playing until you get out." Pups put on lipstick and smoothed her hair. "She's used to parents barging in, trying to strong arm her. I suggest you butter her up. Ask her about the new recycling program or the greywater project. Then once she's all loose and receptive, gently ease into the subject. You'll have her eating out of your hand in no time."

"Yeah, as long as what's in my hand is vegan!" Pups marched into the school full of confidence. Judy was right. They were fighting the proverbial good fight. Unfortunately, Ms. Gagner believed she was fighting not just the good fight but also the politically, ecologically, socially and morally correct fight.

"Good morning, Mrs. MacArthur," said Ms. Gagner warmly extending her hand.

"Thanks for seeing me," said Pups. "My goodness, you've done wonders with this office. It's so ... interesting. When this was Sister's office, well, it was nowhere near as fun as this." In little more than a year, Ms. Gagner had managed to turn Sister Mary Faith's Spartan office into a cluttered junk-laden eco workshop. Everywhere you looked, was something that was eco, green, organic, sustainable, fair-traded or recycled. What used to be a workspace steeped in faith was now a workspace steeped in Kombucha tea. Gone were Sister Mary Faith's framed copies of the Lord's Prayer and the Hail Mary, replaced by a poster of a vaguely ethnic woman preparing a meal in a typical American kitchen. Black dots speckled the woman, the room, and the food she was preparing. Upon closer inspection, the black dots were actually bugs. "If frogs go extinct, you'll know" was written across the top of the picture. "Yes. I re-decorated," said Ms. Gagner. "Or should I say, re-purposed. Everything you see here used to be somewhere else. Too much waste."

"Absolutely."

"The Lord gives us so much and what do we do? We mess it up. We pollute and we decimate. We use and we don't replenish. Our culture glorifies the fastest solution, the quickest route, the easiest way when just the slightest bit more effort might actually be the solution God wants us to choose." Ms. Gagner stared out the window, as if, at that very moment she was searching for some slow, inefficient and expensive God approved eco-solution to a problem. "So, what can I do for you?" she asked.

"I'm here as a concerned parent. One of many

concerned parents as a matter of fact."

"Excuse me Mrs. MacArthur, but I'm trying to move away from the label "parent" and use "special person" instead. It's less judgmental. We don't want to stigmatize children who are being raised by grandparents or are in some other guardianship situation."

"Okay, as I was saying, this on-going, eh … problem with the lice has been a nightmare for all of us … special people."

"I know. It's been awful. Imagine how much valuable teaching time we would have lost if the children had been forced to miss school."

Pups smarted from the swift sharp sting of Ms. Gagner's first wallop. "Yes. Um. Actually, that's why I'm here. To talk about the no-nit policy. We'd like you to consider re-instating it. The entire school of parents … "

"Special people."

"Sorry, special people believe that the only way to get this problem under control is through a no-nit policy."

"I see."

"Um. We also think that it would be prudent to have the children wear head coverings until this problem is completely arrested."

"Head coverings? Like hats?"

"Yes. Um. We've actually made kerchiefs for the girls and do-rags for the boys."

"Do rags?" asked Ms. Gagner, stifling a smirk.

"Yes. They're like caps that boys wear … " Pups felt overwhelmed. The idea of being mocked by the likes of Krista Gagner was making her sweat.

"Oh, I'm familiar with do-rags, alright. Just not in the context of what makes an appropriate uniform for a Catholic school."

"Of course, but these are … extraordinary times."

"You've obviously given this a lot of thought."

"Actually, I have … " said Pups taking a deep breath as she readied herself to state her demands.

"Mrs. MacArthur, while I certainly empathize with what everyone is going through, I hope you understand that the school itself is also impacted. The teachers, the administration, we are all impacted. But it is my job, as principal to ensure that one thing is not impacted—the education of our students. A no-nit policy stands in direct contradiction to that mission."

"But, we believe that NO no-nit policy is impacting the education of our children. It is also impacting their health and their home life."

"I'm sorry about that, but I disagree," said Ms. Gagner digging the cruelty free rubber heels of her Toms One for One shoes further into her organic turf.

"What about the head coverings?"

"I disagree with that too. I'm not sure where such an idea originated but … "

"Except for the Wollacks and the Clamps, every single family in the school signed our petition," said Pups handing Ms. Gagner a stack of papers.

"Couldn't get the Wollacks or the Clamps, huh? I'm not surprised," said Ms. Gagner pretending to read the petition. "Mrs. MacArthur, my decision is final. Our current school policies will remain in place. So unless there is anything else … "

Pups was outraged. She stood up to leave but realized that her one big hurrah was about to be over. It was the first, last, and only time she would see the principal without being labeled a troublemaker and greeted with attitude, or a schedule that had no openings. Determined not to let her golden moment pass by with nothing to show for it, she turned back to Ms. Gagner and said, "Now that you mention it, there is one thing."

"What's that?"

"How dare you monkey with Thanksgiving."

"I'm sorry?" said Ms. Gagner, taken aback.

"Thanksgiving. You can't just willy-nilly make it an international appreciation day. It's American. Americans giving thanks for America. Can you tell me why the Thanksgiving program that we have done for eons suddenly wasn't good enough?"

"Mrs. MacArthur, it's not a question of good enough. The traditional pageant was wonderful. It's just that times change, and it was time to be a little more inclusive. That's all."

"Inclusive? If by inclusive you mean, everyone is welcome to join in—of course. But if inclusive means expanding the meaning and the intent and the origins of the most American of American holidays? No. A foreign song has no place in our Thanksgiving pageant."

"That song had every right to be in the show. We live in a free country. One that allows us to sing any song from any country on holidays or any other days. In other countries, people are persecuted if they sing American songs at their holiday pageants because they aren't free."

"Is that so?" said Pups. "So you're telling me that, in Swaziland, they would sing "Five Little Turkeys" at their annual yam festival if they could, but they can't because they fear persecution?"

"Yes."

"Persecution from authorities? Like thought control? Or persecution from other Swahilis who might think that singing American songs at their yam fest is ridiculous. And disrespectful. And if you're all for singing American songs, maybe you're not getting invited to the neighborhood yam fest potluck. There's persecution, and there's persona non grata. There is a difference," said Pups.

"Mrs. MacArthur, we're way off topic here. And I do have a busy schedule today."

"Sure." Pups turned to leave, but first, she had to ask, "Ms. Gagner, I was just wondering, is Holy Family free of persecution."

"Meaning … ?"

"I mean, some of the … special people think you keep a record of special people's visits to your office?

Something you might review when it's time to bestow character awards on those special people's children. Will this go into my children's file?"

"Mrs. MacArthur. As you said yourself, there's persecution ... and there's persona non grata." She smiled sweetly and tapped the brown, natural fiber folder in front of her.

-twenty-one-

CONFESSION

The day after the cupcake war, Brophy was sent home from school. Again. This time, he would not be invited back until he had a physician's note certifying him as lice free. If he had escaped being labeled common, freeloading trash before, now it was a done deal. Mary Ellen had no idea what people were saying since she had cut off all contact with Claudia, the only Prep insider she considered a friend. Jackie Johnson called a few times but never left a message. Mary Ellen assumed she was looking for her deposit money. Jackie seemed like such a decent person, she was tempted to take a chance and answer it, but in the end she figured that rich people don't like being ripped off any more than poor people and just let it ring.

She could write a manual detailing the ins and outs of virtually every delouser on the market, from all natural tea tree oil to prescription strength lindane which the package insert says is toxic to the brain and can cause seizures in people who weigh less than one hundred pounds. What she couldn't write about is how to effectively rid your family from this pestilence, once and for all, because no matter what she did, they returned. And each time they returned, they were stronger and more resilient than before.

Lice were not the only things making Mary Ellen's headache. Each day, the Packinghams fell a bit deeper into the hole they had gotten themselves into, and at some point, probably soon, they would hit the bottom of said hole and then what? Sit there and wait for someone or something to lift them out of it? And who would that be? Kenny? Ha! Things were so bad that being pulled out of their misery by some external force was such an implausible resolution that not even Mary Ellen, with all her fairy dust and beautiful endings could come up with a decent rescue fantasy. When Mary Ellen found a stray twenty-dollar bill in the pocket of a coat she hadn't worn since last year, she felt like she had won the lottery.

Throwing caution to the wind, she decided to spend her windfall on ... herself. She pulled her special pants out of the drawer and high tailed it over to Humble Warrior Studio. James greeted her like the prodigal daughter saying, "Mary Ellen! You're back!"

"Hi. Yes, just a drop in."

"That's wonderful. It's wonderful to see you."

"Here you go." She handed him the twenty-dollar bill. "Great," said James leaning in and lowering his voice. "Thanks for giving us another chance, *everything* has been dealt with." He raised his eyebrows and nodded his head as if the two of them shared a special secret.

"What?" she asked, immediately thinking that he was somehow referring to her credit card issues.

"*They* have been dealt with."

Another pronoun. Mary Ellen stared blankly, so James leaned closer and whispered, "You know. The L- I – C –E." Mary Ellen was shocked.

"You mean … you had … "

"Boy oh boy did we. Lost a ton of customers. Regulars like you. We finally took those darned Navajo blankets out back and burned them. Yep, just set them ablaze while we chanted. And now, the air is clear and we've got nothing but good karma."

"Great."

"Oh yeah. That's totally behind us. Suki … well, she kind of took the whole thing personally, but anyway, welcome back and Namaste." The studio looked the same except for the empty shelves that used to hold the lovely Navaho blankets. The room was only about half full, some new people and some of the old regulars.

Mary Ellen offered a smile to the few familiar faces and unrolled her mat. She really needed this. The muscles in her back and shoulders felt like they had seized. Whenever she moved her neck, she heard a bunch of cracking sounds and her jaw was tight from gritting her teeth so much. She hoped a good relaxing stretch would help her feel a little more like her old self.

She couldn't stop thinking about what she heard in the bathroom at Prep. Was it possible that she had somehow misconstrued the situation? Once you opened your mouth about these things, your statement defines you. Could she stand to be "the mother who called Wenn Mann a sexual predator," for the next four years? If he threatens murder for simply inquiring about your kid's grade, what's he do when you accuse him of deviance? On the other hand, she felt that what she heard was something that needed to be revealed. If that wicked man was really doing anything to that boy ... the mother in her was sickened at the very thought.

Suki, looking a lot more buff than Mary Ellen remembered, marched into the studio. She turned the heat up, dimmed the lights and punched a few buttons on the iPod station feeding the sound system. Holding the remote audio controller, she asked the class to take a comfortable seat.

"Place you hands at your heart center, consider what possibilities this day holds for you. And inhale."

The class took a collective breath. "And as you exhale, consider something else ... " Suki pumped up the volume way past normal yoga class mood music. A heavy base with an equally heavy drumbeat filled the room so thoroughly Mary Ellen could actually feel the rhythm flowing through her.

" ... consider what you are going to make of those possibilities. Are you going to passively observe what the universe offers or are you going to stir things up?" Suki shouted over the driving beat. "I mean, a lot of you set your intention each day. And what is it? To be accepting? To be joyful? To be connected? Inhale."

The class breathed inward.

"All that is fine, but really, when you think about it, it's bullshit. Who needs accepted when you can accomplish? Who needs connected when you can conquer? Design your own destiny, don't just accept it." Suki pushed a few buttons on the remote control. "And if any of you are offended by the word "fuck," I apologize." As if on cue, the voice of Eminem rose up over the instruments. Mary Ellen was amused. Imagine, her being offended by the word fuck. Her. Wife of the original white rapper, Kenny "The Fuck-King" Packingham. It was a song Mary Ellen had heard many times on the radio while driving the kids around. Mostly, she ignored it, but given Suki's introduction, she paid close attention to the lyrics.

"DOWN DOG. PLANK," commanded Suki. "CHATURANGA. UP DOG." The pace was much quicker than the slow deliberate stretching Mary Ellen was used to. Within minutes, she was panting in the heat and working hard to keep up.

"DOWN DOG. THREE BREATHS. And while you're doing all that breathing, ask yourself, what you set out to be? Are you doing it? Are you tearing down those balconies? WARRIOR ONE, LIKE YOU FUCKING MEAN IT."

All at once, Mary Ellen felt overwhelmed. She was doing nothing. Not tearing down balconies. Not stirring up the pot. Not doing anything more than spraying the giant steaming pile of shit that was her life with Febreze.

"RAISE YOUR RIGHT LEG," Suki barked out orders but sometimes the volume of the music drowned her out. As Eminem continued to spew, the women in the class moved with militaristic precision from one pose to the next. "If you think the music is too loud and you can't hear my calls," said Suki. "Just do whatever the fuck you feel like doing."

The music wasn't too loud, Mary Ellen heard Suki just fine. But after years of hearing much worse spewed directly at her from the person who was supposed to be her soul mate, she had an epiphany. She was offended. Offended by the language and the venom and the plain ugliness of it all. Offended that yoga, like the rest of her life was now full of obscenities. She rolled up her mat. And she left.

* * * * *

"Bless me Father for I have sinned. I haven't been to confession in ... well, it's been ages."

Mary Ellen worshipped many things; high society, designer clothing, and exquisite interior design among them. God, not so much. At least not in a genuine faith sort of way. For her, Catholicism was more like a club she belonged to. It put her in a certain circle and to stay in that circle she had to profess the same beliefs espoused by everyone else in the circle. It's not like she disagreed with those beliefs. The trinity, the saints, the sacraments, they were all honky dory. Her parents had raised her as a Catholic, and she just followed the path they had set her on. She made her first communion and would have made her confirmation if not for her mother's hiatus from life. Now she took her own children to church when she could and sent them to Catholic school so they would learn the faith in a way she never had. It was a fine religion. Admirable even. And she hoped her children would find some sort of peace or inspiration in it. She didn't. It never offered her any comfort. At least not in the same way a new purse or new shoes did.

And now here she was in a confessional, a place she hadn't been to since she was nine-years-old. What sins could she possibly have confessed to at the age of nine? And how many sins had she racked up over the past thirty years? She was supposed to go to confession when her children received the sacraments, but she and Kenny, and most of the other parents, for that matter, clung to the sticky wooden church pews as their children marched off to rid themselves of guilt and affirm their relationship with the church. The fact that she hadn't gone then made the fact that she was here now—in the chapel at Washington Prep on a cold October day to confess her sins to Father Bills—strange indeed.

Getting to this point. Seeing this act as a reasonable solution to a difficult situation was a long and exhausting process of asking tough questions and searching her soul for difficult answers. All this, during a time of nearly unbearable duress exacerbated by her total estrangement from Claudia. If Claudia didn't see Brophy as one of *"them"* there was no point in continuing their relationship, but it would have been so much better to have someone like Claudia to help her through this. Mary Ellen pushed those demons to the back of her mind.

"Welcome back, my child. We've been waiting for you," said a cheerful Father Bills, sliding confessional screen open, so they could hear each other.

"Really? Thank you."

"Yes. Of course, our door is always open. No matter how long it's been."

Delivered as it was by a priest, sitting in an ornate broom closet within a magnificent palace of a chapel that was situated on the campus of an exclusive boys academy, in a wealthy part of the most powerful region of the country—the world for that matter—it was hard to accept his statement at face value. Who was that door open to if no one but Prep students, former students and their families even knew this chapel existed?

"Thank you, Father."

"What brings you here today?" he asked.

Mary Ellen took a breath and reminded herself that she was doing something good. The right thing, but at the moment, it didn't feel very right.

"So ... I, um, tell you my sins now?"

"Yes."

"Okay. Um, I have lied. I have had impure thoughts. I was looking over the list of things you are supposed to ask yourself before you confess, and honestly, in thirty years, I've probably done all of it. But mostly I have coveted. I'm a big time coveter."

"I see."

"You know how the commandment says thou shalt not covet thy neighbor's ass? I literally did just that. I know that's not what was meant, but that's why I started going to yoga. Anyhow, I am truly blessed. And in my heart, I know that. But for some reason, Father, I can't see it. All I can see is what I don't have."

"Why do you think that is?"

"I don't know."

"'For where your treasure is, there also will your heart be.' That's Matthew. Maybe you need to find your treasure."

"Okay." Mary Ellen wanted enlightenment but his words only confused her.

"Are you sorry for all your sins?"

"Yes."

"I want you to say three Our Father's. Now, my child, make an act of contrition." Father Bills started to mumble words of prayer.

"Hold it. Is that it?"

"Pretty much."

"Oh, well. I have something else I wanted to tell you. It's not about me exactly. It's about someone else. Someone who works here at the school."

"You're going to confess on someone else's behalf?"

"No, I need to tell you something … something I think someone else should confess, because it was wrong. But, I don't think he will, so I'm going to do it for him."

"I don't understand. If you have a problem with the school, you should make an appointment with Dr. Brennan. This is … "

"I know that. But I don't want to talk to him. I

don't want to be involved. I just want you to know about it. Something I witnessed here that I feel I must confess ... in good conscience. Even though it had nothing to do with me."

"I'm afraid you lost me."

"Father ... I was in the ladies room. The one near the college counseling office. And you know how the wall ends and there's still about five feet of open space before you get to the ceiling? And on the other side of the wall, is the men's room?"

"I never really thought about it, but now that you mention it, I suppose I do."

"When I was in the ladies room, I distinctly heard ... um ... a teacher having ... relations with a student."

"In the ladies room?"

"No! Gosh. No, I was in the ladies' room. They were in the men's room."

"I see. And you know what they were doing because ... "

"I heard them Father. I saw the teacher walk into the men's room. Then I went into the ladies room. While I was in there, I heard them."

"You need to be more specific. Miss, I really don't think this is the right place ... "

Mary Ellen took a gulp of air. "I heard the teacher's voice say, 'Bend over.' And then after a pause, I heard him make a loud growl. And I heard the boy kind of squeal. And then I heard the teacher tell the boy not to tell anyone about it or they would both have to leave the school."

There was a long silence on the other side of the partition. Finally, Father Bills said, "How do you know it was a student?"

"Because when I walked out of the ladies room, I saw them, the teacher and the student. They were walking out of the men's room."

"I see." Another long pause, followed by "Do you know who it was?"

* * * * *

The sun was beginning to set, and the wind cut through her camelhair coat as she hurried to her car. She had parked over by the athletic center so no one in the chapel could watch her get into a car; a precaution in case anyone in the chapel recognized her. She was being overly cautious. Hardly anyone went to confession—especially here. When she entered the chapel, she saw that her hunch was correct. There was an elderly woman praying the rosary in the front pew and two old men wearing black overcoats in the center. A young man was arranging things on the altar, preparing for the 6:00 Mass. Now, a mere twenty minutes after she had arrived, all of the dread and foreboding she felt had evaporated. It was hard to say whether it was the unburdening of her own sins or the confession of someone else's that made her feel so giddy. She practically skipped the last few yards to her car.

She started the motor, turned up the heat and as she reached down to release the parking break, all those good feelings vanished. The beautiful gold medallion from her right Tory Burch flat was gone. Completely missing. She was wearing one beautiful embellished shoe on her left foot and an ugly naked one on her right. She stepped out of the car and looked around, but it wasn't there. It was somewhere between the car and the chapel, but she couldn't very well go back. That would blow everything. Those shoes cost so much. She loved them so much. And now, she couldn't wear them. Ever. And there was no way she could replace them. Not now.

-twenty-two-

MRS. ROBINSON

"**D**o you have a tux?" Five of the sweetest words ever said over a cell phone. Do you have a tux? She wanted to see him. She was back and she wanted to see him. Elation. "Sure do." The truth, of course, was no. Not unless you count the white dinner jacket and black trousers with the satin stripe down the leg he wore to his high school prom. A bit too 007 for anyone over the age of eighteen and besides, it was currently in the closet at his parents house. He could rent one just as easily. It had been over three weeks since they talked. Hearing her voice, knowing that she didn't want it to end, at least not yet, gave him new life. She told him she had gone by Monty's on Wednesday hoping to surprise him, but was surprised herself when he wasn't there. Phinn, who incidentally is very sweet, she said, told her that Jazz Wednesday had been suspended until further notice.

He winced at the memory of Jazz Wednesday. One bit of poetry in his otherwise prosaic existence. Gone. Snatched by a conniving witch. A witch who discovered creatures in her head. And since she wasn't a total slut of a witch, she had no trouble figuring out who left those creatures there. Perhaps if he had called her back or taken her to dinner, all this could have been avoided. But when it was clear to Cullen that she had been used and discarded, she did what any modern young internet savvy witch would do, she whipped up a witches brew of vitriol and hard feelings and cast an electronic spell that annihilated Monty's Jazz Wednesdays. She went on the Socials website and posted a rant so vile and so detailed, there was no mistaking which local louse gave her lice. Eschewing all things modern, Wenn had never seen a blog, never posted a post, and declined the frequent email invitations to join Socials. So Wenn was the last to know that from Dupont Circle to Adams Morgan, young Washingtonians were enjoying the online adventure story known as LiceMann. He knew something was up when he arrived at Monty's and as usual, opened his arms towards Phinn for the traditional Prep alum hug/greeting and the big guy jumped back like he was covered in shit and told him Bric needed to see him. "Dude, I know it's stupid. But that stuff really registers with my customers. Bugs and booze don't mix. We're going to have to put this jazz thing on hold until it all blows over. We can't have the entertainment giving customers the willies now can we?" With his perpetually red eyes and bulging belly, Bric was the spitting image of his fat fuck of a father. A guy who made millions buying and selling stuff you could never hold in your hand. Wenn left Monty's, vowing never to return. Fuck them.

"Yeah, they're putting in a make-your-own-taco bar. They need the space," he lied.

"I want to see you. I'm going to this thing tomorrow night. Black tie. My escort bailed on me. So if you're game … "

Escort? Hoping it wasn't Todd Baylor he was replacing, Wenn gave her an enthusiastic, "Sure. Sounds great." He didn't give what the "thing" might be, a second's thought.

"I've got the company car with a driver tomorrow. We'll pick you up at your place and go from there." His place? Fuck. What was the address of his place again? He looked around his desk for the yellow slip of paper on which he wrote the key points of his fake life. "What's your address?"

Address. Where was it? He held the phone at arms length and started to talk. "It's in … " He pushed the end call button then switched the whole thing off so when she called back it would go straight to voicemail.

* * * * *

Standing outside The Bethesda Arms, a nondescript apartment building on Elm Street for what seemed like hours, Wenn watched a bunch of teenage girls practicing some kind of cheer in the park across the street. They were flailing their arms and stomping their feet in unison. He wondered why. What's cheering going to accomplish?

A bunch of other whys filled his thoughts. Why did he break down and fuck Cullen? Why didn't Elizabeth ask him to this thing first? Why would a professor at Georgetown live in a shitty apartment in Bethesda? And why hadn't he thought his transportation situation through better? Since meeting Elizabeth, the pile of pink parking tickets on his night table had grown. He meant to pay them, but he had run out of paper checks and didn't own a credit card so settling up required him to physically go to the DMV with his debit card. Bethesda was in Maryland and the tickets were from D.C., but he was pretty sure they were close enough to share information. He couldn't risk getting another ticket, or worse, a boot on his tire, so he took a bus down Rockville Pike to Bethesda. As he stood there, in a black tux with a black satin vest and a black bow tie, he realized how stupid his plan was. If he didn't go home with Elizabeth, she would drop him off here. How late do buses run anyway? Walking or running back to Prep didn't bother him, but what if it's pouring down rain? What about the tux?

A black Lincoln Town Car pulled down the deserted street. "Sorry, we're late," she said when he opened the back door. "Totally my fault. I could not get ... " He climbed in and not listening to a word she was saying, he leaned in to kiss her. She kissed him back. All was right with the world. "I missed you," he said coming up for air and looking into her eyes.

"Oh my God, what happened to your hair?" she said with that same kind of horrified look Phinn had given him.

"Right. My hair," he said feeling the top of his hair for some kind of answer. He had grown so accustomed to his emerging tonsure, he almost forgot about it. Cole's locks hadn't faired much better. As mind expanding as ever, that doobie they shared sent Wenn on a long whimsical tangent where it became absolutely necessary to teach the young man about the finer shadings of jazz guitar. While sampling Django Reinhardt, John Coltrane, and Earl Kluge, he lost track of time. Apparently, leaving that shit on for more than ninety minutes isn't good. Ever since then, his thick gold-tipped locks had been falling out in clumps from the top of his head leaving him looking more and more like Friar Tuck with each passing day. "Um. I don't know if you know this, but they recommend that you re-apply the treatment for the lice a second time. Just in case."

"I told you that. It was in the directions, remember?"

"Um, anyway I did. Re-apply that is and while it was on, I got sort of … distracted and I left it on way, way, *way* too long."

"Your beautiful golden waves," she said running her fingers through the thatchy mess on his head and unintentionally pulling a substantial clump out in her hand.

"It's not permanent," he said sounding more hopeful than certain. "I'm thinking of shaving the whole business off this weekend. Try the Mr. Clean look until it grows back."

"But I loved your waves."

Bored with the hair talk, he made his move for round number two, but she put her hand on his leg.

"Listen. Before we get there, I need to set a few things straight." His stomach flipped. Looks like it was going to be the bus or a long walk in shiny black shoes. "I haven't been exactly up front about a few things. Minor things, mostly."

"What?"

"Well for one thing, I don't work at a small publishing house. I'm the publisher of *The Washington Tribune*. My family, the Sherwood family, has owned *The Tribune* since 1924."

"Okay," he said, wondering if she was trying to impress him or scare him. He didn't care where she worked or what she did for a living. And he hoped she would feel the same about him if he ever decided to tell her. "Wherever you work is fine with me. Really." He started his move again from the top.

"And another thing," she said. "My kids. They're a little older than I told you. I didn't want you to think I was some pathetic old cougar woman."

"I would never think that about you."

"Well, my oldest is fifteen. He's in high school. He actually takes Latin believe it or not."

In hindsight, flashing red and yellow lights and those whooping all hands on deck alarms and the difficult to ignore endlessly annoying tone of the emergency broadcast system; should have all gone off in his brain. Simultaneously. But thanks to that damned lizard, all he heard was the sound of her lips beckoning his lips.

"Age is irrelevant," he said leaning in and finally hitting his target.

The drive was short, and soon they were pulling into the long sweeping driveway of The Presidential Club. Wenn was too busy making out to see that Charlie was on duty in the guardhouse. When the limo finally stopped, Elizabeth took a minute to fix her lipstick.

"Holy Christ. We're at Presidential?"

"Yeah, don't get too excited."

Excited was not the word he would have chosen. Shocked, panicked, ready to jump out of his skin, those were much better descriptors for what he was feeling. "I don't ... I mean I can't ... "

"Oh come on. I promise it will be painless. We don't have to stay long. *The Tribune* is underwriting the whole thing. The Lombardi Cancer Center is our biggest charity. I just need to show my face, and we're out of here." She closed her lipstick case, pursed her lips and as the driver opened the door, stepped out. Lombardi Cancer Center? The Lombardi Cancer Center is his parent's biggest charity. He was paralyzed.

"Come on."

Couldn't he just wait for her in the car? It was so comfortable. Or better yet, she could climb back inside and they'd just drive around all night and have sex in the car like in *No Way Out*? He'd be up for that. She stood there waiting for him, and he knew it was over. As he stepped out of the car, a photographer called out. "Ms. Sherwood. Look over here so we can get a photo for *Washington Life Magazine*."

She looped her arm through his and smiled. As the flash went off, he knew he looked like a deer in the headlights, but he also knew his new tonsure would make him unrecognizable to anyone who might be casually flipping through *Washington Life*. When they got into the lobby, he leaned in, gave her a kiss on her cheek and told her to go ahead. He'd catch up.

"Could it be Wenn Mann? Jeeze, how long has it been?" asked Nick the bartender as Wenn entered The Grillroom.

"Hey Nick. A very long time."

"I see your brothers. Mikey was here this morning. And your parents. They're here all the time. But you? What, like two years?"

"At least. Bourbon, rock."

"Still a one cuber?"

"Yep."

"Everything alright?" asked Nick, as he made the drink.

"Yeah, why?"

"Cancer benefit and all …"

"Oh, you mean this," said Wenn running his hand over the smooth top of his head. "No, nothing like that. Just a … shampoo accident. That's all."

"Well, even with that, you still look good. Ah, to be young," said Nick wistfully. "You must be living the dream."

"Something like that," said Wenn. He took a good swig of his drink and stood up.

"On your dad's tab right?" asked Nick.

"Yeah." By the time he walked the short hall from the bar to the ballroom, he was ready for another drink. Before he got one, however, he had to get by Mr. and Mrs. Carmichael, who lived across the street from his parents.

"I don't believe it. Wenn is here. Oh my God, your mother said nothing about this."

"Hi Mrs. Carmichael."

"Where've you been hiding yourself these days, Wenn? Making it big on Wall Street?" asked Mr. Carmichael who sported quite a nice natural tonsure.

"No, sir … "

Looking stricken, Mrs. Carmichael jumped in to correct her husband. "Wenn is teaching Latin at Prep. Remember? I told you that." She looked embarrassed. It was hard to say if that was because Wenn was wasting his life, or because her husband was an idiot. "He forgets," she said, as if clarification was needed.

Wenn smiled stiffly. She looked at him like he had some sort of incurable disease. The kind it was best not to mention because mentioning it only reminded everyone that you were going to die. Soon.

"No big deal," said Wenn. He ditched the Carmichaels at his earliest convenience and walked toward the bar set up in the corner of the room. "Bourbon," he said, thankful to have found one of the few Presidential bartenders who hadn't known him since birth. He lingered near the bar, scanning the crowd for Elizabeth, his parents perhaps, other people he didn't want to have anything to do with. He finally understood the value of actually memorizing names and faces. It helps you know who to avoid. Half of the room looked familiar, but he didn't know any of them.

"Mr. Mann?" said a red-faced guy.

"Yes."

"Hey, good to see you. Al Sutton Senior."

Fuck. Big ASS, father of little ass—a kid who couldn't translate a wave into the word hello.

"Hello, Mr. Sutton," he said shaking Big ASS's hand.

"Boy, does little Al love Latin."

"Really?"

"Oh yeah. It's all we hear about. How much he loves Latin."

"That's ... eh ... great. Glad to hear it. Mr. Sutton, could you excuse me?"

"Oh, sure. Good to see you."

Wenn thought he saw Elizabeth standing a few tables away. He tried weaving through the crowd to get to her, but every five feet, there was another land mine he couldn't avoid. He lived out his worst nightmare as one parent after another, buoyed by the free flowing liquor, approached him with their tales of woe, their thinly disguised bribes and a few who went so far as to threaten him if their son didn't start to improve.

Just when he thought he couldn't take much more of this long painful detour to the underworld, Jim Barry, the local anchorman bounded onto the stage. "Hello all you fine people. What a crowd. Your support of the Lombardi Cancer Center has raised $1.5 million dollars; money that will fund cutting edge research in our on-going war on this dreadful disease." The crowd erupted in thunderous applause for themselves. "So tonight, we want you to enjoy yourself. Drink up, eat up, and then drink some more. We have our live auction before dinner and believe it or not, the more you drink, the more money we raise at the auction." Everyone laughed. Wenn scanned the crowd for Elizabeth. He spotted her near the stairs leading to the stage. "Let's get Rachel Sasser, chair of this wonderful evening, up here," said Jim. The crowd applauded as a perky little woman hopped up the stairs and threw kisses to the crowd like she was Miss America. Profound sadness overwhelmed him. He was defeated. There was no way he was getting out of there without her knowing that he was just an ordinary high school Latin teacher. More than anything he wanted to be close to her. To touch her. "Next, let's bring up Dr. Xavier Palermo, director of the Lombardi Cancer Center." The crowd applauded as a bald guy with glasses wearing an ill-fitting tuxedo marched up the stairs. From across the room, she smiled at him. She was his. He knew that. And watching her from across the room, he knew that he loved her. Not in the same way all these barely living old fucks loved. The ones who smothered love with things. With words, and expectations. With bigger houses and better cars. With memberships and engagements. And other mind-numbing stuff.

"... and tonight, her company, *The Washington Tribune*, is underwriting everything." The crowd applauded as Rachel continued. "And to get just a little serious here for a minute ... "

She haunted his thoughts. Every pore on her body was etched in his memory so he could see them in his head whenever he wanted. When he thought of her, he thought of her. Not her job, not what he had to do for her or what she had to do for him. Just her. Purely her.

"... received a positive diagnosis of breast cancer," said Rachel in a scary tone of voice. The crowd emitted a collective gasp.

Who? Who is she talking about? Dread forced its way into his gut.

"... it's too soon to know for sure, but the doctors say they caught it early, so her prognosis is excellent. Elizabeth, could you come up here please?" The crowd erupted. They were mad with admiration for her. Elizabeth made her way up the stairs.

Stunned, Wenn found himself doing what everyone around him was doing which was clapping. Applauding this wonderful woman waging war on cancer. A projected winner. *How long has she known? The whole time? Did it slip her mind? She just kept forgetting to tell him, just like she forgot to tell him her last name and he forgot to ask what it was?*

"Thanks, Jim. I am very fortunate. I have excellent doctors and my own personal cheer squad, which if you don't mind indulging me, I'd like to invite up here with me. Three people who mean everything to me. My children, Cole, Lewis and Dagny."

Cole? Did she say Cole? How many Coles could there be besides his student and Cole Porter? That was it. The complete list of people named Cole. By way of an answer, a tall, nicely built young man with a thatchy tonsure, similar to his own, climbed the stairs to join Elizabeth. There was no need to wait for him to turn around. Wenn slipped out the door of the ballroom and fortunately, he knew exactly where the men's room was. The heaves started as soon as he was through the door. When he was finally empty, he splashed his face with cool water, helped himself to a little plastic cup of mouthwash from the wall mounted dispenser and perused the selection of sprays before spritzing himself with something called Febreeze odor eliminator, Axe body spray, and for good measure, a little Pantene hair spray to help hold what little hair he still had, in place. Feeling like himself again, he walked back out to the hall where two ghosts were waiting for him.

"Hello son," said his dad. His mother looked smaller, frailer than he remembered. She rushed over to him and wrapped her arms around his shoulders. It was just what he needed. She soothed him like she did when he was a baby, by softly rubbing the nape of his neck. In seconds, his father had his arms around both of them.

He knew they thought he was overcome by emotion at seeing them after so long. And that must have been a part of it. But mostly, he was overcome by the woman he loved. Someone he never met. As his mother rubbed his head, a clump of sticky hair formed in her hand. "Oh my God. What happened to your hair?" she asked in horror.

He spent the next hour in the bar sipping club soda with his parents. Not surprisingly they were exactly the same. Aside from a kitchen renovation and a vacation in Bermuda, nothing happened. Nothing changed. They were their same stagnant selves. His dad went to the office four days a week. Played golf or tennis three days a week. And his mother busied herself with charity galas like this one. They gushed over their full active lives, vowing to slow down and "smell the roses." But all he saw was time cluttered with meaningless shit. They were as vibrant and successful as two fifty-five-year-olds could hope to be, but all he saw was stillness. Like the stale unflowing C&O canal in August.

They asked about his job at Prep. Said they had heard he was a bear of a teacher, in a good way, of course. They asked if he had a girlfriend and he said he used to, but not anymore. Eventually, they left, but not before he agreed to join them for lunch sometime soon. When they were gone, he ordered a plate of roast chicken and drank copious amounts of water. His mind was a salad spinner of thoughts. He would sort out his parents some other time. All he could think about was Elizabeth. Cancer. What the fuck? Cole. How did that happen? It was close to midnight, and he hadn't seen her all night. Maybe she left without even saying goodbye. Then, a warm hand gently touched the small of his back. She slid onto the stool beside him and ordered a Chardonnay. He ordered one too.

"You know, wine, being a fermented beverage has a certain amount of sugar," she said.

"So I've heard. I need something, and I don't think I could handle another bourbon at the moment. Are you alright?" he asked.

"I think so. They caught it early. It's stage zero DCIS. I have no idea what that means except it's about as good as cancer gets."

"Because Cole was sort of wondering if you were being honest or trying to spare his feelings."

She tightened her lips a bit and looked down. "Yeah."

"When did you know?" he asked.

"About the cancer?"

"No, about me."

"Cole … he kept talking about his really cool Latin teacher. And I kept thinking what are the odds that there could be two cool Latin teachers in the world. I mean, no offence, and you are certainly the exception, but as a group, you guys aren't rock stars. When did I know for sure? Four days ago when Cole showed me his report card, and next to that A in Latin, was the name Wenn Mann. How about you?"

Wenn looked at his watch. "Two hours and twenty minutes ago."

"Really?"

"Yeah. Why didn't you tell me? About the cancer?"

"A purely selfish act on my part. You were my quick getaway from cancer."

"Then why did you ask me here tonight?"

"I missed you."

He nodded. "Were you really out of town for all that time?"

"No."

"I didn't think so. What was it? Exactly?"

"Just … I don't know … It was too intense. And … the cigarette smoke. The way you smelled of cigarette smoke."

"But … it's not that big a deal."

"Believe me, I smoked when I was younger. Back when I was invincible."

"But what does that have to do … "

"That Wednesday afternoon was when I got a phone call that my mammogram showed some "irregularities," as they put it. And I was spooked. Then there you were, so young, so blissfully unaware of how precious time can be. Which is exactly how you should be, but exactly how I'm not. I can't. Before, you made me feel young. Like anything could happen. But that cigarette smell … I just never felt older."

"I'm sorry," he said placing his hand over hers. "So what, am I supposed to do now? Run a race or something for you? Run for the cure?"

"Run a race? No. Running a race won't do anything. Winning a race might. You win a race and all of this goes away." She smiled.

"So what now?" he asked.

"Hmm," she said. "I don't know. Cole and his siblings are on their way back to their dad's house so I'm open. How about you?"

* * * * *

The town car turned off main road and slowly

rolled past the nine-hole golf course and down the long drive. When they got to the guardhouse, Wenn rolled down his window and waved to Watkins, the night guard. Watkins, who had been dozing, waved back without looking to see who else might be in the back seat of the limo. The car proceeded around the circle and stopped in front of Roland Hall. If anyone in the dorm happened to be up at 2:00 a.m. that night, they would have seen two figures emerge from the limo and enter through the front door. They might have heard whispering and the sound of someone stumbling followed by the sound of someone stifling a giggle in the back stairwell. And if they were early risers, they may have seen two figures wearing Washington Prep sweats get into Mr. Mann's classic red Alfa Romeo Spider and drive off the campus.

"I always saw myself as Elaine, but I guess I have to face the facts."

"What?"

"I'm Mrs. Robinson."

"What?"

"You know. This car. It's the same one … "

"*The Graduate*. I know."

"I loved that movie. I always felt closest to the Elaine character, but I'm not. I'm Mrs. Robinson."

"Mrs. Robinson was my favorite," he said. They drove the rest of the way to her place in silence.

-twenty-three-

M . O . M . S .   A G A I N S T
L I C E

The MacArthur residence went from typical suburban home to state of the art command center, as the "special people" of Holy Family waged war on a double headed monster; lice and Ms. Gagner. Six volunteer mothers sat around the dining room table scheduling follow up appointments on their cell phones. In the kitchen, one mom answered the constantly ringing landline while two others used their cell phones to receive updates from the field. The number of Pink Zin girls swelled to thirty as their cause caught fire. In what used to be Patrick's study, the top ranking PZG's, namely Pups and Judy mapped out their plan of attack. In two days, they would stage a "hat in," with every student wearing either a kerchief or a do-rag to school. What was the worst that could happen? Ms. Gagner would force them to remove their hats? Doing so would be a dicey move on her part; especially since their reconnaissance team had turned up a few choice teachers who secretly supported the movement. Gagner could not afford to draw a line in the sand over the head coverings. It would only reveal how little support there was for her side. "I'll bet she gets wind of what's planned and doesn't show up. There's a good chance she'll make Scofield take the heat," said Judy.

"That wouldn't be a terrible scenario for us. Scofield is soft on mothers. Always has been," said Pups. Scofield was the male vice principal who started at Holy Family as a math teacher, and would have happily remained a math teacher were it not for his demanding wife, who forced him to apply for a promotion he never wanted. A teddy bear of a man, he had neither the stomach nor the backbone to be a good henchman.

Whatever the outcome of the "hat in," it wouldn't fail from a lack of planning. The PZG's were masters of planning operations right down to who was taking out the trash when they were done. If Pups and Judy were the brains behind the operation, Angie was its heart. She called on her background in customer service to keep "clients" the term they used instead of "parents" happy. She enjoyed both the bustle of the office and being on the inside of all that planning Pups and Judy were doing. As office manager, Angie also kept close tabs on their ever-increasing bank account. What blossomed out of a need within the community was quickly turning into a lucrative business.

At first, they charged only a nominal fee to cover their costs, but when Mary Ellen Packingham referred them to her highbrow friends in the upper income brackets, they raised their prices and no one seemed to mind. They raked in the dough as fast as they raked out the nits. Pups was more popular than the free sample lady at Costco. Angie came up with a full menu of services ranging from a hunt & peck, to a one-time treatment, to a multi-treatment with 100% guaranteed elimination or your money back. It turns out, rich people would pay anything you wanted to charge so long as they themselves didn't have to do the dirty work. Mr. Tran took a leave of absence from the pharmacy to devote himself full time to mixing up solution. They were using copious amounts of what was now called, MadDawg's Omnipotent Medicinal Solution Against Lice. Abbreviated, it was M.O.M.S. Against Lice. It was all Mr. Tran could do to meet the Pink Zin Girl's demands for the stuff. The field workers, the ones who actually treated heads became hourly employees, as did Angie, and Judy. Pups and Mr. Tran, however, owned the newly formed company and since Angie took care of the banking, she knew they were making a killing.

One of Mary Ellen's referrals was so taken with their business, she mentioned it to her friend at *The Washington Tribune*. When a small feature article buried in the Metropolitan section of the paper appeared, the phone did not stop ringing. In just a month's time, she became a satellite sweetheart, appearing on *Good Morning America, The Today Show,* and *Roberto in the Morning*—all right from her own front yard via satellite. While Pups was becoming a celebrity, Patrick retreated to their musty club basement to watch TV and the kids stayed holed up in their rooms each night, emerging only for whatever take out dinner Pups had ordered. Poor Maddox became the Pink Zin Girls' mascot. As he wandered through the daily commotion searching for Pups, every toddler-adoring woman in the house picked him up, squeezed his cheeks, and spoke to him in ridiculous hyper loud babyease. He cried a lot. He missed his mother. Cady, Willa, and Virginia longed to hear her ask them "who did it and ran?" and Patrick was adrift without an anchor. Grant, being a teenage boy, was happy as a clam to have a little more breathing room.

Patrick and Pups were two people cohabiting, sleeping in the same bed without so much as sharing a smile unless they were in public or around the children. As many times as Patrick attempted to apologize or seek some reasonable way to atone for the past and move forward together, Pups would shut him down. She no longer had time for him. Lice were her life.

When hat day arrived, gangs of kerchief and do rag-wearing youngsters entered the school. When the first wave of half-day kindergarten students was release at 11:50, mothers were delighted to see their children still wearing the head coverings. Phone lines buzzed as news of the Pink Zin Girls' victory spread. When the rest of the school was dismissed at 3:00, every single student still had their heads covered. The jubilation was short lived, however. Over the next few days, separate teams of officials representing the EPA, the FDA, the Maryland Department of Health and other official agencies called on both the MacArthur residence and the Tran garage. Until further notice, M.O.M.S Against Lice was shut down. No more treatments pending further investigation. There had been complaints of soil contamination, improper toxic waste disposal, child endangerment, threatening public health, zoning infractions and a host of other charges and accusations. The feds wouldn't say who made those complaints, but they didn't have to. Krista Gagner was a formidable opponent. Pups and Judy gathered the troops and broke the news. The feds had them over a barrel. The Pink Zin Girls were on hiatus until further notice. They sent the battalion home which wasn't such a bad thing since their families were also suffering from neglect. Angie, whose children now felt more at home in the MacArthur house than their own, stayed on to finish some invoicing with the hopes of scoring another dinner. She was so used to eating with the MacArthur's she hardly ever food shopped anymore.

The glorious sound of nothing was wonderful. Pups put her feet up on Patrick's desk and enjoyed the silence. For about five minutes. That's when the doorbell rang.

"Jeez, when will the parade of Krista Gagner inspectors ever end?"

"Do you want me to get it, Pups?" asked Angie.

"Relax. I've got this one."

Two more official looking guys in cheap suits were at her door. "Good evening, Ma'am. We're from the Baltimore office of the FBI. We'd like to speak with you if we could."

"You guys bringing up the rear of the posse? Don't worry we have halted operations. If you want to leave the paperwork with me, I will make sure we take care of it."

"I think you may have us confused with … "

"No, no, no. All those other officials were here already. The EPA, the Consumer Protection Agency, Food & Drug … they were all here and we're cool.

We have stopped our operation."

"Are you Mrs. MacArthur?"

"Yes."

"We'd like to talk to you about some Internet issues."

"I don't understand. We don't have a website. We're working on it, but ... "

"Mrs. MacArthur, could we come in? We're here to talk specifically about cyberbullying. Do you have children?"

When Patrick heard his wife calling him from the top of the basement stairs, he thought hell had frozen over, and she was ready to speak to him. He practically danced up the stairs only to have his hopes dashed when he saw two FBI agents sitting on his couch.

"This is my husband, Patrick. This is Agent Trask and Agent Dalton. From the FBI." Unlike Pups, who was a seasoned pro at entertaining feds, Patrick seemed visibly shaken. The men exchanged handshakes and smiles.

"Mr. and Mrs. MacArthur, are you familiar with the term cyberbullying?"

"We watch *Dateline*," said Pups indignantly. Patrick nodded in agreement.

"Well, it seems there have been postings on various websites. Postings that we consider to be verging on cyberbullying. They originate from a computer at this address."

"I only use the internet for email. And to see the weekly sales at Safeway," said Pups.

"I haven't been able to get on the computer at home in weeks," said Patrick. "Not since my study was taken over." Pups glared at her husband. He obviously resented her success.

"Most commonly we find that teens are the perpetrators of cyberbullying. How old are your children?"

Patrick and Pups exchanged worried looks. "Our son Grant is thirteen," said Patrick. Agent Dalton took a file out of his briefcase and handed it to Patrick. "Print outs of some of the postings. As you can see, it's some rough stuff." Patrick scanned the papers then handed them to Pups. She looked at the paper full of acronyms and didn't understand most of the words on it.

"I don't understand what this is."

"It's a lot of online lingo in there. It really is like a whole new language. Do you mind asking your son to join us?"

"Um. What exactly are we looking at here?" said Patrick. "I mean shouldn't we have a lawyer present when he talks to you?"

"Of course, that's your prerogative, but honestly, this not a criminal matter. What has occurred to date is something that warrants a warning and perhaps a bit more diligent monitoring of the teen's online activities by you, his parents. That's why we'd like to speak with your son."

As she climbed the stairs, Pups was quickly

reacquainted with her long lost companion, dread. Her heart was pumping, her throat constricted, and her back was slick with sweat. Grant was in his room working on his math homework with the door open, clearly the behavior of a child with nothing to hide. "Grant. Do you want to explain the presence of two FBI agents?"

"What?"

"Two FBI agents are sitting in our living room, apparently to discuss some particularly foul-mouthed postings on an Internet site?"

"What?"

"Don't you 'what' me mister. There are two FBI agents here right now. Like I need this on top of everything else. Let's go." Grant got up and followed her out to the hallway. Before they got to the stairs, she turned and raised her pointer finger at him. "So help me Grant, if you … "

"Mom, I don't have the foggiest idea what you're talking about."

Curious about all the commotion the girls tried to follow Pups down the stairs. She twirled around, "Virginia, you take your sisters and Maddox and lock yourself in my room. Put the TV on. Loud. I do not, repeat, do not want to find you eavesdropping. Understand?"

"But … "

"JUST DO IT," said Pups in the unique combination of a whisper and a shout she used when she wanted to shout at her kids without having another grown up know that she was a shouter.

"Gee, officer, I'm not really sure. I mean, I have guys over all the time. Any one of them could have done it. And there's all those mothers. Who knows what they've been up to?"

Pups and Patrick exchanged looks. "Well, as we said, we are here to inform you of this activity," said Agent Trask. "It's really up to you how you wish to deal with it. And of course, should it continue this could certainly turn into a more serious legal matter."

"Of course. Thank you officer," said Pups, realizing too late that they weren't officers. As she walked them to the door, Pups promised to get to the bottom of the matter. She assured them that unlike some parents, they were not the kind who believed their children were incapable of wrongdoing. There would be no more posts, obscene or otherwise from this address. Just before they went through the door, Pups asked, "Do you know who made the accusation?"

"Yes, Ma'am. A Mr. George Merkel."

Who in the world was George Merkel? What a mess. She went into Patrick's study to Google George Merkel and there was Angie with her eyes cast downward, busy stuffing yellow invoices into cellophane windowed envelopes.

"I forgot all about you," said Pups.

* * * * *

The only thing that spreads faster than lice are rumors. Within hours of the FBI's drop by, wagging tongues were turning the MacArthur's friendly, non-criminal warning into the biggest federal bust in history. While Grant pushed peas around his plate at the family dinner table, gossipmongers reported that he had been taken from the house in handcuffs and was being booked and finger-printed before they hauled him off to juvi. That was the main rumor, but there were others, tiny offshoots that flared then faded without a trace. Grant was the one who stole all that loose change out of the parish poor box. Grant was the one who wrote "Gagner sucks" all over the boys' restroom. Grant cheated on his standardized tests, how else could he have done so well? For as many rumors as Grant spawned, there was only one common response, "No wonder. Look at who his mother is."

For all her good deeds and ability to rally troops, everyone knew that Pups MacArthur was a sanctimonious phony. Who did she think she was barging into people's homes and slathering God knows what on everybody's children? The Lice Nazi? If only she had focused on taking care of her own kids instead of telling everyone else how to take care of theirs, this wouldn't have happened. And didn't she always make you feel completely incompetent, the way she would just take over doing something? And what about her bizarre need to take on the grossest, most disgusting tasks—things that turned your stomach when you did them for your own family— she did for other people? Did she expect them to clean her toilets in return? And did you ever notice that once she felt like you were no longer needy or that you didn't appreciate her enough, the Pups chill set in immediately. Her nose would be out of joint, and her tone of voice would get a little pitchy, and she would affect the face of a woman who suddenly finds herself in the middle of a dog park in her best high heels.

The truth was that as much as Pups gave, she expected far more in return. Not in the form of manual labor, she would be horrified to have someone clean up her mess. No, what Pups sought was complete and utter allegiance. It wasn't that much really. It would be nothing at all if Pups was in any way likable. But she wasn't. That was the Pups parallax. People followed her, but they didn't like her. Angie was not the first one to be flattered when Pups started focusing her personal spotlight on her. It was almost unbelievable that someone so wonderful could suddenly appear out of nowhere really, and make life so fun. Everything was better with Pups in your life. She helped you out, she built you up, she got you through whatever was ailing you. She was a Godsend, until you didn't need her as much. When you wanted to go out with other friends for lunch or when your children asked other kids over to play, you could detect the slightest glimmer of hurt in her voice. When you declined one of her invitations or you couldn't do her a simple favor like pick her kids up from school, the honeymoon was over ... and removing yourself from the situation was going to be a long drawn out and extremely painful ordeal. As brutal as some of the nastiest divorces. None of this was obvious until it was too late and her hooks were sunk deep into your innards. By then you knew it would hurt just as much to pull them out as to live with them. Most didn't have the strength to eliminate her from their lives so they hung around, at arms' length, calling her every so often, paying her the odd compliment, helping her out when they couldn't possibly avoid it; while waiting for the golden day of liberation; which apparently had arrived in the form of Grant's rumored crime spree. For the long line of pseudo friends preparing to jettison Pups, the fact that her long overdue fall from grace came in the midst of her grandest hurrah was epic.

The relative calm of a lice free life was a welcome if short-lived recess for the MacArthurs. The day after the intense federal shitstorm that rained down upon them, the forecast was for a cold but very sunny and pleasant day. Not a cloud in the sky said the weatherman who obviously didn't have his super Doppler 900 trained on 45 Peachpit Lane. Because there, directly over the MacArthur house, was an unmistakable low hanging cloud. A putrid yellow cloud so heavy with the smell of sulfur it brought tears to your eyes. A cloud Pups would be living under for the foreseeable future.

"Everybody knows. And I mean everybody," said Grant storming into her Suburban after school.

"Knows what?" asked Virginia climbing in behind him.

"How could everybody know?" Pups asked in disbelief.

"Did you tell all your lousy friends? Because Mom, no joke, every kid in school knows. And they believe it."

"Know what?" asked Willa, who had front seat privileges for the week.

"I did not tell a soul," said Pups. "Even your sisters don't know."

"Know what?" asked Cady as she stood on the seat next to Grant then dove into the way back seat. Pups looked around the parking lot. Was it her imagination or did the mothers seem just a little more joyful? Sure they were all pleased at the success of hat day, but that was last week.

She unbuckled her seat belt. "Stay here. I'll be right back," she said.

Pups hopped out of her Suburban. As she walked through the parking lot, she could feel hundreds of eyes focused on her. She kept her head held high and with a cheerful, if somewhat tight smile on her face, approached Señora Alvarez who was standing with a bunch of mothers. "Hola, Señora!"

"Hola, Mrs. Pups," said Señora. "So sorry for you."

"Sorry?"

"He's a nice muchacho. Don't worry, Mrs. Pups."

Don't worry? Señora looked at her like she was some pathetic charity case. Pups looked around. They were all looking at her like she was a pathetic charity case, except the ones who were looking at her like she was a conniving bitch who finally got what she had coming.

* * * * *

Pups missed her comfy old sofa, and watching TV with the kids after school, something she had never actually done, but would now like to. She missed her old life. The quiet ordinary life she used to have. Looking up at the ceiling Pups thought about all that had happened in just a few months. She loved her business. She loved being in charge of something that didn't talk back or whine or ignore her. She also loved being a mom. She hated being called the Lice Nazi. Though she wouldn't admit it to anyone, in her heart, she knew that Grant was probably guilty of cyberbullying. Patrick seemed to think so too because the one time they talked about it, he pretty much said so. Regardless, she had Grant on a short leash. No computers, no television, nothing with a screen and to help him fill all his extra time, she doubled up on his chores.

"I hope he learns his lesson," she said. "I just wish it wasn't all so public. But I guess we have Angie to thank for that."

"Yeah!" said Patrick. "Grant's a good kid no matter what. We know that. But unfortunately, there's a big difference between being good and being thought of as good by others."

"You're right," she said. "Sometimes good people do bad things."

It was the first non-hostile conversation they had. It made her realize just how much she really missed him. He was still hibernating in the basement when he got home from work, afraid of getting her riled up by another attempt at reconciliation. As her thoughts wandered, she looked up at the ceiling light, expecting to see a big pile of stinkbugs inside the glass cover.

But she didn't. They weren't there. Patrick had finally cleaned it. Without being asked. Public humiliation was about as painful as she thought it would be, but Pups was a tough cookie and she knew she was stronger than all of them. She refused to give in to the part of her that wanted to hide her head or avoid people. That was for wimps. She put herself out there in the parking lot every day. She looked people in the eye and laughed when they said anything about Grant and his "problem." She responded with the truth. That Grant didn't have a problem. That the whole matter was really nothing, and the only problem is that busy bodies seem hell bent on keeping this non-event alive.

She did avoid Angie, and she hadn't said more than a few words to Judy. All the others; the crowd of onlookers who took such delight in her troubles didn't hurt one tenth as much as being brazenly hung out to dry by her two best friends. Everything they say about mean girls was true, but what nobody talks about is that those girls grow up to become women and they bring their mean genes with them. One bright spot in all this was that once they got the go-ahead from the authorities, she would have a thriving business to return to. Mr. Tran, who was back working at the pharmacy full time, assured her that every single ingredient in his potion wasn't just safe, it was edible. She had been deceived by practically everyone she knew, but for some reason, she was confident that Mr. Tran would not let her down.

There were two bits of unfinished business on her list. And the first one, she felt compelled to see through, just to get some closure. She still wanted a reversal of the no-nit policy. It was a tough one. Insiders, aka, mothers who could still enter the school building without fear, said that Gagner seemed more peeved than usual. The hat day humiliation she suffered would not soon be forgotten. But to get the no-nit policy change, Pups was going to have to go into Gagner's office and negotiate alone and without backup.

Under any circumstances, that would be a challenge, but with the entire school now buzzing about Grant's cyberbullying, Pups no longer appeared quite as righteous as she once did. And she had every expectation that Gagner would use it to her advantage. Without any trustworthy friends, she asked Patrick to go in late one morning. She needed him to watch Maddox while she met with Gagner. "Be sure he makes it to the potty at least once an hour, we almost have this potty training in the bag," she said.

"No problem," said Patrick. Every time he looked at her, it seemed like he was going to burst into tears. He had been in the doghouse too long. He was the second thing on her list. It was time for this to end. When she got back from school, they'd talk. Like a real general leading absolutely no one into battle, Pups entered the school determined not to give up until all her demands were met.

twenty-four

RULE BREAKER

On Sundays, the campus was quiet. Many of the borders went home, not to return until 5:00 Mass on Sunday evening. There were no scheduled sporting events. And aside from the priests, the resident staff, and the remaining borders, the campus was deserted. Dr. Brennan, who normally spent Sunday's prancing to and fro atop an aluminum piste in a brightly lit cinderblock warehouse defending his rank among local fencers, had to sacrifice the day's contest. Father Bills urgently needed to speak to him. On that particular day, Dr. Brennan was to challenge Vladimer Putchki, the Russian diplomat who was currently first to Dr. Brennan's second in the veteran men's division. Withdrawing at this late hour meant forfeiture. He was not happy.

When he got to the school, Father Bills was waiting for him in his sanctuary. Decorated in the style favored by stodgy old billionaires, with mahogany paneling, world class works of art (miniatures but highly valuable, nevertheless), a vast collection of prized first edition books lining the built-in shelves, and a bar stocked with fine spirits worth more than a year's tuition at the school, the room represented the very best of material wealth.

Father Bills saw no conflict between the opulence of his sanctuary and the high-minded mission of the school—"Non Ministrari sed Ministrare" which means, "To serve not to be served." The irony did not go undetected by the rest of the school who wondered if the acquisitive priest confused the Latin translation into: "Not to serve but to be served."

"Father?" said Dr. Brennan from the doorway.

"Dr. Brennan, come in. Sorry to have spoiled your Sunday. But I'm afraid we have a bit of a situation." Father Bills proceeded to describe the unorthodox confession he had heard, and as if to prove the existence of the confessor, he held up an odd, gold-toned disc embellished with a cryptic cross. "This was in the confessional after she left." Dr. Brennan looked at the disk. There were no pins or loops attached to identify the object as a piece of jewelry, which is what he would have thought it was. That the object was of a religious nature, gave credence to the words the woman spoke.

"What is most distressing … is that the accuser is anonymous. We have nothing to back up this charge, but its nature is serious enough to warrant some sort of action. Don't you think?"

For Dr. Brennan, this revelation was not the shock Father Bills seemed to think it was. In fact, he had been waiting for just this sort of thing ever since Wenn Mann took the job. "If at all possible, I would like to leave Cole Reardon out of this. He's a fine boy, excellent student and from what I understand, recently found out his mother has cancer. There's no need to add to his burden."

"I fully agree Father. If ... anything did take place, he was surely the victim. At the same time, we cannot simply dismiss Wenn Mann for an accusation from a nameless, faceless accuser," said Dr. Brennan. "However, it does seem that this woman was acting honorably. I suggest that before we go any further, you allow me to confront Mr. Mann, informally, of course. Perhaps if the charge is correct, he will cave in before we even bring this up in any official way."

"I think that's a reasonable plan. Will you speak with him today?"

"As soon as I leave your office."

"Thank you, Dr. Brennan."

"We'll get to the bottom of this, Father."

Dr. Brennan rose to leave. As he neared the door, Father Bills added, "Oh and Dr. Brennan, if you don't mind, I'd prefer if you don't bring my name into your discussion. The Mann family has given to the school so generously over the years."

"Of course," said Dr. Brennan, wondering if there was anyone Father Bills wouldn't take money from.

* * * * *

After he dropped Elizabeth off, Wenn went out for a run. A long twenty-miler to get his thoughts together. Returning to his room, tired, covered in dried sweat he found Dr. Brennan sitting on a folding chair outside his door.

"Mr. Mann. Can I trouble you for a minute of your time?"

"Okay."

"Why don't you clean yourself up a bit and then come see me in my office."

He wasn't surprised to see Dr. Brennan. He'd been expecting something like this for a while now. He showered. Shaved. Put on fresh clothes, then went down the marble staircase to meet his fate.

Dr. Brennan's office was nothing like Father Bills's. There were some Currier & Ives prints; a framed diploma bestowing upon him the title of Doctor of Philosophy from the University of Maryland. The furniture was early American.

"Have a seat Wenn." Dr. Brennan hadn't called him Wenn since ... ever. Even when he was a student, he called him Mr. Mann. "You have a long and distinguished history with Washington Prep, both as a student and now as a teacher. You have been among the finest teachers of Latin we have had in recent memory."

"Thank you."

"So it was with great ... shock when we ... the school, that is, was contacted by a concerned party who wishes to remain anonymous but who, nevertheless, suggested that perhaps you ... how shall I say this? That you have not been following the rules of this academic institution. Now, mind you, I'm speaking principally about your position as dean of residents."

Broken the rules? Like almost every single one. No pets, check. No alcohol, check. No controlled substances, check. No conduct unbecoming a practicing Catholic. Check. No having sex with your student's mother in your room. Check.

"Um. That's probably … "

"Please let me continue. And if some of the school rules have, in fact, been disregarded, this person also suggested that your actions went far beyond our rules. That you may, in fact, have broken state and even federal laws while under our roof."

"I see."

"Wenn, I'm not going to ask you what you have done. In fact, it's better for both of us if I don't know. However, I want to ask you to examine your conscience and should you discover any … indiscreet acts, anything that might reflect poorly on the school or even bring in the authorities, that you do the honorable thing and submit your resignation."

"I see." Wenn thought for a moment. "How does that work, exactly?"

"Well, if you choose not to resign and a situation does arise … "

"No sir. I mean how exactly do I submit my resignation? Do I have to write a letter or is there some sort of form I need to fill out? Or do I just tell you?"

-twenty-five-

JANUARY THAW

The list of things that can level life's playing field is long, but right there at the top, is humiliation. It gives the mighty a taste of being meek and it gives the meek an opportunity to see that even the mighty cannot completely shield themselves from the occasional shitstorm. As a mother of triplets, Suzanne Nuttin was no stranger to humiliation. When her children were infants, she never managed to make it out of the house without something smeared across her shirt or down her pants. When they got a little older, they took great delight in repeating every snarky, judgmental, politically incorrect thing she and Corn had said about someone to their face. It cost her two gardeners, a housekeeper and a few friends before she learned not to speak in front of her children. But that kind of humiliation was nothing compared to what she faced when she became the stupid mother who could not figure out how to effectively treat her children for head lice. Six times in six weeks, the triplets were sent home from school for posing a threat to public health. Whenever one of the nurses at the very exclusive, very expensive, yet very humble Quaker school the Nuttins attended found a nit—dead or alive—all three Nuttin kids were rounded up and sent home. And each time they were sent home, all those peace loving pacifistic bitches could barely contain their glee that the Nuttins had lice again! When she had tried every remedy money could buy, Suzanne raised the white flag and surrendered. She was no match for the pernicious little creatures. She was seriously considering homeschooling when Mary Ellen mentioned that their old friend Pups, the odd, animal loving girl who lived across the street from them as kids, had become something of a local celebrity for her lice busting talent. Suzanne immediately invited Pups over, challenging her to put her methods to the test against the triplets.

For Pups, the timing couldn't have been better. Suzanne's call came just days after all the final reports from the government agencies cleared her of everything but a minor zoning infraction for operating a business out of her home. Not only was Mr. Tran's formula effective, it was safe and they had reports from six government agencies saying so. When she called Mr. Tran to tell him the good news, she asked the question she had been too afraid to ask through all those months of treatments. "So, how is it that your formula is so safe, but you put that 'not safe for pets' sticker on every bottle?"

"Citrus oil. It's mostly okay for dogs but highly toxic to cats. I don't have a 'not safe for cats' sticker."

Pups pulled her last bottle of MOMS Against Lice out of the garage, got her best hair rake, a pair of high quality, double thick, latex gloves, and drove to the other side of town to treat the Nuttin children.

Ten days later, she went back for a follow up. And that was the end of that. The lice were gone, and apparently everyone at the Friends school knew it. As peace loving and pacifistic as the mothers of the Quaker school were, they were just as petrified as anyone about being labeled lice heads. When the Nuttins were back in school for two weeks without so much as a scratchy temple, Suzanne's phone began to ring. Everyone wanted to know her secret. She told them and soon, Pups's phone began to ring. And ring. And ring. One afternoon, she picked up the phone, and she heard, "Mrs. MacArthur?"

"Yes."

"This is Christine Smith from the Office of the First Lady, can you hold please?"

The president's children were students at that high brow Quaker school. The next day, Pups put her politics aside and did her patriotic duty by visiting the White House and treating the first children. It was supposed to be on the down low, but like most stories about parasites in Washington, once the press got wind of it, Pups was in the national news.

There had not been a single louse on any Nuttin, Packingham or MacArthur since before Christmas. To celebrate the end of Suzanne Nuttin's humiliation, the start of Pups Inc., and the bitter end of the plague, the Packinghams and the MacArthurs were dressing in their classiest sportswear to join the Nuttins for a day at "The Club." It was Suzanne's way of showing her deep gratitude for all the help and support given to her by Mary Ellen and Pups. They had battled the bugs and won.

Suzanne had loaned Mary Ellen the money to return her customers' Plaid-IT-tudes deposits. Mary Ellen didn't tell Suzanne about her family's tenuous financial situation, only that Kenny was being a dick. It was an easy lie to tell because "Kenny was being a dick" could so easily explain any problem to anyone who knew him. Without cash or credit, however, she couldn't buy catalogues or hold trunk shows, so the Plaid-IT-tudes endeavor, was put on hold for the time being.

As Kenny told her, or rather shouted at her a million times a day, "We're not in the fucking poor house. Not yet." But she felt like they were. And if that's where they were headed, she wouldn't mind getting a look see so she could start to figure out how she was going to decorate. They were just barely able to pay their mortgage and the tuition bills, the car, and the electric company. But the credit card bills were killing them, as was the one certainty of suburban living; things break at the worst possible time. In recent months, the Packingham's dryer broke, Mary Ellen's car needed new tires, and their dog Winston ate an entire dark chocolate cake one Saturday night, prompting a trip to the emergency vet for a stomach pumping. Kenny juggled the bills like a master, but at the end of each month they were always tapped out and "declined" came up more than "approved" on those electronic swipers. They were alive, but they were dying. Like a modern day version of Prometheus with the finance charges, late fees and overdraft penalties eating tiny bits of their liver, a little at a time. They somehow managed to make it through each month only to wake up in the next billing cycle with a whole new completely intact liver—more food for the vultures.

They were not the only ones celebrating. All of Washington was enjoying a glorious January thaw. With temperatures pushing upwards of 60 degrees, the running trails, tennis courts and golf courses were inundated.

Getting the Packingham boys out the door so they could hit the links at Presidential was an ordeal. Tanner couldn't find socks. Kenny spilled Gatorade all over the new white golf shirt he got for Christmas, yelling at Mary Ellen even though she was in the laundry room trying to find socks when it happened. When he changed, it was to a hideous fluorescent green polo shirt that made him look like a walking tennis ball. Mary Ellen didn't have the strength to fight him over the shirt. Despite all of that, when they finally did get in the car, they looked as happy and as normal and as capable as any upwardly mobile family. Better even. No one would ever guess that Kenny was a few hundred dollars from insolvent, Brophy was a few points from failing Latin, Doyle was having social issues, Tanner was showing signs of inheriting his father's ADD, Kier was obsessed with Candy Crush, and Mary Ellen was losing her power to smooth every wrinkle out of their increasingly scrunched up lives. As many times as they had been to Presidential, the contrast between what her life was and what she wanted it to be was so vast, emotions overwhelmed her as they pulled past the guard house.

"Christ, Mary Ellen," shouted Kenny.

"I'll be fine," she said, dabbing her eyes.

"Well, Hal–le-fuckin–lu-ya! You'll be fine." He said it so loud that it made her ears ring. It felt like the words were etched into her eardrums, which in a way, they were.

* * * * *

His parents were waiting for him in The Grillroom. In daylight, they looked more like he remembered them and less like the ghosts he saw that night of the cancer ball.

"It's good to see you, son," said his dad.

"Same here," said Wenn and he meant it. The last few months had given him nothing if not a bit more sensitivity.

"Your hair's growing back," said his mother nervously. "I hear you're not at Prep anymore."

"Nope."

"So … what have you been up to?" asked his father without the slightest bit of judgment in his tone.

"Nothing. I've been up to nothing," he said. It wasn't entirely a lie. He wasn't working. He wasn't earning his own living. Instead, he was living in Elizabeth's formerly sparkling white apartment. The decor was still white, but it was losing its sparkle as bits of his crud ground into the creases of the sofa and the edges of the carpet. Elizabeth underwent a lumpectomy at Georgetown University Hospital soon after he resigned from Prep and they both camped out in the apartment while she re-cooperated and waited for the pathology report. When it arrived, the news was good. It was as the doctor initially predicted, contained and entirely treatable. After the surgery, Elizabeth got her own tattoo. Not a cat, but a few freckle sized dots that would tell the technician where to aim the radiation beam into her breast five days a week. She worked as much as possible, but when she needed time to rest and to heal, Wenn took care of her. He rubbed her neck. He made her roasted chicken for dinner. He found vintage foreign films to watch with her.

A few weeks after moving to Elizabeth's, Wenn ran in the annual Capitol City Marathon, and at Elizabeth's insistence, he started with the rest of the pack. Two hours and twenty-four minutes later, he crossed the finish line. First. As nice as winning was, it was even better to have someone waiting for him at the finish line. Someone to cheer for him. Elizabeth's cancer had given him his first taste of humility. It changed him outside and in. Wenn Mann no longer looked like a God. He looked like a hero. His parents would neither understand nor appreciate any of that which is why he was being completely honest when he told him he was up to nothing.

* * * * *

Stubby Hill was in a hurry. The tennis courts, like the two golf courses, were teeming with activity. Unprepared for the onslaught brought on by blue skies and sunshine, he was without his usual battalion of teenage helpers to fill the water coolers, keep the cups in steady supply and answer the phone for the mobs of people calling to reserve court time. When his assistant, Julio finally made it in, Stubbie gave himself a well-deserved break. He climbed into the Tennis club cart and hightailed it over to The Grillroom for lunch and a couple of beers. He stayed at the bar a little longer than he planned and had a few more beers than he planned. Life at home was not going particularly well for Stubby. His wife was constantly haranguing him about everything. Stuff they needed, a new car, a new house and apparently, a new Stubby. To move them from the barely affordable outskirts of Bethesda to the utterly unaffordable outskirts of Chevy Chase, he would have to make more money, which meant he would have to expand his list of private clients.

Feeling that he had reached the peak of his ambition, Stubby had no interest in taking on more work. He had taken to stifling his frustration with an hour and a half at The Grillroom bar, but on such a busy day, he had to cut it short, so he practically gulped his drinks down. Drunk and pressed for time, Stubby turned over the ignition of his golf cart and took off across the fairway. As he traveled down the green, he decided to stop at The Ninth Hole for a beverage to go. Something to help the afternoon pass quicker. He floored it and had that little cart careening along at full throttle, before taking a sloppy left turn into the cart parking area. He misjudged his speed and accidentally tapped the front of a parked cart that began to roll slowly backwards.

Gaining momentum, it swooped downhill towards some guy in a tennis ball colored shirt who was balancing a beer in each hand. So focused on not spilling the beers, the guy didn't see the cart rolling towards him until it was too late. It pushed him backwards, pinning him against a large old oak tree. Given the terrain and the velocity at which the cart traveled, it came to rest with its front wheels in the air and the back edge of the roof nestled tightly against the man's windpipe. What was amazing to onlookers, the thing they brought up every time they recounted the story of what they saw was how long he held on to the two beers he held in his hands.

* * * * *

Sitting in the waiting room of the Georgetown Hospital surgery center, Mary Ellen wondered whether she was a wife or a widow. She did not allow herself the luxury of anticipating what would happen next, for once, choosing to remain in the present. In the present, every outcome was both possible and completely out of her control. She finally understood why it was the most comfortable place to be.

When Patrick had entered the Presidential Grillroom to tell her what happened, Mary Ellen saw chaos approaching and summoned her yoga Zen to kick in. Her breath became slow, steady and controlled, and for once, her focus was in the moment. Pups took the three youngest Packinghams home with her and Suzanne escorted Mary Ellen and Brophy to the hospital. Poor thing, he was a mess. He had seen the entire awful accident. Saw the blood oozing out of the side of his father's mouth and heard the screams and gasps as people realized what had happened. Thank God for Patrick who put his battlefield experience to good use, pulling Brophy away from the scene as soon as the magnitude of what happened became apparent.

When the afternoon became the evening, Mary Ellen asked Suzanne to take Brophy home for some dinner. At first, he refused, but Mary Ellen assured him that they would not know anything for a long time anyhow. It was an assumption since all the surgical liaison told her was that the cart had crushed Kenny's windpipe, it was a miracle that he was still alive. In the best-case scenario, he would need extensive surgery and rehab. Though her demeanor was calm, almost comatose, Mary Ellen developed a bad case of the shakes shortly after the sweet surgical liaison left. The words "best case scenario," introduced the notion that there was also a worst-case scenario, which the surgical liaison did not go into, but Mary Ellen could easily fill in the blanks herself. Before leaving, Suzanne went to the nurses' desk and got an orange fleece blanket to wrap Mary Ellen in.

Over the next week, Mary Ellen kept vigil at the hospital, while Kenny lay in a drug-induced coma to give his body time to rest and heal. She played out best-case scenarios, worst-case scenarios, and in between case scenarios. She thought about Kenny and her marriage, and the scenarios went in one direction, but then she thought about her boys and their father, and they went in another. One afternoon, she was so immersed in her various plot lines, she didn't notice Brophy coming into the waiting room until he plopped down in the chair next to her.

"Any news?"

"No. Nothing. Did you eat?"

"Sort of. Wasn't very hungry."

"You look terrible," she said, smoothing his

bangs out of his eyes, which were already welling up with tears.

"Oh, baby, don't worry. Your dad is a strong ox. He's going to be fine," she said, even if she wasn't convinced of that herself.

"I know … but … Mom … " Brophy broke down in tears.

"It's okay, Brophy. It's okay."

"Mom, I drove the cart."

"You weren't driving when the accident happened. Patrick said you guys were on the green."

"Yeah, we were, but Dad said I could drive, even though you have to be sixteen. He said no one would know. *I* parked the cart."

Mary Ellen could see her son struggling.

"Mom, I'm not sure I put the parking brake on."

"Oh Brophy … that's not important."

"But if I didn't, this could be my fault. At least a little." Mary Ellen looked into Brophy's eyes and suddenly, the Zen train Mary Ellen had been riding for the past week came to a screeching halt.

"What?"

"I mean, maybe the parking brake would have stopped it from rolling down the hill."

"Listen to me," she said sounding like her old self. "YOU had ABSOLUTELY *NOTHING*. Do you hear me, *NOTHING* to do with this accident? That tennis guy is 100% to blame. Whether the parking brake was on or not, it's his fault not yours. Do you understand me?" Brophy looked at his mother suspiciously. The frail, helpless woman who was sitting there when he first walked in transformed into raging lioness.

"Things happen. We're a fine, together family one minute, and the next minute some crazy drunk tennis jerk swoops in out of nowhere and crushes your father's windpipe and in the process, every single one of us. I do not for one second want you to think that you are responsible for any of this. Not for a single second."

She wrapped her arms around her oldest son and gave him a hug. Then she looked him in the eye. "Are we together on this?"

"Yes."

"So, good. What's going on at school? How's the new Latin teacher?"

"I'm getting a B, but he's no Mr. Mann. Tough as the guy was, we all kind of miss him."

Mary Ellen kind of missed him too. Not so much Wenn Mann but Heath. She missed Heath a lot. With all the stress she'd been through, a good old fashioned fantasy romance would have offered a little respite from the nauseating hospital stench and the endless parade of people in white telling her things she could never remember ... but of course, there was no way she could carry on with him after all that drama with his alter-ego. Heath took it hard when she broke the news to him, but in the end, he understood. Before getting on the plane to Namibia, he whispered in her ear, *"... no matter what ... we'll always have yoga."*

"Yeah," said Mary Ellen. "Too bad he left so suddenly. I'm sure it's for the best. Give the new guy a chance. Maybe he'll grow on you."

"I seriously doubt it," said Brophy. "Every day there's a new phrase on the board. A Latin translation of a modern saying. Today's was, 'Vescere bracis meis.'"

"Which means?"

"Eat my shorts. Mr. Mann would have a heart attack if he knew."

"You probably won't learn as much. But a college doesn't really care how much you learn. All they want to see are those good grades."

"I guess," said Brophy. "Father Bills called me into his office today. That place is totally tricked out."

"What did he want?"

"Just to see if I was okay. Tell me he's praying for us and all that."

"That was nice."

"Yeah. He's a nice guy when you get to know him. Really knows a lot about lacrosse. Says it's going to be a great season." Brophy reached into his pocket. "He even gave me something for you."

"For me? What in heaven's name would he give me?"

"Well, we were sitting there talking. And I was, you know, checking out his amazing office, and I look over to this shelf behind his desk, and I see this." He held up Mary Ellen's long lost gold Tory Burch shoe medallion and placed it on her lap. So I say that my mother lost a gold cross exactly like the one on the shelf. I asked him where he got it, because I thought it would make you happy if I could replace yours, but he insisted that I take this one. Wouldn't take no for an answer."

Mary Ellen was stunned. Tears welled up in her eyes as she held the medallion in one hand and leaned over to give Brophy a hug with the other. "My treasure!"

EPILOGUE

Everything she owned was boxed up and ready to go. She would miss the house, the only home her children had ever known. She would miss the neighbors, and even though they all vowed to get together, she knew they never would. Why should they? It's not like they would be traveling in the same social circles. Not any more. The Packinghams were moving to Chevy Chase. To a beautiful red brick colonial with a circular driveway, newly refinished hardwood floors, a kitchen that was to die for, and two fresh coats of Home Depot White White paint on every wall in the house. Best of all, it was just a short, ten-minute drive on the beltway to their new home away from home, Presidential Club. Mary Ellen was learning to play golf and hoped to join one of the less competitive ladies golfing groups. Kier and Tanner swam and played tennis while Brophy and Doyle had joined the junior golf league.

When Kenny was injured, Mary Ellen expected everything to get a lot worse, but, in fact, everything got better. Kenny had great disability insurance, so they actually started getting a regular paycheck for the first time in months. Then, after the dust settled, Mary Ellen got herself a lawyer and when he was done, the Packinghams walked away with a seven figure cash settlement and lifetime memberships to the club for all Packinghams current and future.

As for Kenny, he was in the hospital for weeks and in a rehab hospital for months. When they finally woke him up from the drug-induced coma, he was on a ventilator so he couldn't speak. The first time she went to see him after he woke up was emotional. Tears welled up in her eyes. She squeezed his hand and told him how much she had missed him. Kenny picked up the pad of paper and pen from the bedside table and wrote her a message:

"Why the fuck would you want a dickhead like me back?"

She smiled when she saw it. Not even death's door could change him. It was a question she had asked herself often when it was clear he would recover. The thing was, Mary Ellen could not move into a stately old home in Chevy Chase as a single mom. That was not the dream. The dream was to be a family. To have it all, every single little bit. You can't send out custom made Crane Christmas cards with a photo of a mom and her sons. No one would talk about how great they looked or how beautiful the house looked in the background; all they would talk about was the missing dad.

In time, Kenny fully recovered. The doctors swore that what saved him was his unusually thick neck. Aside from the pronounced scar on his throat and the hole they had to make for the breathing tube, he looked as good as ever. The only lasting effect of the accident was that never again would Kenny be able raise his voice above a whisper, which was just fine with Mary Ellen.

Though she didn't know it, Mary Ellen's new

neighbors were none other than Mr. and Mrs. Wenn Mann, III. They lived across the street from the Packinghams, but it would take a very long time to discover their mutual acquaintance because the Manns were preparing for a long trip that would keep them out of the country for a few months. They were going to Ponza, a small island off the southern coast of Italy to visit their son, Wenn, IV.

Nursing Elizabeth through her radiation treatments had kept him busy for a while, but once she returned to work full-time, he had nothing to do. Though she would need regular check ups, she was no longer a cancer patient, and he was no longer her caretaker. He read, and played music and exercised all day while he waited for her to come home. Each day was a battle against giving in to the slothful tendencies he had successfully squelched a few years back. If he didn't get some kind of occupation, it was just a matter of time before he slid back into those size 38 pants he kept in his suitcase to keep himself motivated.

Given the circumstances of his resignation, he couldn't try for another teaching position and there wasn't that much else that interested him. He spent hours playing guitar—even penning his own compositions, but had no desire to resume his performances at Monty's. Idleness made him grumpy, and soon life with Elizabeth was not all about anticipating great sex and then having great sex. They actually quarreled. Little things upset her, like when he forgot to clean out Gay's litter box. She was tired of his peculiar eating habits. She didn't understand why he was so reluctant to go out and socialize with her.

When it was clear that their relationship had run its course, Wenn packed up his stuff and returned to Italy. He traveled around, but when he took the boat to Ponza, his travels were over because soon after he arrived, he met Lucia, the woman of his dreams. An olive skinned beauty with a wild mane of dark waves and beautiful brown eyes, she was the daughter of a family that owned one of the few small cafés on the island. From the first time they laid eyes on each other, they were inseparable. He leased a room on the island and started playing jazz at her parents' café four nights a week to make money.

Ponza was Wenn Mann's utopia. Like him, the sleepy resort town made no effort to try and impress anyone or keep up with the rest of the world. There was no upscale neighborhood. No status zip code. In fact, no one even had an address there. Lucia lived in the yellow house. That was her address, Casa gialla. Mail was addressed to Wenn Mann, Ponza, Italy.

Lucia spoke only a few words of English. Wenn knew a little Italian, but he pretended not to which kept their relationship fresh for years. Lucia had an i-Phone, and when they really needed to communicate, she had a translation app. They would type in what they wanted to say and read the translations. It was perfect.

Mr. and Mrs. Mann were going to Ponza to see Wenn and Lucia get married at the island church, St. Silvarios. They would also get to meet their newborn granddaughter. After who knows how many generations of Mann men, they finally had a girl. Her name was Wendy Quintus Mann and she was exquisite.

For Pups, two years had been a whirlwind. Shortly after her visit to the White House, her notoriety grew beyond belief. There were multiple appearances on the *Today Show, Good Morning America,* and even *The David Letterman Show.* She had a book deal, and there was talk of a reality show called *The Lice Buster.* The MacArthurs also moved to Chevy Chase, but not before Pups won her battle against Ms. Gagner. Not only did the principal re-instate the no-nit policy, she actually presented Grant with the school's highest honor, the Good Character Award. Where petitions, logic and demonstrations had failed, good old-fashioned idolatry succeeded. As it turned out, Ms. Gagner was a rabid Ellen DeGeneres fan, a fact that Pups used to her advantage. When the *Ellen Show's* producer called to invite her on the program to check Ellen for lice, Pups suggested bringing Ms. Gagner along to give the segment a more educational flair. Now, when parents visit the principal's office they no longer have to look at that awful giant bug attack poster, because in its place, is a giant autographed photo of Pups, Ellen, Ms. Gagner, and Sarah Jessica Parker (the program's other guest that day) on the show together.

Lice may have opened the door to Pups's celebrity, but bugs were not her claim to fame. Her no nonsense approach to everything registered with a certain demographic and soon, Pups was a sought after celebrity. She made frequent appearances as a guest speaker, and though her oeuvre was rapidly expanding to politics and world matters, she never forgot what got her there—bugs. Which is why she always began every speech she made with the same exact story …

"At the Nazi concentration camp known as Auschwitz, a barracks of Jewish prisoners became horribly infested with lice … " Just as she ended every speech with this bit of wisdom …

"There are those who see life as an open road—with endless twisting and turning possibilities. Others see it as a ladder jutting straight up into the heavens, a challenge to see how high they can get. And some people are so engaged in a prolonged and ultimately unwinnable game of existential dodge ball, they never actually have time to think about how they see life. They are too busy getting out of the way.

"Regardless of whether you're moving forward, climbing up or standing still, wrestling fate will never turn out the way you planned. Because even when things go the way you want, behind every corner, lurking in every abandoned hat or riding down the trail on a Cannondale bike or across the green in a revved up golf cart, wonders and shockers await all of us in equal number, ready to appear, seemingly out of nowhere."

Acknowledgments

Many thanks to my family for supporting, encouraging and inspiring me. My husband, Dominic who once again designed my beautiful cover and took care of all the tech issues for me so I could concentrate on the writing. Nicholas, Caroline and Caitlin for always listening to my ideas, giving me their honest feedback.

Also, special thanks to my parents, Ed and Pat and my in-laws, Lucy and Dominic for your effusive enthusiasm for my work.

Most of all, a million thanks to Bruce Shaw, the best friend a writer could ever have! My novels have benefited tremendously from his input, but more than that, I have benefited from his kindness, generosity and friendship.

I would also like to express my gratitude towards everyone who helped me along the way and gave my book a chance. Beta readers, reviewers, friends, and the Story Girls who gave me so much confidence. Merci! I hope you enjoyed the novel.

About the Author

Michele Harris graduated from NYU's Tisch School of the Arts where she studied film production. She has written and produced video and television programs for a long list of corporate, public interest and government agencies. She currently works as a newspaper reporter, covering the arts, entertainment, and food. The mother of three, she lives outside of Washington, D.C. with her husband, Dominic. When she's not writing or reading, you can find Michele working out at the gym or running the trails alongside the Potomac River.

You can reach me at micheleharris@verizon.net